YOU BENEATH YOUR SKIN

YOU BENEATH YOUR SKIN

DAMYANTI BISWAS

**SIMON &
SCHUSTER**

London · New York · Sydney · Toronto · New Delhi

A CBS COMPANY

First published in India by Simon & Schuster India, 2019

A CBS company

Copyright © Damyanti Biswas, 2019

The right of Damyanti Biswas to be identified as author of this work has been asserted by her in accordance with Section 57 of the Copyright Act, 1957.

1 3 5 7 9 10 8 6 4 2

Simon & Schuster India
818, Indraprakash Building,
21, Barakhamba Road,
New Delhi 110001

www.simonandschuster.co.in

Paperback ISBN: 978-93-86797-62-9
Ebook ISBN: 978-93-86797-63-6

Typeset in India by SŪRYA, New Delhi

Printed and bound in India by Replika Press Pvt. Ltd.

MIX
Paper from
responsible sources
FSC
www.fsc.org   FSC® C016779

For Baba, who taught me to read

1

❧

Anjali Morgan wanted to get hold of Nikhil, and smack him. He could have hurt himself jumping out of the moving car.

I told you he'll be the death of you one day. Mom's voice played in her ears. *You never listen.*

'Get back in the car,' she yelled at Nikhil, but he'd disappeared, leaving Anjali stranded at the narrow, sloping exit tunnel of the capital's largest shopping mall. Two drivers honked behind her. She wanted to turn and yell at them, but held back. *You know better than anyone else he can't help it.*

She needed to clear her head before she spoke to him again. He wouldn't go far. *Deep breaths.* She leaned out of the car door and inhaled, only for the petrol fumes to hit her, along with the smog and that dusty smell unique to New Delhi. She forgot it most times, but now she choked on it and coughed.

Anjali stepped out of her car, the yellow overhead lights blinding her for a moment. Five cars now queued up behind hers. The driver in the first car had seen a teenager throw a tantrum in front of his harried mother. He slammed the horn, and the rest followed suit. She spotted Nikhil's gangly form down the slope, cantering away.

'Madamji.' A short Nepali guard in a beige uniform hurried up the slope towards her, his whistle shrieking. '*Yahan* parking allowed *nahin hai*.'

'I'm sorry.' Anjali tried to remember the Hindi words, but they'd fled, along with her composure. 'My son has run away.'

She was about to sprint after Nikhil when the guard overtook her and blocked the way.

'No parking here,' he pointed at the cars queuing up behind her. 'This is "Exit".'

Down the slope behind the guard, Anjali watched in horror as Nikhil turned into the parking area and disappeared. The cool air of a November evening made her shiver.

'I need to go get my son. What part of that can't you understand?'

Anjali loosened the scarf about her neck, parted it from her jacket. In her last therapy session with Nikhil, the two of them had been taught to cup their hands and take deep breaths when in a trying situation. She tried it now, but terror clogged her throat. Her breaths came gasping, short.

'Big boy only, *mil jaega*.' The Nepali guard gestured towards the main road, and spoke in a mixture of Hindi and broken English, 'Make one round and come back. Where will he go?'

How was she to explain to this man that she couldn't afford to lose sight of Nikhil? By now he may have tripped and fallen down an escalator, screaming like a horror movie hostage, or thrown a fit when a stranger brushed against him in the evening crowd.

'Move your car,' another guard appeared, his eyes trained at her chest instead of her face. 'You are making jam.'

A supervisor. Making jam, indeed. Strawberry or apricot?

She needed to get past the honking cars, the petrol fumes in the exit tunnel, and this cranky supervisor eyeing her up.

'Get into car, madam.' The supervisor continued. '*Gori memsaab*,' he muttered under his breath in Hindi, '*samajhti kya hai apne aap ko*?'

The sight of a light-skinned, blonde-haired woman, taller and broader than him, had clearly pissed this man off. Twelve years in Delhi, and it still got to her. The guard didn't know she understood his comment: '*What does she think of herself?*' and the way he chewed on the words '*gori memsaab*' behind his moustache. *White Madam.*

She wanted to punch his face, show him what a big 'white madam' might do, but that wouldn't get her any closer to Nikhil. Quite the opposite. Two more guards jogged towards her from the parking lot.

'I will find him, madamji,' the Nepali guard spoke up in order to be heard over a renewed spate of honks, 'you go and come back. I saw him. In black t-shirt and jeans, *hai na*?'

'Yes. But please don't touch him, he gets upset.'

Anjali scrabbled through her bag, 'Here's my card. Call me please, when you find him.' She dropped it, 'Sorry!' snatched it up again, 'Oh, his eyes are blue.'

The cars blasted their horns, and the supervisor edged towards her. Anjali stepped back, her hands shaking. Would she lose Nikhil the evening after his fourteenth birthday? She slid back into her car and drove off. Speed-dialling Maya, her landlady and best friend, she crashed her gears. Maya may not have found a taxi near the mall entrance yet. She could help look for Nikhil.

***

Anjali tried to steady her fingers on the steering wheel. Stuck amidst other cars in the afternoon traffic on Mandir Marg, with bikes edging past her and picking their way to the front of the congestion, it would take at least another ten minutes to turn back into the mall's parking lot. She prayed for Maya to find Nikhil before he got into trouble.

Should have checked the child lock on his door, Mom's voice piped up inside her head. But how was she to know Nikhil would run? No point in worrying about that now. Take *deep breaths* when you feel under pressure. When you hear a critical voice. Anjali had grown up with that voice, and even though she had moved thousands of miles away from Mom, Mom still lived within her. Anjali counted her breaths. Her Lamaze classes came back to her, days with Nate Morgan sitting behind and breathing right along; when Nikhil was a part of her and couldn't kick other than from inside her belly.

She could no longer shelter her son within her body, or absorb his punches and tantrums. Even as a baby, he'd refused to nurse. Later, he lay alone, keeping his gaze on the red toy airplane buzzing in circles over his crib, unhappy when Anjali picked him up for a nappy change. According to Nikhil's therapist, Dr Bhalla, he would become more amenable as he grew up.

Anjali watched a woman stirring a pot on the pavement not five feet away from the traffic, her baby's feet hovering over the fire. *Be careful*, Anjali wanted to tell the mother, *please be careful*. Despite the cold, toddlers ran barefoot, in torn sweaters. Wrapped in large, shaggy blankets, elderly men sat smoking beside flimsy homes fashioned out of tarpaulin and cardboard. Pedestrians sidestepped makeshift beds, and hurried past migrant children who came to the capital in search of a better life; outsiders, like her, only far less fortunate. Behind them, a huge, lighted hoarding showed pale-faced models, wearing tuxedo suits and gowns, next to large television screens.

Sweat beaded her upper lip. She didn't feel very fortunate right this minute, merely stupid. Why hadn't she taken that guard's mobile number? Like an idiot, she'd told him about Nikhil's blue eyes. Nikhil usually kept his gaze to the floor—what if that guard tried to get a look at Nikhil's eyes, and he freaked? *We'll find him*, Maya had assured her on the phone not ten minutes ago, *don't panic*. Maya was more family than friend, and good with Nikhil, so she was a good bet to locate him. Anjali tried to reach Maya again. She inhaled, and listened to the unanswered phone. Instead of a ring, Maya had downloaded a caller tune, a peppy Punjabi number.

Catching sight of her face in the rear-view mirror, Anjali flinched. Faded makeup, wrinkles under her eyes, greasy hair. Mom would have cackled if she saw Anjali like this. *Stay with the face God gave you. Vanity is a Sin.* Nikhil had aged her, by a dozen, no twenty years. Long work sessions at her Bhikaji Cama clinic, taking him for a group therapy session with Dr Bhalla, and now this shopping trip from hell. She thumped her hand on the horn, emitting a series of sharp honks to hurry along the cars at the green light.

Remember to take deep breaths, Nikhil's therapist's words came back to her, *for him, and for you*.

What if this was her punishment for earlier today when

she let him skip lunch after a tantrum? Dr Bhalla said she must remain consistent, not give in when he went into a meltdown during his daily routine. Nikhil was bound to be hungry by now, after a chocolate shake and not much else for lunch that afternoon. *No, Anjali, focus. Find him first.* She sighed and dialled her friend again.

Maya finally picked up as Anjali turned into the mall parking area.

'Can't find him, Anji. I've looked everywhere. He's not at the toy shop. Should I call Bhai?'

Anjali sprinted up the escalator, two steps at a time, sweating despite the chill. If they didn't find Nikhil soon, she must get the mall security to make an announcement. He may have lost his way to the toy shop, a long walk and three floors up from where they'd parked. Trying to look calm, she approached the handbag-check, where the lady guard in a khaki saree delicately swirled the metal detector through her bag, as if stirring a curry. Wanting to scream with each wasted second, Anjali crossed through the sliding doors, and headed for the information desk. She had taught Nikhil to look for one if he got into trouble. Would he remember?

Reaching the main courtyard, Anjali squeezed past a bevy of perfectly-coiffed women in salwar-kameezes laden with shopping bags. Out of breath, she stopped beside Nando's, where a family sat with two kids about Nikhil's age. *To manage an episode,* Dr Bhalla said, *use the right aids, at the right time.* Nikhil did not allow touch. Anjali grabbed a smiley squeeze ball and his favourite blue blanket out of her handbag and scanned the crowd for a skinny boy with tufts of hair jutting up at the crown, a shambling walk, hands fisted.

She spotted him near a hair salon. She wanted to call out his name, but that would scare him into running, or throwing a tantrum.

He started when she touched his sleeve, but the face was a lot older, filled-out, with a moustache. Not Nikhil, but a salon employee, a bright red tag on his black tee-and-jeans uniform. Anjali blurted out a stream of hurried apologies and sprinted on.

Nikhil wanted to get to Hamleys and buy that airplane. He already owned one in black, but he wanted the red one, he'd said, and the blue. Anjali should have said yes, instead of handing him a squeeze ball and showing him his schedule for today. It specified that he could stay in the mall from 6.30 to 8.30 pm, pick one slice of Black Forest cake at the pastry shop to eat after dinner, and buy one airplane of his choice. Not two, or three, just one.

She called Maya. 'Did you see him?'

'Not yet. I'm at Hamleys. I think you should go to the information desk.' Maya paused, 'Bhai called to ask if I was on my way. I had to tell him.'

Great. Within minutes of each small crisis in her life, one of Delhi's top cops knew. Mr Jatin-Worried-Bhatt, Maya's doting older brother, would call any minute now. Please, not him, not now.

She cut the call. Stopping to catch her breath, she closed her eyes. She needed to collect herself, not panic. A low whine floated up, but once she opened her eyes, there was only the buzz from the throng of shoppers that surrounded her.

2

As the Special Commissioner of Crime, Delhi Police, Jatin Bhatt's phone never stopped ringing. He had forgotten to switch it off before the meeting, and now it buzzed in his hand, like a giant beetle bent on escape.

Across from him sat Commissioner D. M. Mehra, the top dog on the force. At sixty-two, Mehra wore the same trim moustache as Jatin, though his was streaked with grey. He was no match for Jatin's worked-out physique, nor was he as tall. Yet, Jatin felt his boss's upper hand today as in his eighteen years of marriage to the man's daughter.

'So, as you can see,' Commissioner Mehra continued in his gravelly voice from across the wide table, 'we must stay on top of this Sabharwal case. The new home minister has issued a series of directives: I'll have them forwarded to you. If we don't sort it out, it will go for an enquiry.'

Jatin switched off his buzzing phone, and sat up straighter. The Sabharwal debacle: Jatin's biggest headache, and the highest profile case under his charge at the moment—an ex-finance minister of India, a member of the erstwhile ruling party contesting a major State election in two months. A man in the current Opposition who could be a state Chief

Minister if he won. The government wanted this man gone, and they would hang a noose on anyone at all in order to do it. It was that simple.

Initial evidence pointed to culpability on the part of the ex-minister, but that minister's colleague, the previous home minister had asked Commissioner Mehra to avoid certain lines of enquiry and bury the leads that had taken hundreds of man hours from Jatin's team.

If the case went for a Central Bureau enquiry, Jatin could kiss his promotion, and maybe even his job, goodbye. Heart beating faster now, he watched as Mehra flipped through the papers in the file. Jatin stared at the badge on Mehra's shoulder, the crossed swords and State Emblem epaulette that marked the Delhi Chief of Police—he wanted it when Mehra retired next year.

The door swung open. How dare anyone enter without knocking? Ready to dress down a clueless junior officer, Jatin turned to find a tall, broad teen dressed in a woollen maroon jacket and grey trousers. His son, in school uniform. Something was wrong. Varun never dropped by his office on week days.

'Varun?' Jatin heard his question echoed by Mehra.

'Hi, Dad,' Varun said with a wide grin, 'Namaste Nanaji.'

The smile angered Jatin, because it meant his son had disturbed them for no reason at all. He needed to get back to the meeting.

'*Jeetey raho, betey,*' Varun's grandfather lit up in an answering smile. 'Come, come sit down.'

The old man brushed off his wife or his daughter if he was busy with something he wanted to focus on, and should have shooed off his grandson. Instead, Mehra seemed relieved at the interruption.

While his father-in-law rang for snacks and tea Jatin rounded on his son.

'You know you're supposed to call first.'

'Sorry, Daddy.' Varun lowered his head, 'But I called, so many times. I needed money at school.'

Jatin remembered ignoring his phone, then switching it off.

'We're raising funds for a boy whose mother died,' Varun raised his eyes, 'and I wanted to donate. So I came here instead of going all the way home.'

It was hard to stay angry with Varun because he was so quick to apologise for a mistake. But rules were rules, and meant to be followed.

'You entered without knocking.'

'They told me it was only you and Nanaji.'

'This is still an office.'

'Quit harassing my grandson,' Mehra interrupted him and turned to Varun, 'So *betey*, have you forgotten your poor Nanaji in his old age? Come, sit here so I can look at you properly,' Mehra dragged a chair up next to him. Varun rose and walked around the table to sit with his grandfather.

As if any seventeen-year-old would want to 'hang out' with his grandparents rather than his friends. Jatin watched Varun talk, his son's English so much better-accented than his own. The boy sat up straight, and his voice was pitched just right. Varun's school ranked amongst the top five in all of India. He had slipped a few grades this year, but promised to make up for them before his school trip to Manila. His friends belonged to good families, one of them the son of the new

Union Home Secretary, and Jatin's college classmate, Dayal Sisodia. Everything considered, his son made him proud.

An orderly brought in tea and snacks. Jatin noticed that the cutlery needed replacing, like most things in these headquarters—the projector screen behind Mehra, for instance, the old frames on the walls, the curtains. The entire building could do with a new coat of paint. If Jatin snagged the top job next year once Mehra retired, he would have that screen changed, and update the entire Connaught Place office building—more software, fewer paper files lost or chewed up by termites.

Fifteen minutes later, when Varun stood up to leave, Jatin reached for his wallet. But Mehra already held out a slim wad of thousand rupee notes.

Jatin was about to protest, but Mehra stopped him.

'It's for a good cause.' The commissioner put an arm around the shoulders of his grandson, who stood a hand taller than him, 'Here, let the old Nanaji chip in this time. Good job, *betey*, we must always help those in need.'

While walking his grandson to the door, Mehra turned to Jatin, 'I have an appointment before our 11 o'clock meeting. See you then?'

'What about the Sabharwal case, sir?' Jatin still called Mehra 'sir', at the office and at home. It galled him, especially in Varun's presence, to 'sir' his father-in-law.

'Bye, Dad!' Varun waved at him, 'I have to rush back to school! Bye, Nanaji.' The door swung shut behind him.

'All right then,' Mehra cleared his throat and fiddled with his Rolex, 'Let me quickly give you the basics.'

Still straight-backed and broad-shouldered despite the

years, Mehra handled media and ministers with a calm face, and no-nonsense replies. He never looked uncomfortable, so watching the old dog shift in his seat made Jatin uneasy.

'Joint Commissioner Arvind Rathi will be the in-charge for the Sabharwal case from now on.' Mehra raised his hand before Jatin could interrupt, 'Not my decision. He'll coordinate with you, of course, and need the files on the case. But he'll report directly to me on this one, for the time being.'

With those words, Mehra snatched a big case from Jatin, and turned it into a ticking time-bomb under his chair. From what he knew, Rathi was a recent, sudden transfer from the home minister's constituency in Rajasthan, straight to Delhi's Crime Branch. After all of Jatin's cover-ups at Mehra's bidding, this new minister wanted a mole to nose through the dirt. Jatin had run into Rathi—a tall, thin man, who wore rimless glasses. Pansy bootlicker.

Jatin played the case back in his head, the sequence of events, the orders from Mehra. No written instructions to bury the leads, not once. *You can handle this, can't you? Nobody has to know.* Most of the communication was verbal, some non-verbal—a shake or nod of the head as they discussed the case. Jatin could not have asked for written memos from Drishti's father.

'I know it's a change, Jatin. But we must follow orders.'

Mehra's phone rang, and picking it up, he walked to the end of his large office, near the windows. Jatin heard the murmurs, but couldn't make out the words.

He ran his hand through his hair. Commissioner Mehra couldn't possibly risk losing his pension one year before retirement. With no proof against him in writing, Mehra could deny all involvement. Jatin made a note to play nice with Mehra's daughter in the coming weeks.

No matter how hard Jatin had tried to hold their marriage together over its first few years, his increasingly skinny wife had run to her father with complaints: Jatin's long hours, how he paid her no attention and never took care of the kids. It never bothered the good commissioner that his darling Drishti was hardly ever home, that she didn't care for Varun like a mother should, that she hadn't bloody slept with her husband in years.

Jatin missed Anjali. He longed to watch the swing of her hips, and trail his fingers through the straight fall of her dark-blonde hair, over her dimpled chin, her neck, her smooth back. And *Rabji*, her skin! Indian women used cream bleaches and white teenagers took to tanning beds in pursuit of the skin tone Anjali had inherited from her American mother and Indian father.

Her dark eyes and thin lips made her long face appear stern, but he didn't mind. Her wide, movie-star smile slayed him, as did her throaty moans, the way her legs drummed against his back when she came apart in bed.

The knock at the door startled Jatin.

'Yes,' Mehra said. Joint Commissioner Rathi walked in.

He wore an emerald for career growth, a sapphire and a cat's eye to prevent misfortune. Unlike Jatin, Rathi seemed to believe that stones and astrology could change fate. Jatin yearned to make the man double over and cough out a tooth or two, but forced himself to smile, and give the limp, jewelled hand a firm shake. If he didn't do this right, he might have to wrap up his private dreams of becoming the youngest commissioner of Delhi Police at forty-six. Jatin nodded at the right moments as Mehra spoke, made polite noises, but was relieved to hear a knock at the door.

His assistant, Assistant Sub-Inspector Kusum Netam stood waiting. She cut a salute like a veteran, and Jatin noticed Rathi's eyes widen behind his glasses at this woman who looked like a short teenager in police uniform.

'We're finding that lead, sir.' Kusum said, 'The SHO is calling you.' Her dark tribal face seemed calm, but Jatin sensed the excitement underneath.

Jatin had worked all of last week with a Station House Officer who reported to one of his underlings, a Deputy Commissioner currently on leave. The SHO must have located the suspects: a gang on a rampage of loot and rape on the Yamuna Expressway. A case with four murders and multiple rapes within a family travelling to Agra had made TV headlines that week: the women were raped at gunpoint in front of their hapless relatives, who were then murdered.

Jatin nodded to Kusum and made his excuses to Mehra. 'The Yamuna Expressway case, sir.'

'Keep me updated.' Mehra said. 'We need to show results in fighting crimes against women.'

Jatin needed to sort more cases like this one, and make sure his boss took note, while he found a way to avert the Sabharwal disaster.

3

Maya couldn't understand why Anjali never mentioned her problems to Jatin Bhai. After all, her Bhai was not like most men. He was with the police, and if Nikhil was lost, Bhai could help. Maya continued scanning the crowd flowing past Hamleys for a boy of Nikhil's height and build. Dumping her overnight bag on the floor, she gathered her mass of curls, snagged them behind her head with a neon pink hair tie, and jammed in a few bright hair clips to contain the escaping curls. Not the sort of look Anjali liked on her, but to search for Nikhil she had to move, and her hair got in the way. She pulled down her sleeves as low as they would go, picked up her bag, and trained her gaze on the passing crowd.

Anjali must be freaking out by now—she held herself to impossibly high standards when it came to Nikhil: his schedule, his diet, his therapy. Anjali made those her priority, and sometimes, when Maya was being honest with herself, she felt jealous of that boy. She'd known Anjali ever since she herself was a teen. Anjali had held her, and kept her together through the months after Ma's death. On some nights, three-year old Nikhil, and Maya, then sixteen, slept on either side of Anjali. She comforted them both, with lullabies, stories, and in her case, cuddles.

As Nikhil grew up, Maya watched as Anjali's attention shifted—she wanted to make her son an 'optimal outcome' she said. She took him to Hridayog, the charity where she helped out, in order to better socialise him with other children, fought to keep him in the regular school Bhai got him admitted to. Maya hoped it was not all in vain—Nikhil seemed to turn more aggressive and disturbed around Anjali, and today he had run away again. He'd done this a few times, but always from home, and only as far as their street in Safdarjung Enclave. After they found him, Maya decided, they must talk about Nikhil. Nikhil's therapist said that it was Anjali who set him off—her energy and attitude. They had started on group therapy, but Anjali sounded grim after each session with Nikhil's therapist and her boss, Dr Bhalla.

Maya walked further down the long mall corridor and surveyed another, unending swarm at the sprawling lower floor. It was growing cold outside. The mall was bright and warm, luring in young, hungry-eyed men wearing knockoffs, trying to mix in with the office-going crowd and flocks of women in designer jeans and branded jackets. These men roamed in packs, grinning, slapping each other on the back. Maya scrolled to find Anjali's number, but didn't hit the call button: Anjali needed to focus, and they had agreed that unless Maya found Nikhil, Anjali would be the one to start a call. They didn't want their phones engaged with calls to each other. The security guard might contact Anjali with news about Nikhil.

The phone vibrated in her hand as she turned back to Hamleys.

'Found him.' Anjali panted into the phone. 'Come down to the rear exit.'

Maya jogged through the corridor, and ran down the escalator. The overnight bag smacked against her hip, hurting her, but she needed to get to Anjali, and help her contain her son if needed. Nikhil often resisted being taken back home.

At the exit, Maya found Anjali crouched over a cowering, whimpering Nikhil. Anjali held out his blue blanket, whispering. 'Shh…Nikhil, I'm here. Shh, baby…Take this, here.'

Maya couldn't remind Anjali that Nikhil hated being called anything other than his name, not when she noticed Anjali's clenched hands, at odds with her calm face, and soft words. Nikhil rocked back and forth, holding a yellow smiley squeeze ball. Maya stood beside Anjali, watching as people gathered around them.

'Deep breaths, Nikhil,' Anjali said, 'Remember to count as you breathe in. Breathe in, breathe out. There, much better.'

Maya heard snatches in Hindi and English: *Mad or what? Paagalpan ka daura hai, they shouldn't leave him alone! There are asylums for kids like this*!

Before Maya could react, Anjali drew herself up to her entire height and faced the bystanders down.

'Nikhil.' Maya said, 'Stand up. You want to go home now?'

Nikhil whimpered, but made no move to rise.

Maya heard the muttering of the crowd, and turned to find men, with the air of a hunting pack, idling. Some of them wore loud t-shirts, with frayed jackets and jeans; others had shawls wrapped about their broad shoulders. Anjali had shut these men up without saying a word, but they still lingered, with jacket collars raised, and chests puffed up.

'Let's get out of here,' Maya whispered, eyeing the mall entrance.

Pavement fires glowed on the other side of the empty parking lot. Fog curled around the yellow halogen lights of the road opposite the mall, making it look as if the boundaries between worlds had blurred, and ghosts or monsters would step in any moment. The dull, chilled air tasted of tobacco, petrol, liquor, wood smoke. Maya drew her jacket closer about her. They needed to get Nikhil inside, away from the chill. Maya crouched beside Nikhil, her voice shaky as she tried to get him to stand up while Anjali faced the men. A low wolf-whistle from the back of the ragtag group made Maya's hackles rise.

Two of the goons drew nearer. One was muscular, bearded, and the other jangled a chunky metal bracelet on his wrist. Anjali drew herself up, and signalled to Maya with the slightest of nods. Maya knew Anjali would whip out her pepper spray, use it, and then make a dash for the entrance. Maya urged Nikhil to stand up. This time, the boy listened, and grabbed the blanket from his mother's shoulder. The men advanced upon them, all murmurs and jeers, their eyes bright in the glow from the mall's glass doors.

Anjali's ringtone cut through the charged air. The security guard. She told him about finding Nikhil. Around them, some of the men melted away, but the two big goons leered forward. Three security guards strode out of the automatic doors, whistles and walkie-talkies in hand. The guards escorted them to Anjali's car, all friendly chatter and smiles. Anjali tipped them, giving her thanks. With Maya beside him, Nikhil walked towards the car now hugging the blanket. Maya huffed a sigh of relief. Delhi put you through extremes: be it with its weather, or its people.

She teetered on her heels, her head level with Nikhil's earlobes. An arm's length separated them. Nikhil turned to her and pulled her sweater, a soft tug seeking comfort. Maya tugged back at his t-shirt. She noticed the slight fuzz of hair on his chin, and above his lips. He looked like any other teen, walking with his mom and aunt after a family dinner.

Turning to Anjali, Maya noticed her drawn expression, the smudged makeup, hair askew. Anjali touched up her face every chance she got, painting it first thing in the morning, and wiping the gunk off after everyone had gone to sleep. Anjali's hands trembled as she scrambled for the keys.

Maya helped settle Nikhil in the backseat, and having dumped her bag in the boot, walked over to Anjali.

'I'll drive,' Maya took the car keys. 'You sit with him at the back.'

Anjali did not protest, and Maya knew she had made the right decision in skipping her stay with Bhai and Drishti Bhabi, and staying back with Anjali instead.

***

The Safdarjung Enclave home loomed in the darkness as Maya turned into their quiet street. She had lived here all her life—the home belonged to her grandfather, who had died much before she was born. Their neighbourhood once used to be all bungalows and gardens, but with the years, some of the old bungalows had given way to apartment buildings. Since the housekeeper Ira had left for the day, Maya stepped out of Anjali's car, reached up on her tiptoes to unlock the gate at the top, then shoved with all her might.

Her first clear memory of the bungalow was learning to open this massive iron gate while sitting on Bhai's broad shoulders. That was also her first memory of Bhai: he had left for the USA when she was three, and returned just after her fifth birthday. Ma was very ill at the time, and for a few weeks, Bhai babysat Maya, tied her plaits with his large clumsy hands, fed her breakfast, sent her to school. And when he brought her back from school, he let her sit on his shoulders and push open the gate.

She drove the car in, dropped Anjali and Nikhil at the porch, and parked it in the garage at the side of the bungalow. She came back to find Anjali waiting with Nikhil on the cane chairs under the porch.

'Sorry, forgot you keep your house key along with the car keys.' Maya handed Anjali's keys over, and unlocked the main door with her own. They stepped inside. Things were so different now. She lived upstairs, while Anjali rented the rooms downstairs.

When Anjali first arrived twelve years earlier, Maya had helped carry the sleeping two-year-old Nikhil inside. After the long flight from Washington with a toddler, Anjali had looked almost as dishevelled as she did now, but the home had been very different then. Bhai, Drishti Bhabi and Varun stayed in the rooms downstairs, Maya had her room across from Ma, upstairs. A few weeks after Anjali's arrival, Bhai had moved out with his family to police accommodation, despite protests from everyone, including Anjali.

Maya put Nikhil's things away, then headed upstairs with her overnight bag.

'Meet for a drink upstairs?' she called to Anjali.

'Sure.' Anjali replied from Nikhil's room. 'See you in a bit.'

Once in her room, Maya made room on the bed by pushing away the pile of clothes, earphones, notebooks, jewellery. It used to be Ma-Papa's bed, the one place in the home she never ventured before their death. Papa had a temper, and often, as he sat on the bed with a drink on the side table, he would refer to her as his *budhapey ki galti*, a mistake in his old age.

Once she'd showered and changed into her pyjamas, she checked her phone. Drishti Bhabi had left a message. She had been to the dry cleaners to pick up the clothes she'd promised Maya, and wanted to drop them off.

When Drishti Bhabi arrived, Maya ran to the gate. Her frail Bhabi struggled under the weight of the boxes, so Maya gave her a hand. Bhabi's short hair was all tousled, and she looked exhausted.

'You're never going to wear all of these?' Maya hefted the packages on to the living room sofa.

'They don't fit me. I brought a few extra, the ones you don't like I'll pass on to my cousin.'

'I get first dibs?'

'Of course, always.' Bhabi smiled. 'I brought some of Varun's clothes as well. They're hardly worn, and might fit Nikhil.'

'Clothes for Nikhil?' Anjali walked into the dining room, her hair and makeup back in place. She wore sleek t-shirts and lounge pants at home, and mostly managed to look as if she'd stepped right off a magazine.

'Hi,' Bhabi turned to hug her, 'how have you been?'

'Great,' Anjali hugged her back. 'All of this for Nikhil?'

Maya explained how she'd seen all her Bhabi's gorgeous clothes hanging unworn in her closet, and asked for them. The dry-cleaners was not far from Safdarjung Enclave so Bhabi had decided to drop them here.

'I also brought this.' Bhabi placed a large cake on the table.

'Cake?' Maya said.

'Black Forest.' Bhabi tucked her fringe behind her ears, and patted the short hair at her neck, 'I got it for you, but now that you're not coming this weekend, I thought I might as well bring it here. Nikhil loves this cake too, right?'

Maya went upstairs to grab the packet she'd bought for Varun, a new set of gloves for his boxing classes. That boy worked out like a madman. She came back down to find Bhabi unpacking a box, showing some of her clothes to Anjali. Bhabi picked two long embroidered kurtas, the same design. She made Anjali hold one up while she held the other.

'Which one do you like better?' Bhabi said.

Maya looked up at the two women she loved best. The smiling, rail-thin Bhabi, the curvy, tall Anjali making a face, and pointed to the light-coloured one her Bhabi held up.

'That one.'

Bhabi left with the darker shade kurta, for her cousin. In the uneasy silence that followed, Maya helped Anjali gather the clothes together.

'Time for that drink.'

They watched TV for a while, then chatted about work. Women-led detective agencies in New Delhi were few and far between; and women psychiatrists shared more than a few of the same challenges: difficult clients and chasing payments. They agreed that following up on payments was almost as difficult as running after Nikhil today.

'Only we care less about clients.' Maya laughed.

'Yes. We found him, though. That's what matters.' Anjali sat back in her chair, swirling the ice in her drink.

'You'll speak about this to Dr Bhalla tomorrow?'

'I'm thinking of changing Nikhil's therapist.'

'But he's your boss.'

'Bhalla keeps talking about me and Mom. I need someone to focus on Nikhil, give *him* ways to cope.'

'What did Bhalla say this time?' Maya caught a ringlet of her hair in her fingers and pulled it straight. She wished for sleek hair like Anjali's but straightening only made her hair dry and brittle. She would never look like Anjali: tall, graceful, put-together.

'Dr Bhalla thinks I need to connect with Mom. If I resolve things with her, he says, I'll be better with Nikhil.'

'Why not give it a shot?'

'He has never met my Mom, nor have you, or you wouldn't say that.' Anjali's voice rose, the way it did each time she spoke about her Mom. Maya knew when to back off.

'Sorry, Anji.' Maya rose from her bed, walked to a drawer and picked up her cigarettes. She opened the window, lit one, and inhaled. She pulled her sleeves down, but that exposed her shoulders. She quickly let go of the sleeve. Anjali was familiar with the discoloured patches all over Maya's arms. She had taken Maya to doctors, been defeated, along with Maya, by that word, *vitiligo*. Maya wanted to hide the marks on her body, and Anjali the scars of her past. She stubbed out the cigarette against the window frame, and walking to Anjali, hugged her.

'We'll not talk about your Mom again.'

4

Jatin walked towards his office, Kusum by his side. The tube-lit corridor led off to various offices, with doors marked in golden lettering, and the occasional ventilator that opened to the outside and brought in a little of the cold, smoggy air.

The SHO called. They had put the hideout in Noida on watch, and once he was sure he had all the gang members in there, they would swoop in. He thought it might go down by 7 pm.

Three hours. It might take up to an hour to reach Noida, so he must leave right away.

'I'll be there.' Jatin said. The arrest needed to proceed without a hitch.

'I'm going with you, sir?'

Kusum's keenness, and her English made him smile. She needed polish, but at least she spoke and understood the language. You couldn't get far in the Delhi police without English.

'You have all the reports to type in.'

'At your desk already, sir.'

Jatin wanted to find another excuse to say no, but this young Sub-Inspector's eyes, bright with excitement, stopped him.

'Please, sir. I'm needing to speak with you about something I'm noticing on the ZIPnet. Only five minutes on it sir, and then I'm giving you the details during the drive to Noida? I can take notes on today's emails when we reach there as you're waiting with the SHO.'

This girl didn't give up. He did have a lot of emails to get through, and it would be a good use of his time to dictate some of them as he supervised the arrest.

'Ok, five minutes,' Jatin said, 'and then we leave.'

They avoided the long corridors from the conference rooms to his office, taking the shorter exterior route that led past the lockup area. Bracing himself against the cold haze outside, he strode out under the row of *gulmohar* trees, their tiny yellow leaves strewn along the paved road that ran parallel to the walls of the Delhi Police Headquarters. Jatin stared up at the tall mural of Mahatma Gandhi. The artists should have painted a few other leaders, not left the bald old father of the nation, with his sad, droopy lips, quite so lonely.

As Jatin neared the lockup area, drunken shouting, abuses in Hindi and Haryanvi and the growls of police jeeps made quite the racket, broken by the guffaws of policemen going about their business, herding drug addicts, snatch thieves, and men who had upset one member of Parliament or the other. Jatin sighed—he no longer dealt with that mess, thank *Rabji*. The cawing of dozens of crows on the trees above and the honks of traffic from outside the walls followed them as they strode past, and Jatin felt the beginnings of a headache. He needed coffee but there wasn't time.

Kusum walked off to switch on her computer, and soon enough, walked in with a file and a small tray. 'Coffee, sir.'

This girl had read his mind. Jatin thanked her and followed her to her computer, where she pulled up the ZIPnet site. He usually inspected files from the assistant commissioners these days, and got briefed by his underlings on important cases, without any need to check the police network database.

Settling back in his chair, he studied the department office while he waited for the page to load: he longed to get away from the politics, the kowtowing, the drab walls, the posters of Gandhi and Nehru, the maps of India and Delhi. He needed Anjali; hadn't seen her in three weeks. He hated meeting her in secret, and Anjali's terror of someone finding out.

He tried not to acknowledge her fears, the same way he firmly ignored his own gunshot wound received in the second year on service, nearly nineteen years ago. It had pierced his shoulder bone, missing his heart by a few inches. His shoulder hurt on cold days: he couldn't raise his arm and needed to use a hot pack to soothe it. The scar tingled now, declaring itself. Winter had begun.

'Here it is, sir.' Kusum brought him back to the matter at hand.

Scrolling down the screen, Kusum showed him the details of an unidentified body discovered two days ago, in the Pul Bangash area.

Jatin settled down with his coffee a few feet away so as not to crowd Kusum, and waited, ignoring her smell of jasmine and sweat. Kusum must learn to present her case. Before giving his assistant his complete attention, Jatin checked his watch. They had a few minutes.

'My friend, constable at Pul Bangash branch, telling me

about it.' Kusum hovered the cursor over the case account. 'Some rag-picker children finding the body in Madipur, in black plastic rubbish bags. Face gone, sir, all melted. When the PCR van reaching the scene, they asking few questions, just writing FIR only, sir.'

'Ok.'

'She being poor slum woman, sir.'

Dozens of people died on Delhi's streets each week. Police mostly responded by filing First Information Reports and shoving them into files, because there was often no other way for eight hundred Police Control Room vans to patrol a city of twenty-five million. Those who bribed the police for their safety when filing reports got help, be it on the street or at police stations. PCR constables hardly received enough salary to justify the long hours they worked and needed money to change hands 'under the table'. That was the appeal of most government jobs, you made up for the low salaries and delayed promotions. Slum-dwellers, with little or no money to offer, got the shortest shrift: that was the way of things.

Face melted away? Unusual. It didn't seem like the deceased was one of those homeless drug addicts, the sort of deaths that Delhi police categorised as 'beggar-type'. Jatin examined the photograph. Her hair was not matted, and her hands looked like they were used to labour.

'I'm looking at some more records, sir. Last few months.'

He checked his watch again. This was interesting, but they needed to leave soon.

'ZIPnet having similar cases before.' She showed him the records. 'Two in last three months.'

'No photographs?'

'I'll show you while we are driving, sir. Dilawar is getting the car.'

Constable Dilawar, his driver, a tall giant of a man, who had just had a son. Jatin reminded himself to pick up a few of the vouchers he crammed in his drawer for such occasions. He had helped Dilawar in getting the job several years ago at the request of his father, an old acquaintance. The Constable had since proved his worth as Jatin's trusted man.

'Not the Sumo.' A police Sumo would be recognised, and put the entire plainclothes operation in jeopardy.

'Right, sir. I will go and change also, sir.' Kusum said.

Dilawar navigated the car along Mathura Road, where the evening traffic rush was about to begin, leaving behind the green-and-yellow auto rickshaws, shiny delivery trucks, and dented vans. Sleek saloon cars flanked their car at the traffic light. Jatin tried to relax in the back seat. Dilawar was doing a good job of trying to reach on time, given that they had no siren on this car—Jatin didn't want to risk it.

Not recognising it as a police car, a throng of beggar children knocked on its windows: dark eyes, chapped lips and hands, grimy faces, voices shut out on the other side of Jatin's car window. They held aloft steel cans with handles wrapped in bright-yellow marigold garlands. He had listened to Anjali chat with similar kids over the years, ask if they wished to go to school, but they only ever wanted coins for their cans filled with sesame oil, for *Shani-puja*.

Anjali had laughed when he'd first explained. *Shani-puja?* She had said, *Worshipping the planet Saturn on Saturday, so He won't send bad luck?* Jatin had watched that laughter fade when he explained that beggar cartels sent these kids out on the street to bring back money. The coins never reached the temples, and some of the kids never saw adulthood.

He'd grown used to such faces, but they moved Anjali, and after spending years in her company, he saw them through her eyes. She helped a charity in a slum, which took care of kids like these. At a gesture from him, Kusum reached into the glove compartment for the packets of granola bars and biscuits stashed there. Lowering the window, Kusum handed them out. Some of the children grabbed the packets, but most carried on with their chorus for coins, *ek rupaya, doh rupaya dedo madamji*.

Once the vehicle moved again, Kusum turned to him. 'As I was saying earlier sir, there are more cases.'

'You have the photographs?'

The reporting constables hadn't bothered to upload pictures on ZIPnet, but Kusum had sent for them. Despite the blurred shots on her second-hand smartphone, Jatin recognised the similarity in the unclothed, defaced bodies huddled in trash bags.

'Where were these found?'

'Slum areas, sir. One in Pul Mithai, the other in Madipur Colony.'

This could turn out like the Nithari serial murder case, but different. Someone had murdered, disfigured, then dumped slum women in the past few months. If the case proved the work of a serial killer, it could blow up. Journalists on channels like India Tomorrow would cover it round-the-clock, screaming till their throats hurt. If Jatin fed the media the right information at the right time, this could claim the airwaves for much longer than the Yamuna Expressway case. That is, if the investigation panned out.

He glanced at his phone. The SHO had sent a text. Things had moved according to plan. The gang was meeting up. Jatin looked up at Kusum, 'The photograph you showed me earlier? Do they still have the body?'

'Yes, sir. Should we be asking for post-mortem?'

He noticed the way she said 'we,' as if they had teamed up on an undercover mission, but said yes.

'Ok, sir.'

If he discussed the case at the upcoming weekly briefing, it might pass to an underling, a joint commissioner or a deputy commissioner. On the other hand, if it emerged much further into an investigation led by him, and escalated into a media frenzy, it would boost his profile in the force.

'Kusum, remember what I said about on-the-job training?'

'Yes, sir.'

'*We* can solve this one together, but we need to keep it quiet.'

Kusum nodded, her eyes bright.

'Dilawar?' Jatin needed to make sure Dilawar understood the need for secrecy.

'*Theek hai*, sir.'

He would bring Maya in on this, to help from the outside. Kusum and Maya would work well together, Kusum providing information from the inside, and Maya doing the grunt work Kusum couldn't do within the police while keeping it quiet. Jatin held back a smile. Maya and Kusum were almost the same height, and both possessed the same mulish drive.

Two years earlier, tired of listening to Maya insist that she wanted to sit for the Civil Service exams, he had set her up with a small detective agency. He found her a divorce case or two from among his contacts and named the agency Vigil, expecting it to shut down in a few months. But his then twenty-five-year-old sister had not only finished those first assignments, but gone on to receive more via word-of-mouth. She and her assistant had helped with legwork on a few crucial police cases, too, allowing Jatin to crack them.

Jatin sent Maya a text, but when she didn't answer, called her number. It was late, about to be dark soon.

'You're still coming to stay with us tonight, Gudiya?'

Gudiya, or doll, a name he and Ma had called Maya since the day she was born, a few days after Jatin's nineteenth birthday. Such a tiny little thing she was then, her head soft and downy in his palm.

'I'm still at the mall.' Maya said.

Jatin heard Maya huff into the phone.

'Why do you sound like you're rushing? Where's Anjali?'

'She's lost track of Nikhil.'

That boy was unpredictable. As he grew taller and stronger, he got tougher to handle. Anjali and Maya together often failed to hold him down during one of his panic attacks.

'Want me to come down?'

'She says we'll find him any second.'

'Tell me when you do.' Jatin paused, 'We'll see you this evening?'

'Yes, Bhai.'

At Noida, Jatin worked on the arrest with the SHO. Policemen in plainclothes surrounded the crumbling building where the gang was to meet. Jatin placed eyes on all exits, and monitored movements from the informal control room they had established. The team took final positions, and waited. In the lull, Kusum finished replying to a bunch of emails, her hands flying over the keyboard.

In the next two hours, the team nabbed the men, with no shots fired. Jatin called Mehra, informed him of the success.

'Well done.' Mehra's voice floated across the line.

'I've been taught by the best, sir. Would you like to address the press briefing this evening?'

'No, you do it.' Mehra said. 'Ensure you make the point about women's safety.'

'Of course.'

'I'm going for a round of golf with the usual set this weekend. Want to join us?'

'Sorry, sir. Drishti has made plans for the weekend.'

Jatin was planning to attend a house-lunch party with Drishti, but only because it was at Dayal Sisodia's home. If things became hairy with the Sabharwal case, the Home Secretary would prove a useful ally. He headed back to his car.

'I've arranged for the post-mortem, sir.' Kusum trotted along to keep pace with him.

With the entire force buzzing about crimes against women, Kusum might have stumbled across the right case. This one, if it played right, could prove useful in either distracting attention from his role in the Sabharwal mess, or balancing it out. Much harder to bring down an officer seen in the public eye as a fighter of crimes against women in New Delhi.

He might yet replace Chief Commissioner Mehra next year.

His phone beeped. In the flurry of activity, he'd forgotten all about Maya, Anjali, and Nikhil. He dialled Maya's number.

5

In the mellow light of the lamp, Anjali watched as Jatin poured their drinks, clinking ice into the glasses, adding a large measure of scotch into his. She studied his almost-but-not-quite sharp nose, his trim moustache, the cleft chin, the frown on his bushy eyebrows as he focused on his task—she never got to look at him from a distance. He was either in her bed, or in a social situation where it would be inappropriate for her to stare. He'd slung on the hotel towel robe, the belt loosely tied, his tall, broad frame casting a shadow against the pale wall. He worked out, calling it *dand-baithak*, two hundred sit-ups and push-ups a day, no matter how tired he was, and the results showed. Anjali tried her best, but these days she had to exercise much longer and harder to stay trim.

Leaning against the headboard, she pulled the covers up to her throat: Jatin liked the air conditioning turned high and its cool draft produced goosebumps on her arms. The blanket was softer than the one she used at home, and there was something about the crisp white sheets and the firm bed beneath her bare body: she felt cocooned, far removed from her domestic troubles.

'Cheers,' Jatin handed her the glass, and clinked it against his own.

Anjali shifted back into the bed to let him sink in beside her, lay his head on her chest. He murmured a few soft words, sipped his drink, whispered a few more. Jatin recited couplets when he was drunk: he loved *shayari*, the soft, mellifluous Urdu words Anjali didn't understand.

'You must write for me what you recite.'

'Too sentimental for you, Jelly.' He took another sip. 'Leave them be.'

'When did you first start with these? I never heard them in Florida.'

That was a lifetime ago, when Jatin was her Dad's student, his favourite. When Jatin used to hang out in their living room, chatting with her Dad about social justice. Keen on his law studies.

'You were such a gangly girl in those days.'

'I was seventeen when you returned to India.' Anjali shifted, prompting Jatin to sit up. 'And you still haven't told me when you started reading these poems.'

'After my father died, funnily enough. He used to love them.'

'You never talk about him.'

'You never talk about your Mom either.'

You don't know what to say to a man, when to keep quiet. Mom's voice returned to her from years earlier when she was so full of advice about Anjali's marriage. How to keep a man, things to say to him, when to hold back. *At this rate, you won't stay married for long.* How prophetic of Mom. Anjali had divorced Nate Morgan after six years, and was left with only his last name. She had kept it because that was the name on her degrees and certificates, and she didn't need the hassle of changing them back to Gupta. No point dwelling on that ancient history now. Jatin waited for an answer.

'You've met her.'

'Yes.' Jatin chuckled, 'Can't say it was a pleasure.'

'Your Dad loved poetry?'

From all accounts of Jatin's dad from Maya, he was a tyrant. A lawyer who beat up his wife and son.

'I've hated him all my life, but I hated him even more for dying, you know? For going almost bankrupt, for using the house as a collateral. I had to come back after he died—Ma was sick, I had to join the force, marry Drishti. I never wanted to be powerless again.'

Anjali knew Jatin had given up his dreams of studying law in the USA, settling down in that country, but she understood the depth of his bitterness only at moments like these. She stroked his hand, the long, thick fingers, and laced hers through them. In the stillness, she imagined Jatin as she had seen him last in the US, a bright, talkative young man of twenty-four. Jatin remained silent for a while, and she didn't speak either, leaving her fingers interlaced with his while she sipped her drink.

'You know,' Jatin turned to her, 'at that time, when I appeared for the police force exams, gave tuition classes on the side to pay the bills and Papa's debts, I needed something to hold on to, other than Maya and Ma. I found Papa's books of poetry, and began to read them. They made sense of things, somehow.'

Anjali squeezed his hand, and rose up to kiss him, letting the covers fall. Jatin reached for her, and for the next hour Anjali tried to tell him with her body what she couldn't say in words, that we are each alone, and we need to make sense of this mixed-up world, and she was there, if he needed her. That's what friends were for.

'Dinner?' he asked later.

'Nah,' she said, 'dessert,' and drew him back in. He chuckled, did not resist. For the next few minutes Anjali got to play games, use her mouth to give pleasure, or deny it. No arguments with her boss or son that she couldn't win, no memories of a past she couldn't change. In bed with Jatin, she had control. He gave her that.

After they'd showered, Anjali began to dress.

'You could stay.' Jatin watched her from the bed, his wet hair combed, his eyes relaxed, sleepy.

'You say that each time. Why?'

They had their routine: they coordinated via an email, with a software to keep it untraceable, and they used it for the barest of communications. They did not message or call, unless in family situations. They arrived in different cars, parked far away from each other, entered the hotel at different times. Jatin said no one could trace the hotel bookings back to his name. They tried not to repeat the hotels too often. Jatin usually stayed the night, while she left, but not too late.

'You worry for Nikhil, but Maya is at home, and your housekeeper, Ira, has stayed back.'

'You know Maya will find out one day.'

'It's been ten years. We're careful. Can't stop living, Jelly.'

'Drishti dropped by the day before with clothes for Nikhil, and Maya now wants me to go shopping for Drishti's birthday.'

Drishti meant well, no doubt, but Anjali did not appreciate it. She hadn't asked for Varun's old clothes: she was capable of meeting Nikhil's needs. Talking about Drishti to Jatin seemed too much like complaining—no matter how things stood between the two, Drishti was his wife. Anjali had no desire to keep house for him.

'Sorry about that.' Jatin said, 'Gudiya can be so dense. You can always make an excuse.'

It was a good thing Maya was dense about such things. Anjali put final touches to her makeup and checked her face in the mirror. Behind her Jatin made himself another drink.

'I have a favour to ask you, Jelly.'

She liked this about him. When he needed help, he came straight to the point. Both Maya and Jatin referred to her when they needed an opinion on a case. Anjali read files, went through crime scene photos, analysed suspect interviews. Gave them her thoughts on possible motives. At other times, she helped Jatin with counselling a colleague or rehabilitating orphan kids caught in the dragnet of crime investigations.

'A case.' He put his hand on her shoulder, 'But this time it isn't photographs I need you to see.'

'No?'

'You'll have to visit the morgue. The body is at your hospital.'

She'd worked part time at the Safdarjung government hospital under Dr Bhalla for almost eleven years now. In all that time, she'd never ventured near the morgue.

'Must I?'

'I'll owe you a big one. Can't have Drishti's father finding out about the case, so no profile from the forensic psychologists at the Central Bureau.'

'I'm not trained for this, you know that, right?'

He told her about the case then. The women: raped, murdered, defaced, and dumped off.

'It could mean my job, Jelly. Besides, you have worked in the slums. That will work for you.'

'Why do you need to keep it from Drishti's father?'

'The less you know about all this, the better. Will you help?'

'Do you need to ask?'

Jatin had made room for her in his life and within his family. Her Dad had been his professor and mentor for the two years he'd spent in the USA. Ten years later, when Dad had called him to say she was moving to India with her toddling, special-needs son, Jatin had promised to help her and ensure her safety. He had done both. Even now, years after her father had passed on, he continued to support her in a hundred different ways. Of course she would help him. Not just because she felt obliged, but because she wanted to. For him, and those women.

'I'll owe you.' Jatin said.

He gulped down his drink, and walked over to her. He handed her her silk scarf, then decided to drape it around her neck. He turned her towards the mirror, and met her eyes in the reflection.

'You look fantastic,' he said, and whispered another couplet, his voice a soft husk over the whir of the air conditioning.

'What does that one mean?'

'I'll tell you some day.'

He hugged her from behind. She stared at the picture they made, Jatin's strong arm around her waist, his face on her shoulder, her hair tangled under his chin. She liked that he was so much taller than her five feet nine, and she liked him when he relaxed into her, lost his hard edges.

'I like that your father gave you this love of poetry.'

'He didn't give it to me.' Jatin's eyes turned wistful. 'I got it from him. I'm trying to do a better job as a father. Everything he never gave me, I'll give Varun.'

6

❦

Varun's phone rang, and he picked it up with a wide grin.

'*Abey saaley*, now only you're calling me?'

Felt amazing to talk to Bunty this way, so informal. Bunty was so chilled out he didn't mind, even though he was twenty-one years old, and studied in college, second year. Bunty's father worked as the Home Secretary these days, powerful enough to give orders to Varun's grandfather, the great Commissioner D.M. Mehra himself, but Bunty had called to invite Varun to a house party.

'Yes, of course I'll come.' Varun said. 'Was only taking your trip ya…chill *mar*, no need to be so senti.'

Bunty called him Vicky, not Varun. He said it matched better with Vish. Vish for Vishal Singh Sisodia, Bunty's formal, princely name. Big men called themselves a string of names and nicknames, Bunty said often. He was the sentimental types: small mistakes made him angry. He got pleased equally fast, thank God. Send him a hot video or a joke and he was all happy emojis again. You just said yes to Bunty, basically, whenever he asked for things.

Mostly, *daaru-shaaru*, whiskey and beer from Bunty's father's cupboard, and driving on Varun's bike. Because of the security that tailed him, Bunty didn't take his car out much. Varun picked him up on the bike, and they both went on drives, Bunty smashed and swaying like a proper *talli*, singing off-key. Varun acted as his sober driver, helped him up to his room via the back entrance to their mega-sized bungalow with its swimming pool and jacuzzi, where they all partied whenever Bunty's father went out of town.

It was all worth it because Bunty lived or died for his friends. *Yaron ke saath jeena-marna*, he said, and meant it— he'd rescued Varun from different scrapes: a traffic accident, and twice from worse. Varun didn't want to think too much about those times, but he would stick by Bunty, come what may. Let no one call Varun Bhatt an ungrateful bastard. He might have a thousand things to do, but when Bunty called, he dropped everything and answered.

Varun must arrange the booze for tonight's party. Also the girls and the hard core stuff. Given the current scene, it was difficult. The cash, for starters. Mummy was at home. And then he needed to call the guy for the drop. Such a bore ya this Bunty was sometimes. Why throw a party this week with Varun's tests in a few days? Daddy wanted him to clear the tests, or no school trip to Manila.

The answer was simple. Vishal Singh Sisodia wanted to party because his father Dayal Sisodia was travelling, doing the Home Secretary thing. Varun must bring it, or become toast. When Bunty got upset, he called Varun by his formal name, not Vicky, and that spelled trouble.

'You can trust your Vicky,' Varun sank into the sofa, 'I'll fix everything.' He cut the call.

Talking Mr Jatin Bhatt and Mrs Drishti Bhatt into letting

him stay over at the Sisodia bungalow was a breeze: Mummy and Daddy never said no. Too busy doing important things in their lives to talk to him, or worry too much. He had trained them well. Varun smiled to himself as he blasted off messages on the group about tonight's party. Parents. Buy them at one market and sell them in another, they'll never know. He also made a few calls—some of the boys didn't like a message invite. Ego-shego and all.

He wasn't called *Jugaadu* Vicky for nothing. He will find some *jugaad*, a way to get things done despite the last-minute notice. At least the *tota* girls weren't a problem for Bunty's parties. Vish and Vicky threw the best parties, the girls said, and clicked selfies, made all kinds of chat videos and more.

Varun checked himself out in the mirror. Must lift a few weights before this evening, to keep his arms the right shape for the *tota*s.

His phone rang. A private number. A smile spread across his face. His message had gone through.

'Hello?' Varun cupped his hand over the phone and walked into his toilet. *'Tere friend ko mera message mila? Aj free hai kya tu? I need a drop ya, Vish ki party hai.'* Varun opened his medicine cabinet, where he hid his stuff in regular pill boxes. *'Chal*, ok, done. How much have you got?'

7

~~~

Drawing her scarf closer about her neck, Anjali stepped out of Kusum's jeep at the Safdarjung mortuary. The sooty air made her cough, the chill about her face like the touch of a spiteful ghost—light, yet unmistakeable in its malign intent. It was far colder where she was headed.

A *harshingar*, still blooming in early November, had left a carpet of stale flowers on the ground beside the entrance. Nikhil loved to crush the orange stems of the tiny white flowers. He was the one who had taught her its name. Daylight had dwindled, and at this run-down building behind the main hospital, Anjali heard no sound other than the distant chitter of roosting birds in the trees bordering the parking lot.

'Are you all right, Anjaliji?'

Anjali liked this policewoman Jatin sent with her. Dusky, muscular. The relaxed face of someone who slept well at night with an unburdened conscience. Kusum's presence reassured Anjali, though the woman's head barely levelled with Anjali's shoulders.

'Sure, let's go in.' Anjali zipped up her fleece jacket.

'I'm going to find the doctor.' Kusum smiled. 'You waiting for me?'

The temperature had dropped to six degrees that afternoon. Nikhil had smashed a flower vase and a few plates at lunch; Maya and the housekeeper Ira struggled with the season's first flu, and Anjali felt as if she'd drunk too much coffee and wine all at once. Each hotel-room rendezvous with Jatin ended with a crash. Her body ached, and her mind grew numb with the effort of trying to tamp down her guilt.

She dabbed Vicks under her nose. It stung, but helped fade out the stench of detergents and bleach that layered the mortuary corridor, and the butcher-shop odour lurking beneath the chemicals. That smell took her back to her childhood grocery trips with her Dad on Sundays, where they chose steak for Mom, chicken or lamb for her and Dad. She might have been American, but her Hindu father had insisted she not eat beef.

Right now, she must drag her Hindu-American butt through the long corridor lined with racks and drawers, and study a corpse without flinching or throwing up. Must study it and find her way to the killer—not think about how it had once been a living, breathing person or how it would soon be turned into ash and charred bones. The cold afternoon seeped into the narrow corridor, and Anjali drew her scarf tighter. Her gut told her to upchuck her lunch and run, but she needed to go through with this. For Jatin.

She wanted to hold his large, reassuring hand while she walked down the corridor. Kusum stood in front of her instead, with the doctor-in-charge, a balding, soft-spoken old man with a straggly beard. He wore a lab coat over his sweater, no other barrier against what could be a whole host of infections. He offered them coats, masks and gloves, and while Anjali accepted, Kusum waved hers away. Along with all the protective gear, Anjali donned her listening 'shrink' face, and followed the other two into the morgue.

'We've had it for forty-nine hours,' was all the warning the doctor gave them before asking an orderly to drag out one of the drawers in a wall cabinet.

Years ago, on a college trip to Europe, Anjali had visited an exhibition of preserved human bodies: sinew, kidney, lung, blood vessel and bone all turned to plastic, then placed inside glass cases. She'd felt a shiver go down her body, goose-bumps on her bare arms. All that backlit lace of blood vessels, the swirling weave of nerves, the bulge of muscles, the vacant eye sockets and grinning teeth—all of that worked inside of her, too. She'd half-expected to smell a whiff of decay, but detected none. No formaldehyde either, that funk which clung to her through modules during medical school.

No such luck now. Under the white glare of halogen bulbs, the plastic-sheet-covered body on the slab smelled like meat past its use-by date. Anjali clenched her jaw, but no amount of preparation could have contained her gasp. She stared at the face, if you could still call it that, stewed away, leaving behind a slick mess, with stubs of bone poking out. The body had bloated to almost twice its normal size, like an alien from a B-grade sci-fi movie. Anjali shoved her hands into the pockets of the lab coat, and dug her nails into her thigh. The Vicks protected her somewhat, but she saw Kusum raise her knuckles to her nose.

'What happened to her face?' The question shot out of Anjali before she could stop herself. Jatin hadn't warned her about this.

'Tests show industrial grade sulphuric acid,' the doctor said.

He lifted the green plastic sheet to just above the chest. The acid had found its way to the woman's chin, her throat, it flowed down into her chest in mottled pink-brown tracks.

Anjali looked at Kusum, who pulled the entire sheet off. The old doctor's jaws went slack.

'Are you sure?' He hurried forward, and reached for the sheet.

Most Indian males, especially the older ones, treated women either like doormats or fragile fairies.

'Yes.' Anjali raised her hand to reassure him. 'I need to see it all, for me to be of any use.'

'Blood work shows traces of Propofol.' He cleared his throat, and regained his professorial air. 'Physical examination indicates vaginal bruising from repeated rapes, but no evidence of any seminal fluids. Condoms may have been used. Other bruises on the body, and bite marks from more than one individual, but with the decomposition, we can't be certain how many. Maybe two. The acid was used after death.'

'Propofol? Isn't that...'

'Yes, it is one of the drugs used to induce general anaesthesia before surgery.'

Unlike sulphuric acid, cheap and readily available at roadside shops, Propofol wasn't sold over the counter, only at a hospital. Anjali stared at the body and tried to marshal her thoughts, despite her churning stomach and the stinging bile rising in her throat. She didn't train for this. What went through that woman's mind when those monsters grabbed her?

Stretch marks on her abdomen. Definitely a mother,

many times over. No vaccination marks on her arms or thighs—couldn't be from a very educated family. Cracked, dirty heels, uneven, chipped toenails. A woman who walked in the dirt. Tan lines on her arms and chest. Wore short-sleeved, deep-necked blouses. Unusual. Not many poor Indian women wore revealing clothes.

'We found these bruises,' the doctor pointed to dark marks on her arms and legs. 'Someone might have held her down. They strangled her with a cloth, that's the cause of death.'

She ignored Kusum and the doctor, and breathed in the Vicks. Gang rape occurred before they poured acid on this woman's face and torso. To prevent identification. This was not a caste murder, like the ones in Haryana and Uttar Pradesh where higher caste men raped and killed as a lesson to the lower caste. This seemed more personal, intimate. To burn and disfigure a woman this way, the perpetrator must hate women. At least one of the men, the leader, and there was always a leader, had wanted to not just hurt or kill this woman, but to erase her from existence. He possessed medical knowledge and access to hospitals.

Anjali crossed her arms, bracing herself against nausea.

'We also found these on the body. It was hard to prise them off.'

The doctor held up a small ziploc bag containing two silver rings.

'These looking like toe-rings, the sort we're wearing in the village.' Kusum took the packet from him. 'Nothing else?'

'No.' He said. 'I double-checked.'

Anjali watched as Kusum turned the packet this way and that, making the rings slide about. They looked delicate, with tiny daisies at both ends to twist and adjust to various toe sizes. Anjali turned away from the doctor. A few more minutes of this might give her a migraine. She turned around to find Kusum watching her.

'I think we seeing enough.' Kusum held Anjali by the elbow.

The doctor replaced the cover and moved the body back to its place. All three of them stepped out into the corridor, and Kusum let go of Anjali. Anjali's feet, her hands, her entire body felt numb.

'Are you filing a report?' Kusum walked ahead with the doctor.

'Not yet,' the doctor said. 'I need it signed off.'

The two of them continued talking as they walked, but Anjali didn't want to hear any of it. She strode ahead to return the lab coat, trashed the gloves and mask, and hurried out to the police jeep. Darkness had claimed the parking lot. She felt thankful for the light from the entrance. The air tasted grittier and colder now; but she welcomed it after her time inside. She checked her watch: twenty-five minutes. It had felt like two hours.

She needed to fix her face, but the thought of a hospital toilet discouraged her. She swallowed large gulps of air, her nose burning with the Vicks. Her contact lenses stung, making her eyes water. Easing out the PET bottle of sanitiser from her bag, she rubbed her hands clean, then hunted for some tissue to dab at her nose, nearly losing her grip on her bag in the process.

Dad carried white handkerchiefs. Mom insisted on tissues, but Dad never got used to Kleenex. On long road trips across Florida to see Mom's folks, Mom would ask her to bite on tissues and lean back to keep from throwing up. Car-sick and dazed, Anjali wanted to hurl herself out of the window, but stayed buckled in, soggy tissues wadded between her teeth. Dad would stop after a while under a clutch of trees or at a gas station. He let her out, soothed her with a cool damp kerchief on her forehead, a pale lemon scent dabbed on it to make her feel better. He mumbled songs and prayers while she gulped in mouthfuls of air by the empty roadside. She missed him sometimes. Through the decades of his life in his adopted country, Professor Gupta had stuck to the set of beliefs and habits he carried from India—his secret aversion to concepts like privacy, his teeth-grinding accent, his weird Sanskrit sayings like, '*Ghrane ardh bhojanam*—smelling is half-eating.'

Had she half-eaten that corpse? Decomposing cells had risen and made their way through the mask, her breathing mouth, into her stomach. She felt her phone vibrate inside her bag, but ignored it. That woman, now no longer a woman, lying there in the cold. Anjali wanted to slough away the images, but they refused to go, and the thought of the murdered woman's orphaned children, clueless, bereft, made her want to rush home and see Nikhil.

***

'Are you okay?'

The voice scared her for a second till she recognised it. Jatin stepped out of the dark. What was he doing here? Part of her wanted to launch into his arms, but she stared at him instead, at his squared jaw and eyes crinkled in concern. The police driver sat in the jeep behind him and the mortuary guards gathered around the tea stall, chatting and laughing, warming their hands over a small fire.

'I'm on my way to see Maya.' He answered her unasked question. 'Thought I'd pick you up.'

Anjali couldn't focus on his words, couldn't forget the woman she'd just seen. Tears prickled her eyes. She swallowed, wanting to go home and offer herself up to a hot shower. She focused on Jatin's face, his lips forming the words as he spoke. She wanted to stay anchored in the moment, rub her hand against the emerging stubble on his cheek, feel the prickle of the short tapered hair against her fingers.

'I've told Kusum I'm dropping you back. My driver will wait and take her to the office in her jeep.'

He steered her towards his jeep. They met publicly either at family gatherings, or when he visited Maya, but hardly ever walked beside each other. He wore the dark long jacket she'd gifted him last year, and for a moment she imagined herself wrapped around him.

The distraction didn't work for long. Her contact lenses irritated her eyes, and tears blurred her vision. *You must always look your best beside your man*, Mom had ranted at her after she'd worn t-shirt and shorts when Nate Morgan first visited their home. When Nate left the marriage, Mom said: *it's all your fault. I warned you. A woman needs to know how to keep her husband.*

Mom never smiled at her, thanked her grudgingly when she did chores or planned a special surprise for Mother's day. Was Mom a narcissist, incapable of empathy? Or maybe a mild case of Munchausen by proxy: abusing Anjali to gain sympathy for herself. All of Anjali's mentors cautioned her against trying to analyse her own parent, but she couldn't help herself.

She was her own Mom, she decided, she would hug herself better when she got home. Her inflamed eyes made a foggy nightmare of the slow-moving tail lights on the road ahead, watching, blinking. She wanted some place warm and safe: her Safdarjung Enclave home, her bed.

'You ok? Are you crying?'

'No, just drive home, please. I've got to wash my eyes. They've been troubling me this week.'

'Do you keep eyedrops at home?'

'I'll ask Maya.' Anjali clasped her hands together to keep from rubbing her eyes.

The car turned into a lane, and Anjali looked up at him. What was he up to?

'We'll stop at the pharmacy to pick up the drops.'

He parked the car in the lane, lit by a lone, flickering yellow streetlight.

'Lock yourself in.' He strode off.

Anjali clicked the lock to his door, and sat back. Outside in the lane, smog curled around the lights from various windows. Customers stood in front of a small shop, under a huge billboard advertising second-hand mobile phones and electronic repairs. Someone played television loud enough that Anjali could make out the music and the canned laughter. A woman came out onto a second-floor balcony and hung a saree to dry, its length falling all the way to the satellite dish on the balcony below. Cyclists and bikers passed by, trying to peer inside the parked car. Anjali pushed her seat back into the darkness. Just ahead of the car, a fight broke out between two stray dogs. They scuffled over some scrap, growling and snapping. The police had discovered the woman's body in a rubbish dump. What if no one had found it? Would dogs have squabbled over her flesh? That half-rotten meat smell came back to Anjali, and with it an upswell of nausea.

Deep breaths. She inhaled and tried to visualise her breath going down into her lungs.

When she got in trouble at school, when the kids called her Bindi, Curry, Fatty, her Dad had said: *Be like a boat. All the water in the sea can't drown a boat unless it springs a leak. Don't let it get to you.* All through her school and college, she imagined herself skimming over the surface of muddied waters, not a boat, but a girl in a boat. After she found Nate, she'd dropped anchor.

Here she was, twenty-four years after she first met Nate, sitting in a car on a Friday evening with another man. Not an ideal Friday evening, and not quite her man, but still, a man who had gone to buy her eyedrops. Nate Morgan was the senior at her school everyone wanted to snag, and he went for her. Against all advice, against Mom saying, *You can't trust an orphan, an immigrant* (Why did she marry an immigrant orphan then?) and her father's warnings, *Nate has no sense of responsibility*, Anjali went for the beach wedding she'd always wanted. At twenty-one, she had a real family— far away from her mother's hard words and hands, and her father who never raised his voice and said things like *You know how she is, she's stressed out, she means well.*

You'll suffer, you watch, Mom warned, but Anjali laughed

it off. Nate loved her, made no secret of it. At each family gathering, Fourth of July, Thanksgiving, Christmas, when he held her by the waist, planted a kiss in her hair, or nuzzled her neck, Anjali met Mom's eyes to find a cold, disgusted stare.

Four years later, Anjali was ecstatic to find out she was pregnant. But with Nikhil came trouble: wild fits of crying, anger, and finally the diagnosis: *He's on the spectrum.* For a moment she had wanted to turn it into a joke—spectrum, like the colour spectrum? Autism, they said. With treatment he'll get better, he's high-functioning, but he'll always be different. Over the next few months she had fought with Nate, tried to persuade him that Nikhil was worth it. She battled for Nikhil, but lost his father in the process.

Now she had Jatin: part closet-poet, part patriarchal jerk, enthusiastic bed-mate and best friend: exasperating and endearing in equal measure. Anjali watched him walk back towards the car through the dimly lit, smoggy air, a large shadow against the dark evening.

'Here, we can put this in your eyes.'

'I must take out my lenses. Let's go home.'

'You don't need to. I asked the pharmacist.' He helped her put on a pair of gloves, and picked up the bottle. It looked tiny in his large hands. 'Tell me when you're ready.'

'I'll do it myself.' A serial blinker, she didn't want him grumbling as the eyedrops landed everywhere but her eyes. 'Why did you buy the gloves then?'

'So you can hold your eyelids. That's how I put eyedrops for Maya when she was young.'

'Don't tell me I didn't warn you.'

'Relax. Try to picture something beautiful.'

Anjali's mind drifted back to the Jacaranda trees of her childhood, their pale purple blossoms nodding in Florida's summer breeze. Dad, his brown face under the sun, laughing at something she'd said. When the drop entered her eye, her fingertips remained firm on her eyelids.

'Close your eyes.' He lifted her index finger and touched it to the inner corner of her eye. 'Put your finger here.'

Jatin stroked her wrist while she waited in the dark, her eyes cooling down. She heard him flick off the light. Leaning on his shoulder, she felt his breath on her hair, soft and regular. He switched on the light after a while, and repeated the process with her right eye.

'You know, Jatin, the woman...'

'We don't need to discuss it today.'

'No.' She didn't want to dwell on the morgue any longer than she must. 'Let's finish with it on the drive home.'

'We'll eat first.' Jatin turned the car out of the alley, 'Maya isn't feeling well, she will meet me another day. She wants us to pack food because Ira also has the flu. Paranthas?'

Nikhil liked paranthas, and Anjali didn't mind them herself. A piping hot aloo parantha would warm her up before she reached home. While Jatin drove through the congested traffic, Anjali described what she'd seen. When he asked her further questions, she answered them on autopilot. Facts, her conclusions, and pointers on what avenues to investigate.

At the drive-by stall, Anjali sat back in the car as Jatin stepped out to order food, and came back with tissues, a squeeze bottle of disinfectant soap, and a bottle of water. Anjali washed her hands, taking her time, letting the water run into the dry earth beside the pavement.

A tousle-haired boy, definitely a minor, came running with their packages. He refused a tip, but Jatin forced it on him. The street urchin left with salutes and grins and thankyous. A lad like that should be at school, studying.

This was why, despite hours at her Bhikaji Cama private clinic and part-time consultancy at the Safdarjung Hospital, and all the evenings taken up with Nikhil's therapy activities, she carved out time to volunteer at Hridayog with Mr Lahiri.

'This boy is new at the shop?' Anjali opened the packet of paranthas, handed one to Jatin on a tissue. The fragrance of *ghee*, the spice of the potato filling invaded the car.

'Yes. And before you ask, yes, he's underage. I can get Kusum to call the beat constable to check if this boy can go to Hridayog night school.'

The one aspect of Delhi Police she loved: they tried to home at-risk kids with non-profits whenever they could. Jatin went out of his way to help her—the best way to beat crime, he often said, was to prevent children from getting into it.

She laughed. 'I'll have to persuade Mr Lahiri yet again.'

Mr Lahiri said they needed to think of practical concerns, but in the end, he always gave in. Anjali occasionally wondered where he got the money from. She'd never seen him run a fundraising campaign. Rumours spoke of a falling out with his rich family, and his inheritance money used to fund Hridayog.

'Oh.' Jatin said, 'Grewal sends his regards.'

Ravinder Grewal was Jatin's school friend, an SHO in Delhi Police. His sister, an aspiring fashion designer, had tried to commit suicide earlier that year, because her family rejected the man she wanted to marry. Anjali had given her five months of trauma counselling at reduced rates.

'Grewal's sister is planning to design a trousseau for you, he says, for when you get married.'

'Right.' Anjali dipped a warm piece of parantha in pickles, then yoghurt, and popped it into her mouth, letting the clash of spices fill her mouth. Warmth, at last, after the creeping chill of the last hour spent with Kusum at the morgue.

'Any marriage plans I don't know about, madamji?' Jatin copied Grewal's accent.

Anjali laughed as she ate. She watched as Jatin polished off his parantha, packed the trash, tied it up and tossed it into the backseat. He changed gears and joined the traffic heading back towards Safdarjung Enclave. The police found the woman in a trash bag secured with twine—the report said that the rapists had tossed her from a moving vehicle. A sob escaped Anjali.

'Jelly?'

'That woman,' Anjali struggled to find the words, 'I just can't…'

Jatin pulled over in a lane behind the Green Park market. Deserted, with lights twinkling from the buildings on both sides, it looked like a street from a haunted city. The trees seemed distorted and large in the dark, like enormous, mythical beasts.

Unbuckling his seatbelt, Jatin reached for her.

'I know,' he tightened his grip on her back. 'I know.'

Anjali held on to his shirt collar and wept. She felt her makeup streaking down her face, but didn't care. His calloused fingers ran through her hair, across her back, stroked her arms and hands. He kissed her forehead, her eyebrows, ears, but when their mouths met, the kiss became a hungry, living thing; it demanded to be fed. For a second, Anjali tried to think, to remember where and who they were. *Deep breaths*, she tried to tell herself, *be a boat*. But that other, fierce, fearless part of her took over. *Relax*. She sagged beneath him. *Nothing is in control*.

8

Maya walked down to the living room to find her giant teddy bear of a brother squinting at the newspaper. He refused to get glasses—they made him look weak, he said. That teakwood rocking chair he sat on had belonged to Papa when he was alive, and now to Bhai, each time he visited. Everyone else left it alone. Ira wiped it down every day, and polished it each weekend, making the place reek of turpentine.

Kusum sat on the corner of a sofa typing away at a laptop. She greeted Maya and went back to work, leaving Maya to approach Bhai, who had so far ignored the mountain of pakoras and the tea things that sat in front of him. Before she could say hello to her brother, Maya heard Pawan's bike powering down outside the gate.

Bhai heard it too, because he simply raised his head and said, 'We'll do standard fees this time.'

No hello or good morning. Bhai never got into pleasantries at home, behaving as if he still lived here and had seen everyone a few minutes ago. Maya nodded and turned away, placing a few pakoras on a plate instead, pouring a cup of tea, and taking them to Kusum. She would not let Bhai see her joy at being told Vigil was now worth professional rates. She handed him his tea, and poured one for herself.

Pawan strode in, and Maya's heart did that funny flip-flop thing it tended to do around him. Her assistant wore jeans, a black jacket, and a grey sweater that complimented his wiry build. He strode in with an easy grace, his smile wide, his red muffler setting off the typical Punjabi square jaws and strong chin. But in the end, it was his eyes that got her. He kept them lowered most of the time, but when he gazed at her with those hazel eyes, she wanted so much to walk up to him. Her assistant, four years younger than her, Drishti Bhabi's cousin. Maya huffed a sigh and tucked back the runaway curls from her haphazard knot.

'Good morning, Maya. Hello, Jatin sir.'

Pawan bent down to shake Bhai's hand.

Maya loved the way he said her name. It had taken her a month of corrections and threats to get him to call her Maya, not Maya*ji*. Worth it, in the end, though he still used the super-polite Punjabi *haanji* instead of 'yes' every time she gave him an instruction.

'What's that?' Bhai pointed at the covered shopping basket Pawan had carried in.

'Dr Bhalla thinks Nikhil needs to connect with a pet.' Maya took the basket from Pawan and opened it. 'So we got these two from a shelter.'

She took out one of the puppies, and stroked its black woolly fur. It yawned, stretched, but didn't open its eyes. She wanted it for herself: a live soft toy, its tiny black legs the size of her fingers, its ears floppy bits of velvet.

'Aren't they too young?' Bhai put his teacup down. 'Are you sure?'

'Bhalla said smaller puppies will work better.'

Pawan had set the puppies down on the carpet, one jet black and the other pale brown—shiny wet noses, closed eyes. He held them by the scruff, and they nuzzled against his feet, squealing softly.

'Where did you get them from?' Nikhil spoke up from behind her.

She'd meant to go call him, and was surprised he'd come out of his room by himself. He shuffled up to her, clutching his half-finished model airplane, his arms too long for his loose sleeves.

'Did they run away?' Nikhil said. 'Their mother scolds them, too?'

Oh man, poor Nikhil. Poor poor Anjali. The pups, now half-awake, stumbled towards him. Nikhil took a step back, as if he'd seen cockroaches. He stiffened, and grabbed Maya's sweater. Beside her, Bhai stood up, and Kusum at her sofa, ready to intervene. Pawan scooped the puppies up, and put them back in the basket. He took off his jacket, readying himself for the meeting.

'Hello, Nikhil.' Bhai said. 'How are you?'

Nikhil didn't look at Bhai. Maya wanted to jump in, ask the boy to talk. *Talk or you'll turn out like me*, she wanted to say, *I don't have any real friends, other than your mother.*

Pawan asked her to put the basket in Nikhil's room.

'Don't be an idiot, Pawan.' Nikhil swayed the airplane right and left, following it with his eyes.

Bhai's shoulders stiffened. He wasn't used to Nikhil. Maya put her hand on his arm so he wouldn't speak.

Pawan turned to Nikhil, 'How would you like it if people called you names?'

Maya loved the Punjabi rasp in Pawan's voice, so like her brother's. Her assistant never lost his head.

'They call me names all the time.' Nikhil slouched down in his chair. 'Blue-eyed bastard. *Harami sala*, *Gore ka poot*, so many more.'

This was new. Maya would have to tell Anjali that Nikhil got bullied at school.

'You should tell them not to.' Pawan walked towards Nikhil.

'I don't have muscles like you.'

'You can if you want.' Pawan leaned on the sofa across from Nikhil, letting the light from the ceiling lamp shine on his arms.

Besides his other qualities, Maya had hired Pawan for those biceps and his karate. She had once watched him handle a big man swearing away and hitting his wife. Pawan had reached out and held the man in a chokehold, making him go limp in a few seconds.

'Can I get a black belt like you?'

'It takes time. You must work hard,' Pawan straightened, 'but you'll be able to tell people not to bother you.'

Pawan picked up the basket and headed towards the kitchen. Nikhil followed him.

A few minutes later, Pawan returned. Nikhil had settled down in the kitchen with a piece of cake, he reported, and agreed to go to the gym with Pawan three times a week, in return for helping Ira take care of the puppies.

'Well done,' Bhai nodded and gave Pawan one of his rare smiles.

Bhai leaned forward in his chair, no longer a teddy bear.

He looked every inch the Special Commissioner of crime, even though he wore a casual navy sweater and trousers.

'This case is top-priority, and the usual non-disclosure agreement applies.' Bhai began, 'You'll talk about this case only with Kusum and Anjali.'

Maya took notes as Bhai told them about the serial murder case Kusum had uncovered, about Anjali's conclusions at the morgue. Kusum sat by, a stern expression on her face, but Maya could sense her eagerness. Bhai's phone rang, and after a glance at them, he excused himself to take the call.

When he came back, he called Kusum to the door. Maya couldn't make out all that he said, but the words Sabharwal, documents, Rathi, floated back into the living room. Kusum nodded, and began collecting her things.

'Everything all right?' Maya said.

'Kusum has to leave,' Bhai settled back in his chair, 'because she needs to work on something important. But I'll continue.'

Once Kusum left, Bhai said, 'There have been some developments at the office. I want you to put this case on priority.'

'We're here, Bhai.'

'So far, we know this.' Bhai summed it up. 'We have multiple offenders, a gang if you like, dumping bodies after committing similar crimes: gang rape, murder, acid on the dead body. At least some of them are young: Anjali agrees that such gang crimes are usually committed by young, mostly unattached men. They used Propofol, a drug they can find only in hospitals, to make their victims unconscious, then molest them, and dump the bodies in black trash bags. She says they must be choosing spots they're familiar with as dump sites: either near their homes or their work place.'

'We can begin with a list of where the bodies were found.' Maya unfolded a Delhi map.

Pawan and Bhai opened it out on the large centre table. With a red marker, Bhai circled the two sites in Pul Mithai and the latest at Madipur Colony, and joined them in a triangle.

'Pul Mithai is in Old Delhi, Madipur Colony is in the West.' Bhai said. 'We don't have reports of any missing women from those places. Kusum has checked.'

'So these women are being dumped far from places where they live?' Maya said. 'Otherwise, if a woman is missing from an area and the body is found, people would assume it is the missing woman, right?'

It took at least an hour and fifteen minutes to drive from Old Delhi to West Delhi during high traffic, and no less than forty minutes on emptier roads at night.

'If they are moving the women, then the killers must own some sort of vehicle.' Pawan peeked into the profile notes Anjali had given them. 'They can't move them on public transport. And, they must take the women to a hideout.'

'We must try and identify this body.' Bhai said, 'Kusum has arranged for it to be checked against reported missing cases from all over Delhi. This woman had children, and may have worked as a prostitute, Anjali says. Police have disposed of the two other bodies from Pul Mithai. So this one is all we have to go on.'

'Pawan can start with Madipur Colony tomorrow.' Maya said, 'Check if anyone has gone missing and not been reported. I can use one of our freelancers if I need help at the office.'

'I can go there in my gear, blend in.' Pawan said.

'Your gear?' Bhai turned to Pawan.

'He changes into different clothes when needed, Bhai.'

A lot of their work involved landlords, money lenders, tracing employment histories or missing persons, but the agency also gathered evidence for divorce cases. It was tricky work, tailing cheating spouses, because they were a paranoid lot. Pawan had been part of a theatre group in college, and used wigs and accessories when needed.

'A disguise?'

Pawan explained to Bhai, showing him pictures of some of his looks on his phone. Bhai chose one, and they discussed what Pawan would do, and the best spots to collect information at a slum.

'The BCs will keep getting away with these if we can't identify this body soon.'

Bad Characters and Anti-Socials. The Delhi Police used funny names for criminals—when they first began working together, Maya had teased Bhai about it.

'We'll do our best, sir,' Pawan stood up. He needed to go out to collect payments from a client.

'Good job with Nikhil today.' Bhai shook Pawan's hand. 'But do you think karate is a good idea for him?'

Maya hadn't voiced it, but she feared karate might make Nikhil more difficult to deal with. Nikhil had turned angry as he hit puberty. Dr Bhalla said it was his hormones, and his inability to relate to people.

'It will help channel his energy, sir.'

Pawan took his leave, and Maya began gathering her notes.

'Nikhil makes me uneasy,' Bhai said.

'What about our Varun? He's *toh* all perfect only, na?'

'*Kya matlab?*' Bhai's voice rose in a challenge. 'What's wrong with Varun?'

He switched to Hindi whenever he got annoyed.

'Your son spends money like he earns a salary, not an allowance, returns home late at night after loafing about with that Dayal Sisodia's son, misbehaves with Nikhil...'

As usual, Bhai didn't let her finish. Varun could do no wrong.

'He's just a boy.' Bhai picked up his phone. 'He'll grow out of it. And Bunty Sisodia is from a good family.'

'And that makes him a nice boy? Remember what his father did to Anji?'

Dayal Sisodia was Bhai's friend from his college days, who had once tried to grope Anjali at a party, and she had slapped him. Bhai had apologised to Anjali, and stopped inviting Dayal to their home. But he kept up with their stupid golfing weekends, sending him mangoes each year from Papa's farmhouse at Sainik Farms, exchanging gifts each Diwali. Dayal was from a royal family and now the Indian Home Minister's top man.

'His mother died recently. It is natural for him to act out. I'm glad Varun can support him at this time.'

Helping a depressed friend was fine, but how could Bhai not see that Bunty, an older, college-going boy, who had once stayed in jail overnight for harassing a girl, was not good for Varun? Bhai turned away from her and swiped at his phone, as if flicking his finger on the screen could make the conversation go away.

Bhai's phone rang. 'Yes.' He walked off to answer it. 'Ok, fine.'

He said those words to Drishti Bhabi whenever he was angry with her. Always busy fighting, these two. She had to make them see what a good thing they had: family. Maya herself could never marry: she had accepted this after spending years with the spots on her body. But she had to make sure nothing broke up Bhai's family. That was all the family she had left, too.

A piercing cry broke into her thoughts. It grew louder with each second, the high-pitched squeal of a puppy in trouble. Another voice joined in. This time it was Nikhil, screaming. She ran towards the boy's room, Bhai close behind her.

9

Jatin didn't wish to be right this time. Watching as Maya and Pawan introduced the puppies to Nikhil, Jatin had wanted to ask them to stop.

Now, Nikhil held the squirming black puppy by the throat. With his other hand, he pounded the mattress in time with his words, 'Go, go, go!' He sat on the bed, rocking to and fro.

Maya rushed to him, Jatin behind her.

'Nikhil, what's wrong?'

'Go, go, go!' Nikhil sobbed.

Jatin wanted to move in, grab Nikhil's hand and get him to let go of the puppy, but Maya stopped him, her small hand on his forearm, her gaze focused on Nikhil. He stepped back. Other than Anjali, Maya understood the best way to handle Nikhil.

'It's ok, Nikhil. Put it down.' Maya stopped a few feet from the bed.

'Take it away!' Nikhil shook the drooping black body in his hand. 'It got my airplane!'

Maya inched closer to the bed, and repeated her words to Nikhil. 'Just let go of it. It will be ok, I promise.'

The tiny black body had gone limp. If Nikhil didn't let go very soon, this pup wouldn't make it.

'Stay back. Pull down the blinds and ring Anjali,' Maya whispered to Jatin, and to Ira she said, 'bring me a soft cloth bag.'

Ira handed Nikhil's stress ball and blanket to Maya, and rushed out.

Jatin lowered the blinds while dialling his phone, then stepped out. Anjali picked up at the second ring, and he didn't bother with greetings, giving her the bare details.

'Come home now, hurry.'

Jatin returned to the darkened room and stood behind Maya as she tiptoed closer to the bed, prepared to grab the tiny body the instant Nikhil let go. The room smelled of urine; the puppy must have wet itself.

'My airplane!' Nikhil's voice came to her in a high whine. He repeated the two words, again and again, his head lowered, the puppy clenched in his hand. Maya took the bag Ira returned with and held it open.

'Here,' Maya placed the bag beneath the puppy, 'Drop it in here. Take your blanket, come on, Nikhil.'

Jatin let his Gudiya coax and plead with the boy. Anjali had suffered because of her son, lost a husband, her home, and even to this day, this boy ruled her thoughts, her priorities. If Nikhil were a normal boy, she wouldn't live from crisis to crisis. *Not Nikhil's fault*, he repeated to himself the words Anjali often said to him, but it didn't work.

'Well done, Nikhil.' Maya said, 'Look, Ira has taken it away. It can't hurt you now. Breathe.'

Ira carried the bag away. Nikhil swung his hands about as Maya tried to hand him his blanket. To Jatin, he seemed crazed now, throwing blind punches and kicks.

Just as he decided to step in, Jatin heard a car screech to a stop at the driveway and hurried footsteps in the living room. Anjali.

He walked out to meet her. 'Maya's with him. I can help if you need me.'

Ashen-faced, Anjali nodded and walked past. He followed her into Nikhil's room, just as the boy took a wild swing at Maya.

'I'll call Dr Bhalla,' he said to Anjali, but she held his arm.

'Hold on a few minutes. We won't use medication if we can avoid it.'

Maya turned, and a look of relief washed over her face. She made way for Anjali to approach Nikhil.

One of Nikhil's punches landed on Anjali's arm. She didn't flinch.

'Come now, come.' Anjali said in a low hum, 'It's ok. There, there. You're ok now.'

Anjali arranged the pillows Nikhil had scattered on the bed, draped Nikhil's small blue blanket around his shoulders. She handed him a pillow, making soothing noises, all clucks and whispers. Nikhil droned on, words Jatin couldn't understand. He headed out to look for Maya.

In the kitchen, he found her and Ira bent over the puppy, trying to revive it. He checked the puppy and told them what he had feared all along. The puppy was dead.

Under the Flame of the Forest tree in the backyard, Jatin drove the shovel into the moist earth. Maya looked calm, but from her stormy expression and the way her lips quivered once in a while, Jatin guessed his sister had taken the puppy's death to heart.

Maya's eyes welled up with tears. 'All because of me.'

'Gudiya, it was an accident.' Even as he said the words, he found himself disagreeing with them. Nikhil strangled that puppy. It might have been an accident, or not. That boy was already a little taller than Maya, and his punch thwacking Anjali's arm must hurt. As Nikhil grew in strength, he would become more of a challenge. Jatin resolved to broach this with Anjali the next time they met.

10

Anjali liked visiting Hridayog on holidays. Today felt special because it was a Monday, but a holiday nevertheless, because of the festival of Mahavir Jayanti.

Pre-schoolers chased each other on the terrace, playing tag as their laughter and shrieks rose on the chilly afternoon breeze. Songs floated down from the Special Section across the alley. She breathed easy in the knowledge that Nikhil would be happy and safe there for the next two hours. After yesterday's puppy incident, she couldn't afford to take chances.

She didn't have counselling sessions scheduled today. Instead, her students, twenty women in colourful sarees, sat soaking up the winter sun on mats spread across the terrace, heads bent over exercise copies and alphabet books. She wished she could do this at her private clinic. Her clients at Bhikaji Cama might benefit from therapy sessions outdoors.

There was no furniture on the terrace, only mats, but the straggling group of mothers in front of her couldn't afford any better. Their neighbourhood was named Sanjay Colony, as if it were a decent locality with proper amenities like water, sewage and electricity, not a rubbish-clogged slum beside the Okhla industrial area.

One of the women read the lesson out loud and the others repeated it after her. On the vibrant indigo walls of the attic, flowers bloomed, painted during the drawing classes for older children. Mr Lahiri, the bald, portly man who sat at a table not far from them, ran the classes. He looked like a battle-worn retired lawyer—his sagging jowls didn't detract from the strength of his jaw.

He'd set up Hridayog, and run it for the past ten years. The place helped many women and children in their studies. With the benefit of an education, that woman at the morgue might have led a better life, away from the streets that claimed her.

The woman haunted Anjali, as did the puppy. She should have stayed home yesterday instead of listening to Dr Bhalla, followed her own instincts, knowing that Nikhil got bullied. India didn't possess adequate infrastructure for kids with ASD. Despite knowing this, she had fled here all those years ago, in a bid to run as far as possible from it all: Nate's rejection, her troubled, fledgling career, Mom's relentless bickering. Weak and naive, she'd mistaken distance for escape.

Too late to regret that now. So many New Delhi moms raised kids like Nikhil. Nikhil's school boasted some of the best teachers in India and very inclusive policies. Anjali needed to trust herself. After all, she'd handled him yesterday, made him fall asleep, just like the children in the tuition class opposite her on the terrace, taking their afternoon naps curled up in the sun.

She called for a break, and the sombre-looking women relaxed. They cracked jokes and laughed, their faces half-hidden behind the ghunghat of their sarees. These women who owned so little, yet found laughter, inspired in her a certain lightness, a willingness to embrace life, warts and all.

She needed to speak with Mr Lahiri while the women enjoyed their break. With two cups of tea in hand, she headed towards him.

Despite six years of working together, and Anjali's relative youth, Mr Lahiri still called her Anjaliji. She protested, but he remained stand-offish. She knew that he was unmarried, came from a well-off family he no longer kept in touch with, and used to work at a pharmaceutical college, but that was all. She hadn't ever heard him mention friends or relatives. He never answered the phone in her presence, and ate his meals alone.

'You're sure about this?' Mr Lahiri pushed aside the answer papers once she had said her piece, and pressed his pudgy hands on the table. Anjali nodded. The story came to her from one of her brightest students—Usha, a smiling, round-faced woman, who had looked distracted over the last few days. This woman's friend Sujni, a single mother, had been missing for the past week, along with her oldest son, Ram Sharan.

Sujni's youngest son, a toddler, now stayed with this woman. Police had picked up Sujni's two middle kids, but no one knew why. Anjali helped out in such cases, because thanks to Jatin, she had access to the police.

'They asked me to talk to you.'

Not one woman approached Mr Lahiri for help unless Anjali mediated.

'Maybe Sujni has run away?' Mr Lahiri said.

'Her son is missing, too. You've met him before, remember

Ram Sharan? He joined the after-school classes for a while, then dropped out.'

Ram Sharan began at Hridayog as a strapping happy-faced teenager, always ready to shift the rickety blackboard, or place the mats on the floor. Over a few months he lost a lot of weight, turned surly, taciturn, and then stopped coming in altogether for the weekend lessons. According to Sujni's friend, the boy had taken to drugs.

'So many of them come in each year,' Lahiri said, 'They come and go as they like.'

Anjali wanted Hridayog to find a way to support Sujni's children until they located her, but Mr Lahiri didn't seem keen. For the most part, he sympathised with the women who came to Hridayog, but today, his face had taken on a hard cast.

Anjali had met Mr Lahiri at the Safdarjung hospital years ago when he came to get some kids treated. She had liked his quiet manner, and understood that her counselling and teaching might help him and the other staff. 'I'll see what we can do.' The chair creaked as Lahiri settled back. 'But I can't make promises.'

Anjali stood up. A mother who had taken care of her children so far wouldn't abandon them and run away. Granted, Sujni's friend said she walked with men into the alleys. Anjali tried to imagine what she would do in that woman's place: no husband, no education, but with four children to feed. Selling her body might have been Sujni's only option. Mr Lahiri wouldn't understand. So much for compassion at Hridayog.

***

The next afternoon, Anjali stood under the Modi Mill flyover, traffic streaming on both sides of her: two-wheelers, green-and-yellow auto rickshaws, crawling buses, and cars of all makes and sizes.

'Are you sure,' Anjali turned to Kusum, 'this is it?'

Exhaust fumes clogged her throat, and amid the honks of taxis and scooters she lost Kusum's response. The shadow of the flyover cloaked a jostle of makeshift shanties, and the nip in the breeze made her shiver despite the old fleece jacket she wore. She repeated her question.

'Yes.' Kusum said, and walked ahead, her short figure trim in a khaki sweater and uniform. Anjali followed her. They picked their way around piles of rubbish, torn bits of newspaper and colourful plastic packets, empty water bottles, rotting scraps of fruit peels, crumpled aluminium foil. Fruit-sellers and tea vendors lined the pavement on the opposite side, where customers in sweaters and mufflers stood around shopping, negotiating prices, sipping at steaming cups of tea.

Anjali was to meet the kids of the missing woman, Sujni. Kusum had located them last night in police custody and offered to take Anjali to see them. Police would find their mother much quicker if Anjali managed to speak to them for some leads.

'You can make sure they will be no trouble, Anjaliji?' Lahiri had said. He didn't want these children, but couldn't say it outright.

Less than a few hundred metres of slum roads separated this flyover from Hridayog. A throng of young boys loitered on a culvert next to the slum: laughing at shared jokes, breaking out into mock-fights. Behind them, from a vent in the blue tarpaulin 'wall' of a shanty, a child peeked, big eyes in a dark face. Anjali and Kusum came to a halt in front of riffraff structures made of tarpaulin, wood, bamboo, old printed cardboard and the odd brick or stone. This tumble of habitation made the other brick-walled slum dwellings in the interiors of Sanjay Colony look like regular homes. Anjali visited the alley that was home to Hridayog, far neater in comparison.

Surrounded by the stench of refuse, urine and beedis, Anjali wondered if her decision to meet in this area made any sense. She'd hoped that the brother and sister would open up in their own surroundings, talk about their mother, and they could pick up any personal belongings that made them feel secure during their stay at Hridayog. She'd never imagined such homes, couldn't bear to think about the 'belongings'. Nikhil had left for his first session at the gym with Pawan today, to learn self-defence moves. She and Nikhil struggled, true, but this family endured problems on an entirely different scale.

'They're here.' Kusum hurried forward to meet a man in a khaki jacket and uniform, escorting a little girl. He handed Anjali forms for Mr Lahiri to sign in case he accepted them at Hridayog. The other guy would bring along the boy soon, he said.

'*Kya naam hai tumhara*?' Anjali bent down, her nose level with the little girl's face. Asking names was as good a conversation starter as any.

'Sakhi.' Sakhi looked up, surprised at the question in Hindi from a white woman. Her voice floated up in a soft whisper, nearly lost in all the traffic noises.

Sakhi shivered in a boy's vest, and a pair of frayed, oversized black pants held to her hips with the help of some string. A dirty black cardigan, all the way down to her knees, completed the outfit. Anjali wanted to stop questioning Sakhi and get her cleaned and fed instead.

Kusum and her colleague retreated a short distance, but stood in strategic directions, their eyes trained on Sakhi. They clearly expected the little girl to make a run for it at any moment. According to Kusum, Sakhi had tried to steal food from a snack vendor, got caught, and her brother had joined the fray, fighting with the vendor and his friends. Some policemen eating their lunch at a nearby stall picked them up, and shoved them in a lock-up. Anjali knew that the police picked up such children on a regular basis, to make a little extra from the hapless parents.

The other policeman marched up with Sakhi's brother, Radhe. Tall and skinny, the boy gave his captor a hard stare. Had Anjali not been watching him, she wouldn't have believed that expression on a young boy—a caged predator prodded with a sharp stick. With his spiky hair and angular face, he looked like a smaller version of his brother Ram Sharan. She would know him anywhere.

'Why don't you just let us go?' The boy's voice must have broken recently, because in his tone, Anjali heard the man he would become one day.

He wore a faded shirt one size too small, a torn leather jacket, trousers frayed with age and dirt, and fake Nike shoes, their red stripes fading into brown. But he carried himself like some wannabe Bollywood hero wearing high-street fashion. He reminded her of Nikhil, his tantrums and rage at not being understood.

'We must find your mother first.' Anjali said.

'My Mai?' Sakhi asked her, her eyes wide.

'Yes.'

'Where is your home?' She needed to get the girl to talk, because the boy stood sullen, arms folded across his skinny chest.

'*Us taraf!*' Sakhi pointed, brightening up. She trotted off, and Anjali followed her, casting a glance at the three in khaki, who tagged along with Radhe. They made their way between tents and makeshift huts. Sakhi wore slippers, her feet cracked like an old woman's. Anjali glanced at her own feet, snug in sneakers that squelched in the mud. From the ramshackle homes nearby, she heard snatches of television, music, women shouting at their children. They followed an open drain running in front of the thresholds, passed open-air dustbins and toilets, and a tiny blue-tiled temple for Lord Shiva, its squeaky-clean walls decorated with a prayer in bold red Sanskrit letters.

The slum opened out to a field with runty trees and shrubs, and at the edge of this field, Sakhi stopped.

It looked like a nightmare version of hobbit-land, large circular entryways covered with blue and yellow tarpaulin flaps. Looking closer, Anjali recognised them. Enormous pipes either abandoned or 'stored' by the Public Works Department for unknown purposes: drainage, or water supply. For now, squatters had taken over.

Sakhi was one of those squatters. She pointed regally to a circular doorway, lifted the flap and walked in, her head short of the drainpipe roof by several inches. Voices around them alerted Anjali to their audience: Sakhi's neighbours now surrounded the three in uniform, looking curious. Radhe smiled at some of them. Bad move, coming in here. A glance at Kusum confirmed Anjali's concern—Kusum didn't like this at all.

'Come in, madamji,' Sakhi stood peering out of her circular doorway, holding the tarpaulin open as if welcoming her guest to a mansion.

Anjali couldn't enter, not unless she crawled in on all fours.

'Not now, Sakhi,' Kusum came up, her manner brisk. 'Madamji must go to work. Why don't we step out for a while? It is cold, and a cup of tea would be nice.'

'But Mai…'

'Your mother hasn't returned yet, Sakhi,' Anjali bent towards the little girl, 'do you want to help find her?'

'Yes.' Sakhi raised her stained face. Her rough, yellowish hair caught the rays of afternoon sunlight.

Without waiting to talk further, Anjali reached for Sakhi's hand, turned, and strode off.

'I don't want your dirty food,' Radhe spoke in a high half-sob, but Anjali didn't pause. Sakhi's small hand gripped in hers, she crossed small open drains and heaps of trash back to the main road.

In the distance Anjali heard the metro rail, the cawing of a single crow somewhere in the field surrounded by shanties, pigeons cooing above them in the tangled electrical wires, a woman's voice risen high, selling incense. She turned to the sniffing girl beside her, and vowed to get a good meal in that little stomach.

Radhe wolfed down the roti-sabji, slurped at his cup of tea, and then polished off a second helping. Nikhil was a fussy eater, but when served chicken kabab or daal makhani, he gorged himself just like this boy. Images of Nikhil's episode two days ago came back to her, and she closed her eyes for a brief moment. She had an appointment with Dr Bhalla this evening about Nikhil's new medication. She couldn't rest the last few nights, in anguish each time she remembered her son and the puppy. Watching these two eat brought her the first measure of peace in some time: this meeting of a simple need, within her powers to fulfil. It made her feel less helpless; she couldn't succeed as much as she wanted to with Nikhil, couldn't change the lives of these two siblings overnight, but she could fill their bellies. One small job done.

Anjali asked Radhe if he wanted more after he finished his third helping.

'*Bas.*' Radhe said, '*Main theek hoon.*'

I'm fine, said in the tone of *Please back off.* Radhe reminded her of a street cat she once fed that bared its fangs when she tried to pet it.

Sakhi ate quietly, but it was clear that she hadn't eaten in a while. They sat at a roadside dhaba, with some of the tables laid out on unpaved ground, but she looked around, bemused as if in a new and strange land.

'Can I keep this plate?' she pointed at her steel plate, 'Mai will like it!'

Anjali put down her cup of too-sweet, milky tea.

'When did you last see her?' she asked Sakhi.

'That evening,' Radhe answered, 'She fought with Ram Bhaiya.'

'What about?'

'Money. She said he stole from her.'

The policemen and Kusum leaned forward, and Anjali struggled to keep her own face neutral as she asked her next question. 'They both disappeared right after that?'

'Ram Bhaiya went out. Mai went out much later, for the delivery of the paper packets she and Sakhi used to make.'

'Alone?'

'Yes. But someone joined her down the lane. I couldn't see in the dark.'

'How tall?'

'Taller than her.' Radhe said, 'Like Ram Bhaiya.'

If Ram Sharan had something to do with his mother's disappearance, Hridayog might need to support the kids much longer. Anjali asked Radhe if he could show them a picture of his mother and brother.

'Where will I get that, madamji?' Radhe looked at Anjali's phone on the table. 'We don't own big-big phones like you.'

'Talk properly to madamji,' Kusum snapped.

'Let us leave!' Radhe said, his voice louder than before. Several heads turned at the surrounding tables.

'Not until we find your mother or brother.' Anjali spoke before the two cops could intervene. 'In the meantime, you will stay at Hridayog.'

One of the men in uniform, the burlier of the two, explained Radhe's choices to him: he could go back with his sister to the lock-up, or he could go to this madamji's organisation. Not how Anjali would have put it, but it seemed to work. Anjali packed a few paranthas, in case they got hungry at night. While the waiter cleared the tables, Kusum opened her bag and began sorting its contents: a notebook, some packets, stationery.

While paying the bill, Anjali heard Sakhi from their table at the back. She rushed back to find the girl wailing, her voice rising with each word.

'You took my Mai! That's my Mai's! Give me back my Mai!'

11

Pawan missed his phone. A labourer smoking a beedi at a slum tea-stall wouldn't talk on a smartphone, so he had left it behind.

Other than that, his get-up kept him comfortable in the smoggy cold of the mid-November morning. He had ordered tea, and taken his time drinking the first cup. Under his layers of torn t-shirts and sweaters, paired with his father's shabby wool pants, he wore warmers. On his head, a muffler wrapped like a turban, milkman-style. A wig and a bushy false moustache completed his gear.

Maya would laugh if she saw him right now, but she was in Mumbai. She had phoned him early to discuss work. She wouldn't be back over the weekend, she said, because the DNA test to confirm if the dead body was Sujni's would take longer than she thought.

Sakhi had recognised the toe-rings, and Radhe had confirmed it, but Jatin sir didn't want to take any chances. He asked Maya to fly to Mumbai, to match the dead woman's DNA results to that of Radhe and Sakhi, without a soul in Delhi police force any the wiser. Luckily Vigil had snapped up a client in Mumbai, so Maya could double up on some office work.

Betting that Sakhi was right, Pawan had spent some time here, in Sujni's neighbourhood, but he hadn't found anything useful so far. Kusum continued to monitor all missing persons' reports as well as bodies logged in by the Delhi police. Well, at least Sanjay Colony was easier to reach than Madipur or Pul Bangash. It was near Vigil, and also Maya's house in Safdarjung Enclave, where he'd left his bike.

'Two cups of tea, *puttar*,' a bulky elderly man settled down on the bench, keeping his distance from Pawan.

'Namaste, Dharam Chacha! One minute.' The chaiwala scrambled to fill two glasses from a large aluminium pot.

Dharam Chacha's friend, a thinner old man and also white-haired, sat down and put on a pair of glasses. He flicked open his *Navjagran Times* and began to read. For a while, Dharam Chacha glared around him, hacked a few times, spat in the drain flowing under the bench. Pawan tried not to cringe. These two old uncles were regulars at the stall, and might know the gossip.

The air smelled of fresh tea, drains, and traffic smoke from the nearby road. Dust covered the few trees at the end of the alley, the tarpaulin draped around the shops, and the bikes and dented cars parked behind the tea stall.

This area reminded him of his childhood home in Chandni Chowk, in one of the cramped alleys. Pawan had lived on his own in Pitampura the last two years, away from his mother and her home-cooked Punjabi meals. His Beeji could no longer give him hourly reminders of chores not done, food not eaten. Now that she had fallen sick, the entire joint family pestered him to move back. But he'd made his escape from the crowded alleyways, the home packed with cousins of all ages, where no one was allowed to keep a secret, and did not wish to go back.

Pawan cleared his throat, making it deep and chesty like men used to heavy labour, and sat with his feet gathered together.

Once the chaiwala served the tea, the thin old man put his paper down.

'What days have come, I tell you.' A Jat from Haryana, from his Hindi accent. Pawan smiled to himself. At the very least, this might be fun.

'Why, now what happened?' Dharam Chacha took a long sip from his glass.

Pawan lit a beedi, and waved for one more cup. The bench opposite him filled up with young boys, ribbing and joking about their tuition classes. The noise from the traffic meant he must keep his ears sharp if he wanted to catch every word from the two seniors.

'These women. Now this one wants to do her *swayamwar* on TV. Choose her own husband. Imagine that.'

'Women earn money these days, so they wear the pants in the household,' Dharam Chacha said. 'Now God only knows what will happen to this country.'

Pawan sipped tea to hide his smile. What would Anjaliji and Maya have said? Anjaliji remained calm most of the time, but Maya, such a tiny woman, but a firecracker. The kind of girl his mother hated—Beeji thought her son needed to stay away from these *madern-tip-taap* girls who talked too much.

'Modern, Beeji,' he would have said to her, 'tip-top, not

tip-taap. Speaking English and wearing Western clothes doesn't make them bad girls. Just look at Maya.'

He caught his wandering thoughts, and returned his attention to the two men who had fallen silent. He drank his tea with loud, slurping noises, copying them.

'What to say of the country?' The old man in glasses started again. 'Take this colony itself. All these women going to this Hridayog-Lahiri's building, learning about writing and beauty parlour work, and what-not.'

'What is bad in that, Uncleji?' A young man sitting on the opposite bench spoke up. He wore jeans and a t-shirt, and had bought two packets of snacks for his friends. 'Good only na if the women can help with the running of the home? You have seen the rising costs these days or not?'

'It is because of boys like you that women fly high.' Dharam Chacha came to his friend's defence. 'You don't know how to keep them under your thumb. A man's job is to go out and earn for the family. Women should stay at home.'

'Hridayog is doing good work only, Uncleji. Take our alley itself. So much better after their cleaning drive.'

'You call this cleanliness? Dirty, that's what it is.' The thin, white-haired 'uncle' rolled up his newspaper, as if to beat some sense into the young man. 'You think we don't understand how the women are earning their extra money? We're old, not blind.'

Dharam Chacha took the rolled newspaper from his friend's hands, unfurled it and flipped it open with a snap.

The young man stood up only for his friends to draw him away.

'Let it go, *yaar*. Old men only, what to do?'

The students paid for their tea and left. Pawan pretended to make a call from his run-down mobile phone, but he kept his focus on the two cronies.

'Yesterday's runt, setting out to teach me!' The thin uncle pushed up his glasses and sniffed.

'Last week I spotted boys in school uniform behind that Lahiri's building, smoking. Some of them our local boys, and others from outside.'

'Not just smoking. They do drugs, I tell you. *Nasha*. There will be trouble one day, mark my words.' The thin man spoke in a whisper, his glasses sliding down his nose.

Maya said that Sujni's older son, Ram Sharan, had fallen into bad company and drugs. Why did that boy disappear at the same time as his mother? Did Lahiri know boys smoked up behind Hridayog? Anjaliji worked at the place. Pawan couldn't just go and blab gossip to Maya, he must verify it first.

After grumbling for a few more minutes, the old men shuffled off. The chaiwala was busy on his mobile, taking calls and sending his boy into the alley to deliver tea. Pawan had polished off four glasses. He could not remain much longer. The traffic noises behind him grew louder. Ear-splitting honks from autos and trucks, the impatient beeps from cars. Dust and smoke replaced the morning smog.

He stood up and stretched.

'These uncles who were talking. Really, the women in this place go out with...?' Pawan let his question hang in the air.

'Why?' The chaiwala turned to him, his gaze a challenge.

'No, just like that.' Pawan lowered his eyes, 'I stay away from my family, here, so...'

Pawan copied the man's Bihari tones in his own Hindi. 'You want some *jugaad*. You're new here?' The chaiwala's hands remained busy arranging his things, but he didn't seem upset at the mention of prostitutes. Quite the opposite.

Pawan looked up. 'Someone spoke of a woman called Sujni.'

The man stared straight into Pawan's eyes. 'Where do you stay?'

He had found a job nearby at Tughlakabad, Pawan said, and was searching for a room. He did not know Sujni, someone at the factory in Okhla told him she was good. Now that he earned a salary, he could spend some extra.

'You leave your phone number with me.' The man said. 'I see if someone wants to talk to you. You said you wanted a room?'

Pawan kept his gaze lowered. He noticed the pots and pans under the table, and the flies buzzing about a forgotten bowl of cream. He paused before making his reply, as if taking his time to think.

'Thank you. Yes, something on the cheap.' Pawan passed him three ten-rupee notes. 'What is your name?'

'Manoj. And yours?'

'Mukesh. I will wait for your call, Manoj Bhaiya.' Pawan refused to take back the change. 'No, no, keep it. Thank you for your help.'

He couldn't be seen giving a large tip, but a labourer flush with new money could afford the price of an extra tea. He gave Manoj his phone number.

'Thank you,' Manoj said. 'We have good stock.'

By 'stock' Manoj meant women. Pawan nodded, and tried

to seem eager. *When you show your hand, hold your temper,* Pawan's karate teacher often said. Pawan would come back here later—either in the same get-up if Manoj called, or in another, to check out Hridayog's neighbourhood. He made a note: he needed a pair of eyes on Manoj.

12

Anjali stood in the kitchen staring out at the Flame of the Forest in her backyard, its dark branches like charred, tortured arms. Each year its last leaves clung on till late into December; but this time it had lost them early.

She touched her face, and pictured the same tree in February, when it stood crowned in shameless, flame-red blossoms. The crushed petals gave off colour. She wished she could use some of it to stain her cheeks, because despite the tints from her make-up box, her reflection on the cabinet door looked like that tree. Dark, and bare. Nikhil claimed the tree spoke to him at night. He was the reason no one supported the step she was about to take.

Especially not Jatin, who stood phone in hand at the kitchen door, having roasted her about her decision, now letting her stew in her own juices. Anjali chuckled, rueful at her own choice of metaphor, and chose to continue it. Jatin would carve her up soon enough, and maybe she deserved it, but there was no way she would let that little girl slip through the cracks of a system that was indifferent at best, and relentlessly abusive, at its worst.

'So, have you decided?' He stopped typing on his phone, and looked up at her.

'I'm fostering Sakhi for the time being.' She added a smile, though she knew it wouldn't thaw Jatin.

'Explain to me how that makes sense.'

'Sakhi may be mistaken. That toe-ring could be someone else's. They found her body in Pul Bangash, the other end of Delhi.'

'Maya will bring the evidence we need. If that's not her mother, then we can file a report. We can find her another place to stay for now, an orphanage. She'll be safer.'

Anjali didn't want to go over it again, nor tell him how insulting it was to be told that a child would be unsafe in her home. It wasn't his business anyway. Why did he have to show up all huffy like a husband, putting up objections against her personal decisions, about *her* household?

'She *will* be safe here.' Anjali strained the tea that had steeped the last few minutes. Jatin liked his tea dark and strong.

'Like that puppy that died was safe? Like the other one is still safe in Maya's room upstairs? Consider what's best for the girl.'

Jatin got under her skin, hitting her where he knew she was vulnerable. She hadn't been able to protect that first puppy, and she couldn't bring herself to send the second one back either. Maya had agreed to find a home for it.

'I didn't ask for your opinion, or your help.'

'You don't have to, Anjali.'

She started at his use of her full name, but then realised Ira had just come in from the backyard after hanging out the washing.

'I didn't need to ask you to take care of Maya, or pick

Varun up from school when he was stranded, or drive Drishti to the hospital when she fell down the stairs.'

She couldn't argue with that; so she tried a conciliatory tone.

'It will only be for a few days. Once Kusum locates a proper foster home, Sakhi will move out.'

'Keep her at Hridayog.'

Jatin could be heartless when he chose. Anjali arranged the tea things on a tray, all the while wanting to toss one of the cups out the window, or at him. Yes, hundreds of children lost their mothers and then themselves were lost, but Anjali hadn't met them. She remembered Sakhi's large eyes, her inconsolable wailing for her Mai, and she wanted to protect *this* girl. Was that so hard to understand?

'Hridayog doesn't have the right facilities to keep a young child. Their dormitories are for older boys. Kusum is bringing her here for now, and that's that.'

'Kusum works with me.'

Anjali was about to raise her voice in response, when she spotted a bearded man in her backyard. He wore a turban made of some old woollen cloth, ill-fitting, mismatched clothes, and walked towards the back door of the kitchen as if he belonged there.

Alarmed, she walked out to confront him: *'Kaun ho aap? Kya chahiye?'*

'Wait, Anjali.' Jatin spoke from behind her.

The man smiled and said, 'Anjaliji, it's me. Pawan.'

'Pawan?'

Now that she looked at him closely, she recognised his eyes, and his build. Her relief came out in a chuckle. Ira had mentioned he would drop in soon to collect his mother's medicines from her.

'I just need to change into office clothes.' Pawan smiled at her through his fake beard, 'I left my bike here because this place is close to Sanjay Colony.'

Anjali walked in, and let Pawan head to Ira's room, where he kept some of his gear. She carried the tea and followed Jatin into the living room.

'Kusum is on her way,' Jatin settled into his usual chair, 'I just want you to remember that I warned you against this.'

Anjali thought of Sakhi at the doorstep of her 'home'. She would not lose this kid to the system.

When the bell rang a few minutes later, Anjali rushed to open the door. 'Come in, come in, Kusum.'

Kusum seemed to be alone.

'Where's Sakhi?'

'*Woh* Anjaliji, Sakhi crying very badly. So I'm getting her brothers in the car.'

'Radhe and Chotu are here? My son is home, I told you about him…'

'I know Anjaliji,' Kusum said. 'I'm having no choice.'

Anjali turned to check inside, only to find Jatin looming near.

'You see?' he grumbled, 'The trouble has already begun. I'll go and check.'

'You'll only frighten them.' Anjali said.

Pawan stepped out from behind Jatin, 'Sir, let me go and speak to them, and bring Sakhi inside.' He had changed back into his normal clothes and looked like his real self again.

Anjali liked Maya's assistant, and suspected Maya did, too. She watched him stride out towards the gate.

13

Pawan saw three children in the backseat—a thin boy holding his sister by the shoulder, and a young one squirming in her lap.

'You're Radhe Shyam Misra?' Pawan said.

The boy nodded, and gripped his sister tighter.

'Look. I know the people in this house. They will keep Sakhi well.'

'Sakhi can stay with me at Hridayog.' The Bihari accent in Radhe's Hindi was strong. 'She doesn't need rich people from big-big houses.'

Chotu scrambled off. Sakhi caught the toddler, and gave him an end of her shirt to play with. Pawan strode over to the other side of the car, and opening the door, asked Radhe to step out.

'She can't stay at Hridayog.' Pawan closed the door behind Radhe with a thud.

'Why? Lahiri saab said she can stay. Our mother is gone, we don't know where our older brother is, and you want us all to stay apart. Why doesn't she keep us all then? She has such a big house; she can afford to feed all of us if she wants to.'

To live on the streets, be orphaned and separated from your siblings—Pawan couldn't imagine what that must feel like. But Radhe made Pawan uneasy. It was in the way he spoke, never meeting Pawan's eyes.

'Anjaliji wants to, but she can't right now. Let her take care of Sakhi. Your sister needs it.'

'You don't worry, saabji. I can take care of Sakhi. I can get work if I want. I have friends. Just ask madamji to let her go.'

'*Dekho betey...*' Pawan toned his voice down and softened his Hindi. 'This is temporary. For the next week, go along, okay? I'm sure things will work out.'

Kusum walked out of the gate.

'Fine, saabji. But I want to be able to see her in between.'

'I'm sure they will arrange it. Anjaliji goes to Hridayog quite often.'

'Madamji has to give Sakhi back soon.' Radhe clenched his hands. 'I want her back.'

Ten minutes later, when Kusum left with Radhe and Chotu, everybody except Pawan and Jatin had tears in their eyes. Sakhi had wailed at being separated from her brother, but now she had subsided into sobs and hiccups. Anjaliji took her inside.

'Did you find anything useful?'

'Not yet, sir. We'll need a little more time.' Pawan could not speak without proof.

'Keep me updated.'

Jatin looked grim as he left with Kusum.

Ira Chachi, her large body wrapped in a shawl, walked up to Pawan.

'Here are some medicines for your beeji, puttar,' she handed him a packet, 'she knows what times of the day to take them, I spoke to her this morning.'

The way she called him puttar reminded him of his Beeji. He thanked her and turned to go but she stopped him.

'This is Ayurvedic medicine. It will help, but only if she is happy. Go back home and stay with her for a few weeks.'

Beeji wanted him beside her, wanted him to marry, and lend a hand in the shop run by his joint family—exactly the opposite of Pawan's dreams. He would deliver the medicines this evening. But before that, he must verify the drugs and prostitution rumours about Hridayog, report to Maya once she returned. Something about Radhe didn't add up. That boy hadn't looked at Sakhi throughout, not once. Pawan's phone rang—it was Varun.

'Why are you getting that boy to come practice karate with us? He's just a beginner.'

14

Mummy didn't know what was good for her ya, always just not eating this and not eating that, as if that would make her feel good. She ran in the morning, did yoga in the evening, every single day, and in between it was office, office, office. Calls about colour coordination, match the curtain swatch to the sofa and contrast it with the wall colour, all in her interior deco business in her stupid English with that *theth desi* Punjabi accent she tried so hard to hide.

And now she wanted him to stick with that stupid freak, go to the gym and practice with him and Pawan.

'Breakfast is ready!' Mummy knocked at his door.

'I know.' Varun called out, 'I'm brushing Laddoo.'

Laddoo, his chocolate cocker spaniel with the melty eyes, looked up at him at the mention of her name.

'I have to leave soon, Varun. Come out now.'

By the time he finished powdering and grooming Laddoo and walked to the table, Mummy was done.

'Ask the cook to get you your breakfast,' she patted his shoulder and picked up her scarf, 'I told her to get it when you came out so it is hot.'

'Yes, Mummy.'

'And no more parties before your exams.' She made a stern face, but that was all it was, a face. She didn't have the time to sit down and be stern with him. All that discipline shit was beyond her, unless it came to her assistant, who she shouted at on the phone non-stop.

'Yes.'

'Make sure you eat well.' She called out over her shoulder and ran out the main door. 'Don't forget your karate clothes.'

Even the freak's mother was better than this. Varun had seen her sit down with a plate and spoon-feed her son, even when he had one of his hissy fits. Just lock him up and be done with it; but no, everyone walked on tiptoes around poor fragile Nikhil. A load of bullshit it was, bloody *nautanki*.

'I'm not practicing with Nikhil.'

'You will do what your Mama says.' And she was gone.

Pawan Mama. He was Mummy's distant cousin, a karate black belt, and just six years older than him, but behaved like he was bloody fifty or something. But dude could kick the shit out of people, royally take their happiness, and Varun wanted to learn how to do that.

So yeah, he had to train with Pawan and ignore that freak. Varun sat down and called for his breakfast.

At the gym, Varun couldn't wait for the session to end. Pawan was his, Varun's, uncle. Why did he spend so much time with *that* woman's son? *Gaandu saala*, this Nikhil, couldn't look a person in the face even.

How did Pawan think Nikhil could learn karate?

Saala puppy-killer. Varun knew it all—Daddy speaking to Maya Fufee, consoling her about the puppy, telling her it wasn't her fault, it was an accident.

Varun could hear each word spoken in Daddy's study—it used to be Mummy's home office earlier, with a connecting door to Varun's room. When Mummy moved out to a proper office, that room became Daddy's study, and the common door got blocked with a large almirah. If Daddy darling ever checked Varun's room, he would know Varun heard everything. But he didn't, did he? He only came home to sleep, or play host at his boring old parties.

Varun kicked the air hard enough to break a door or plank. Pawan had asked him to go over the old stances and routines, while he helped Nikhil practice the basics. The air reeked of sweaty socks and stale cologne, but Varun liked it here. He felt like he belonged, and the stares from some of the girls didn't hurt. Desperate, every last one of them.

'Just make him run, Pawan, let's build his fitness level first' he'd said to his uncle, only to get a stare, and a rude, 'Get back to your practice!' in reply.

What a bore ya, this uncle of his. Couldn't he find anyone else to do his charity? Varun's Daddy paid for these extra lessons. Did *that* woman pay for her son?

His father, Special Commissioner Jatin Bhatt, paid for a lot of things. The chunky silver bracelet for instance, just like his hero Salman Khan, but with his own name engraved on the plate under its blue stone. He left it on the pile of dumbbells beside him as he swung his body through his routine.

Varun sweated through the last set of exercises and checked himself in the mirror, rolling his biceps this way and that. *Saala* Nikhil, he'll never stand a chance no matter how much karate-sharate he learned.

Once Varun was done, he shrugged on a sweatshirt, and grabbed his bracelet. He checked his messages, then made a call.

'*Arey main hoon na*,' he walked out to the corridor in front of the gym, and muttered into his phone, 'I'm there I'm telling you. I'll set it up. *Haan* I have my sources, *tu thand rakhiyo bas*. Just chill, ya?'

Varun zipped up his jacket as he spoke, because the corridor felt cold after the heated gym.

'Varun.' Pawan stood behind him.

How much had his uncle heard? Varun gazed into Pawan's eyes, and let his mouth go slack. Having practiced in the mirror as a child, he knew what he looked like: the 'good boy' they all wanted to see. Eager to please, happy, no hassles. He had made that face so many times to so many people at school and at home, he almost believed it himself.

'Yes. Sorry, I got a call.'

'I'm walking downstairs to the Starbucks. We can wait for you to change if you want to come along?'

And watch that freak dribble all over his chocolate cake? No, thanks ya. Besides, he needed to take care of a few things.

'No, Uncle, some other day.' Varun said, 'Thank you.'

'Ok. See you next week, then.'

Pawan walked out. Nikhil followed him, watching each step as if about to fall. Before bringing him here, Pawan had called Varun to explain how difficult it was for Nikhil to come to a new place, the freak couldn't adjust very fast, Varun must not scare him.

Nikhil kills a puppy, and people took him to the doctor and for karate practice. Everyone made time for Nikhil, made sure they didn't make him angry. Mummy Daddy both paid more attention to that weirdo space cadet than their own bloody son. Nikhil's mother didn't go out in the evenings; she sat with him repeating everything—twice, thrice, more, with index cards. No one cared what happened to Varun other than Bunty. Bunty was the only decent *banda* he knew, seriously.

No, also Laddoo. Laddoo loved him, waited up for him to eat dinner, gave up food when he stayed out on vacations. Laddoo-dog and Bunty, two friends he could count on never to let him down. Varun decided to pick up a few treats for Laddoo before he headed home.

If that *behnchod* Nikhil ever stepped near Laddoo, Varun would have his head on a plate.

15

Anjali tried to keep things simple at her private clinic in Bhikaji Cama. The beige office walls bore no decoration. Muted lights, a few plants, and some orange-scented potpourri at corner tables completed the decor. Her only indulgence was the gallery in the corridor beyond the consulting room. She brushed a finger across the *noumen* mask acquired on a work trip to Japan last year—the glazed cheek, smiling eyes, half-parted lips. The face of a girl in the first bloom of her youth. She pictured a grown-up Sakhi. Sakhi would have the same smile, but bigger eyes. After a week in Anjali's household, the girl's cheeks had filled out, and her hair now felt silky with all the oil and shampoo Ira had lavished on it.

The *noumen* seemed to mock Anjali for losing her cool this morning with Dr Bhalla. The Risperidone he prescribed after Nikhil's episode seemed to have worked to calm her son down, but her discussion with the doctor hadn't gone that well.

'It could lead to problems with this girl you're fostering,' Dr Bhalla said.

With his small face and huge eyes, he looked like a lemur

in a zoo enclosure. The high turban he wore did not help his cartoonish appearance.

Anjali assured him, 'I'm with them when they share the same space.'

'Place that girl somewhere else. Best for everyone concerned.'

Bhalla's face had looked like the *kijinmen* at that point, the old demon masks next to the *noumen* in Anjali's lighted gallery.

She paused before the masks for another moment, and mumbled *deep breaths*, Bhalla's mantra, the one thing she agreed with a hundred per cent. With her final client for the day gone, she needed those breaths in order to face the last item on her schedule. Out at the reception, Radhe Shyam Misra had showed up with a friend, demanding to see her. She'd asked her assistant to organise sandwiches and soft drinks for them, and then leave. She wanted to talk to the boys in peace and quiet.

Unforgivable to keep newly orphaned siblings from seeing each other, but Anjali's schedule at home and work had permitted no time to arrange a meeting between Radhe and Sakhi.

'Namaste madamji,' Radhe rose as soon as Anjali entered the reception area. It sounded more like a taunt than a greeting.

With him was a tall, burly boy. She had seen him before—Chander, a frequent visitor to the small gym at Hridayog. With red eyes and pursed lips, he stood up to loom over Anjali, making her step back. Both boys smelled of the streets, of traffic smoke and unwashed bodies. They looked like the comic version of a puny goon and his hulking sidekick.

Still dressed in his jacket from earlier, Radhe dismissed all her queries about his well-being with a curt nod.

'Sakhi should be with me.' He came straight to the point. 'I'm her family.'

'I know,' Anjali gestured for them to sit down on the sofa and dragged a chair for herself. 'I wish you could stay together, too. But Sakhi is too small, there's no proper place for her at the boy's hostel where you're staying. Till we find your mother or your brother we'll do our best for her.'

Talking to Sakhi in the last few days had improved Anjali's Hindi.

'My mother is dead, my brother gone who knows where. Sakhi is my sister. I need her and Chotu to attend Mai's funeral.'

Anjali tried to stay calm. Police hadn't traced Ram Sharan, and Jatin couldn't confirm Sujni's identity as the dead woman at the morgue. No DNA test results so far despite Maya's best efforts, ten days after Sakhi first saw those toe-rings.

'We don't know that's your Mai. She might be alive, Radhe. You must be patient.'

'I want Sakhi back, *bas*, I'm not leaving without her.' Radhe stood up, along with Chander, and for the first time, Anjali felt afraid. Granted, Radhe was a runty fifteen-year-old, and Chander not much older, but their postures meant business. The reception area seemed to shrink under their glares.

'You must leave.' Anjali said, her voice loud, firm. 'I'm trying to help you and your sister. But behaving like this won't make it any easier, for me, or you.'

'Are you going to give him his sister back or not?' Chander banged the glass table as Radhe stood by him, fists clenched. He had quit addressing her with the formal '*aap*' and descended to the downright rude '*tu*'. Up close, his eyes had the too-bright, kite-high look Anjali had seen in some of her patients. Anjali lifted her phone. 'I'll call security right now.' She ignored Chander and focused on Radhe, 'If I can get you out of jail, I can put you back in.'

Anjali dialled her phone. Radhe stepped back and put his hand on Chander's arm.

'We're leaving, but we'll be back. You can't keep Sakhi, got it?'

Anjali closed the glass door behind them and locked it. She walked back into the corridor towards her consulting room. The *noumen* on the wall faced her, the expression unchanged, and Anjali allowed herself to smile. She would give Sakhi the best chance she could. One day, that girl would grow into a bright woman, and her face shall glow with a *noumen*'s bloom of health.

16

Pawan almost didn't make it despite changing into his gear. It felt wrong.

He dragged his feet the whole day, unable to stop thinking of his meeting in the evening. *It was just a job*, Maya reminded him over the phone from Mumbai. He kept repeating this to himself, like a chant, but that didn't help. He was a well-brought up boy from a respectable family, a Sikh, a *surdar*, though he wore no turban. Sikhs fought for honour. They protected women, did not disrespect them. And in his meeting with Manoj, he was set to do the opposite.

Late in the afternoon at his place, he checked his reflection in the mirror. His puny, symbolic *kirpan*, the sword meant for the fights of the righteous, would cause less damage than a shaving blade, but he always carried it with pride. Today, he left it behind on his dressing table, along with the assortment of wigs and pins, and set off. He walked past his bike—Manoj wouldn't expect a labourer to own one.

In the bus, he tried to calm himself. He was making progress in his life. He worked a job, paid Beeji's medical bills, a far cry from his teenage years when she bore insults from the family because he got into fights, broke cars and shop windows after his father's death. But his Sensei, a middle-aged man who taught karate at the school grounds, managed to draw him away from that. Karate saved him in the next ten years, taught him that the fight for justice took not muscles alone, but patience and focus. Having met Delhi police officers, he understood that he was twice as fit as an average officer, and quite as smart. But his Beeji wouldn't let him join—she couldn't bear to see him wear the same uniform that the men who murdered her husband had hidden behind.

Some day, his Beeji might come around. At twenty-three, he still had a shot at sitting for the Civil Service Examinations. Until then, he must learn whatever he could on his job, and get into Jatin sir's good books. This case, more complicated and darker than all the others Vigil had helped with, could give him the break he craved.

Kusum had visited Vigil yesterday, and showed him some photos.

'This may be one of the two women found at Pul Mithai.'

'How do you know?' Pawan peered at the passport size photo of a middle-aged woman, with a round face and crinkly hair.

'I checked records of all missing persons' cases.' Kusum said in soft Hindi, 'And I found this one's hair matched one of the dead bodies. We don't have the body anymore, only photos of it.'

Kusum wore a business-like expression as she clicked on the crime scene photos, but her hand shook.

'This one has the same type of hair, right? The height and the body shape also match the description in the missing person's report. I checked the police notes.'

'Where is this woman missing from?'

'The slums at Dilshaad Gardens. Missing from around the same time when police found the body. '

If Kusum was right, the woman had been picked from Dilshaad Gardens and the body dumped at Pul Mithai, at least an hour's drive away. This would confirm the pattern. If the other dead woman whose DNA was being identified in Mumbai was Sujni, then she had been kidnapped from Sanjay Colony in South Delhi and dumped all the way in Madipur Colony in West Delhi: another journey of about an hour.

Even if they took DNA from this Dilshaad Gardens woman's relatives, there was no dead body to match it to. No way of positively confirming her identity. But Pawan agreed with Kusum, they needed to keep trying. Their main focus must remain on Sujni, and that meant Manoj.

Manoj could give them leads, Pawan told himself as the bus jerked to a stop. He must steel himself, pretend he was a married man away from his wife, in need of comfort.

At the last minute, Manoj had called to change the venue to a house of prayer, of all places. Pawan wrapped his shawl closer about him, the evening breeze cold against his face as he waited behind the Durga temple near the slums of Sanjay Colony.

A chorus of voices praising the *devi maiya*, the Mother Goddess, rose in loud singsong, along with the tolling of bells and clanking of cymbals. Roosting birds on the trees in the temple backyard seemed unafraid and quite chatty, unlike Pawan who felt sweat trickling down his back. The stench from the dustbin on the opposite side of the road floated in, and Pawan covered his nose with his shawl. He couldn't get over the fact that he was meeting a pimp behind a house of worship to check out pictures of prostitutes. *Beda garak ho is* Manoj *ka*, he muttered a curse, and saw the object of his foul temper turn the corner.

'*Raam-raam*, Manoj *Bhaiya*.' Using God's name to greet a pimp at a temple. Pawan cursed himself again, under his breath.

'*Raam-raam*. I had to bring my wife for her prayers,' Manoj said in his Bihari accent, 'and I couldn't show you the pictures of the goods at the shop,' he laughed, 'so I called you here. Good only, after our sins we can pray to repent.'

Pawan clenched his fist behind his back. This rat with his thin nose, a long vermillion tika on his forehead and mocking eyes just made fun of the Goddess. Pawan wanted to rearrange this fellow's face for him, break that nose, split up the fat lips, bruise his cheeks all shades of purple. His mind flowed through the karate stances that would do exactly that.

He faked a smile. 'You could have sent them to my friend's phone. On his phone we can see pictures.'

'Not for new clients, you understand. This is side-business only. You can't be too careful these days.'

'Yes, you are right, Bhaiya.' Pawan smiled, trying to appear humble yet eager at the same time.

'Here you are, then,' Manoj slid out a shiny smartphone from his pocket, 'check and tell me, each one has the price written on it. Per hour, per night. Very reasonable rates.'

Pawan willed himself to look at the pictures as Manoj stood by. Women—tall and short, skinny and fat, fair and dark, all in bright sarees, cholis and salwar kameezes. Each with a dark-lipsticked smile that didn't reach her kohl'd eyes. Pawan kept scrolling through dozens of pictures till they all blurred and he reached the end.

'Nothing catch your fancy? Maybe your tastes are...ah...a little different?'

Manoj grabbed the phone from Pawan's nerveless hands, flicked his fingers on screen, 'Check these then,' he handed the phone back.

The first picture made Pawan freeze. A young girl, her little breasts thrusting out of a tight choli. 'Oh, come on. No need to be so shy, all *randis*, each one.' Manoj snatched the phone again, 'They know their job, too. Here, let me show you.'

Picture upon picture lit up the screen, chubby cheeks, rounded bellies, some girls as young as six or seven. Pawan's head spun. He knew this happened in India. In Mumbai, where girls got sold to monsters, but not so close to home.

'Some are quite cheap, look.' Manoj pointed to a dark-eyed child on the screen. 'It can all be arranged.'

Pawan recognised those dark eyes, despite the different hair, clothes, that lipstick. Little Sakhi.

17

Twelve days after Sakhi moved in, Anjali sat down to dinner, unable to contain her smile.

Nikhil ate his dinner at 8.30 pm each evening with Maya and Anjali at the table. He made his displeasure clear if they tried to make any changes. But today, he had successfully dealt with two.

First, Ira sat next to him instead of Maya, because Maya's flight back from Mumbai hadn't landed yet. Secondly, Sakhi sat beside Anjali, diagonally opposite Nikhil. Not too close to him, but a change, nevertheless.

Anjali had worked with him using Sakhi's picture—a small girl, she told Nikhil, a guest who didn't understand English, with no other place to stay at the moment. She'd explained the facts and repeated them, over and over again.

'Why can't she stay with her mother?'

'Because…her mother died.'

'Like the puppy?'

Nikhil talked about the dead puppy often. Why did the puppy try to bite his airplane? Why did it die? What happens when you die? Would he die? Would Anjali? What happened to the other puppy? He didn't know the other puppy was in Anjali's room, unnaturally quiet for a dog so tiny, along with Sakhi. Anjali couldn't find the heart to separate the two orphans.

Anjali passed the chicken curry, Nikhil's favourite dish, to Ira, so she could top up his plate. Checking on Sakhi, she found the girl staring into space, not eating. This sapped her joy in Nikhil's good behaviour.

Nikhil slept alone since age two, the year they came to India. He never needed help with his homework. As per Dr Bhalla's evaluation, Nikhil was at the *high-functioning end of the autism spectrum, with an above-average intelligence.* Nikhil *wanted* to form relationships, he said, but didn't know how. She must try and meet him all the way.

Anjali took Sakhi's roti, tore a piece, dipped it in chicken curry and held it to the drooping mouth. Sakhi looked up, surprised. She opened her mouth and Anjali popped the morsel in, like with Nikhil more than ten years ago. Most of the time, he spat the food out or howled, or both. Sakhi, on the other hand, seemed to have no enmity with food, only a disinterest in life. Anjali watched as Sakhi swallowed and stared down at the table, making no move towards her plate. She had picked at her breakfast, and according to Ira's report, not eaten much for lunch. So Anjali fed the little girl her dinner.

Sakhi usually slept in Ira's room, so when Anjali hunkered down on her yoga mat to get in a few stretches, she didn't expect to find the kid under her bed. The little brown puppy pattered about her, trying to lick her toes, face, anything else it could reach. Anjali heard soft hiccups.

'I'm scared,' Sakhi said when Anjali asked her why she was crying, 'The roofs here are too high.'

Anjali recalled the abandoned drainpipe Sakhi called home, with just about enough room for Sakhi to stand straight.

She looked about the room, then arranged a few pillows on her bed, constructing a quick tent with some sheets and the blanket.

'I've made a small home for you.' Anjali pulled at Sakhi's arm.

The kid came out without resistance, and the puppy scrambled after her.

'You can hide if you feel scared.' Anjali pointed to the pillows. 'This is your igloo.'

'Igloo?'

'A place to hide.'

'Thank you.' Sakhi nodded her approval. 'We all need a place to hide.'

It startled Anjali, the bizarre grown-up lines Sakhi sometimes came up with. The little girl's expression often took on the cast of a knowing old woman, a sort of unnatural maturity Anjali had seen often in slum children.

'Manku can go inside igloo?' Sakhi peered inside the makeshift tent.

'Manku?'

'The puppy.'

The word meant nothing, but it suited the puppy, the white stain on its forehead. Sakhi scuttled into the igloo, and Manku followed, curling up in Sakhi's lap.

'Mai says everyone has a name.' Sakhi turned inside the igloo to face her, all huge eyes, like a squirrel peeking out of a burrow.

'You know what your name means?'

'No.' Sakhi shook her head. Anjali loved the way this girl swayed her head, slow and deliberate, hair swishing over her smooth brown face. Anjali wanted to plait it, but she'd left Sakhi's appearance and hygiene to Ira. No point in getting attached.

'Sakhi means "friend",' Anjali straightened some of the sheets draped over Sakhi's shelter. 'And what's my name?'

'Jali Aunty?'

Anjali shook her head. 'Uh-huh. My name is Anjali.'

'An-ja-li Aunty?' Sakhi stammered, her brows crinkled with effort.

'Yes, but you can call me Jali Aunty if you like.' Anjali patted her knee. Indian kids never addressed adults by their name.

'When will I see Chotu?' Sakhi said, 'Radhe Bhaiya?'

Anjali couldn't tell Sakhi about her Radhe Bhaiya, how he'd come to meet her and wanted to keep Sakhi with him.

'Radhe must stay in school and study, so we can't disturb him. But we'll go meet Chotu this week.'

'Mai? Where is Mai?'

'We're trying to find her.' Anjali crossed her fingers behind her back. God, let that be true. Let that woman at the morgue not be Sujni.

Sakhi clambered out of the igloo and into Anjali's lap, as if she did it every day. Manku followed suit. Anjali had never held Nikhil this way. Cuddling Sakhi's soft weight to her breasts, Anjali leaned back and tried to remember the last time she'd held a child in her arms. Her friends' kids, a few children of the women she counselled at Hridayog.

She relaxed against the bed as girl and puppy snuggled into her.

***

'You'll cramp your neck.' Maya's voice woke Anjali.

Her neck did hurt. She sat up and checked her watch: it felt like she'd slept a long time instead of an hour. Sakhi and the puppy lay fast asleep in her lap, the puppy's nose nestled against the girl's throat.

Maya picked Sakhi up, laid her on the ottoman and covered her with a blanket. The puppy woke and followed, so she put him next to Sakhi, where he immediately curled up. Anjali laid a blanket over the two of them. Maya flicked on her phone, and trained the camera at the two.

'Cuteness overload.' Maya's fingers traced her screen. 'If she weren't involved in a case, this would have gone on my profile.'

'What about the DNA results?'

'A match, I'm afraid.'

A match. Sakhi would never see her Mai again. Anjali stroked the little girl's hair, and Sakhi snuggled deeper.

'I must talk to Mr Lahiri about this. Sujni was from Sanjay Colony.'

'No, Anji. It's an active investigation. You can talk to him about it later. We need to find out more about this Ram Sharan. When you next go to Hridayog, check if anyone can tell you about him. Pawan has been working there, but I haven't had a proper chat with him yet. We need to be careful.'

Anjali considered telling Maya about Radhe and Chander.

Maya might report it to Jatin, and he would get Radhe tossed back in jail. Sujni had suffered too much for her kids to go back to their old life.

'Want a drink?' Maya said, her face haggard.

'I'll catch you upstairs.'

Anjali put a pillow under Sakhi's head. The kid didn't stir. She threw on a jacket and took the puppy out for a walk in the garden. In the dark, the Flame of the Forest in the back garden frightened her, its black, bare branches reaching towards the sky. Despite the security alarms Jatin had fixed around the house, she couldn't shake off the prickly sensation of being watched. She quickly made her way back inside.

She remembered Sujni's burned-off face, and that made her shudder even after she returned to the warmth of the house. She needed to look in on Nikhil.

He'd kicked his blanket off. She covered him and then reached up to stroke his hair, the way he never allowed her when he was awake. She sighed. Sujni would never see her children again, never touch them like this in their sleep.

Upstairs, Anjali found Maya stretched out on the couch in her room, holding a drink in one hand and a lit cigarette in the other. In her frilly, full-sleeved nightgown, Maya looked like an underage drinker, even more so as she puffed away.

Maya lit a new cigarette from the stub of the last one.

'Slow down.'

Anjali had tried over the years to get Maya to quit. She still made token attempts, like a ritual. This was perhaps the best reward friendship offered—the comfort of familiarity, repetition.

'Cheers,' Maya clinked her glass against Anjali's. 'Why slow down? Life is short.'

'Don't make it shorter.'

Maya sucked in a drag of her cigarette, and Anjali curbed another urge to protest.

'What about Christmas shopping?' Maya's voice cut across the drone of the TV. 'Three weeks to go.'

'Next weekend?' Anjali offered. 'I'll ask Ira about the tree.'

Her first December in Delhi, Jatin's mother had helped Anjali cook during Christmas. It moved Anjali that Jatin's mother, despite being a traditional Hindu woman, tried to make her feel at home. Anjali was happy to be rid of Christmas, because the year-end holiday reminded her of Mom baking, cleaning, telling her to straighten the sheets or the room, *Do it right for once, get the lights out of the attic for God's sake, be of some help with the Christmas tree.*

Unaware of this, Maya and her mother insisted they wanted to help Anjali bake a liquor-soaked Christmas cake and decorate a tree. The following year, the year after Maya's mother died, Anjali did it to cheer Maya up, with Ira's help. It became a tradition—the entire Bhatt clan gathered at Anjali's for lunch on Christmas Eve. Nikhil loved decorating the tree, eating Christmas cake, the only cake he craved besides Black Forest.

'What should we get Bhabi? I'm organising a dinner for her birthday tomorrow.'

Anjali didn't reply, so Maya continued, 'Bhai won't, I know. They're always fighting, Anji. I want to make things good between them again.'

'Sure.'

Maya took a long gulp of scotch and thunked her glass down on the table. 'I can't do anything right, even the puppy...'

'Shut up.' Anjali held Maya's hand. 'Nonsense, and you know it. Come on.'

Drishti had married into Maya's family six years before Anjali came to India. Maya wasn't very close to her Drishti Bhabi, but they were 'family' and Anjali the 'outsider.' Nothing would change that. Anjali felt her eyes brim with tears. *Drishti didn't sleep with her own husband, so what did she expect?*

She didn't expect you *to sleep with her husband!* Mom's voice taunted her.

Drishti made it clear she stayed with Jatin for the sake of the children, and Jatin agreed. A divorce from D.M. Mehra's daughter would spell disaster for his career. Why should Anjali guilt herself out about sleeping with him then?

Because he's a married man, dear Anjali, Mom said, *and you're making excuses.* For once, Mom was right.

'Hey! You're crying!' Maya sat up. 'What's wrong?'

Anjali said it was her contact lenses. Maya, the tiny child-woman, told her off, then felt sorry about it, and said so.

'I forgot,' Maya rose and walked over to her handbag, 'I got you these.'

A bunch of roses, six long-stemmed peach beauties, a tad wilted. Anjali laughed, and kissed Maya's curly mop of hair. She walked into the bathroom, ran the tap, and put the roses in a vase.

'Don't forget to make enquiries about Ram Sharan.' Maya said as Anjali made to leave.

'Will do. He was a good boy.'

'He may be involved. They disappeared on the same day.'

'That was his mother, Maya! And it wasn't a simple murder.'

'A mother he fought with. He was a drug addict. And with men, who knows?'

Much later, exhausted and not a little drunk, Anjali began her routine before settling down for the night. At the dressing table, she grabbed her bottle of facial toner, and peered into the mirror.

Treat your face like the fragile treasure it is, Mom's sister used to say, *take care of it and it will make your life easier*. Vivian, (*Call me Aunty Viv, dear*), gone these many years at the age of forty-seven. She peered at her cleansed face— patted the few freckles on her cheekbones. *Too much sun, girl*, Aunty Viv's voice came back to her, *Remember: the sun is your enemy*. No matter how exhausted and depressed, Anjali always followed her aunt's advice.

She cleansed, toned, moisturised twice a day, avoided greasy food, binged on vegetables, cut down her drinking, slapped on the face packs, never missed a facial, saved up for her botox shots. And yet sun spots marred her face now, a wrinkle on her forehead, those horrid lines across her throat like canals fading into a desert.

In bringing up Nikhil, she lost her friends, her budding career. Nate. But she had battled too hard for her appearance to lose it without a fight. A mixed woman's golden skin, but Indian dark hair at her armpits and on her legs. A white woman's calf muscles, but an Indian's heavy hips and stomach. During her teenaged years, she'd spent hours at the gym, and all her waitressing money on skin-care and makeup, shaved and waxed and whipped herself into the right shape, become the popular chick and landed a white boyfriend.

Later in her bed, sleep eluded Anjali. Life was slipping away from her. Nikhil. The poor puppy. Her son was fine now, and tolerated Sakhi, but he still had a long way to go. Under the night light, Anjali considered the girl and the puppy curled together amid blankets. What if she had a daughter like Sakhi: no fuss, affectionate, healthy? Or a son, handsome and big-built like Varun, always the polite, well-behaved child?

Her ears burned at the thought of Varun as a child.

It was eleven years since that day at Jatin's cousin's wedding, but she could still hear the chorus of songs and laughter, smell the garlands of jasmine with which the women decorated each other's hair. After she freshened up following a spate of traditional dancing, Jatin ambushed her in a cramped alcove on her way back from the Ladies Room. Jatin's mother had been dead for less than a year at the time. A tortured, needy soul, he ogled her through each of the rituals they witnessed. His sudden attack was as thrilling as it was unexpected. She didn't protest. That first time between them turned feverish.

With Jatin's head buried at her breasts, she glanced over his shoulders and spotted a small white face. It belonged to six-year old Varun, who watched them with teary, scared eyes, his mouth hanging open. Maybe he was hungry or wanted to go out, or pee, but couldn't find his voice.

Anjali pushed Jatin away with all her strength, but by the time they turned, Varun had disappeared. He peed himself later that evening and developed an upset stomach. His mother took him home.

After that, Anjali broke it off. But Jatin convinced her Varun didn't understand what he'd seen, and would never remember it. She went right back for more the minute their eyes met, whenever she heard the growl in his throat, or felt the brush of his fingers on her back.

She sat up. Whatever existed between them, it had gone on too long. She rubbed her hands together, and pressed her palms against her face. From her bedside table, she picked up the bottle of perfume she'd bought for him yesterday. On his skin, it drugged her—she'd gifted him this very same brand all these years, so he would never run out. This would be the last one.

Enough was enough. She would focus on her son. Wouldn't listen to Jatin anymore. She would meet him this weekend, gift him this bottle and break it off. For good, this time.

18

Jatin needed to mute his tweet notifications, because the damn phone kept buzzing against his thigh and wouldn't let him focus on his meeting with the weasel Rathi.

The hashtag #PunishPervert had taken over Jatin's official Twitter timeline—a German woman from her country's news agency went jogging near India Gate, and claimed a man had flashed her. Why did these foreign women in skimpy clothes want to jog on Delhi's polluted streets when they could work out in the safety and comfort of air-conditioned gyms? The media got wind of it when the Home Ministry gave its assurances.

This Twitter circus must end. Period.

Jatin had asked Kusum to put through the SHO on the #PunishPervert case if he called with updates. He glanced at his desk phone, willing it to ring.

'But sir, this shows Mr Sabharwal was in Delhi at the time.' Rathi's jewelled fingers drummed on the file. 'Yet that line of enquiry was not followed.'

Of course it wasn't followed, on Commissioner Mehra's instructions—but Jatin couldn't say that. So he did the next best thing.

'Everything was done at the time to follow all the leads. Mr Sabharwal's movements on the night were examined, and the department did its best to interview all possible witnesses who could shed light on this.'

Be as vague as possible and shut the man down with all kinds of formal language: Jatin had seen Mehra do this often enough, but he wanted to ask Rathi to go take a hike, do his worst. Just bloody quit with this harassment. A lot of the paper trail ended with Jatin, and he couldn't prove he didn't take some of the decisions when the files showed otherwise. He hoped his father-in-law would step in when needed, that Kusum would be able to keep the most crucial papers from Rathi and this case would linger, get lost in mounds of files.

'Here is a list of my findings so far, sir.' Rathi passed him a print out, 'for you to take a look. Once I receive your responses, I can make a report on reopening the Sabharwal case.'

Jatin made a show of looking at the paper, and put it aside.

'I'll speak to Commissioner Mehra about this, and we will get back to you.'

'Sure, sir.' Rathi lowered his voice this time. 'Sir, this is purely part of my work, but I was asked to examine the assets and properties owned by all the officers who handled the Sabharwal case.'

To ask such questions, sitting in Jatin's office, this man must have plenty of backup.

'An audit?' Jatin said, 'Isn't that the job of the Vigilance or the CBI?'

'I'm only to make a report for now sir. When I looked at

the records, there's a bungalow at Safdarjung Enclave, and a farmhouse at Sainik Farms in your name, other than your official quarters at Punjabi Bagh. I just wanted…'

'Both belonged to my grandfather. My sister owns the Safdarjung Enclave bungalow now. You can check the tax records on the farmhouse, if you like.'

The phone at his desk rang, and it was the SHO. His team had surrounded the office of the man who exposed himself to the German tourist, but the media supposed to cover the arrest hadn't turned up. Since the Home Ministry wanted to tweet pictures of the arrest, Jatin must ensure the presence of the media. Phone pictures of a similar arrest had received poor feedback from the ministry. Jatin would normally ask one of his juniors to take this up, but this time, he reassured the SHO on the line and rose from his chair.

'Let's talk about the rest of it another time, Rathi.'

'Yes, sir,' Rathi stood up, 'Sure, sir. I'll get in touch again.'

As Rathi left, Jatin exhaled. That Twitter #PunishPervert fellow, whose penis had made Delhi Police lose sleep for the last thirty-six hours, was some good, after all.

19

Hospitals were supposed to be quiet, but each time Anjali stepped into any of the lobbies of the Safdarjung government hospital, it seemed like a marketplace or a railway station, with its deluge of signboards, noise, people.

India's poor flocked here for treatment by qualified doctors, offered free of charge, but like all government hospitals in the country its infrastructure didn't compare with those in the private sector. Families accompanying patients spread blankets on the floor, and if they couldn't find a spot in the hospital corridors, they set up tiny camps in the open and burned small fires to keep warm. This evening, at the main exit, Anjali came across security guards warming their hands over one such fire, exchanging paan, beedi, jokes, their raucous laughter mingling with honks from cars and buses on the busy road just outside the hospital walls. From the lobby behind her came a tang of air-freshener, disinfectant and the low hum of desperation and grief.

Eighteen days to Christmas. The air flicked at her collar with chill fingers. Though Delhi would never see snow, it matched a lot of other cities in terms of the cold, and the smog that now crawled in from all directions, shrouded the hospital in its breath. Anjali felt a twinge of misgiving about reaching her car parked at the back of the hospital. Since her trip to the morgue two weeks ago, her workplace didn't feel as secure. Her assistant at the department, the elderly, ever-smiling Mr Pande, hurried out, spotted her and stopped.

'I will bring your car for you, Doctor?'

'Aren't you running late?'

'Five more minutes only it will take. It becomes dark so early these days.'

True. At 5.30 pm, fog curled around the yellow halogen lights, making them seem ghostly. She had dealt with enough ghosts for the day.

'Thank you,' she handed over her keys, and waited.

One of her patients, a woman set on fire by her in-laws for failing to bring in a dowry, broke down during the consultation session today. The scars on her face had healed, and with each operation, her skin improved. But in her eyes, Anjali saw the husband and his mother, forcing this woman down, pouring kerosene on her. She might belong to a normal middle-class family, be married, but her fate was similar to Sujni's. Sakhi would escape the cycle, Anjali wanted to make sure of that. Maya had called about needing to discuss Sakhi tonight, after her Bhabi's birthday party.

Anjali's old Hyundai turned the corner and Mr Pande stepped out. One of these days she must buy a new car. With Nikhil's school and therapy fees, maintaining the household, and what Maya called Anjali's 'vanity' bills—facials and botox injections, there never seemed to be enough money.

When she insisted on dropping Mr Pande to the Metro station, he gave in. Behind them, other cars queued up. Their lights reflected off the fog, the milling patients, the gilt-framed donation notices in the lobby. The glimpse of bent old men, pregnant women, ragged children in her rear-view mirror made her want to open her door and ask them to come away from the cold and into her heated car, but this swelling river of desperate people would never fit.

'Sorry about making you late, and thank you for your help, Pandeji.'

'I saw a boy near your car, Doctor. I did not get a proper look, but he wore black clothes, like Nikhil, and walked off when I called to him.'

'Must have been someone else. Nikhil is at home.'

She drove to Safdarjung Enclave, following the red eyes of the traffic ahead. They blinked and dipped through the fog, staring at her pale face, her clenched hands on the steering wheel. Watching her, always watching.

***

Anjali didn't find Nikhil in his room. Strange. She called to Ira, but no one seemed to be home. She dialled Ira, but the phone kept ringing. Worried, Anjali ran from room to room, downstairs and upstairs, yelling Nikhil's name. On her way down, she heard the landline ring.

'Anji, thank God I got you!'

'Where's Nikhil?'

Maya didn't know. Anjali ran to the kitchen, but kept the cordless to her ear as her friend explained. Ira had tried to call Anjali but couldn't reach her phone. So Ira called Maya, who gave her permission to go to a ceremony at her home and take Sakhi with her. Maya was due home in a few minutes. But she was now stuck with a broken-down car, and hadn't been able to get through to Ira or Anjali since.

Anjali checked the kitchen. Darkness cloaked the garden outside. Ira had left the front door unlocked. Had Nikhil gone out into the street? Had Pandeji actually seen Nikhil at the hospital? Impossible.

'I can't find him. He doesn't seem to be home.'

Anjali opened the back door, walked out into the garden.

'I'm so sorry, Anji. I thought it will be a few minutes… wait, where's Manku?'

Maya's voice spilled from the phone, but Anjali half-heard, transfixed at what she saw.

In the light spilling out from the kitchen window, Manku lay on the grass, gnawing on a piece of tree bark. Anjali spotted Nikhil not far from the puppy, eyes closed, headphones on.

'Found Nikhil. Talk later.'

She decided not to mention either her scare, or the fact that he had unlatched her room door, got the puppy out and ruined his clothes by lying down on the wet grass. She clapped to get his attention.

'What do you want now, Anjali?'

The short answer? She wanted her son to stop calling her Anjali. She wanted to hug him. She wanted to strangle him.

'Go change now.' She said, 'We're going out for Drishti Aunty's birthday. They make good chicken tikka at Nazaakat, remember?'

Nikhil could demolish large quantities of chicken and still want more. She felt grateful for this one thing—his bottomless appetite. Just like Varun, or Radhe.

Nikhil stood up, 'I'll stay home.'

'You can't stay home alone.'

'I just did!' Nikhil stamped his foot.

Anjali began the long process of persuading her son. She sent him off to shower, while she laid out his clothes on the bed. She decided she'd wrap up getting ready by the time he emerged.

When she returned to his room, there he stood, all showered, dressed, hair combed. He'd learned to do these things much later than his peers, but at least he did them now. About to give him a smile, Anjali stopped. Nikhil hadn't worn the clothes she'd laid out. He wore a pair of army black pants, a moss green t-shirt, and a black leather jacket with a knitted hood attached. Varun's old clothes hung loose on him.

He'd dug out them out from the bottom of his cupboard where she'd stuffed them, meaning to give them away.

'You can't wear those clothes.'

'Look, this is a fighter plane,' Nikhil pointed at the graphic on his t-shirt. An airplane. Anjali checked her watch—they were late, but she couldn't let Nikhil wear those clothes and risk Varun provoking Nikhil at the table. She considered dropping out of the evening, but Maya had called her a few minutes ago, and asked her to collect Drishti's birthday cake.

'I know,' she stood her ground with Nikhil. 'These are good clothes, but not this evening. These are Varun's. You can wear them on the weekend.'

'I'm wearing these.'

***

An hour later, Anjali sat in her car outside the South Extension market. Nikhil hunkered beside her, headphones on, stress ball in hand. He still wore Varun's clothes. For the third time that evening, Anjali tried to get her son to do as she asked.

'I'm not coming out.' Nikhil stared at the foggy street. 'This wasn't part of the deal.'

He was right; she hadn't foreseen having to park the car so far from the cake shop. South Extension during the evening rush hour was chaos.

'I can't leave you here. I'll be gone a few minutes.'

'Why?'

Because the last time she got separated from him at the mall, she'd almost lost him. And today, when she couldn't find him at home, she'd been terrified. She couldn't go through that again, nor could she say that out loud.

'I'm not coming out.' Nikhil cowered back in his seat, and clung to his seatbelt. She didn't blame him: she couldn't distinguish one shop from the other in the dense smog, and the dim streetlights cast warped shadows. She tried to call the shop and request them to come out with the cake, but didn't get through. Her phone battery wouldn't last much longer.

'It's Drishti Aunty's birthday. How can we celebrate it without cake?'

'Black Forest?'

No, not Black Forest, but some sort of vegan vanilla Drishti liked. Anjali couldn't lie to him, because she would pay hell at the restaurant later.

'What if I...'

'No.'

'Nikhil. Come on. Now.'

Why did her son have to be so stubborn on top of everything else? If this were Sakhi, she would have stepped out without a word. Had it been Varun, Anjali could have reasoned with him. But with Nikhil, nothing worked.

He flicked his finger, the first sign he might launch into a full scale tantrum. Anjali needed to pre-empt it.

'Nikhil, here, hold on to your blanket,' Anjali laid the tattered blue cloth on his shoulders.

'I don't want to hold anything, all right?' Nikhil swept away the blanket and in doing so, the back of his hand came towards Anjali. Anjali didn't duck in time, and caught his entire backhand on her face. Her head spun from the impact.

'Nikhil!' Her voice came out broken, husky. She felt on the brink of tears.

Nikhil rocked back and forth, mumbling, no, no, no no no. Anjali sat with him, trying to calm her own breathing, wondering if her right temple would bruise or swell. It felt sore.

'Ok. If you sit and just listen to music, I'll let you stay in the car. But this is an exception, okay?'

Nikhil stopped mumbling. Anjali checked her watch. If they didn't leave soon, Drishti's cake would never reach the dinner on time. She sent off a text to Maya, telling her they might be a little late, and to start without them.

'You'll sit here, and wait for me.'

Catching sight of her dry, patchy face in the rear-view mirror, she sighed. She remembered what Sakhi had said to her the other day.

'It is not real.' Sakhi touched her made-up face. 'You are pretty in the morning, with your real face.'

Anjali smiled at the memory of the little girl's precocious, all-knowing ways. For once, Anjali agreed—today her face looked like a painted mask. Not a flawless *noumen*, but one that told the world of her utter, bone-deep weariness.

She shut the car door, debated locking her son in, then decided against it. He might panic if he heard the locks click. She'd be gone only a few minutes. Without looking back, Anjali strode into the fog.

***

Minutes after she stepped into the shop, Anjali wanted to bash the cake on the bald pate of the man behind the counter, and watch it crumble over his unapologetic face. His shop had misspelt Drishti's name, written 'Happy Anniversary' instead of 'Happy Birthday', and used normal icing in place of the special reduced-sugar version specified on Maya's order. The salesman stood there, arms folded, after pockmarking the cake while trying to replace 'Anniversary' with 'Birthday'. The cake was paid for in advance, he informed Anjali, and she couldn't get a replacement.

By the time Anjali picked one of the readymade affairs, got the correct words on top, and paid up, she'd left Nikhil alone for the better part of twenty minutes. She ran out the glass door, intent on reaching Nikhil. Fog closed in around her, diffusing the streetlights. Her eyes itched. She stumbled towards the general direction she'd left the car, half-blind, paper-box in hand. She would sort out the problem with her contact lenses first thing tomorrow.

From behind her, she heard someone called her name. Nikhil? How had he come this far?

When she turned, she felt a liquid sloshed on to her face.

Water? No, too warm. Tea? No, it grew hotter, oh Lord so hot it burned. What had Nikhil thrown at her?

Dropping the box, she clawed at her face to stop the hundreds of needles digging into it, and the rotten-egg smell. A low laugh in the distance, then Nikhil tugged her scarf, and splashed her face and throat again. Screams, loud, like an animal in pain calling to Nikhil, but those screeches came from her throat. Anjali saw a blur of light, and ran towards it shrieking for help, before colliding with a glass door.

Water, she needed water. She stumbled into the shop, yelling, *paani, paani,* water, *bachao,* at the top of her voice, drawing air into lungs that burned. The pie-faced man she had wanted to choke only minutes ago turned and stared at her—if he could see her steaming face he would get her water, wouldn't he, but he just stood staring instead, as if he'd just swallowed something, and held her hands when she collared and shook him, begging, demanding, ordering, him to get water—her face, her face, she must douse it before it seared clean off and killed her.

She went scrabbling, gasping, gagging, till someone tipped a bottle of cold water on her, then brought her a pail to hold and told her in half-broken, freaked-out English, to dunk her face. The same person also asked madam to please give him a phone number, that he had called the police, but he needed her family number. Anjali said Maya, Maya Bhatt. He said they were coming, and he would get more ice.

Nikhil, where was Nikhil? What had he done? She asked this man, this very kind bald man with the horrible sweet English, this provider of water and ice and life, to go outside and find her son, Nikhil, she cried, and the man said, a catch in his voice, 'Is that one standing there your son, madam?'

20

Late, as usual, and they'd lost the table at Nazaakat.

Jatin could pass his name card to the new manager, loom over and explain who he was and why they needed to find him a table, but he didn't feel up to it tonight. Rathi had sent him an email asking for a sit-down discussion with Commissioner Mehra and Jatin. Jatin needed a solid break in the Sujni case before he got stuck again with Rathi's questions. Maya had brought confirmation of Sujni's identity, Kusum had found a lead on one of the bodies, Pawan said he had information regarding a prostitution ring and Hridayog.

'We need to sit down and discuss all the developments on the Sujni case.' Jatin turned to Maya, who stood chatting with Drishti.

'No work-chat at Bhabi's birthday dinner,' his sister said, 'we can talk about it tomorrow evening, if you like.'

Jatin was about to protest but Maya laid a hand on his arm, 'Please, Bhai.'

Jatin nodded, and tried to make himself relax. At the very least, he could look forward to a family event without Drishti's parents. The in-laws had travelled out of town for a wedding and wouldn't attend their daughter's fortieth birthday.

Music floated out of the hotel restaurant, a *ghazal* Jatin couldn't identify. Maya had chosen the place because of its live music, the kind Jatin liked. Maybe he would corner the manager after all, so they could go in. He looked around, his eyes seeking Anjali, but she hadn't turned up yet.

'Is Anjali on her way? I'll try and get us a table.'

'Should be here soon.' Maya glanced at the lobby entrance. 'She's picking up the cake.'

'Did we really need a cake? It's not like I'm all that young anymore.' Drishti spoke to Maya, but her eyes wandered, taking note of the flower arrangements, the dresses of the other women, and the chandelier that lit the five-star hotel lobby. Jatin liked her dedication to her work, but couldn't she pay attention to her family for once? Would it kill her to be nice to Maya, who had taken so much trouble for her birthday?

'Hey, come on Bhabi, who said you're too old to cut cake?'

Maya, the peacemaker. His Gudiya might argue with him in private, but when with family, she tried her best to get everyone talking to each other.

'Besides, the kids love cake,' Maya's voice carried across the lobby, loud and cheery.

Jatin spotted her assistant, chatting up the restaurant manager. Pawan had a way with people.

Still no sign of Anjali. Jatin glanced at the door and found his wife in a long sweater and a pair of skinny jeans, taking pictures of the flower arrangements. Drishti had shrunk like a stick insect through the last ten years. Her breasts knobby and small, her hips and butt all skin and bone. Like any hot-blooded Indian male, Jatin liked his women lush, with

YOU BENEATH YOUR SKIN

enough flesh to squeeze and hold on to while he rocked them in bed.

The manager walked up to Jatin. Their table would be ready in five minutes. Finally. Pawan ushered everyone towards the restaurant, but Jatin hung back when his phone beeped. Not Anjali, like he'd expected, but Kusum, with his schedule for the next day.

As he scrolled through the text, he watched Varun whisper to Bunty Sisodia in the background. The two boys had become staunch friends in the last five years, ever since Bunty first stayed at Jatin's place for a few days when his parents went on a long trip abroad. What did they talk about with such serious faces? They might be up to some mischief, but boys would be boys—beer, girls, the usual. Only a fool would lose a friend from the Sisodia family. A royal family from Rajasthan, the Sisodias had gifted the nation no less than two Members of Parliament, a Defence Minister and a Rajasthan Chief Minister. Inviting a son of that family to a private dinner showed off Jatin's status—it would have shown his father how Jatin had made a success of himself, on his own.

Maya was right. He did indulge his son; but what did he work so hard for, if not to give his son an easy time? His own Papa grudged him every rupee, starting from the bike he wanted as a teen, to the dollars that went to supplement his scholarship in the USA. Varun could do whatever he wanted. Jatin didn't wish to check his son's mettle or make him worry about bills. Varun Bhatt just needed to be a fine son and a good man.

***

Once inside Nazaakat, Maya pleaded with him and Drishti to sit together.

His Gudiya refused to see facts staring her in the face. His marriage with Drishti had become defunct long ago, like an appendix in the human body; remembered only when it gave trouble, but otherwise left alone.

His sister cared for Drishti, because as a new bride, Drishti had cared for her. As a child, Maya had once developed very high fever. Jatin was out on work. Drishti, despite being pregnant with Varun, tended to Maya all night, took her to the hospital next morning. The doctors said Drishti had saved Maya from possible paralysis. Maya had stood up for her Bhabi ever since, even when that led her against her Bhai.

Jatin ignored his sister's pleas and settled down at the head of the table, with Bunty and Pawan on either side of him. Drishti walked to the other end, next to Maya. Maya spoke to Drishti while she nodded, her eyes on her smartphone—in fact everyone was busy scrabbling through theirs—Varun, Bunty, Pawan. Ten years ago, no one knew what a smartphone was, and now look at the lot of them. Phones had replaced manners.

Three men sat on the podium, with a harmonium and a tabla between them. The lyrics of the old ghazal they picked next seemed to echo Jatin's thoughts, surrounded by a family who made him feel like an unwanted outsider.

Na kisi ki aankh ka noor hoon, na kisi ke dil ka karar hoon
Jo kisi ke kaam na aa sakay main wo ek mushte-gubaar hoon

Jatin had left his days of poetry behind, but he murmured to himself the lines in English, and the translation his Papa used to mumble when drunk: *Neither am I a source of light to any eye, nor any comfort to any heart, I am merely a handful of dust, not of any use of any sort.*

The unfortunate Bahadur Shah Zafar penned those famous lines. He was the last Mughal emperor in India who built the ruined Zafar Mahal in Delhi's Mehrauli area, a humble thing compared to the celebrated Taj Mahal built by his ancestor. Thinking of Bahadur Shah, who was exiled by the British and died a pauper in Rangoon, made Jatin feel cold. Death was real, a journey on which he couldn't take anyone along, not his son, nor Maya or Anjali.

Shaking off the gloom, he asked everyone to decide their orders, when Maya's phone rang.

'Hello. Yes?' Maya's wary, questioning tone got his attention. A dissatisfied Vigil client?

'Yes. I know Anjali.' Maya's voice rose, and everyone turned to her. 'Yes. Who is this?'

Something was amiss. Jatin stopped himself from snatching the phone from Maya, as she listened, her face losing colour. Her eyes widened, and she gripped the phone tighter.

'What? Where?' Maya left her chair, 'We're on our way!'

She snatched up her handbag and strode off without looking back. She threw back gasped replies to their questions and broke into a run. Jatin waved to the dumbstruck manager and followed her out. His heart hammered in his chest as they ignored the lift and tore down the stairs to the car park. Behind him, he heard the others. He had stopped praying after his mother's death, but now he found himself pleading, *No, please let her live, Rabji. Please, let her be okay, please.*

21

When Maya called back the man from the cake shop about Anjali, he blubbered words like acid, water, police. Maya could hear Anjali's groans in the background. Poor Anjali had stopped by South Extension as a favour; she shouldn't have been there at all.

Jatin Bhai barely gave her time to jump into his car before swerving out of the hotel's car park, tyres squealing. He sped through no less than three traffic lights, sirens blaring, making one call after another on his hands-free to Kusum, to other policemen. He asked her to call her doctor friend for advice, but beyond that, didn't seem to register her presence right beside him. Maya prayed for Anjali, prayed that it was a small burn. Only her hand, maybe.

Maya had once seen an acid attack survivor at Safdarjung talking to Anjali—stared at the blind white eye, the black and brown patchy skin, the burnt-off nose and eyebrows.

Not her Anji. Anji was fine, who would want to hurt her? Did someone want Maya hurt and find Anjali instead? One of those husbands or wives from the marriages Maya helped break up due to her work at Vigil?

'We'll look into all angles,' Bhai said when she asked him. 'Let's reach her first. You must stay alert, all right?'

Maya nodded. Her head buzzed with the flash of car headlights whizzing by in the opposite direction, the screeches and honks of traffic and the way Bhai's jeep growled each time he revved the accelerator. She needed to discuss so much with Anjali. Pawan swore the girl in Manoj's phone was Sakhi, so Sakhi was in real danger. She would talk to Anjali as soon as they took care of her injuries. Even minor burns hurt like hell—better wait till tomorrow.

The drive to South Extension, at times through dark, twisted shortcuts and alleyways, made Maya queasy. When they came to a halt, she unlocked her seatbelt and turned to Bhai. She expected him to pat her, tell her Anjali was going to be okay. Instead, he looked at her once, then banged his door shut before she could react. For the very first time in her life, she saw fear in his eyes.

Inside the shop, Anjali sat on a low bench, her head dipped in a small pail a bald man held for her. Nikhil slouched in a corner, his headphones snug on his ears, eyes closed. Two or three other people milled about, a tall man shouted into a phone. Bhai made straight for Anjali.

'Are you ok?'

From within the pail they heard Anjali moan. Bhai got the salesman to bring more water bottles, which he emptied in a trickle over her hands and forearms. The rest of the party trooped in a little later. Pawan, Bunty and Varun ran about trying to get more water. Someone got a packet of salt and a new pail. Maya focused on Anjali, whispering to her she would be ok, help was on its way, the ambulance would reach any minute, the salt water spray would cool her. Bhai sat on the other side, holding Anjali. Bhai was too much—asking Anjali if she'd seen who did this, did she spot anyone outside the shop when she stepped out, could she hear them—and so on and on, but Anjali shrieked or grunted or asked for Nikhil. This was no minor burn. Anji would never be the same again. Maya whispered on, trying to keep her voice steady and not burst into tears.

She heard Pawan, Drishti, their words rising and falling around her, the phone calls. The splashes of water as Bhai or someone else sprinkled Anjali; on her head, her body, everywhere, making the floor slippery under Maya's sandals. Nikhil let out a yell. About to rise, she saw Pawan go to him, and settled back at her post.

Maya gritted her teeth, because from Anjali came a rotten egg smell, the smell of melting flesh. The acid ate into Anjali's face right in front of them. The ambulance was working its way out of a jam, so the family couldn't do much other than stand by and listen to Anjali grunt and scream. Anjali's voice grew rattled and coarse like an animal's and once in a while she gasped out a few words. Maya caught *pain, hurts, dying, Nikhil*.

The minute they heard the ambulance siren, Bhai helped Anjali stand up. Maya flinched at the sight of Anjali's pale ghost-like-white face, straight out of a low-budget Bollywood horror flick. Not red, as Maya had expected. The eyes had swollen shut, the lids rubbery grey-blue like dead jellyfish Maya once saw on a beach trip to Puri.

She kept a hold on Anjali's upper arms, and climbed into the ambulance with the nurse.

***

'Calm down madam,' the nurse said, 'or it will hurt more.'

Maya shushed through Anjali's wails, and helped the nurse snip away Anjali's top and wrap her in a hospital gown.

Bhai flashed his card and clambered in, demanding that the nurse give the patient a painkilling injection. But she only had instructions to keep all the affected areas bathed with sterile water.

'We're right behind you.' Pawan's face was calm as he spoke to her. He dumped in a carton of bottled water as backup, and banged the door shut on them.

She sat down beside Anjali, while Bhai stood with his head bent, looking out of the window as he mumbled into the phone. Maya couldn't make out the words above Anjali's cries. They stopped with a jerk, minutes later. Above her, Bhai cursed into the phone. She stood up. A quick glance out the window on her side showed her the entire stretch of clogged traffic. She couldn't make out anything other than blinking headlights in the fog on both sides of the road. Not one car gave an inch to the ambulance's blaring sirens.

Each movement of the vehicle brought a yelp or shriek from Anjali. Maya couldn't take away the pain; just hold Anjali's arm and talk useless nonsense. Bhai tugged off his jacket and hunkered down beside Anjali.

'Jelly, come on,' he whispered. 'A few more minutes, darling. I'm here—shh.'

What did Bhai just call Anjali? Maya looked up, expecting to find someone else, or that she'd misunderstood, but Bhai continued with his soft words: *Darling, Jelly, just a little longer, you're my brave little sweetie, aren't you?*

This must be a nightmare. She couldn't be awake to

see Anjali hurt this bad, nor Bhai calling Anjali those names.

The ambulance moved slowly in crawling traffic. Looking out, Maya saw the dim glow of lights behind them. The nurse kept trickling water on Anjali, and Maya did her best to mop up the excess with towels. She tuned Bhai out, refusing to hear a word, or think at all.

Anjali's voice was now hoarse like an animal's, *Help Nikhil Jatin Maya burning stop this help oh God can't take this please stop* and on and on, despite Bhai and Maya doing their best to calm her.

The ten kilometres from South Extension II to Okhla felt like fifty. Maya focused all her energy into her hands, into the water trickling down from the bed, as if that would make the ambulance go faster, make Anjali stop screaming, make her whole again.

Or dial the evening back, to earlier, when her car broke down, so she would go pick the cake, not Anjali. Why Anjali? No one could mistake Anjali for her.

She heard Bhai again.

I'm sorry, Jelly, hold on just a little longer. We'll be there soon darling, I promise. Just listen to me, don't you always listen to me?

Bhai slammed the partition separating them from the driver, swearing under his breath. They felt the traffic pick up speed. Bhai came back again, murmuring to Anjali. This was why Bhai was so horrid to Bhabi sometimes, why he didn't even sit with Bhabi today, on her birthday.

Maya's profession led her to help break marriages. Maybe this was her punishment—to never get married herself and to watch her brother's marriage crumble to bits. And Anjali? She never let on. Did it begin recently or were they together all along and Maya, Bhai's baby sister, poor foolish Maya failed to see it?

Maya's thoughts raced on but in the next few minutes, the ambulance eased to a complete stop.

Bhai answered a call, and the nurse took his place.

'Use whatever you have to.' He chewed his words into the phone.

Anjali thrashed harder now, and Maya held her down by the shoulders. She felt Bhai hunker beside her and looked up at him.

'The Home Minister's nephew is getting married. They have blocked a few roads for the procession. They're saying we should turn towards Safdarjung.'

'Safdarjung?'

That was a government hospital, its corridors crowded with patients seeking free treatment. That was no place to take a patient in such a serious condition.

'I know. But we'll get there sooner, and she can get first aid. They have a good burns unit. She also works there, so we could get help if needed.'

'Let's do it.' Maya patted the stretcher with towels. She couldn't bear Anjali's screams for help, nor Bhai's desperate, *'Darling'*, *'Jelly'* for much longer.

Maya dropped the soaked towel and reached for another.

Avoiding Anjali's burnt forearm, Bhai gripped her upper arm with both hands, and whispered. He prayed, mumbling words from the *Chaupai Sahib*, praying to the *Waheguru*, *Rabji*, begging for his protection.

Hamri karo hath de rachcha, puran hoi chitt ki iccha,
Tav charanan mann rahe hamara, apna jaan karo pritpaara

He continued with the long prayer, each word clear, same as Ma used to recite them.

Maya hadn't seen him pray aloud while waiting for the birth of his kids, or when they lost their mother. But Bhai prayed now, and Maya joined in, drowning out Anjali's cries.

22

The hospital, when they reached it, became a blur around Jatin.

Kusum had got the word out. An inspector with his men stood ready to clear the way for them across the corridors. Throughout, Jatin held Anjali's right arm and Maya her left. They ran with the gurney, jostling through the patients who thronged the corridor, as the ward boys wheeled it into the Safdarjung Burns unit.

The door slammed shut on them. With nothing left to do but wait, Jatin looked around to find Kusum and a few men in uniform whispering among themselves, their faces serious. His gaze clashed with Maya's. She glared at him like he'd grown another head, and turned away. His Gudiya was shaken, but that look she gave him wasn't friendly.

He turned to Kusum. 'Go to Anjali's office tomorrow, and get all the CCTV footage for the last month.'

'Yes, sir.'

This could have been one of Anjali's patients, someone unable to adjust to therapy. Or maybe a patient's relative or ex-spouse, who resented Anjali. Jatin paced the corridor, weaving among people curled up in blankets, camping for the night.

A few minutes later, Drishti entered with Varun, Pawan, and Bunty. Maya walked up to them, but Jatin made himself sit down. All around the corridor, people milled about. Unlike private hospitals, this one was filled even at night with a loud hum of patients, attendants, orderlies and other staff. Jatin called Kusum and asked her to contact Anjali's boss, Dr Bhalla. Best to inform everyone on staff that one of their own had been admitted. While making a few other calls, he noticed Nikhil, who sat stone-faced, his headphones stuck on, staring out a dark, dusty window.

They were on the second floor, and the window beside Nikhil overlooked the parking lot. Jatin watched Nikhil for a while, but the boy didn't turn around. Where was he when Anjali was attacked? Did he see the attacker? Maya said Nikhil hadn't wanted to go out with Anjali. Did he get angry with her? Jatin remembered Nikhil with the puppy—it took very little to provoke him.

Walking past Anjali's son, Jatin spotted a hole on the front of the boy's black hooded jacket, another on his t-shirt. Jatin considered talking to Nikhil, but those holes on his clothes could be from anywhere. Speaking to him would only stir him up and cause a scene. He dialled Kusum instead.

'Ask someone else to get the CCTV footage.'

'Right, sir.'

'Take some men with you, and search Anjali's car. Report back to me.'

There was a pause before Kusum replied. 'Yes, sir.'

Jatin could not sit still. Bracing up against the wall, facing one way or the other did not ease the knot inside him—Anjali would never look the same again. Jatin physically jerked himself away from that thought. He wouldn't worry about that, not yet. She would live, she would be fine.

If he could have traded places with her, he would. He didn't give a damn what he looked like. As a man, he was stronger.

'The kids are hungry.' Drishti walked up to him. 'We should get them something to eat.'

'Take Pawan and Maya with you,' Jatin rubbed his hands on his face, feeling the beginnings of stubble scratch at his palms.

'Maya wants to stay here.' Drishti said, 'Bunty's father is on his way to pick him up, and Varun wants to go to Bunty's place for the night. You're sure you don't want to eat?'

In place of the usual emptiness and sarcasm, he saw a spark of interest in Drishti.

'I have to be here. And I might as well meet Dayal.' Jatin said. 'The men will pack me something, don't worry.'

Before he got a good look at her face, she turned away. He watched her whisk up her hair in the fishwife knot he hated so much, the one she often tied in the middle of an argument.

'Hello, sir.' Joint Commissioner Rathi came in, a large phone gripped in his delicate hand.

'The attackers will have acid spots on their clothes.' Jatin said. He didn't want to tell Rathi about Nikhil's clothes, so he didn't elaborate.

'That must have been a big splash, sir.'

A splash that changed Anjali's life. *Please let her be all right, Rabji. Protect her.*

'The men are searching the area, I'm in touch with the

SHO there.' Rathi's long face drooped more than usual. 'Should we get a word out to the TV channels, sir? We may receive some leads.'

The channels, with their loud crime reporting and flashing images, would give out Anjali's name sooner than later. He didn't want her mother to know, not yet. Anjali wouldn't want that, and if Nikhil were involved…he couldn't finish that thought. Besides, media coverage right now would show Rathi in the limelight, and Jatin couldn't afford that.

'We'll see.'

Jatin called Drishti, made sure she took Nikhil along to their home after dinner. Ira wouldn't be able to handle him all by herself. Drishti could ask their male housekeeper to help if Nikhil kicked up a fuss. Next he called Ira, briefed her and asked her to take care of the little girl. He wanted to ask Maya to go with Nikhil to help settle him, but a glance at her pale face and swollen eyes told him she wouldn't budge. He stretched his arm, trying to soothe the pain of the old injury at his shoulder. A hot pack usually reduced the swelling, but today he would go without.

His phone beeped. Kusum's text said: *Finding drain-cleaner in car.*

Drain cleaner contained acid, the sort that might have been used to attack Anjali. He called Kusum.

'Get in touch with the SHO. Rathi has spoken to him. Get forensics on to that car asap.'

***

'Jatin.' Dayal Sisodia strode in, his security detail in tow, 'So sorry to hear this.'

Jatin stood up to greet his college friend, who put an arm around him. Dayal wore a beige Nehru jacket typical of Delhi's bureaucrats. Two straight-backed, wary-looking men on his detail wearing similar suits, but in cheap grey, stood behind him. Three others formed a loose cordon, keeping curious onlookers at bay. Dayal was the shortest of the lot, more than a head shorter than Jatin, but no one watching them would fail to recognise the man in charge.

'I was at the wedding when Bunty called.' Dayal took off his glasses , tucked them into his breast pocket, and pinched the skin between his bushy eyebrows.

Dayal mentioned the wedding of the Home Minister's nephew as if it were the only wedding in Delhi, and not one of an epidemic of loud shindigs that plagued the city each winter. Jatin wanted to tell Dayal where to shove 'the wedding'. It had cost Anjali unbearable pain, possibly deeper burns, and landed her in a government hospital instead of a private one where she would have received much better care. But he kept quiet, and instead waved at Maya, Bunty, and Varun returning from the cafeteria.

'There's your son.'

He watched Rathi rush down the corridor, but lose the wind in his sails when he saw Dayal's arm around Jatin. He saluted Dayal with his ring-laden hand, got a greeting in response, but not much more. Rathi was the Home Minister's stooge, and the Home Secretary didn't acknowledge him— that was encouraging.

'Call me if you need anything.' Dayal patted Jatin's arm, 'Anything at all.'

Jatin didn't flinch from the pain that jolted through his

inflamed shoulder. Dayal knew about his injury, but never remembered it. They walked out, Jatin by Dayal's side, followed by Varun and Bunty within the ring of security men.

Half an hour later, he came back to find Maya waiting in front of the Burns unit, and sat down next to her.

'Did Pawan leave?'

'Yes,' she rubbed her temples and tied her hair up, 'he went with Drishti Bhabi, to help settle Nikhil in.'

Turning her face away, she closed her eyes. Maya was clearly angry for some reason, but it wouldn't do any good to talk to her right now. He knew his Gudiya—she was best left alone when upset. Talking to an angry Maya was like going for a walk in a minefield.

With the corridor lights dimmed, Jatin settled down beside his sister to wait for word on Anjali.

He woke with a start much later, a crick in his neck, and looked around, dazed. No Maya. He stood up, sleep gone in a moment. You couldn't let a woman wander alone at Safdarjung Hospital at night. Jatin picked his way through the corridor between people sleeping on the floor, wrapped head to toe in sheets and blankets. They looked like so many abandoned dead bodies in a haunted building.

He stumbled through one corridor after another. No trace of Maya. Ready to dial her number, he spotted her blue shawl and stopped himself from calling out to her. She had her head on a man's chest, under the shadow of a staircase. Everyone around them slept, even those who ought to have been awake—the nurse at her station, and the security guard on his chair at the end of the corridor.

'How dare he?' Maya's whisper carried in the silent corridor.

'Maya.' A male voice said.

Pawan had rushed back all the way to the hospital from West Delhi. Even without traffic that would have taken him no less than half an hour.

'He called her nicknames. "Jelly", "Sweetheart". And I went and scolded him the other day about how he dragged her to a morgue. I'm *such* a fool.'

She sagged against Pawan. They stood like that for a while, Pawan's hands caressing Maya's back. Jatin clenched his fists, but thrust them into the pockets of his coat.

Maya's next set of whispers got smothered in Pawan's jacket, and Jatin couldn't make out the individual words. His sobbing, angry Gudiya in her assistant's arms. Jatin made himself turn and walk away. He needed her right now, for the case, for Anjali, but most of all, for himself. His little sister had worshipped him all his life. Back in the corridor beside Intensive Care, he slapped the wall, startling the relatives and attendants scattered on various benches. His palm burned.

Maya never got angry without good reason, but once someone pissed her off, she stayed that way. Over the years, Anjali had warned him this would happen, but he had not listened.

***

Word on Anjali did not come in till almost 3 am. Anjali was out of danger, but still under sedation. Maya had returned by then, and sat huddled a few chairs away, Pawan by her side.

The attending doctor had rushed out for another emergency operation. A nurse led them to the viewing window in the Intensive Care Burns unit. Anjali lay on a high steel bed, under a white sheet. Her face—that couldn't be her face. It looked brown-red and splotchy despite the dim light, and her head seemed too large, like an alien's. The swelling would go down, the nurse assured them. Maya did not react. She stood staring, her nose flattened against the glass, till Pawan led her back.

Jatin had taken one glance at Anjali and looked away. At Maya, the walls, anywhere but back there. He couldn't bear it. *Ho chukka Ghalib balaen sab tamam, ek marg-e-nagahani aur hai*. For all these years he had read the poet Ghalib, he hadn't understood these words, but he got it now—*the readiness to face anything at all, now that the worst had come to pass.* He would give up anything, his job, his son, his life as he knew it, to have Anjali back. The realisation stunned him, and for a while, he could not put another thought together.

He wandered out to the car park, following Pawan and Maya, who walked in step, Pawan's hand at Maya's elbow. Pawan wished him goodnight, but Maya didn't say a word.

Jatin turned and walked back to Intensive Care where Anjali slept.

The cake salesman had seen Nikhil walk in behind Anjali. Anjali had left her keys in the car. They had found drain-cleaner in the boot. Jatin didn't know what to think of this till the forensic reports came in. He would call Dr Bhalla in the morning and talk about Nikhil.

23

Darkness slow and deep, quiet, still, unmoving, un-breathing in a dark, sugary sleep: no pain, no joy, no sight, no sound, no taste, she remained floating, distant. She wouldn't wake up, she'd stay in this cotton-wool world, its soft-sleepy music lifting her up through the roof, the banisters, the rooms up above, through the entire weight of the building, its steeple. She rose like a wisp of cloud. Didn't need pain, could leave it behind.

The pain insisted on waking her up though, jabbing and pulsing; she needed to make it stop. Her eyelids were glued shut—that had never happened before, no matter how severe the hangover. All she needed was to stretch her arm for the packet of painkillers on the sideboard and sneak in a pill before her agony worsened.

It usually hammered at her head. This persistent throb in her face, her throat, her chest was new, and it hurt to lift her hands.

'Dr Morgan?'

She didn't recognise the voice. Soft but firm hands pushed her down when she tried to rise.

'You can't sit up yet,' the voice in the dark continued. 'Do you feel pain?'

Who was this and how did she enter the bedroom? How did she know about the pain? Anjali couldn't place that voice. An older woman, not as old as Ira, but definitely middle-aged and more. She spoke with an accent from southern India—the rolling of the tongue, the stressed t's, the heavy emphasis at the end of each word. If Anjali focused on this dream voice, she might distract herself from the pain.

'You need to relax. Anjali, can you hear me? Dr Morgan?'

Anjali clenched her teeth and tried to rise, but something was wrong with her palate, her gums. The woman pressed her shoulders back down on the bed, gently, but her insides hurt, her windpipe, her stomach. She gave in, and lay back down, trying to breathe against the shards of pain. It hurt to swallow. What was wrong with her mouth?

'We've called the doctor. Please try to relax, okay?'

Doctor? Why would a doctor come to her bedroom? What did she need a doctor for?

'An accident,' the woman said in response to Anjali's silent question. 'Your face and chest are affected.'

It came flooding back. That warm liquid on her face and the burning. Nikhil. Affected? No, much worse than that— her face had melted—she must check. Nikhil had thrown this at her. She rose again, but this time an additional pair of hands held her down.

She struggled in earnest. *I want to look; don't you get it? I must see what my son has done!* But no voice emerged. She tried to open her eyes, but they stayed shut.

'I'm Mary, the head nurse,' the woman holding her said. 'You are doing much better than last night, but if you keep moving we must sedate you. Do you understand?'

She tried to wrestle her arms out of Mary's grip, and kicked against the darkness with all her strength. Despite the pain searing through her face and chest, she kept at it till a needle sank into her arm.

***

She walked on the pavement wearing a silk dress the colour of egg yolk, and the weight of air. It caressed her thighs and whispered while she strode under the jacaranda trees, treading on dried blossoms. She gazed up at the purplish-blue-white canopy, from which flowers drifted down like fragments of blessing, or the first snowflakes of winter.

During her childhood in Florida it never snowed. She had tasted snow for the first time, light as froth and melting cold on her tongue, on her first visit to DC. She was back from college now, and Nate walked towards her, his eyes blue like the sky, dancing with laughter as he said hello.

Those eyes, so different from her own or her parents' or anyone else she knew—a blue that startled her like a sudden wave of surf and made her thoughts sweet-molasses-slow, made them turn to sunlight, birdsong, reckless laughter. Those eyes always spoke to her.

The two of them walked, Nate's cool, dry fingers sliding up her elbow.

Even as she watched him, the eyes lost their warmth, became icy cold. The smile stretched into a sneer, and the next time he turned to her, his face had changed into Nikhil's. She screamed and ran, and when she looked back he stood there under the row of jacaranda trees, still smiling in that half-grimace, flowers stuck in his hair.

'Nikhil!'

Where had Nikhil gone? She needed to find him, keep him safe. She tried to search the next street, and there, at the end of it, sat Nikhil on a bench. She sagged with relief.

She stroked her face, but her fingers touched plastic. She took it off, a *noumen* mask, smiling at her its benign smile. But when she touched her face again, her skin came off. Pain seared down her chin and throat, her skin and flesh dribbled on her chest. She ran, searching for water. In front of her, rain dotted the pavement. She stood, her face stretched upwards, letting the water wash over her, but instead of cooling her down, it heated her up. Her face steamed, didn't hurt, but when she touched it, she found hard bone.

She jerked away her hand, but brought it back, slower this time. Her fingers didn't find skin; they went inside the hollow where her cheek had been. The rain had stopped, and her face splattered all over her white and yellow dress, smeared in blood skin lipstick rouge.

She let out all her breath in a wail that went on and wouldn't stop, caught a small hand in hers, a soft, familiar hand. Maya. She couldn't see, her eyes still closed, but she grabbed Maya's hand and called her name. She heard a whisper rasp from her throat and a burn, all the way up to her tongue.

'Anji. I'm here.'

Anjali let those three words fall on her like a thing of grace. She wasn't lost. That was a nightmare; she would wake up.

24

Not often, no, but every once in a while, like this Saturday, Jatin let himself sleep late. Last night he'd turned in past midnight, and once in bed, sunk into a nightmare. Trapped in the ambulance with Anjali and Maya, he saw marshes outside, jungle and snakes. The vehicle filled with Anjali's cries for help, and he flailed about as she burned. He fell back into the empty darkness, and woke up trapped in clammy blankets, calling Anjali's name.

At the breakfast table an hour later, Jatin found Varun at his usual seat, tall and handsome in his maroon-and-white school uniform. The woollen jacket sat square on his broad shoulders. Varun would clear high school soon. *Punjabi gabru jawan*, Jatin murmured. Ma used to call Jatin those words, pride shining in her eyes.

'Good morning, Daddy!'

'All set for Manila? In five days, right?'

'Four.' Varun wiped his mouth, having finished his glass of lassi, 'Need to buy a few things for the trip. May I take your card?'

'What about your report for the school test you took last week?'

When Varun's grades slipped in the past year, Jatin had cut a deal: if Varun didn't clear the tests, no Manila trip.

'I'll clear it ya, Daddy, you'll see. Bunty'll pick it up from my school, pass it to you.'

His son would deliver, he always did.

Jatin needed to trek upstairs to get his wallet from the bedroom. Would be so much faster to walk to the safe in his study, right next to the dining area. He tossed the hush money he got from the office into a black bag, never kept track of it. Papa used to say: *Paani mein rah kar magarmach se bair nahin karte*, if you live in water, don't make an enemy out of the crocodile. Accepting that token sum each month made him part of the system, made life easier with colleagues and promotions. He kept his promise to himself never to use that money for himself or his family. *That doesn't make it right.* Ignoring that voice in his head, Jatin walked upstairs and came back with his debit card. Varun thanked him with a huge smile.

Varun asked for what he needed, worked hard at school, was friendly with everyone, polite. A contrast to the last four days with Nikhil in the house. Everyone was wary of his moods.

'Where's Nikhil?'

'Still asleep, last I saw.' Varun waved at him on the way out. 'Thanks again, Daddy. And before you say it ya, *I'll be careful.*'

Jatin did want Varun to be careful around Nikhil. The holes on Nikhil's jacket were from the drain cleaner. Forensics said the boot contained Nikhil prints. The container seal was broken. The acid on Anjali matched the drain cleaner. His call with Dr Bhalla hadn't gone well, either.

'Is he capable of it you're asking me, Commissioner saab?' Bhalla had wheezed over the phone, 'He is. He gets very angry when provoked, or unable to communicate. We're working on that.'

'He was angry with Anjali?'

'All teenagers are angry about something or the other. Hormonal. Nikhil gets frustrated because he can't understand other people, and has trouble being understood.'

'Would his anger be strong enough to want to attack his mother? Would he understand how dangerous throwing acid is?'

'He's intelligent and old enough, he would understand acids. He has attacked Anjali before, but only when he was upset. I don't think he would plan an attack.'

Jatin didn't want Nikhil upset under any circumstance. He couldn't tell Varun his fears, but had warned him to leave Nikhil absolutely alone. Varun and Nikhil had been in a few scrapes when much younger, but that was out of the question now. Jatin prayed he was wrong, for Anjali's sake. They had her sedated, still.

***

The doorbell rang, and a while later, Pawan walked into Jatin's study. Jatin didn't invite anyone into this room piled high with files, crime scene photos, bills and receipts. But he needed a quiet word with Pawan.

'Good morning, sir.' He placed a packet on the table. 'I picked them up last night.'

Pawan had helped out with Nikhil in the last two days, dropping by to coax him to his meals, taking him to the gym for a karate lesson. And now, he'd brought the pills Dr Bhalla had prescribed to keep Nikhil calm.

'Thanks, Pawan. Take a seat.' Jatin walked to the door of his study and called the housekeeper to bring them tea.

'These make him drowsy, sir. You're sure they're good for him? He has skipped school as well.'

Jatin considered his options. If he told Pawan about his suspicions about Nikhil, Pawan might tell Maya. Jatin had collected Nikhil's clothes from the night of the attack for examination, without Maya's knowledge. Maya loved Nikhil, and was at present very pissed off with her Bhai.

On the other hand, Jatin could think of no one else to discuss this with. Besides, Pawan would be the best adult to ask Nikhil questions.

'If I speak to you about Nikhil, can you assure me it won't go beyond this room?'

Pawan's eyes widened for a second, but he nodded.

Jatin began with the holes on Nikhil's clothes, and the forensic opinion. He spoke of the drain cleaner, the fingerprints on the can.

'I've thought about it myself, sir. I noticed the holes on his jacket and t-shirt.'

'You didn't mention it.'

'I noticed his clothes were missing from the washing basket, sir.'

Jatin had okayed him as Maya's assistant because he knew Pawan was respectful, and part of Drishti's extended family. But this boy clearly didn't miss much, and deserved a raise at Vigil.

'What about any CCTV footage, sir?' Pawan said, 'There might have been a camera or two in the neighbourhood.'

'We've got them. But it was foggy that night, and the attack happened in a blind spot. We can only see a figure walking away, in a dark hooded jacket. I have a copy here.'

Pawan examined the video Jatin showed him on his computer screen. The housekeeper served them tea and left. Jatin handed Pawan his cup, and picked up his own.

'The forensics on the case think the height and the build matches Nikhil.'

'I can't be sure, sir, but the walk does not look like Nikhil's.'

'Will you ask him a few questions?'

'I spoke to Dr Bhalla last night, sir. He said we shouldn't mention Anjaliji to Nikhil. His upset routine has already been difficult for him. He might react badly.'

Jatin stared at Pawan, but the young man did not flinch under his gaze. He needed to give Pawan the entire picture.

'Anjali's assistant at Safdarjung reports that a young boy who looked like Nikhil was loitering near Anjali's car, at the Safdarjung hospital parking lot.'

'Mr Pande knows Nikhil sir.' Pawan picked up his teacup.

'He can't be sure who he saw, because the boy walked away quickly. I spoke to Ira—she had left Nikhil home alone for a while, at the same time this Mr Pande saw someone near Anjali's car.'

'But Nikhil never steps out of the house alone, sir.'

'He has run away before.'

Pawan had no answer to that, and Jatin watched as Maya's assistant scrutinised the video again. Despite the hot tea, Jatin felt cold inside. His shoulder hurt, and he wanted to head to his bed. Maybe if he slept long enough, all of this would disappear. Anjali would be whole again, and Nikhil at home with her.

'Nikhil doesn't handle stress well, sir, but I can't imagine him planning all this.'

Jatin put down his own teacup.

'I hope I'm wrong. But unless we can rule him out, we have no choice but to keep digging.'

25

With every word Bhai spoke, Maya wanted to launch herself at him, shake him by the collar and ask him why. Why betray Bhabi, why ruin the family, why lie to his Gudiya? They stood around the table at the Vigil office as Pawan explained what he'd learnt at Sanjay Colony so far: about his suspicions of Lahiri running a drug den. He had proof now.

'Did you tell Anjali about this?' Bhai said.

'I found out the day before the attack.' Pawan said, 'I told Maya the next morning, but she couldn't talk to Anjaliji because of the incident.'

Pawan continued his report, and Bhai added a pin to Sanjay Colony on the Delhi map. He drew lines joining together Pul Mithai, Madipur Colony, Dilshaad Gardens and Sanjay Colony in a quadrilateral, 'The hiding place must be somewhere inside this area. Do we have proof of a drug den in Sanjay Colony? You said you took pictures?'

Pawan laid out the snapshots taken from a shed behind the Okhla railway tracks, close to the buildings Hridayog rented. Boys, syringes, cords, bottles, plastic pipes, blurred in smoke and fog. Poor quality pictures because Pawan had taken them on a cheap phone, afraid to use a camera while dressed as a poor labourer. Police regularly found dead bodies in the area.

'This boy is from Hridayog.' Pawan pointed to one of the pictures. 'But I didn't recognise the others. It was too dark, and the fog made things worse.'

If Hridayog boys used drugs at this place, impossible Lahiri didn't know about it. Maya made a note to ask Anjali if she knew anything at all about this when the police took her statement. She thought of Anjali lying on the bed, her face destroyed, writhing in pain whenever she woke. Ever since she knew of Anjali's affair, she'd struggled between sadness for her friend, and rage at the betrayal.

Bhai fished out his private phone and sent a text. 'I've just contacted the SHO of the area surrounding Sanjay Colony. Ravinder Grewal is a good friend. He could help us.'

'They would not pick up a prostitute from their own neighbourhood. Too much to lose.' Maya turned away from Bhai. 'Who knows, though, they're men only. Men can do anything.'

Maya picked up a few pins scattered on the table under the soft board and stuck them in, one by one, along the bottom of the map. Bhai broke the silence behind her.

'Get someone to enhance these photos.' Bhai spoke to Pawan, 'We need solid evidence on Lahiri and Manoj.'

'*Haanji*, sir, I'll send the photos right away.'

'It will help if we chat up this Lahiri, see if we can dislodge something.'

'I'll go, sir.'

'No, Radhe has already seen you, and he's from that area. I'll get Kusum to send someone.'

Pawan couldn't go, but Maya could.

'I'll give it a shot,' she cut in.

'No.' Bhai sat down, 'Too unsafe. Can't let you go to a slum with a suspected prostitution and drug ring.'

'Lahiri would be less defensive with a woman.' Maya took the chair across from him.

'I'll send Kusum then. She'll have backup with her.'

'I can go there as Anjali's friend.' Maya leaned forward. 'I've met him before at a charity drive Anjali had organised.'

'A woman must know what places to stay away from. Didn't I just say you can't go?'

'You say and do a lot of things, Bhai' Maya didn't hold back. 'Not even you can claim you're always right. And I'm sick of being told what I can and cannot do, ok?'

'I'll go with her,' Pawan said, and when both of them stared at him, he added, 'In different clothes. I'll be on hand if Maya needs help.'

***

'Have you been here since you met Manoj?' Maya spoke from the backseat.

'Twice.' Pawan shifted the cap of his driver's uniform. He wore a moustache, but other than that, he was her Pawan. White suited him better than all the colours she had seen him in. He wasn't her Pawan, she corrected herself. He was her assistant.

A cow stood chewing the cud in the narrow alley they used to enter Sanjay Colony, its ribs standing out of its patchy brown and white hide. Pawan patted it aside and they walked on. They passed elderly women at their doorsteps making packets out of old newspaper, and a tiny grocery shop-cum-tea stall. A tabby cat slept in a patch of sun on one of the low tin roofs. Maya wanted to pat it.

Pawan turned into an alley flanked on both sides by broken shanties plastered with layers of political campaign posters. Having told her the way, he fell back as she walked, skipping over cow dung, side-stepping broken glass and rubbish. He couldn't lead the way, because a driver would be expected to follow his employer. Maya curled her nose against the dust and chemicals from the factories behind the slum. The stink of urine and rot from all corners of the alleyway choked her. She coughed with her hand over her mouth, then walked on.

Anjali came here each weekend—how did she deal with the stench from the drains, with people bathing, shitting and cooking in the same space, with all the honking of the traffic and sirens from the Okhla industrial area?

They walked to the alley that housed Hridayog. In one of the classes, a small boy led a group in reciting multiplication tables in his high, clear voice. Maya took in the neatness of this alley compared to the others, and listened to Pawan as he pointed out the rooms Hridayog rented, with words instead of gestures, in case someone was watching them. In his guise of 'Mukesh', Pawan had arranged an attic room from Manoj on the cheap, not far from the alley, and paid the rent for a few months in advance. He'd made an excuse of a trip back to the village, and locked it up, mentioning that a cousin might visit. The window of the room provided a clear view of most of Hridayog's rooms.

Lahiri sat in his office, working on some files, in a kurta

pyjama, a wide shawl wrapped about him. Maya stopped at the threshold.

'Namasteji, I'm Maya. Anjali's friend.'

'Namaste, namaste, come in. How is Anjaliji now?'

Lahiri waddled over. For a social worker who worked in an office strewn with dumbbells and exercise mats, the Bengali *babumoshai* carried a big paunch.

'She's better now,' Maya said, 'But still in the hospital.'

If he used Anjali as a front, Lahiri would be upset with the attack—she might not come back here for many months. But instead, Lahiri looked uneasy—the sympathy on his jowly face seemed to cost him effort. The head of Hridayog kept glancing at Pawan, perched on a stool near the door.

'You must find it hard to replace her for the weekend classes?'

'No one can replace Anjaliji, but yes, some volunteers have stepped up.' Lahiri pulled his cap closer about his head, and lifted his fat-sweet-simple face. His pudgy hands clenched into fists on the table. A man walked in, went to one of the almirahs and having placed something on it, handed Lahiri the key. *I'll see you in the evening,* he said to Lahiri and walked out, but Lahiri didn't pay the man any heed.

Maya asked Lahiri about Radhe, his studies, and his disappeared brother Ram Sharan, and listened as Lahiri rambled on. He didn't know about Ram Sharan, but Radhe was doing all right. Maya looked around this office where Anjali sat when she came to Hridayog. Did she counsel the children or their parents, too? This slum could have caused the attack. An unhappy parent or husband, any of the boys she must routinely tell off during her classes. One of the husbands she sent to jail for domestic abuse.

'So you don't want to keep Sakhi any longer?' Lahiri said once he had finished talking about Radhe.

'It is difficult, with Anjali in the hospital. But we're going to keep her for now. Can I talk to the boy? Anjali would want to know how he is.'

Lahiri said yes, but he himself wouldn't be able to stay longer because he must rush off to another class. He hurried out of the room, his paunch wobbling ahead of him. He didn't offer her water, tea—nothing, even though she was Anjali's friend. Lahiri hadn't visited the hospital either.

About five minutes later Radhe rushed in, breathless. 'You have come to return Sakhi?'

Maya asked the boy how he was, but Radhe didn't want to talk about that. He demanded that Sakhi be returned to him, to live together again as a family.

'She is doing well.' Maya reassured Radhe, but he stood in front of Maya, his frayed leather jacket collar puffed about his neck like a snake's hood. A year or two older than Nikhil, Radhe must have lived all his life on Delhi's streets. But she could not let him bully her, and she needed to find out more on Ram Sharan.

'Someone has to take custody of your mother's body, and it has to be an adult.' Maya said. 'If not, it will be declared *lawaris*. Where is your brother?'

Radhe broke into sobs.

'Please madamji, save us.' He grabbed her feet. 'We need Mai's body. If we don't cremate her, her soul will never rest.'

Maya curbed the urge to jump away. She bent down and removed Radhe's grip on her feet. 'I need names. Ram Sharan's friends, and where they live. If not, there is no way to save your Mai's body.'

Radhe's thin shoulders continued to rise and fall, but Maya did not speak or move.

'I think he talked about Madipur Colony, madamji. But *kasam se*, I have no idea who stays there. Give me your number and I'll call you if I hear news.'

Madipur Colony. That's where police found the other dead body.

Ten minutes later, they walked out into the alley.

'He might have us followed,' Maya strode ahead, 'that Lahiri and his boy gang. Just to make sure we didn't bring the police in or something.'

Stray dogs ran ahead of them, chasing each other, filling the alley with their yaps and growls.

'You're right.' Pawan said. 'We can go to Anjaliji's place, because they already know you're her friend. We move out separately from there.'

'I gave him your extra number. They won't be able to trace it to me if they try, but you will get the calls. Tell them you're my assistant.'

'That man who walked in when we were there?' Pawan caught up with her, his eyes bright.

'You know him?'

'That was Manoj.'

'Did he recognise you?'

'No one really looks at a man in a uniform, plus I had my cap and moustache.'

Breathing a sigh of relief, Maya considered the facts— Lahiri and Manoj were friends, and ran a prostitution and drug gang together. Anjali had no clue. Lahiri also didn't seem to care all that much about the women and children who came to Hridayog.

Both men fit the profile Anjali had given them—able to spend money, with possible access to a vehicle and a hideout. With his background as a pharmacist, Lahiri might have access to Propofol. But Anjali said at least one of them was likely to be a younger, unattached man. According to Pawan, Manoj was a married man in his forties. Lahiri was single, but not young. The profile might not be a perfect match, but Maya couldn't dismiss these two out of hand.

'You will watch Lahiri and Manoj?'

'Yes.' Pawan opened the car door so she could get into the backseat. Maya could get used to this. *Don't be silly, Maya, he's pretending to be your driver.* She blushed, and to cover up her confusion, said, 'Your cousin will enlarge the photos, right?'

'I've already sent them to him.'

As Pawan drove, Maya discussed Vigil cases with him, the payments of the freelancers, and the clients they needed to chase. Pawan listened and nodded.

A text pinged on Maya's phone. Bhai. Grewal said that he had heard rumours of a drug operation running out of Sanjay Colony, but had no solid leads. They either kept it very low-profile, or carried out small, local business. No direct connection to an international syndicate.

'You were right,' Pawn interrupted as she typed her reply to Bhai, 'That fellow on the bike is tailing us.'

26

This was not the end, half-sitting, propped on a white bed in a white room, her head throbbing, her throat and face numb, her eyes dry and grainy like in a sandstorm.

'You're very fortunate, Dr Morgan, both your eyes are fine. We've managed to sort out the problem with your eyelids. I'm Raghuvir Singh, by the way.'

The white-masked doctor beamed with goodwill, like she had won the lottery. No thank you, Dr Singh, take my fortune, and I will take yours. Anjali gulped down the scalding words. This man wasn't the enemy.

'Now that you're with us, you'll make rapid progress.' He took the chart the nurse handed him, 'How do you feel?'

The nurse beside the doctor stood thin and tall, her eyes pinched, her mouth and nose hidden, like the doctor's, behind a surgical mask. She towered over both the doctor and Maya, and gave Anjali a stiff little nod.

'I can see…better.' Anjali said.

Her voice came through a muddy, sloshy throat—not her throat, someone else's. Maybe she would wake up again, in the right place and bed this time. The nurse wore gloves and gave her eyedrops. Anjali blinked, and the process needed to be repeated. Jatin did it so much better. Where was he?

'Your tear ducts are not functioning, so we will have to do these drops regularly. Keep your eyes closed.' The doctor rustled some papers. 'After we evaluate tomorrow's surgery, we'll plan the next step.'

'Surgery?' Anjali asked the question into the dark behind her eyelids.

'Yes. We could've started before if you came to us earlier, but never mind, we can begin now.'

'Where…?' Her voice stuck.

'You're at the L.K. Hospital.' The doctor pronounced it like it was the Holy Land, to be spoken of only with the utmost reverence. 'We'll work under general anaesthesia.'

'My face?'

'We'll remove the scar tissue first, so we can prevent infections and then figure out the reconstruction. We use the latest technology here, Dr Morgan, don't worry. Now that we have removed your feeding tube, make sure you take in adequate nutrition, we'll do the rest.'

She knew about the debriding of scars, so she let herself drift through the darkness behind her closed eyelids as the doctor droned on. The pain in her head throbbed like a hammer gone berserk. Scars? How bad? How long had she been here? L.K. Hospital? Who paid the bills? Did her insurance cover it?

When she opened her eyes, the doctor had left. Anjali turned to find Maya, wearing a white surgical mask that all but covered her eyes. Her fingers flew over her phone, absorbed in her work, as if she sat in her office. Why wouldn't

Maya look at her? The pain in her face and chest dulled, but remained waiting in ambush.

Water. Anjali needed water, to make the inside of her mouth less dry and gummy. She didn't call Maya. Anjali Morgan—a needy, ugly lump now, who needed to be fed, watered, clothed, and taken to the toilet. She itched to ask Maya about Nikhil.

It wasn't him. It could not have been. And yet, she had heard his voice. Didn't she hear him laugh? She had recognised him.

'Will you be ok by yourself for a few minutes?' Maya stared at Anjali's feet, not her face.

'Maya?' Anjali tried to clear her throat but it remained sludgy, moist. 'How long have I been here?'

'You were at Safdarjung earlier, for three days.' Maya turned towards the door. 'Three days here.'

Six days. She couldn't remember almost a week of her life. Anjali wanted to touch her own face, but they'd tied her forearms down to the bed with gauze bandages, and she couldn't bend her elbows.

'Take these off?' Each word a wound in her throat. She stared at the tapes that restrained her.

Maya muttered about Anjali thrashing in her sleep and hurting herself. Maya's voice faded in and out, just like the doctor's earlier. Was her hearing ruined?

Maya spoke on, vague words about having left Sakhi outside the room, in the corridor. Sakhi came with her because Nikhil might return home. Return from where? Jatin's. Why did Nikhil go to Jatin's? When?

'When can I...'

'The doctor says we will have to wait for the children to visit you.' Maya buttoned her jacket up, her fingers brisk. 'Risk of infections.'

Her eyes still blurred from the eyedrops, Anjali watched Maya. Would her own fingers ever be that nimble again, holding each buttonhole wide and slipping in the button in simple, unthinking movement?

'I'll just be a few minutes.' Maya said, dark circles under her eyes, hair messier than usual, clothes crumpled like she'd slept in them. This couldn't be easy for her, managing work, home, hospital, all by herself.

Water, just a sip would do. Anjali closed her eyes and let darkness, heavy and smooth as a worn shawl, fall over her. She saw Nikhil, walking closer, a cup in hand, a cup that would set her burning. She ran.

***

A light touch on her arm, above the sores. A soft tap, gliding, confident. It could not be Nikhil. He never touched her, or anyone. Mom. Mom would strangle Anjali. Anjali's breath quickened, but she bit down the scream in her throat. Let Mom put her out of her misery. It would hurt, but only for a moment.

Anjali squeezed her eyes shut, but the touch didn't grow stronger. She opened them a crack and saw a red blur. The blur let out a squeak. Anjali screamed too, though only a hoarse bray emerged. Sakhi in a red frock, shrieked at the top of her voice, 'Mummy, mummy, mummy!' her eyes closed, mouth wide open. Somewhere in the distance an alarm rang out and Anjali heard the clatter of approaching feet. Sakhi took off at a run and barrelled into Maya, who'd just rushed in. Sakhi's screams faded as Maya picked her up and hurried out.

The nurse came in and patted Anjali's shoulders, murmuring, 'It's ok, it's ok.'

She held a paper cup to Anjali's mouth, 'Just to wet your lips, ok? Doctor is coming now.'

Dr Singh walked in, then Maya.

'Dr Morgan, I'm so sorry,' he said. 'Children are not allowed in here. I apologise for the trouble.' He gestured towards the nurse. 'Vibha here will take care of you.'

Mummy. The girl had called her a mummy. Like Egyptian mummies, in the movie she had watched with Sakhi, or Mummy as in Mom? Like her Mom? Mom who had dressed her up for that wedding?

Anjali used to love mud, dipping her toes in the soft dark goo. That morning she hadn't meant to walk by that ridiculous little stream. It had seemed so big in those days, and she so small, a puff of froth in pigtails. She'd stumbled, her satin shoes slipping off the track and into the mud. How would she go back to the church now? Mom had warned her not to wander, not before she walked the aisle behind the bride, Mom's friend. She had to hold a bouquet in one hand, and the other bridesmaid's hand in another. Now she'd dirtied her cream shoes, the exact shade of the dress that Mom had driven around one whole day to find.

She didn't remember the wedding afterwards, only Mom's hands dragging her away, her shoes getting dirtier, the flap of Mom's skirt, the *clickety-click-clop* of Mom's heels on the pavement. She couldn't call to mind the lunch, though they must have eaten, but she remembered the backyard, later. Her mother repeating the words, *You like mud, do you? No matter what I do, you want to go into the mud, don't you?* The slaps on her cheek. The spinning in her head. The drawn-out ringing in her ears. Dad behind them at the back door, talking in his low, polite voice, *maybe that's enough, Dorothy. Let her go now, you're hurting her.*

The clumps of cold mud smeared on her face. The blinding of it. The lumps in her mouth. The retching. Her face rubbed in the stinky grass, those fingers boring into her neck. They reached her arms and Anjali twisted away. Not Mom at all, but Vibha, a blur of white uniform and soft words.

Anjali had to see what she looked like. She asked Vibha for a mirror, but no words came out.

Vibha injected a clear liquid into the cannula on Anjali's hand. She didn't want to sleep. What if Mom came this time?

Maybe that was what she needed. To talk to Mom. Dr Bhalla said, *if you are able to face your mother, it might help you with Nikhil. But it must be your decision.*

Anjali had avoided meeting Mom all these years.

Nikhil had done this to her. She needed to understand why. Pain was her constant companion now—she had no choice in the matter. Meeting Mom would be her decision, her choice.

27

At yet another meeting with Rathi, Jatin answered only the questions he couldn't avoid. It had become increasingly difficult to respond to some of them.

The monthly brief took up the rest of his morning. He spoke to various deputy commissioners, helped plan and coordinate operations between different units of the Crime Branch in all of Delhi's eleven districts. On normal days, he enjoyed that part of his role, but not today. It had given him a headache that didn't respond to aspirin. At such times, he used to drop Anjali an email, and wait for a response, then fix up a time and place to meet. All that was gone. He had not been able to protect her, and now, in the two days since she was awake, he couldn't gather the courage to go talk to her. Instead he visited her at night like a thief, when the nurses had already drugged her to sleep.

'May I come in, sir?' Kusum stood at his door, her laptop in hand.

When Jatin nodded, she placed it on his table.

'You're asking for the CCTV from Anjaliji's clinic, sir,' she clicked on a file. 'There was problem with the recording, but with Pawan's help, I'm opening it.'

'Anything unusual?'

'Only on one evening, sir, two days before the attack.'

Jatin saw the two figures, young guys looming over Anjali as she sat on the sofa at her reception. They gestured with their hands, and pointed fingers.

'Find these two.'

'We may have already found them, sir. This tall one is Chander, who we have in custody, for following Maya and Pawan the other day.'

Interesting. They had found smack on that boy, but he had refused to speak. He had fallen ill since—withdrawal symptoms.

'The packet of smack we found on him?'

Five grams of heroin. Since Chander didn't have a previous record, the possession could only get him six months in jail or a fine of ten thousand rupees. Both, if he got a cranky judge or an inexperienced lawyer.

'He is not knowing what it is, he says. Someone putting it into his bag.'

'Has he seen this footage?'

'I just got it from Pawan, sir.'

'Has this Chander said why he was following them?'

'He is saying he is not following anyone—just driving to work on his bike when police arresting him for no reason.'

'He'll change his tune soon enough. And this other boy?'

'I know him, sir.' Kusum cleared her throat. 'This is Radhe, Sakhi's brother.'

'Radhe is at Hridayog, right? Have him picked up.' Jatin said. 'Make sure you do it without alerting Lahiri.'

Jatin knew just the man who could make Chander talk

using that footage. He asked Kusum to pass the footage to the SHO handling Anjali's case, and also make a copy for Jatin himself on a thumb drive. The boy had followed them on someone's instructions—either Radhe or Lahiri.

'Get Chander processed and send him to the Jamia Nagar police station. Once you get Radhe, send him there as well.'

Once he got these two boys to talk, Jatin could get a clearer picture of Lahiri and Manoj, and whether they were involved in the Sujni murder. These boys had also gone and threatened Anjali; did they have anything to do with the attack on her? Or was it Nikhil? Pawan hadn't spoken to the boy yet.

Jatin dismissed Kusum and sent a text to Pawan. The response came within minutes.

'Not yet, sir. I haven't managed to get him alone yet. I'll do it before office tomorrow.'

28

Varun *se panga mat lena*, they said at school: no one messes with Varun Satyaprakash Bhatt.

He had caught the puppy killer near Laddoo-dog. He didn't like it, and he made that clear. But the freak kept going to Laddoo. Varun found them sunning themselves together on the roof the other day. Laddoo never went near the terrace, so it must have been that *gaandu*'s doing.

Hadn't been that hard to get rid of him. Varun knew the basics. Pull the freak's hair, or punch him out of the blue, and walk past. Nikhil Morgan was such a space cadet; he never saw it coming. Catch his arm and twist it behind his back, cuff his mouth if he tried to scream. Do it regularly, but not so as to bruise him. Then, with people nearby but out of sight, kick him, knee him. Goad him to hit you back this time. Fall down and yell for help. Let everyone rescue you.

With Daddy away at a community meeting, Mummy had panicked once Nikhil started hitting and screaming this morning. She'd called Maya Fufee who called the space cadet's doctor. The doctor came with two big men, and collected Nikhil. Mummy and Fufee left for the clinic with him.

'So easy it was a bore ya,' he told Bunty over the phone,

'That *gaandu saala* is gone, they took him to the hospital. Served him right for trying to touch Laddoo.'

Laddoo gazed up at Varun at the mention of her name. Laddoo-dog. Varun combed Laddoo's long brown fur with his fingers. At fifteen, Laddoo was growing old. The vet said the dog had two more years at the most. Varun didn't want to think about life without Laddoo in it. He half-listened to Bunty grumbling away at the other end of the line.

'*Abey bhosdi ke* you'll get me killed one of these days.' Bunty said, 'I asked you to stay chilled, Varun. And you go and do this.'

Bunty meant the swear words as cute nicknames, but sometimes they annoyed Varun. Couldn't Bunty call him a good word once in a while? And why 'Varun' instead of the usual 'Vicky'? Not as if he'd screwed anything up for the great Vishal Sharan Sisodia. Tempted to call his friend 'Vish', a sure way to piss him off, Varun held back.

'Come on, what's that to do with us?' Varun lay on his bed, still patting Laddoo. 'I'm telling you no one knows I got that drop the other day for the party. And even if they do, your father is the home secretary, dude. What are *you* afraid of?'

'Same thing as you, Vicky. The Daddy darling finding out. He wants me to prepare for the IAS this year.'

'Do it ya.' Varun sat up on his bed. 'What have you got to lose? We're catching up for a last hit before I leave? Or you too scared now?'

With Bunty you needed to be careful. He wanted you to joke with him, but only when it made other people look bad. You didn't want a cheesed-off Bunty if you wanted a good hit.

'Come over.' Bunty said, in his bored voice, 'You'll be ok in Manila, dude. Plenty of corner places, even after all their shooting on the streets. Chill *maar*. And be careful at home, ok?'

Varun didn't see what they had to fear. The freak must have injections stuck into his ass now, Fufee and Mummy clucking over him. Nikhil Morgan wouldn't tell anyone the truth. Even if he did, who would believe that psycho piece of shit?

Varun heard voices outside and checked his watch. The women had come back. He said a hurried bye to Bunty, and hung up. No noise at all when his parents were at home. Best way to stay under the radar.

'We can talk here.' Mummy said, 'No one comes here when Jatin's not in. I have the keys.'

They were in Daddy's study. Varun gestured Laddoo to lay still, and the dog closed her eyes. Pushing aside the piles of magazines and clothes on the floor, Varun sank down and crawled closer to the connecting door opposite his bed, so he could hear better.

No one had permission to enter his room other than Laddoo. His parents didn't mind, but not letting the housekeeper in meant he had to clean up the place himself. He sorted the shoes and clothes while he listened.

'No one's home?'

'No, Varun has gone out for a bit.' Mummy said, 'After this morning he needed a break, I think.'

'I'm sorry, Bhabi. All this is new for Nikhil, and he's never been away from home this long.'

Ah, poor, poor Nikhil. Varun leaned closer.

'How long will that girl stay at your place?' Mummy sounded annoyed. She didn't want Nikhil to come and stay here again. Varun fist-bumped Laddoo, who looked up at him with her soft eyes, and tried to lick his hand.

'I don't know, Bhabi. It's a little complicated right now.'

'I don't understand why Jatin won't let you throw that girl out.'

'Anjali brought Sakhi home.'

'Sometimes Jatin listens too much to Anjali. She is his mentor's daughter, but…'

There was silence. What were they doing? What was his dumbo Fufee going to say to his Mummy? Varun stood up, hoping to run into the study to stop her, but it was too late.

'Bhai is having an affair,' his Fufee sobbed out, 'with Anjali.'

No, no, no. Fucking feminazi Fufee. Did all girls have to be so stupid? Now Mummy would go ballistic.

Varun had seen those two together that first time, hands crawling all over each other. *Saala* even then he knew it was wrong. Found out why when he grew up, met Bunty. He kept shut of course, had to. If Mummy-Daddy split up, Mummy would want to stay at the Mehra mansion, and that simply wouldn't do.

The grandparents, Varun's loving *nana-nani*, watched their money like hawks ya. No sneaking stuff from them. Varun typed an SOS to Bunty. This called for a meeting. Their major source of loose cash was about to dry up. He didn't give a shit about Mummy-Daddy. Sissies cared about things like that. He was a man now, cool with stuff. Bunty would know what to do.

As he waited for his Mummy to explode all over his feminazi Fufee, he held on to Laddoo, who nuzzled his throat. Laddoo-dog was Varun Satyaprakash Bhatt's soulmate, the one who understood all his troubles. He hugged Laddoo tight as his Mummy asked Maya Fufee the first, loud, shaky question.

29

Anjali's throat hurt, pain driving sharp spikes through her face and chest as she ran, trying to find Nikhil, to talk to him. When she found him, she was afraid to call out, afraid whose face she would see when he turned.

'Anji.' Maya's voice broke into Anjali's terror. She didn't know if this was part of her medicine-induced dream, but maybe if she tried to open her eyes, she would see Maya. A safe haven. Light.

'Anji? Dr Bhalla is here to see you.'

Anjali opened her eyes, and saw Maya's curly hair, held up by a lime-green band. It was her. Dr Bhalla. Why Dr Bhalla?

Anjali needed to remain alert for this one. Nikhil couldn't stand strange places, so of course he didn't like it at Jatin's home. Took her six months to get him used to his new school. Anjali drew a long, shaky breath, preparing herself for the worst. Maybe they knew about Nikhil, what he had done.

'I'm here,' Maya said, her hand on Anjali's knee. Maya's soft eyes above her surgical mask was all Anjali could see of her face.

That dry touch on an unhurt part of her body set Anjali

sobbing in big, painful gulps. She still had her knee, her legs, her body. Maya, and yes, Nikhil. She would do what she needed to keep Nikhil safe; they wouldn't take him away.

Anjali's hands were now untied. She tried to reach out to Maya, but her arms hurt. Her head felt woozy.

When Bhalla came in, he looked much shorter than he was. Anjali wanted to say *boo*, and watch him jump. How high could he jump on his tiny feet? Lemurs jumped, she knew that from TV. Bhalla rambled on about how she needn't worry, just focus on getting better, the whole department was shocked by the incident. Why didn't he get to the point?

'How is Nikhil?' Anjali said.

Her question agitated her pocket-sized boss.

'I've been telling you,' Bhalla stood taller and raised his voice, 'about the need for stronger intervention with Nikhil.'

Anjali waited for Bhalla to continue. When he didn't, she put his advice into practice: *deep breaths*. Once she felt calm enough, she repeated, 'How is he?'

Maybe Bhalla didn't know about Nikhil, after all. No one had guessed.

'He stayed ok for the first few days, though not interactive. He suffered a crisis yesterday morning. We must hospitalise him.'

'What kind of crisis?'

'He attacked Varun all of a sudden. We've brought him to the clinic, and kept him under observation since last night.'

'You want him to stay on?' Anjali's throat felt dry. When she looked at the bottle beside the bed, Maya brought a paper cup from the side table and held it to her lips.

'You were not well.' Bhalla shifted his weight from one foot to another. 'Hospitals scare him, but with your permission, we need to keep him a little longer in order to monitor his reactions to the medication. Bhatt saab thinks he might be involved in…' Bhalla did not continue.

Anjali's glance caught Maya, who looked puzzled. Jatin had spoken to Bhalla, but not Maya. Anjali's forehead pounded with her effort to focus, and the searing pain inside her throat and on her face came back stronger than before.

'We will put him under intensive therapy,' Bhalla said, his eyes yellow and evil-twinkly. He wore whiskers, didn't he, a lemur's whiskers? No, that couldn't be. Everyone who entered her room wore surgical masks, so it was hard to gauge their expressions. The dry burn in her eyes made her shut them.

'No!' Anjali sat up with a jerk, but Maya made her lie down and rang for the nurse.

'Shh…it's ok, Anji.'

'Nikhil can stay at the clinic tonight…but I need to see him after that.'

Making excuses again for your son? Mom's voice came to her. Yes, she was. So what? All mothers made excuses for their children.

Vibha came in, administered eye-drops. Next, Anjali felt the push of fluid from her cannula into her vein. Vibha said she needed to keep her eyelids shut tight for a while.

Bhalla had sneaked out by the time Anjali opened her eyes, so she made Maya promise: one night, not more, unless they talked to her. Maya's voice stayed soft, but her eyes turned angry. Everyone was angry with Anjali. She'd dragged them all to this room that reeked of cleaning fluids and room fresheners, and each one of them hated her, including Jatin.

She thought of asking for her phone, but changed her mind. Not as if she could hold a phone or dial a number. Anjali tried to resist the pull of drugged slumber. She needed to talk to Jatin, but more than that, maybe it was time she faced Mom.

'Maya?'

'Sleep, Anji. I promise Nikhil will be back home soon.'

'No, not that.' Anjali gasped out. 'I need to talk to Mom.'

***

The clomp of boots on the tiled floor told Anjali someone had come in. She opened her eyes a crack. Whoever it was didn't need to know she was awake. A flash of khaki uniform. Jatin?

'Namaste, Anjaliji.' Kusum waited at the foot of the bed.

'She's here to take your statement,' Maya stood next to Kusum, 'but she can come back later.'

'No, it's ok.' Anjali's head felt clearer. She needed to deal with this, not give anything away.

The window had grown dark. She must have slept for hours. She looked at the two white-masked women, both almost the same height, the one fair, chubby, colourful, the other muscular and dark, in khaki uniform. '6 pm,' they chorused, when she asked the time.

Kusum dragged a plastic chair next to the bed and sat down, her pen poised over her notebook. Her eyes held the careful blankness of a witness taking the stand. Anjali hadn't seen an entire human face in a long time, and she wished she could tear Kusum's mask off, read her expression, and tailor her replies accordingly.

'You're seeing your attacker?'

Yes, I'm seeing him all the time, she wanted to tell Kusum. She felt the liquid as it dripped down her face. She shut her eyes.

Anjali explained about the fog, about her eyes blurred with tears because of contact lenses. No, not a full-grown man, the attacker was a teen. No she couldn't tell if he was dark or fair, or how tall he was. He was a lot shorter than she. Not broad or fat. *Keep it as vague as possible,* she told herself, *but don't lie either. Jatin always catches you out.*

The moment of the liquid hitting her face came back to her. That was the very last moment she was Anjali Morgan, aging but good-looking mother, moderately successful psychiatrist. Not this charred heap on a hospital bed.

'Was he reminding you of anyone?'

Kusum leaned forward on her chair. Anjali tried to smile at Kusum's English—'was he reminding'—anything to distract her from the throb building in her head.

'No.'

'The attacker talking to you?'

Anjali tried to interpret Kusum's expression. 'Am I supposed to recognise him? Have you already found out who did this?'

'No, Anjaliji.' Kusum's frown relaxed, but her mouth still made a tense line on her face. 'But we need your help to get a description of him.'

'He called me by name.' That was the truth. 'But I didn't recognise the voice.' That was a lie, but Jatin always said that all good lies had a trace of truth in them.

'So the attacker knowing you? Can you think of anyone wanting to harm you?'

'No.'

'We are finding a can of drain cleaner in the boot of your car.'

'I had taken one to the Safdarjung hospital, to get the toilet cleaned. How is that relevant?'

Kusum wore a calm smile, but she gripped the pen hard. 'Nikhil was nearby at the time.'

Pain dug its claws into her temples. She had to deflect this. If they found out about Nikhil, he would never stand a chance. They would shut him up, in one of those places with high walls. He would never come out.

'Nikhil? You think Nikhil did this? Have you lost your mind?'

The two women tried to calm her down, to tell her it was routine, that they must follow due process, eliminate suspects.

Kusum asked a few more questions—specifics about what Anjali remembered, if anyone suspicious had hung around her clinic or home, in the days leading up to the incident.

She finally produced a large file with police mug-shots. 'Are you seeing any of these persons before?'

Anjali pointed at Chander, the only familiar face amid the lot. She told them about her encounter with Radhe and his hulking friend at her office. The shouting about Sakhi, the veiled threats. Let them focus on Radhe and Chander, not Nikhil.

'He's Radhe Shyam Misra's friend?' Kusum confirmed the name.

'Yes.'

'Do you know where Radhe could go, other than Hridayog?'

'No, why?' Anjali tried to sit up, 'He isn't there?'

'We're trying to find him. He was with Mr Lahiri yesterday, but not this morning.'

'I'm not sure. Have you asked Mr Lahiri?'

'We didn't know Lahiri as well as we thought,' Maya said.

'What does that mean?'

Anjali tried to make sense of what Maya said next. Hridayog, drug den, Manoj, prostitution, Sakhi. Chander following them, being caught with drugs—no surprises there, but how could she not have known about Lahiri? And who was Manoj?

Kusum scribbled on her notebook, assured her they would find the culprit, and hurried out. Maya went out with her, and came back after a while.

'This man,' Anjali said, 'this Mr Lahiri's friend, showed Sakhi's pictures?'

'I'm sorry.' Maya said, 'We always thought Lahiri harmless just because of his roly-poly face.'

'Are you sure? I must have met this Manoj. Did he groom her?'

'I've spoken to Nikhil's counsellor. She's spoken to Sakhi: Sakhi is all right. She does not know Manoj.'

'He deserves to be thrown in jail.'

'He will be.' Maya said. 'Sakhi's safe—you try and rest now, ok?'

Anjali's eyelids drooped, and her arm spasmed in pain. All of her felt heavy, too heavy to carry any more. *Such a fool, Anjali. Why are you so naïve?* Mom's voice scolded her.

'I wanted to talk to you.' Anjali heard the sorry note in her own voice, and took a breath to calm herself. She shut out the pounding in her head, the throbbing of her face.

'You rest now.' Maya tugged up the zip on her handbag, preparing to leave.

When Maya was hurt, you approached her like you would a wounded animal—by talking softly about other things, never making eye contact, but closing in all the time. Maya *was* hurt, or she wouldn't be caring one minute and indifferent at another. She needed to pacify Maya, but she needed to talk to Mom more. To understand how she had come to this. How to make things better. How to protect her son, not be afraid of him, because yes, as she spoke to Kusum, she was terrified Nikhil would walk in the door and throw more of that liquid on her, and the burning, clawing agony would begin again.

'I need to speak to Mom.' Anjali said, focusing on forming each word so it came out firm, distinct.

'Are you sure?' Maya walked up to the bed. 'You said that earlier, but I thought you were…'

'Hallucinating?' She put all of herself into that word, to fight down everything that swelled up within her, urging her to say, *no, not really. I'm hallucinating. Why would I ever want to talk to Mom?*

'No, I want to talk to her. Ira has her number.'

Maya stood there, staring, as if it wasn't Anjali, but someone else on that bed. Anjali wanted to tell her she was a different Anjali now, a burned Anjali, a desperate mother looking for answers.

'All right,' Maya said, 'I'll call her.'

30

When he stepped into the Jamia Nagar police station the day after they had transferred Chander, Jatin's plain clothes meant he didn't get any gushing and bowing. SHO Grewal, the only man in the entire force who didn't call him 'sir' despite ranking lower, didn't make a fuss either, just waved him to a chair, and ordered him tea.

'How is Anjaliji now?'

Grewal's biceps bulged under the sleeves of his uniform. He hadn't changed much since their school days together: still preferred his clothes one size too small, smoked too many cigarettes, chewed *paan*, and wore his belt way too high.

'Recovering. How's your sister?'

'She's engaged now, to that same fellow. Going to open her shop.' Grewal pushed his chair back, and placed both his hands on the table. 'She's smiling again, all thanks to Anjaliji. You must nail the bastard who did this to her. Is the man you brought related to her case?'

'He could be.' Jatin passed the thumb drive with the video footage to Grewal.

'Both look very angry.' Grewal stared at the screen.

'There's also the drugs we found on him.'

Jatin gave the details of the Sujni murder and the serial cases to Grewal, about how Maya and Pawan had met Lahiri, and been followed by Chander. Grewal paced the room as he listened, his steps soft for such a large man.

Ten minutes later, Jatin walked into the windowless interrogation room, with its lone tube light. This wasn't strictly legal, picking this fellow up and keeping him in a lock-up on remand, not telling him his rights. Jatin had seen it done dozens of times before, and himself sanctioned it often enough on cases that skirted the law, involving one Member of Parliament or the other. So many MPs got away with crimes because they held the police under their thumbs, kept winning elections despite criminal records and murder cases pending against them.

Jatin sighed. This time, instead of a criminal MP, his own interest was at stake.

'You know this boy?' Grewal held out his mobile phone, the CCTV video rolling on the screen.

Chander froze when he saw it, but didn't say a word. He kept his eyes lowered, his hands under his thighs. Despite the damp, chilly room, Chander wore only a light t-shirt and a pair of thin pants. The constable standing by must have taken away his sweater. Under the light, Jatin could see the scars on Chander's forearm. Needle marks.

Grewal caught Chander by the scruff of his neck and shook him, pushing his face into his mobile on the table, still playing the video of Radhe and Chander at Anjali's office.

'So you don't know him, huh?'

The room stank of sweat, urine and vomit. Jatin hadn't conducted such interrogations in a long time. He held his breath for a while then stepped out to check on Kusum's progress with Radhe. They had not found him the day before. Pawan's man had apparently seen Radhe get into a Maruti van at night, and disappear.

'We're still not finding him, sir.' Kusum said, 'Radhe is not at Hridayog, or his shanty, or anywhere in Sanjay Colony.'

'How is that possible?'

'He should be here, sir. We'll keep looking.'

Radhe had disappeared from under their noses. Jatin considered calling Pawan to ask for updates, but he let it go. No point in making a call when he might say things he might regret later. They needed to get it out of Chander—where had Radhe vanished to, why Chander himself had followed Pawan and Maya. Jatin returned to the interrogation room.

Chander was tall, broad-shouldered, but Grewal shoved at him as if he were a loosely-packed bag of grain. Chander's hands trembled: they made sure he kept them on the table. He looked this way and that, as if searching for a friend, and shifted in his chair. With bare walls and a single, barred window, the room didn't offer much to please the eye.

'We will book you, you know that.' Grewal's Hindi carried a soft, polite edge, in contrast to the way he hit Chander on the jaw. 'But maybe we need to help you remember a few facts, first.'

When Chander did not speak, two men in uniform came in and held Chander by the arms, face down on the table. Grewal asked the third to come in with his *danda*, the metre-long police baton, and hit Chander. With each resounding thwack on his buttocks, Chander screamed out loud, tried to kick and rise, begged them to let go, but the

Sub-Inspector with the baton hit with unerring aim, at the same spot. Jatin counted six strokes before Chander let out a long wail and Grewal gestured for the *danda* to stop.

'The choice is yours.' He said once the men stood back. 'We can charge you with the acid attack, because we have the CCTV footage with the lady, and keep you here for interrogation.'

'*Danda milega yahan*,' Grewal added, making a rude gesture, thrusting up with his fist, and his men laughed.

Chander shivered and whined, his legs quaking. Jatin made himself watch, but in his mind he played back the many times he had participated in such interrogations: the way the policemen hit out with all their strength, in some cases to vent their frustration at the unfair terms at work, and the hapless Bad Characters in the lockup who paid the price. The marks on the bodies in places the suspect needed to strip in order to show others. He considered himself a hardened police officer, but today's procedure, carried out solely for his benefit, made him cringe. He wanted leads on Sujni's case, but at what cost? He wanted it to stop—for Chander to give them what they needed.

'Or, you can get charged with the smack you were carrying.' Grewal loomed over the cowering Chander, 'Much faster, and we will take you for *haziri* to court tomorrow. Which do you want?'

'I just met her once, saabji, I swear.' Chander said, 'One time with Radhe.'

'So you *do* know Radhe.'

'His father and mine were cousins, saabji, I only went to support him. We scared her a little, because she refused to return Radhe's sister. That's all, saabji, believe me. Please let me go.'

'What about the smack?'

'I don't know,' Chander hid his face in his hands, his body curled up on the floor. 'Someone put it there.'

Chander jerked back and hacked. Grewal took a bucket sitting nearby, and shoved it at Chander, who threw up, making retching noises. The room filled with the reek of bile, and Jatin tamped down the urge to throw up.

'I can arrange for you to feel better right away.' Grewal put away the bucket and gave Chander a mug of water. 'I can let you snort a little...you will be ok.'

Chander splashed his face with water, slugged down some of it, and glanced up at Grewal for the first time.

'I didn't do anything on my own, saabji. It is that Lahiri. He asked me to take it to his customers.'

'Ok. Record your statement, and you can have your reward.'

Jatin and Grewal left the room, and walked out into the chill air beyond the gates of the police station. Fog blurred the street lights, and in the distance the azaan played out on a mike, the Muslim call to prayer. Jatin took in a gulp of the smoky air, and turned to his friend. A drug addict's confession wasn't worth much as a testimony. They needed to get more on Lahiri and Manoj.

'Will we have enough for a raid?'

'He'll sing now.' Grewal stretched, sticking his massive stomach out, and cracked his knuckles. 'But they must already know he's in; gives them time to hide their tracks.'

'What about the attack on Anjali?'

'He kept saying he didn't do it. He doesn't match the

height of your suspect anyway, he's too tall and broad. The footage from the shop shows a thin fellow, you said.'

'Yes. Keep pushing him about Radhe, though.' Jatin said. 'He knows the whereabouts of that rascal.'

Jatin relished the colloquial slang of Hindi, and the swearing. He spoke refined words these days at meetings, and more English than he liked.

'My men will start again tomorrow morning.'

'Try and find out more about Lahiri. He has a degree in pharmacology. He may be able to cook drugs. And check if there's any way he can access Propofol.'

'That's what you found in the Sujni case?'

Grewal didn't miss a trick. He had the stamina and the brains to rise in the ranks, but chose to remain an SHO. Jatin couldn't understand it.

'You know you can easily go higher up the ladder, right?'

'I am happy here. I'm in charge of about two hundred staff, and even if it is stressful, this is the work I like to do. I cannot do more politics, Jatin, and I cannot push papers.'

'You're calling me a paper-pusher?' Jatin laughed.

'I'm saying I'm happy where I am. Can you say that about yourself?'

***

On the way back to his home in Punjabi Bagh, Jatin looked in on Anjali as he had done each evening since the attack. The hospital noise was muted in her room, and the blinds drawn half-way against the distant street light. It felt strange, being in the same room as her, and not smelling her perfume.

He never ventured close to her bed, letting her face remain

a dark shadow on her pillows. He would have to talk to her soon, but he wanted to avoid it as long as he could, at least until he had some answers about her attacker. And if it turned out to be Nikhil…Nikhil had attacked Varun the day before. With Anjali's permission, he was still at Bhalla's clinic, where he couldn't cause harm.

Stepping out of Anjali's room, Jatin realised that Grewal was right. Grewal was happy where he was, but not Jatin. Not with all the stress the job brought him, not with his empty shell of a marriage, not even with his affair with Anjali. Keeping their relationship a secret had worked all this while, but not now, not when Anjali suffered in the hospital, and he was reduced to the status of a helpless onlooker. He wanted to be with her, hold her hand, stand beside her, take care of her when she got released from the hospital.

Maya already resented it. Funny, how he felt the need to be with Anjali now that she was disfigured; he'd always thought his attraction to her was more physical than anything else. Friendship perhaps. But this went beyond that. Different from what he felt about Maya and Varun—the intensity of his feelings for Anjali made him come undone. Maybe they had always been there, and he had hidden them away. So much easier not to feel, because as he had found out in the last few days, it fucking hurt.

Lost in his thoughts, he didn't switch on the living room lights. He took off his shoes and was about to head to his room up the stairs, when the lights came on. Drishti.

'You haven't gone to bed?'

Drishti had the use of the master bedroom—he usually stepped in for his clothes, but spent the night in the guest room. Drishti slept early, because she left for work at seven each morning.

'Where were you? I called your phone.'

This was unusual. They did not keep tabs on each other, coming and going as they pleased. Perhaps the incident with Nikhil had scared her.

'I went to the hospital.' Jatin said. 'It was too late to meet the doctor. He had already left.'

'You're breaking up our family for her? After I stayed for years, tolerated you, and you are…'

'What is this about?'

'Maya told me everything. I couldn't talk to you yesterday because Varun was home.'

Varun was staying with his grandparents tonight—they lived less than five minutes' drive away.

Jatin hadn't expected Maya to talk to Drishti. He was old enough to be Maya's father, and there was always that sense of discretion between them. No point denying anything now. He had to find a way to control the damage with Drishti's father.

'Anjali has nothing to do with this. She has always refused me, told me to stay with you.'

Even as he said those words, he heard how limp they sounded. Truth could appear flimsy at times.

'How? By sleeping with you every now and then? Is that how your "good friend" sees this?'

'Drishti, it was my fault. She wasn't the only one I went out with, all right?' That was true. In the early days of his marriage, there had been others.

Drishti collapsed on the sofa, closed her eyes and lay her

head back. What had she expected to hear? That he had remained celibate for all these years?

'If you want a divorce, we can do that. Share joint custody of Varun for a year.'

'You have all this planned already?'

No he hadn't. But he found that the word divorce brought with it a sense of lightness. He'd been 'trying', 'thinking', 'discussing' all these years. No more. If a splash of sulphuric acid could change Anjali's life, something equally small could take away his, too. And after that he would have had to spend all of it living with someone he couldn't stand.

'We both know this has been difficult for a while.'

'And who has made it difficult?' Drishti stood up, her nose in line with his throat. She wanted to fight, he could see that in the way she had thrust her head forward. Her tall, starved neck looked rigid.

'What's important is how we move on from here.'

'I don't care.' She shoved herself up as close to him as she could, 'I want to know. Everything. Did you sleep with her on my bed while I was away? Did your colleagues know? Were they laughing at me at each party I hosted for them? When did you meet her—in between office hours? In hotels? Do you have another apartment?'

'Drishti.'

'Don't "Drishti" me. I'm going to know all of it even if it kills me.'

A noise behind them made Jatin look up from Drishti's red, blotchy face, and straight at Varun's.

Varun's eyes stayed on his, cold and strong. A man's eyes, challenging another. When had Varun come back? Jatin hadn't heard his bike power down.

'Varun!' Jatin shoved Drishti aside and walked to his son, but the young man with the hard stare had walked out. He must have broken into a sprint, because by the time Jatin reached the main door, he heard the bike fire outside the gate, and throttle off.

31

Vibha pushed Anjali's wheelchair towards her second appointment with her counsellor. Anjali kept her gaze on the floor. Nine days after the attack, she still hadn't seen her face. She'd repeatedly asked for a mirror, because the bathroom contained none, but the doctor said that her counsellor Fareeda Saigal would decide on this. Until then, no smartphones, no mirrors, or cameras.

Fareeda had asked whether Anjali would prefer the next session in her room again, or at Fareeda's clinic in the other wing of the hospital. Anjali chose the latter, because she longed to see the world beyond her room. She kept her head lowered, despite the giddiness from staring at the shiny floor under the wheels. She didn't want to meet the eyes of those who saw her face. They stopped at a door and Vibha knocked.

Anjali watched Vibha's shrunken face, the way her pale lipstick bled out of her lips, the wrinkles on the woman's forehead, the hollows under her eyes. Earlier, while doing up her face, Anjali used to curse at a pimple—it showed the world she couldn't control her own skin. Now, she'd give anything for a pimpled face, or one covered in hives or wrinkles, even one like the nurse's, who stood talking to the counsellor's assistant.

'Hello, Anjali.' Fareeda Saigal's quiet greeting startled her.

A large, well-rounded woman, grey hair, thick glasses, in a pale blue saree and black cardigan.

Vibha helped Anjali to a sofa, and left, promising to return in an hour.

'Can I get you something to drink?'

The possibility of a spilled drink terrified Anjali. She shook her head, but that lightest of movements tugged at her throat. Some of the scabs felt raw.

'On a scale of 1 to 10, how are you feeling today?' The counsellor straightened up in her chair.

'3.' Anjali focused on Fareeda, and tried to resist the urge to touch the itchy bandages at her throat.

'That's higher than yesterday.' Fareeda said, 'Would you like to talk about it?'

Anjali forgot what she'd said and when. Each hour seemed to merge into the next; mornings, evenings and nights, a haze of pain, people moving in and out of her room, needles, protein shakes, physiotherapy, nightmares. All that she cared about anymore was to figure out why Nikhil had attacked her, and if there was a way forward for them, without involving therapists, and the police.

'Anjali?'

'I'd like to meet Nikhil, if possible, please.'

She kept her gaze on the marble floor. Her throat felt parched, but she wouldn't ask for water. Just her son. She needed to look into his eyes, determine what was in there. She was done being afraid of him, like she'd been the past week.

'We must wait a little longer.' Fareeda shifted in her seat. 'Your son has autism?'

Anjali nodded.

'I think you would understand, that given the circumstances, he's a little upset.'

Yes. Upset enough to attack Varun, who was twice his size, and strong enough to turn him to pulp. That didn't sound like Nikhil at all. Varun had always teased Nikhil, but in the past few years Nikhil had learned how to handle it. His therapy taught him how to react in stressful situations, how to mimic the 'neurotypical' behaviours like eye contact, smiles, cracking jokes. Aggression was a recent trait: the running away at the mall, the incident with the puppy, fighting with her in the car. *He attacked you, Anjali, what about that?* Mom's voice mocked her.

'Are you all right?'

'Yes.'

'Like I was saying, we'll wait for a while before we meet Nikhil. I heard you've asked to speak with your mother?'

'Maya spoke to you?'

'I spoke to both Maya and Jatin.'

Of course. Fareeda would speak to Anjali's family and friends in order to help her with trauma counselling.

'I understand.'

'Maya seemed concerned about your wish to re-establish contact with your mother.'

'Based on his sessions with me and Nikhil, Dr Bhalla has often asked me to work on understanding my relationship with her.'

Anjali expected to be asked more about Nikhil, his therapy, but Fareeda spoke of Mom instead.

'What sort of a person is she?'

Mom. How did one describe a mother who made your headmistress seem more intimate by comparison? She didn't really know Mom. Nothing at all about her childhood, and very little about how she met her husband, Ashok Gupta. And Mom never told stories from Anjali's childhood like other mothers did. She spoke often and loud on just the one subject—Anjali's shortcomings.

'She was stern. Not easy to please. I bonded better with my aunt.'

'Your father's sister?'

'No, my mother's. Her name was Vivian.'

Vivian had died of lung cancer ten years ago. She used to visit them each Fourth of July at their Florida home. Unmarried, with no kids, with spiky, dyed hair and multiple piercings, Aunty Viv at thirty acted like a schoolgirl. Mom mumbled snide comments behind Aunty Viv's back—*God how she dresses, no shame, such deep necklines, why doesn't she dress her age for God's sake.*

'Why did you get along with her, and not your Mom?'

'She was fun, easy to talk to. She let me try on her stuff, bought me gifts.'

'What's your earliest memory of your Mom?'

Anjali closed her eyes and tried to remember a happy memory, but all she saw was Mom dragging her out of the kitchen by the ears, because Anjali had used a stool to climb the shelves, and dipped into the cookie jar. She was four.

32

Jatin hadn't seen his son in two days, not since he'd disappeared on his bike and holed up with his grandparents. He waited for Varun at the departure terminal shrouded in fog. The diffused lights made everything look like the set of an old Bollywood movie, hazy sepia and black. People got out of cars in groups of a dozen or more to drop a passenger or two—entire families to drop a couple. He hoped the Mehra family wasn't likewise headed for the airport with Varun. He couldn't imagine what Varun thought of him. For the first time since holding Varun as a baby, it occurred to him that he might have set a bad example as a father.

Varun wouldn't stray from his marriage, Jatin consoled himself, because he wouldn't have to choose a woman based on his parents' wishes, or how good she would be for his career. Even as the thought came to him, he now knew it to be false. He would have had an affair with Anjali even if he'd chosen Drishti for love. It was him that was the problem. Jatin. He couldn't keep his promises.

He texted yet again, telling Varun where he waited, but there was no response. Varun was sure to spot him where he stood in the light, and though the terminal was fairly crowded, there was no way they could miss each other. He saw the Mehra car easing into one of the dropping points not far from where he stood. He walked towards the car, only to find Varun rushing out of it with a backpack and a small suitcase.

Jatin called out to his son, but Varun didn't turn. Drishti emerged from the car next, and Jatin stopped in his tracks when she looked at him, her eyes bright with tears. She'd been staying with Varun. He didn't know what to say to her beyond what he'd already said—apologised, offered for her to dictate the terms of divorce. By the time he turned back towards Varun, the boy had already reached the gate, and stood getting his documents checked.

Jatin called to Varun, asked him to wait, but Varun did not turn or pause, not even to wave at his mother. He walked straight into the terminal even as Jatin ran towards him. Jatin wished that Indian airports allowed everyone to walk till the check-in counter, but they didn't. He could buy an airport ticket and enter, but Varun was on a school trip, and would be surrounded by friends. It wouldn't help Jatin's cause to embarrass Varun in front of them. He had hurt his son, and now he had to bear the consequences. Jatin turned and walked towards his car.

***

Jatin headed straight to the L.K. hospital from the airport. Anjali's doctor had requested a meeting, and for the second time that day, Jatin found himself waiting. Framed certificates and accolades covered the wall behind Dr Singh's chair. It reminded Jatin of his own office. When Dr Singh came in, his bald pate shining in the white light of the room, Jatin stood up to greet him. Anjali's life was in this man's hands.

Dr Singh said they had temporarily covered Anjali's face with a mask, skin from donor corpses stitched together and placed on her face to help the healing, and save it from infection.

'Dead people?' Jatin said. 'Won't that make it worse?'

'We know what we're doing, Commissioner saab.' Dr Singh smiled and patted his hand, 'Don't worry. The mask will protect her body from heat loss, and we would remove it in about ten days or so. Then we prepare her face for the next major operation.'

'Another operation? So soon?'

'She would have to undergo many procedures. Now that her condition has stabilised, best to start with them as soon as possible, in order to shorten the recovery period. Afterwards, we'll try a dermal substitute all over.' Dr Singh wore the know-it-all face doctors put on when they need to break difficult news.

'What's that?'

'Her wounds are too deep.' Dr Singh drew his lab coat close. 'Won't work if we try to rebuild her face with skin grafts from her body alone. Too much scarring, pain. A dermal substitute is more expensive, but it will help fill up the hollows in her face, give us a frame on which to place her own skin grafts.'

Jatin watched the doctor steeple his fingers on his glass-covered table. The office smelled of cleaning liquids, and stale perfume. Jatin wanted out, but he needed to stay and ask a question important to Anjali.

'Will she look like before?'

Anjali loved her face. She spent hours dolling up. He had never seen her without make-up, not even at five in the morning when she came to meet him. It would kill her to see what her face had become.

'That's a difficult question.' Dr Singh's expression turned even more official. 'We'll take it one step at a time. We'll need your permission to put her in an induced coma.'

A coma. She might never wake up from it. It might damage her. Jatin stretched his neck, trying to release the building knot of tension.

'Unless she's in a coma, she would be in too much pain. She needs to remain completely still to heal well.'

She would improve with each surgery, Dr Singh assured him, remaining cheerful as Jatin asked more questions, about Anjali's recovery, about how much the operations would cost, and what sort of schedule they would follow.

'Control your expressions when you see her,' the surgeon said in parting, 'she will see herself through the eyes of her friends and family.'

'Can she start wearing her contacts any time soon?'

'No.' The doctor sighed. But the ophthalmologist was able to do a lasik surgery on her left eye. They will get to the other one soon.'

So, Anjali would be able to see better than ever before. Thank *Rabji* mirrors were not allowed in her room.

***

Jatin tied the surgical mask onto his face while walking down the corridor to Anjali's room.

Dr Singh said Anjali needed to eat as much as she was able, only then would the healing speed up. Jatin knocked, his usual way of knuckling the door when Anjali was in the shower in his hotel room. Would she recognise it?

The air freshener didn't cover the strong smell of disinfectant. An infection could still kill her.

'Jelly?' He walked towards her bed.

Her eyes were closed.

'Jelly, it's me.'

Thank God she hadn't opened her eyes yet. During his daily visits when she was asleep, he never stayed for more than the few seconds that he needed to reassure himself she would be all right. His first long look at her, and Jatin wished to turn and run. But he made himself stare. The gouged, peeling skin on her throat, the scabs instead of lips, the bandages at her jaw, the blackened forehead, the spiky dark-blonde hair in uneven clumps. Patchwork of skin and bandages. Stitched-up skin and flipper-like hands. A burned-up, twisted mermaid.

Inside of it all was Anjali, his shining golden girl, who smiled with her lips slightly quirked up to the left, making a dimple he liked to stroke. When she threw herself on his bare chest, the light sprinkling of hair on his chest tickled her, making her chuckle. Her laughter used to gurgle right outside his chest, inside hers, behind those fair, peaked breasts that rolled and moved as she twisted and turned in his arms. Jatin smiled at that memory.

When she looked at him, Jatin didn't let the smile in his eyes falter.

'I brought you breakfast.'

'You're here.' She tried to sit up. 'Finally.'

'Wait.' He cranked the bed up, adjusting the lever, wincing each time she whimpered. But the nurse said the patient needed to sit as straight as possible while eating. She also allowed the one-time exception of paranthas, totally against hospital regulations. They were prepared to risk an infection to get Anjali's appetite back, because in the week since removing her feeding tube, she hadn't eaten enough to begin rebuilding lost tissue.

'Where were you all this time?'

He could think of no answer, so he busied himself with unpacking the food.

'Not as if you'll ever say sorry, right?' Anjali said. 'How is Nikhil? Is Varun ok?'

'They're both fine.' Jatin unwrapped a parantha, took out the plastic cutlery. 'I'm here now.'

'Why is Maya upset with me?'

'Can we eat first? I haven't eaten yet.'

He knew he sounded cold, but the doctor didn't want her agitated. He pulled a serious face, and cutting a parantha into tiny pieces, dipped them in yoghurt, and fed them to her one by one. He couldn't let the food dribble on her peeling chin, or her lips. Her lip was a huge half-healed scar. He was glad the surgical mask he wore covered most of his expression.

He chatted to Anjali throughout, the way he used to while feeding little Maya, and later Varun. He rattled on about how cold it was, how one of his staff brought sweets because his wife was pregnant with twin boys, and then moved on to Nikhil, glossing over the details. No of course he wasn't a suspect, was she mad? Kusum had to follow procedure, that was all. He told her how stressed Maya was, at work, home and hospital—it made her snap at times, nothing to worry about.

He didn't tell her about Drishti, or Varun. A basketful of white lies, but he saw no choice. He needed to keep her calm, and eating.

'Now you're full,' he put her empty plate down, and picked up another, 'may I eat too?'

He used to say this to tease her when in bed, food the furthest thing from their minds.

'Okay.' She lifted her webbed hands to her chest.

He stared at his own healthy, unhurt palms and pictured Anjali's hands in them, the long tapering fingers, the manicured nails. He turned away from the bed. He must make himself eat, make it all a normal conversation, like in earlier times when they ordered room service.

He settled the plate on the table far from the bed, and removed the mask so he could eat.

'Maya told me about Hridayog.' Anjali said, 'Did anyone speak to Mr Lahiri?'

'It is an ongoing investigation. We can't talk about it yet. I'll tell you if something turns up.'

Why could he not figure out the bloody culprit? Radhe held the strongest motive so far, though no witness put him at the scene of the attack. Nikhil, on the other hand...

'Are you ok?' Anjali leaned forward on the bed, but he couldn't read the unchanging mask of her face.

'Fine.' He smiled at her.

He wanted to tell her about the fight with Drishti last evening, about the pain the size of a large fist that kept him awake at nights, and how he sank into nightmares about her face each time he slept. She used to cheer him up when he fell into a slump. He intended to stand beside Anjali now, whether she wanted him or not. If he didn't, and cared only about his job, he would turn into the bitter, violent bully, Tathagat Satyaprakash Bhatt. His father. Not Jatin.

When he'd seen Anjali's teenaged face for the first time, decades ago, he'd thought it sad, too strong-jawed, long-looking, to be beautiful. But, in the next moment, the light of her smile had made him stare. That smile was gone, and that face was now covered with dead people's skin.

He kept eating despite the lack of appetite that made the parantha taste like old leather in his mouth. He needed to hear her talk—other than a slight husk, her voice was still the same.

'You really want to speak to your Mom?'

'Yes.'

'Why, after all these years? Why now?'

'I have my reasons.'

'She spoke to me on the phone last night.' Jatin spoke between bites. 'She says she has wanted to talk to you ever since your Dad's death, but she needs to talk to you in person.'

Anjali sat up. 'In person?'

'Yes.'

Anjali went still. Jatin remembered playing one of those games of 'statue!' he used on Maya when she turned too much to handle. Six-year-old Maya would freeze, and he would plait her hair or tie her shoelaces. She couldn't move. Anjali was a statue now, and Jatin was tempted to say 'ease!' the way he said it to Maya, decades ago.

'Jelly?'

'Of course she wants to talk to me face to face now. Now that I don't have one.'

'I'm sorry, Jelly. I'll tell her you want a call instead.'

'I don't even know what I look like, do you know that? Can you bring me your phone?'

'You know the doctor's rules.'

'Fine. Tell her...tell Mom I'll see her.'

Jatin stared at Anjali. Her face had been robbed of all expression, but her eyes glowed with a fierce light. For as long as he had known Anjali, even when she was fifteen, she fled her mother, always finding an excuse to leave any room her mother entered. She had run from her mother all the way to India, grieved for her father from afar because she didn't want to face her Mom. And now, she was ready to meet the very person she had made it her mission to stay away from. He would never understand her.

'Really?'

'Yes. Ask her to book tickets.'

Jatin knew most of Anjali's secrets. He would soon find out more about this one.

33

Anjali waited for Nikhil to come into Fareeda's clinic.

He stood quietly by the door, watching his feet. He seemed thinner and taller—his wrists stuck out of his sweater. He flicked his left hand, and held a squeeze ball in his right. His black shoes, new ones she'd bought a few weeks earlier, looked scuffed, as if he'd been kicking at walls and stones. The hospital divided her life into Before and After. Buying shoes for Nikhil was in the Before, that's all she could be sure of. She waited for her son to look up.

His expression would change once he caught sight of her face, and she wanted to record it. He hadn't yet learned to mask his emotions completely, didn't realise how others saw them play on his face. Reading others' expressions was part of his education with Dr Bhalla. Her heart thumped. As the moments passed, she realised Fareeda was right. It was too soon.

Anjali had worked for this meeting—spoken to her doctor, Maya, Dr Bhalla. Persuaded Fareeda. Bargained with them. If she did not see Nikhil, she wouldn't consent to her procedures. She would check herself out of the hospital. After a day of back and forth, they had given in. She was allowed to meet Nikhil as long as it was in Fareeda's clinic, in her presence. But now that Anjali had her wish granted, all she wanted was to pull her shawl all the way up to her eyes. Disappear.

Lulled by the rustle of Fareeda's papers, the whirr of the heater in the background, the room seemed to go to sleep. Anjali curled her toes further into her socks and peered at Nikhil's black sneakers by the door.

'Nikhil,' Fareeda spoke up, 'Would you like to step inside and close the door behind you? The heater isn't working well.'

Anjali kept her eyes on Nikhil's shoes. She watched them turn, step in, and move to a chair. The chair creaked. He settled down at an angle, facing away from her. 'What did you eat for breakfast, Nikhil?' Fareeda said.

'Omelettes.' Nikhil mumbled, his hands flicking faster now.

Pawan had suggested Nikhil drink eggnog in order to beef up. Nikhil threw up the first time he tried it. 'Tastes like puke,' he'd told Ira. Anjali and Maya had exchanged glances and bitten back smiles.

'Did Ira put cheese on it?' Anjali joined in.

Nikhil liked cheese sprinkled on any meal he found unpalatable. Pasta, paranthas, cereal, curries, plain rice—didn't matter. Cheese made everything better.

'When will you come back?'

This was unexpected on many levels.

Nikhil usually answered if a question was put to him, he couldn't help it. He did not change the subject, especially not one he liked. And, when she went out of town he never asked her when she'd be back.

She answered, as she always tried to do with him, with complete honesty. 'When the doctors let me go.'

'Will I have to stay at Varun's place again?'

This was a tricky one. Dr Bhalla had released him from the clinic after monitoring him for two days. Nikhil would go back home today, but Anjali understood it was a tough situation for Maya: how was she to keep an eye on Nikhil, watch him so that he and Sakhi were never left alone? A part of Anjali felt guilty. By not telling them about Nikhil's attack on her, she might be putting others into another potentially dangerous situation.

Nikhil's aggression needed therapy, but if she told Dr Bhalla about the attack, he might feel compelled to breach patient confidentiality—Nikhil had actually harmed her, and had attacked Varun. They would put Nikhil in an institution, and then there might not be a way back for him. She wanted her son to cope better, not be shut away so he would deteriorate.

'Anjali? Will I stay there?'

'Your Maya Masi will decide. She will take care of you as long as I'm here. You must listen to her.'

Her gaze rose to her son's sinewy hands, so strong when he clutched her arms. She took in his bony, yet slowly broadening shoulders under his heavy black sweater, the reedy neck, the elf-like chin, the pale shadow of a nascent moustache. She raised her eyes to find Nikhil's gaze directed somewhere behind her, like a bird of prey, curious, head slightly cocked to one side.

'Your face is all messed up.' That was her Nikhil. Never sugar-coated his words, didn't know how. 'Can it be fixed?'

He had done this to her face. Anjali considered turning away, not answering. 'The doctors are trying,' she said.

'Will I go to the clinic again?'

'If needed, yes.'

'I don't want to go to the clinic again! I'll miss school.' Nikhil squeezed the yellow stress ball. Why didn't Fareeda give Anjali one? She needed it, just so she could bite down the words at the tip of her tongue. *Missing school never seemed to bother you before.*

When she didn't answer, he turned away to the wall, so she could barely hear him, 'I'm never going to the clinic again. Promise?'

She couldn't make that promise. Boy, she wanted to. Never to see the inside of Bhalla's office again, or listen to a therapist telling her how to handle her son. To let Nikhil do his own thing with no anxiety.

'You don't have to miss school.' She said instead. 'Classes don't start till New Year.'

'Are Varun's parents getting a divorce?'

'Who told you that?' The pounding in her temples grew intense. With each question Anjali felt like someone was pumping her full, like a helium balloon at an overcrowded birthday party. Her skin felt taut, stretched thin. Any minute now, she would explode, and pieces of her would splatter the walls.

'Someone called Maya Masi.' Nikhil squeezed the yellow ball, hard. 'She said you had something to do with it.'

What the hell was he talking about? Jatin and Drishti? Jatin hadn't mentioned it yesterday. She tasted the protein shake she'd drunk this morning, and tried to keep it down. *A divorce, Jatin was getting a divorce.*

The door opened and Vibha walked in.

'Time for madam to go back.'

Nikhil watched the nurse, hands curled inside his pant pockets.

'Is that your son, madam?' Vibha turned to Nikhil without waiting for her answer. 'Hello, what's your name?'

Nikhil didn't react well to being stared at or questioned by strangers. *Can you let him be*, Anjali wanted to say, but defending Nikhil in front of others only seemed to aggravate him. Her son faced the wall and leaned forward, as if the zinnias and azaleas on the wallpaper had caught his attention.

Vibha helped her into the wheelchair.

'Nikhil,' Fareeda called out, her voice soft. 'Want to say bye to your Mummy?'

Nikhil stood still, as if inside a soundproof bubble. He took his right hand from his pocket, and squeezed the smiley ball with all his might.

'Bye, Nikhil.' Anjali called out to him, her throat sore.

'I don't want to go to the clinic!' Nikhil ran out, shoving Vibha, who fell against Anjali's wheelchair, making it move. Anjali tried to stop it with her feet, but the wheelchair slipped out from under her.

34

Maya stood by as Dorothy Gupta, the woman Anjali spoke so much about, strode out of the airport gate. She dragged two heavy suitcases along. Tall and broad, with close-cropped blonde hair, no make-up on her unlined white face, and a voice so loud it made the crowd turn when she greeted Bhai, her head almost level with his. 'I'm Dorothy,' said Anjali's mother, crushing Maya's hand in her grip. 'Dorothy Gupta.' Funny how both mother and daughter had chosen to take the surnames of the men they married, and keep them—in the States, women didn't need to do that.

A porter helped Bhai's hulking driver stack the bags in the two cars. He had asked Maya to meet him at the airport so she could bring Dorothy home in her car. Commissioner Jatin *I-know-best* Bhatt, in his usual bully mode—he had a meeting, so Maya had to play hostess and driver all in one. Despite raring to fight him, the nineteen years between them seemed a huge gulf at times like this. She hadn't confronted him yet, because she already felt she had overstepped by speaking to Drishti Bhabi.

And despite her anger, hating Anjali felt like hating herself. Maya had shared with Anjali each one of her secrets, if not in words then in gestures, holding nothing back. She had taken Anjali into her heart. To find out that her friend hadn't done the same, instead been in bed with…it didn't bear thinking about. Had it been an affair with a complete stranger, Maya would have shouted at Bhai the minute she found out. But it was different with Anjali, and on top of that, she lay helpless in a hospital. Anjali meeting Dorothy would only take matters downhill, but as usual, no one consulted Maya. Anjali and Bhai still treated her like she was fifteen.

Maya made sure Dorothy was comfortable, entered the car, and drove off. Dorothy's voice startled her. It was very different from Anjali's soft timbre.

'Is everything ok?' Dorothy leaned forward in her seat, 'You look lost. How is Anjali doing today?'

Anjali was better, Maya told Anjali's mother. She was scheduled for another round of surgeries soon.

Two hours later, having settled Anjali's mother in the guest bedroom, Maya set off towards Connaught Place to meet a client. The moments in the ambulance returned to her—how Bhai had clung to Anjali's arm, the whispered *darling, Jelly, sweetheart,* the tears he hadn't bothered to wipe, the prayers.

Caught in a traffic jam, she stared at the other cars, the green-and-yellow auto rickshaws. On the pavement sat a shawl-clad old man on a rickety old chair, his head stretched back, his face lathered, eyes closed, getting a shave. Another old man in a torn sweater stood over him, one of those ancient folding razors in hand. What did you call it? Yes, an *ustara*. He reminded Maya of her Papa, confident and precise, who used an *ustara* to shave as well. Over the years, Bhai had filled in for Papa, wrapping a shawl over her head to muffle the sounds of Papa hitting Ma in their bedroom, and later, Ma's sobs. He stopped the cousins who teased her for the patches on her arm, ferried her to different skin specialists.

Maya braked hard, and parked across the road from Nizam's Cafe. Bhai used to bring her here when she was upset, or if she did well in her exams. Maybe that was why he had chosen this place to meet. Entering the cafe now, she was surprised to find that her brother had arrived, but not placed an order. She ordered at the counter, their usual: a double egg mutton *kathi kabab* roll for him, and a single egg chicken roll for her.

She returned to her seat to find him on a call, his long black overcoat slung over the back of a nearby chair. He spoke softly in English, not mentioning names. With the fitted grey sweater on his broad shoulders and chest, his neat haircut and moustache, he was handsome. Maya only ever thought of him as Bhai, but for the first time, while pretending to check her phone, she understood the slanted looks the women at the surrounding tables sent him. Anjali must have glanced at him the same way.

When their order came to the table, she bit into her roll and sighed. The fluffy roll and the spice of the meat remained the same over the years. Her brother cut his call, and stared at a spot behind her. She turned around, and his gaze dropped when their eyes met in the mirrored wall. Had he been talking to Anjali? A rush of anger turned the juicy bite to a glob Maya must swallow. How could she have ever liked this place, with its dim yellow lights, its red table-tops, greasy food, and the loud lunch crowd?

'Did you double-check all the doors last night?' Bhai said.

'Yes. I've told Ira to be very careful during the day as well. She has Radhe's photo. She'll call me if she spots him.'

'Now that Dorothy is here, you'll have help.'

Maya pushed her plate away. 'Why didn't you tell Anjali not to call her?'

As usual, Bhai ignored her question, and took a bite of his roll instead. Maya picked another tack.

'Kusum made some funny queries at the hospital. About Nikhil.'

'Routine.' Bhai shifted in his seat.

'Nikhil can't plan ahead, you know that.'

'Bhalla said the same thing. But the fact is he was there, he has acid spots on his clothes, he argued with Anjali a few hours before the attack. We found an open can of drain-cleaner in the boot with his fingerprints.'

'You're really considering this?'

'He matches Anjali's description of the suspect and the forensics guy working on the CCTV footage can't rule him out.'

'Anjali said it wasn't Nikhil.'

Nikhil had done well since he came back from hospital. He ignored Sakhi, and the surviving puppy, Manku. This morning, he'd stayed calm with his grandmother. No point arguing with Bhai on this: he would give up once he came across evidence that proved Nikhil was innocent. Time to broach another topic.

'You want to divorce Bhabi?' She needed to hear it from him.

'None of your business, Gudiya.'

'If you're having an affair with Anjali, it *is* my business. You're my brother, she's my friend, she rents half our house. Bhabi, the kids, they are my business, my family. *Your* family.'

Her voice grew stronger with each word. By the time she reached the last sentence, she wasn't whispering. Conversation at the other tables stilled.

'I do my best for you, and them. What else I do with my life is not your problem.'

'Are you serious?'

'You went and spoke to Drishti. You could have talked to me first.'

Maya kept silent, and Bhai drove home his advantage.

'You have no idea what is involved at my office. Do you know what Drishti's father can do if he puts his mind to it?'

She hadn't considered that. All she'd seen was Varun, hurt. Nikhil out of control. And Bhai, who took her call, but didn't speak a word of assurance to Bhabi. Only to Varun, a few words asking if he was fine. It wasn't right, the way Bhai treated Bhabi. Marriages weren't supposed to be like this. And all because of Anjali.

'I don't need to tell you how Anjali stood by us when Ma died. Pulled you through.' Bhai ran his hands through his hair. 'Helped tend Varun when your Bhabi was in hospital. I can go on.'

'What about Bhabi? Don't you care about your family?'

'That's between me and Drishti. Stay out of it. I don't comment on you and Pawan.'

The lunchtime buzz around her died as if at the trip of a switch. Such soft words, such a calm face. So, he knew.

Maya scoffed at herself—there wasn't all that much, was there—a few dinners and her breakdown at the hospital. The day Pawan came across the discoloured patches on her skin, it would stop. No one wanted a twenty-seven-year-old virgin with white patches all over her body.

Bhai's phone beeped, and he straightened up. 'Hold on, Gudiya. Bunty is coming in.'

Bunty Sisodia, the home secretary's son. What did he want? Varun wasn't in town. And how could Bhai let anyone interrupt their conversation?

'Hello, Uncle.' Bunty walked up to their table, a hefty envelope in hand. 'Varun asked me to pick this up from his school.'

Under a half-sleeved storm jacket, Bunty wore a tight sweater that clung to his muscles. He looked like a bodyguard, an extra strayed off the sets of a cheap Bollywood movie. When Varun first introduced Bunty to her at his birthday party a few years ago, Bunty ogled her up and down as he said *hello Masi. Ma-si*, means *mother-like*, she wanted to tell him, *the mother's sister. Show some respect.*

She watched the two large men, the older one patting the shoulder of the younger. Bhai spoke to Dayal's son as if to an equal.

'Yes, Uncle, sure.' Bunty said. 'I'll tell Dad. No, no problems at all. I've got to go now.'

Bunty turned to her, and from his towering height gave her a mocking nod. Maya scowled back at him, wishing to launch her plate at Bunty's hulking back. She stood up.

'You haven't finished.' Bhai said.

'Not hungry anymore.'

'I meant your words, not your food. Finish what you wanted to say.'

'What's the point?' Maya sat down. 'You are not going to listen.'

'I need you *with* me, Gudiya. If we team up, we can help Anjali. Not all families are related by blood.'

'She matters that much to you?' Maya hated herself the minute she said it. One glance at her brother's reddened eyes told Maya this wouldn't go away, but she resolved to fight it.

'You can't go on; it is not right.'

'What do you suggest I do, then?' Bhai said.

He used that tone with his underlings—it was a challenge.

'Stay away.' Maya gathered her handbag and rose from her chair. 'Let me take care of her.'

35

Cold, so cold. Anjali tried to pull the blanket over herself, but she couldn't. Her hand trembled, her arms, her legs, her entire body shivered, and her middle did not support her weight. Jelly, she chuckled, Jatin had named her right. She'd had fever before, and she had burned the last few days whenever the painkillers wore off; but this clogged head and throat and nose and this quaking, this was a first. She tried to reach out for the bell, but her hand would not obey. The bedside table moved away the further she reached, and the curtains fluttered closer, as if they had come alive in the night, bringing in the chill and the fog from the night outside. Her feet and palms turned to ice. Maybe after all these years it was snowing in Delhi. Anjali giggled, which set her coughing. She tried to reach the bedside table again.

She had complained to the nurse of the hurt in her neck after the fall. They had dressed the wound, mopping up the blood on her hospital gown, so much blood from her burned ugly skin and Dr Singh had come in, murmuring at her, and later shouting at the nurse outside her room, *how can you be so careless, Vibha, she's to be kept free from injury at all costs.* How careless, the words came back to her, careless of her to not have looked where she was going that night, to not have taken Nikhil to the cake shop with her. *How careless, Anjali,* Mom said, *now you've ruined the entire set of cups, careless just like your aunt.*

Careless to get involved with Jatin. To not know he was divorcing his wife. To let Nikhil near a can of drain cleaner. To not understand how angry with her he really was. And now here she was, cold, trembling, with no one to rescue her.

Anjali would rescue herself. She tried again, almost rolling off the bed this time when Dr Singh's words came back to her. *We can't afford a sepsis Dr Morgan. We have enough to deal with as it is, do not take risks like this again.* Yes, of course it was a risk to see Nikhil, and she had gained nothing by it, but she would risk herself again. Mom, this time, Mom who let Dad put cold compresses on her forehead when she caught fever. Fever, she had fever now, Anjali wanted to tell the nurse, but the door to her room was shut. She must risk injury again, reach for her pillow and swing it at the table.

It landed on the floor with a soft thud. Another. Try again. This time she managed to set the glass and the jug crashing along with her medicines, and she sobbed with relief when the nurse rushed in. *Blanket,* she tried to say, *cold. I can't breathe.* But no words came.

The lights came on, the covers, and then the room became a blur of nurses, machines, and voices, panicked, scattered, *pressure falling,* they said, *hold it,* another replied, *oxygen, 500 milligrams, ventilator,* pin pricks on her arms, someone holding her feet, *Anji, can you hear me,* and then silence, silence and blessed darkness.

36

Lit by faint white street light, Pawan Dahiya practiced his *qigong* techniques on his small balcony, its size barely enough for him to make it through the wide, flowing stances of the Dragon, the Tiger, the Leopard, the Snake, and the Crane. The Sensei started them off on these slow, dance-like movements of *Wudan qigong* to relax the students and prepare them for the karate sessions. As he moved, Pawan tried to *Be Present*, take away all thought. His breath fogged in the cold air, but it was not in tune with his movements.

Anjaliji's mother had landed that morning, so Pawan was alone at the office when Jatin sir called him, asking why he needed to learn about Radhe from Kusum. How *disappointed* he was that they let Radhe slip away. *Beda Garak.* Pawan's informant didn't own a vehicle; so he had watched Radhe enter a blue Maruti car and disappear. So much for trying to impress Jatin sir.

After two days of following all possible leads with no results, he'd borrowed his cousin's bike for a few weeks and handed it to his man, along with money for petrol. He wanted to find Radhe and his brother Ram Sharan. He'd pay out of his own pocket, if needed.

He scrolled through the photos of the drug den on his phone. His cousin might finish processing them by tomorrow. Pawan prayed the enhanced images contained some sort of clue to Radhe. He flicked through the other pictures, of Maya and her family.

When Drishti Didi called this morning, Pawan had remained polite and told her he knew nothing of Anjaliji's relationship with Jatin sir. Her mother was his Beeji's sister, the ties too close to mess with. Besides, he owed his cousin his job, she never let him forget that. He could have found other jobs, but not in a detective agency. His Beeji made it clear he must choose between her and the police. Vigil gave him a little of what he craved—the thrill of the hunt, following up on clues.

Pawan worked his arms in a few quick karate stances and repeated the high kicks he practiced each morning. His thoughts kept going to his informant who kept an eye on that fat *khoosat*, Lahiri. This time Pawan would not allow any mistakes. The phone rang in his hand, breaking off the howling of a few stray dogs in the street below.

'Hello?' Maya said. 'Any updates?'

Her voice sounded hoarse like that night at the hospital, when she had cried in his arms.

'I'm waiting for alerts from Sanjay Colony, but nothing so far,' he told her. 'I could not go today because of the other case briefing.'

He could hear her sob. He was her assistant, not her friend. Or was he? She'd confided in him at the hospital, and on the way back, clung to him on the bike. Things had been a little awkward between them ever since.

'All right. Just thought I should check.'

Maya didn't need to check, and they both knew it.

'Is Nikhil okay?' Pawan wiped off his sweat with a towel, rubbing his neck hard. He couldn't afford to catch a chill.

Anjaliji's Mom had gone to visit relatives from her husband's family. Despite all kinds of tricks from Maya, Nikhil hadn't eaten. Maya was scared he might get hungry at night and throw a tantrum. Pawan looked at his watch: 9.45 pm. She would refuse help. But given what he knew of Jatin sir's suspicions of Nikhil, he must offer it. To his surprise, she agreed.

'Thank you, Pawan,' she said. 'Yes, Mughlai takeout would be nice. Nikhil's favourite.'

From within his helmet, the smogged-up streetlights and the near-empty roads seemed like a misty hillside drive. Pawan whistled a tune to himself. Maya had accepted his help. Not a big deal, but somehow it didn't feel that way. Pawan thrilled in the cold air whipping against him, the way his grip revved the accelerator as he raced to meet her.

***

Mutton do-pyaza, chicken tikka, pudina parantha, and biryani seemed to do the trick for Nikhil. He finished dinner in record time, and called Sakhi to share.

Without her heels, in an oversized fleece jacket, short top, and woollen pyjamas, Maya looked different from the demanding boss at office. By the time they wrapped up dinner, Pawan wanted to carry the pale, about-to-collapse Maya to a sofa and make her ginger tea.

While Ira and Maya washed up and Sakhi trotted along

to help them, Pawan took Nikhil to the living room. He asked Nikhil casual questions, helping him with his airplane all the while.

Yes, Nikhil remembered the evening of Anjali's attack. He stayed in the car while she went out to fetch the cake.

'Anjali didn't come back for a long time, so I went after her.'

'Why didn't you remain in the car?'

'Help me with my airplane.' Nikhil flicked his fingers, 'Anjali is in the hospital.'

'Do you want to go see her again?'

'I want to add the wing here,' he pointed on the plane. 'May I use the computer? They have a tutorial for this one.'

'So you don't want to see her?'

'She doesn't let me use the computer whenever I want.'

'You want her to come back?'

'Anjali will make the rule book again.' Nikhil rocked back and forth. 'No more rules, No more rules, No rules.'

If Nikhil got upset now, Maya might find out that Pawan was questioning him. For now, Nikhil needed to calm down.

'What about some *Flyboys?*' Pawan had watched the little-known movie about fighter planes with Nikhil at least three times. Nikhil could never get enough of it.

Nikhil nodded, '*Flyboys*. Yes, *Flyboys*.'

'Not again.' Maya came in, smiling.

'*Flyboys?*' Nikhil said to her.

'Fine,' she gave in, 'but you will go to school tomorrow without any trouble, all right?' When Nikhil nodded, she continued, 'And because we just ate dinner, we can have only one bowl of popcorn.'

Maya had learned how to handle Nikhil. She would make a capable mother and wife. Pawan felt himself blush at the thought, and turned away. Nothing would ever come of this. Maya was used to this sprawling house, large smartphones and handbags. He couldn't afford any of these, not yet. Besides, Beeji would hate Maya. On top of being *madern*, Maya was four years older than him.

'Sakhi can get Manku if she wants.' Nikhil said, his eyes on the TV.

'Really, Nikhil Bhaiya?' Sakhi brightened up, and dashed off towards Anjaliji's room.

Pawan glanced at Maya. Her wide eyes reflected the surprise he felt, but Nikhil paid them no mind. Pawan must find another way to talk to the boy again soon, maybe pick him up for karate class tomorrow. Nikhil grew so anxious at the mention of Anjali's attack, and angry.

No rules.

Sakhi pranced back, her shiny plaits swinging, Manku bounding along beside her. Nikhil made Maya and Pawan sit on either side of him, and asked for Sakhi to be seated beside Maya, with Manku. He ordered Pawan to keep fast-forwarding to the airplane scenes, and lectured them about popular planes from World War I, about the errors in the film—how the rotary engines were all wrong.

After a while, Pawan heard soft snores beside him. Maya had fallen asleep, her mouth open. Pawan debated waking her, but the next moment her face lowered onto his arm stretched out on the sofa.

Man, woman, children cuddled together, watching a movie, Manku dozing at Sakhi's feet: it felt like a dream inside a warm blanket on a chilly morning. He needed to step out, but each muscle in his body protested against it. He turned to Maya. Her jacket had parted, and the hem of her top had risen.

He'd often wondered why a woman who smoked, drank, swore, and wasn't shy of showing off her shape in tight jeans and tops, revealed so little of her skin. Now he knew.

His boss carried her own secrets on her skin. *Beda garak.*

He wanted to reach out and touch her, talk to her about what he'd seen, but thankfully, before he could do anything stupid, his phone rang. Its shrill tune made everyone jump.

'The fatso is leaving.' The informant sounded excited, 'He never goes out at night.'

'I'm on my way.'

Beside him, Maya sat up. He mouthed 'Lahiri' to her, and she nodded. She picked up the half-sleeping Sakhi. The bleary-eyed Nikhil stood up without protest when Pawan switched off the TV.

Pawan dialled Kusum, hoping she hadn't gone to sleep.

Maya took the two kids, one in her arms and the other trailing her, out of the living room. Manku loped off behind them.

'Wait for me. I'll hand them over to Ira.' Maya turned at the door, 'You can drop me at the hospital? Give me two minutes.'

Pawan stared after her short figure covered from neck to toe. As he shrugged on his jacket and waited, he mumbled the words his Sensei often quoted during class: '...*the wise are guided by what they feel and not by what they see, letting go of that, and choosing this.*'

37

Jatin tried calling his son, but the phone kept ringing. Varun had left two days earlier, but to Jatin it seemed more than a week. He continued to receive updates from the teacher leading the group, but not a peep out of Varun. It was natural for the boy to be upset. A son any father could be proud of, who had never thrown a tantrum or brought shame to the family—Jatin had failed him.

Softness and warmth had disappeared from Jatin's days. He felt the cold hard edges of his marriage breaking. Maya's hurt, brittle and dangerous, like cracked glass. And Anjali, lying burnt on white hospital sheets.

He stared at the Delhi map on the wall in his office, and the four red dots he'd marked on it: Pul Mithai, Madipur Colony, Dilshaad Gardens and Sanjay Colony. At 10.30 pm, after a bunch of painkillers for his throbbing shoulder and more cups of black coffee than he cared to count, the city on the map appeared to him more of a maze than ever. A hopeless crisscrossing of roads, train tracks above and below ground, alleys, footpaths, flyovers, malls, marketplaces, slums, old monuments and new office buildings all jostling for space, just like the eighteen million humans who inhabited it. Like ants, but with none of the organisation of an ant colony.

All the years of investigating crimes hadn't prepared Jatin for this collapsing of his personal and professional life. He had tried to keep them as separate as he could, given that he was married to his boss's daughter, but that had ended after his showdown with Drishti. Mehra would call soon, and with about a month to go until the elections in which Sabharwal could become a chief minister, Jatin needed something big. Something that could splash across media and stand him in good stead if the Sabharwal story broke.

He waited for word from Grewal, or Kusum, who had joined Grewal's team for this night's operation. Grewal wasn't sure he could put the raid together tonight, but Jatin sent in Kusum with his driver in any case. He needed eyes on the ground, and the giant but deceptively quick Constable Dilawar would keep Kusum safe.

These days Jatin participated in a raid only if it was crucial, on suspects with international links and long records. His presence would have set tongues wagging among Grewal's team and sent word all the way up to Mehra. He didn't need that.

His phone buzzed.

'Our informer calling, sir,' Kusum said. 'Lahiri is leaving Sanjay Colony in an auto rickshaw.'

Why did Lahiri have to run off now? Did he get wind of the raid? Jatin's plans involved netting Lahiri, Manoj, and possibly Radhe and Ram Sharan at one go, and breaking the Sujni case open. Now with Lahiri making a run for it, someone must follow him, and make a separate arrest, depending on what the raid uncovered.

'You keep an eye on Lahiri, don't lose him.'

'On my way, sir. Our man is right behind him. He's going out towards Govindpuri,' Kusum said. 'Also, Pawan Dahiya calling, sir.'

'Where is he right now?'

'Leaving Safdarjung Enclave, sir, he's on the way here.'

Safdarjung Enclave? He was with Maya? No time to dwell on that—Kusum waited at the other end for his instructions. Jatin couldn't go to the raid, but Pawan could.

'Tell him to follow the raid, I'll tell Grewal about him. We must find that Radhe and his brother,' Jatin said. 'Keep updating me on Lahiri.'

Jatin unlocked a drawer, took out his Glock, and for good measure, the Auto 9mm pistol as well.

'Tell me which way he's headed.' Jatin shut his files in another drawer and locked it. 'I'm leaving now.'

'But, sir...'

'Just follow orders, Netam. Call Pawan now. I'll see you soon.'

***

Jatin left his office jeep parked in a corner not far from the apartment complex at Lajpat Nagar, and moved into the car with Kusum. An old Santro, unlike the usual police Sumo, to navigate narrow alleys if required, and also a good cover. Kusum wore plain clothes, a kurta and jeans, which made her look like a school girl dressed in grown-up clothes.

'You're sure he's inside?'

'Both our informant and Pawan Dahiya's man following him till here, sir. Dilawar going to talk to our man at the back gate. Lahiri is not going out, sir.'

'Has he come here before?'

'Not since our man following him, sir.'

Odd. Lahiri in a strange apartment in the middle of the night. Another drug den right in the centre of a middle-class residential area? Jatin stretched his arm out and massaged his shoulder. With the combination of coffee and painkillers, the worst of the pain had subsided, but a dull ache remained. He checked his watch: five minutes past eleven, and no sign yet of Lahiri. A car emerged from the smog ahead of them and passed them by, loud Bollywood music thumping, a hand with a lighted cigarette sticking out of the back window. Jatin heard raised male voices, singing completely out of tune. Another hand stretched out from the front seat and sent a bottle crashing into the boundary wall of the apartment complex. Drunken fools. Jatin would have made a PCR call, but he didn't want to give out his location to a police control room just then.

'He's coming out, sir,' Kusum said. 'I'm calling Dilawar.'

Jatin spotted the unmistakeable form of Lahiri waddle into the dimly-lit lobby. He was not alone, though. Two other men in jackets and shawls flanked him, one of them looming and broad, the other thin. Between them, they carried a load to a blue van parked inside the complex, heaved it into the back seat, and drove out of the apartment complex.

Following the van at a discreet distance proved difficult because of the empty roads. Jatin asked Dilawar to stay as far behind as possible without losing their target. At first, it looked like the blue Maruti van was headed towards Sanjay Colony, but instead of taking a right towards Captain Gaur

Marg, it continued left on Mahatma Gandhi Road. So Lahiri wasn't headed back to Hridayog.

Jatin's phone pinged. A message from Pawan: *Raid at Sanjay Colony started.*

The car now sped along an empty stretch of the Geeta Colony Road. The halogen lamps threw a bright glow on the tarmac, but could not dispel the darkness beyond. A lone light or two twinkled in the distance, a few trees scattered behind dark buildings, with an occasional bright window. In Jatin's car, Dilawar shifted his massive bulk and leaned forward on the steering wheel.

The van turned left into a dark alley at the slums opposite Geeta Colony. Jatin asked Constable Dilawar to kill the car lights and heard Kusum check her gun.

The van stopped some distance ahead in the alley. In its backlight Jatin saw the other two men climb out, but not Lahiri. Somewhere in the night a child let out a high wail that turned into a whimper. The two men opened one of the back doors and hauled out the load. What did the bag contain? Did Lahiri move evidence out of Hridayog before he could be nabbed?

Jatin unfastened his seatbelt and checked the safety lock on his gun. He needed to move fast once he got out. His shoulder throbbed now, but he ignored it.

'Dilawar?' He handed the 9mm to his driver. A constable wasn't given a firearm, but Jatin had long since learned to trust this man with one, and never regretted it.

'Ready, sir.' Dilawar nodded.

The men dropped the sack while carrying it to the side of the road. It moved, as if someone were kicking out. 'Move, now!' Jatin stepped out of the car without waiting to check on the other two. The stench of drains hit him like a solid wall, his face registered the sudden cold, and then he took long strides, calling out to the men to stop, raise their hands. Behind him he heard Dilawar and Kusum, and decided to focus on the taller of the two men, who had broken into a sprint.

His shoulder sent out jolts of pain each time his feet hit ground, but Jatin ran on. So long since he'd run like this, in the semi-dark, uneven ground under his feet, giving chase to a suspect, blood humming in his ears. He called out a warning, the same words he had yelled out a hundred times in his career. The suspect ignored it and ran with his shawl trailing him, desperate enough to risk being shot.

Just as Jatin grabbed that shawl, pain spasmed through his shoulder, and he dropped the gun. He stumbled and fell, his face smashed into a rubbish heap of papers, rags and dirt. He rose to see the suspect duck into an alley and disappear. Scrambling for his gun, Jatin shot up, blotting out the now-blinding pain in his shoulder. He ran into the alley, but the suspect had vanished. He switched on the flashlight on his phone, and rushed on, avoiding loose stone and bricks, but beyond a few small pigs curled up in a puddle of mud, he saw no sign of life.

His phone squalled into the silence, and Maya's name blinked on the screen. Why was she calling him at way past 1 am?

'Come soon, Bhai,' Maya sobbed out before Jatin could say hello. 'They took Anji into Intensive Care.'

38

Anjali floated on another cloud. She laughed at her wayward fancy, at her walking on this layer of cotton wool. Why didn't she fall through? The spongy clouds held her aloft, just like the plush carpets from the game arcades of her childhood.

All those kids running behind her, yelling *Fatty, Fatty*, they couldn't catch her now, not this nimble Anjali. Anjali went through tunnels and labyrinths but she couldn't lose their mocking voices, echoing far behind her somewhere in the dark. Aunty Viv and Mom chased her, asking her to stop running. A hooded figure took up the chase, not giving up no matter how many times she dodged it. She sprinted on, sending large black spiders skittering away from her on hard ground strewn with rocks sharp as claws. She cut her feet on them, but kept running. She collided against a warm body and let out a scream. *Shhh…I'm here, Jelly, sleep now.* Anjali relaxed. Safe, at last.

Sea breeze in her hair, Anjali laughed at Aunty Viv's words. Back home for the fourth of July, she and Viv went out, dressed up in some of Viv's sexier outfits, which involved miniskirts, low necklines and lots of glitter. They stood out in the small town where the families went to each other's backyard barbecues, organised bake sales for the latest cause the Father spoke of in his sermon, and welcomed new neighbours with cookies and casseroles.

Anjali laughed, throwing her head back and shaking out her hair. Mom favoured full-sleeved blouses, and flowery skirts swishing below the knees, which is why Anjali dressed up at Viv's, exchanging lipstick, discussing tones of eye shadow and trying out different shoes. Nate Morgan loved it, this short-skirted girlfriend. She couldn't wait to see his expression when he saw her this evening.

She should've just stayed back here, with him, majored in English, like she wanted to. Why did she take up psychiatry? Her parents, an accountant and a professor, both wanted her to grab a doctorate, so they could show off to the world a high-brow daughter. Her parents walked hand in hand, into the Favolosa bar, the threshold of which they hadn't crossed in decades.

'Come home this minute!' Mom said, her glasses shoved high up on her nose, her long, loose dress crumpled. Blotches of red stood out on her thin pasty face, hair escaped from her tight bun.

'Listen to your mother.' Dad stood behind Mom, his voice quavering.

'Aunty Viv,' Anjali put down her mug of beer with a *thunk*, and the music stopped. Everyone turned to stare at them.

'One slut per family is quite enough.'

'Mom!'

Anjali moved closer to Aunty Viv, who held her hand, fingers gripping hard. Anjali's hand hurt as she turned back to face her parents, now dressed like priests, white collar high and ridiculous on her skinny mother, and too tight on her father's large brown neck.

The music began again, an acoustic number with the lyrics, '*Something's gonna get us all*,' and her parents marched towards her, speaking in loud stage whispers: *what were you thinking, getting pregnant? Look at your face, dressed up like a tart, like your...you ought to be ashamed of yourself. Wipe it off*, Mom took a dishcloth from the counter and began rubbing at her face. *You're not my daughter, look at you, all this face paint, just look!*

The music faded out, the cutlery rattled, plates shivered, the room swam, in the air she smelled alcohol gone rancid, medicinal, pungent like phenyl. She wanted to throw off the dishcloth on her face, slap Mom out of the way.

'Anjali!'

A man's voice, Jatin.

'Help! They'll kill me,' she screamed, but her voice emerged in a harsh, tortured groan that burned her throat. 'I hate them, take me away from here...switch on the lights, so dark...'

'I'm here.' Jatin sounded soft, hoarse. Would this nightmare never end?

'Let them help you, they need to finish the treatment.'

Treatment. For this pain. Her reality was confined to these needles biting into her neck, this heavy, heavy head, the darkness, and the bed under her. She had no face now, Mom had wiped her face clean off.

39

In his fantasies, Pawan often led police teams. He threw punches, shouted orders, and nabbed criminals.

Running with Grewal's men in the dark, down the alleys of Sanjay Colony did not compare. Men, women and children scattered from homes, half-dressed, half asleep. Policemen closed in from all sides on Hridayog and other pre-selected buildings, including Manoj's hideout. As they upturned one shanty after another, Pawan's world reduced to shrieks all around him. Warnings, wails, curses, the crack of police *danda* against limbs and heads. The whine of sirens, the smell of sweat, fear, sex, tobacco, *hashish*. The policemen, who began with such quiet, now shouted to each other and the suspects they nabbed. He followed the men, carrying out his own search for Radhe, fighting the rise of confusion, fear, disappointment.

Before Pawan could understand the course of events, he stood next to Grewal, staring at the suspects lined up against a wall, Manoj among them.

Manoj gaped at Pawan, and was about to speak when a policeman slapped him, hard, and told him to shut the hell up. Grewal stood chewing *paan*, hiking up his belt and nodding from time to time as all of Lahiri's rooms were ransacked, and bags of seized packets lined up. Men came in from all directions: no trace of Ram Sharan or Radhe, nor any information about them.

Pawan checked his watch. 2 am. Beeji had called him five times in the past three hours. She felt restless, she said, could he come home to her tonight? He tried pacifying her: he wasn't at his place but out on work at the other end of the city, he said, in the middle of a police raid. She screamed into the phone: always with the *manhoos*, cursed police. One day she would die, while he ran after his work and police. What sort of work was this that a son forgot his duty to his ill mother?

Looking around, Pawan saw no reason for him to stay on. He had tried to find Radhe and Ram Sharan as per Jatin sir's instructions, and a thorough search had shown no sign of either. Lahiri was now Jatin sir's lookout. He was about to dial Jatin sir, when the man himself called. They had arrested Lahiri with an injured woman in his car. Kusum had gone to take that woman's statement. Would Pawan help her?

For a moment Pawan thought of his Beeji. But if he wanted to impress Jatin sir, here was the chance.

'I would go,' Jatin sir said, 'but Anjali is in ICU now, and I'm rushing to the hospital.'

That decided Pawan. He set off on his bike for the third time that night.

Like all government hospitals, Lok Narayan saw its share of crowds even at dawn. Pawan picked his way down the corridors as per Kusum's directions. His Beeji would land up, sooner or later, in a hospital quite like this one. Doctors said last week that it wasn't asthma as they thought earlier, but a sort of arthritis that affected the lung.

Pawan set thoughts of his mother aside and asked directions from the harried-looking nurses. They gave him brisk replies and rushed off on their business. He found Kusum settled in for the interview.

The woman lay covered in a blanket, her face dry and chapped, eyes drowsy, half-shut. Pawan stood back and watched, waving at Kusum to continue.

'Where were you when this happened?'

'Behind my *jhuggi*. I had gone out to...'

Many slum dwellers used open drains as toilets. Pawan peered into Kusum's notes. This woman, named Roli, lived in Kanchanpuri, Yamuna Pushta. Twenty-two years old, married, with one daughter, two years old. Doctors confirmed rape, and had taken swabs. The same drugs injected into her as Sujni: Propofol.

'How many men?' Kusum spoke slowly, her Hindi soft.

'Two-three.' The woman turned away. 'I'm not sure.'

'Can you describe them?'

'It was dark...'

'Ask her if she remembers any of their voices.' Pawan said.

'Many voices,' Roli gasped and coughed.

A nurse gave her an oxygen mask. The doctors said the drug had overpowered her system, and yet she fought on. Pawan pulled up a stool and sat near the bed and waited. Watching this woman suffer because some men hurt her in the worst ways possible, was different from working with photographs of dead women.

'What were they saying?' Kusum said once Roli calmed down and no longer needed the mask.

'At first, they only talked about taking me into the car.'

Roli heard two different male voices. Young-sounding. The first two spoke in Hindi, they pressed a cloth over her mouth that made her dizzy, then gave her an injection in the car. She remembered very little of what happened afterwards, but later there was some English, and more than two voices. Pawan remembered his internet research on the effects of propofol: the drug was given to patients going into surgery, so they didn't remember what went on. Propofol not injected in a controlled way by experts could lead to death.

Roli gasped again as she spoke. This time the nurse came in and asked the two of them to move out. Just as Pawan stepped into the corridor, his phone buzzed, and Maya's name flashed on the screen.

40

Jatin sat with his arm around his Gudiya.

You're responsible, he wanted to shout at Maya, *you said I should stay away*, but the real blame lay at his own door. Anjali needed him. He had let her down. The hospital let her down. They had let Anjali get hurt on their watch, and then let the infection resulting from it escalate to the point of multiple organs on the brink of failure. Jatin held his shaking, hysterical baby sister and told her everything would turn out all right. Anjali will make it. They had taken emergency measures to counter the blood poisoning. She was on a ventilator, now, which would help her breathe. The doctor had said Anjali would be on watch now. Infections these days were stronger, having developed immunity to medication over time. It could go either way tonight. But he couldn't tell Maya that.

'She'll be fine,' he repeated himself.

'How do you know?'

'I called Dr Singh on the way here.' He didn't mention that he had threatened the doctor with jail time.

'I left her alone.' Maya sat with her face in her hands, muffling her sobs. 'I should have come earlier, but I was angry. I stayed back with the kids.'

Jatin patted Maya's head, stroked her hair. He looked around at the empty plastic chairs in the corridor and longed for another sound, anything other than his sister's soft crying.

'The night attendant didn't turn up last evening.' Maya spoke between sobs, 'I asked you to keep away. One of us should…all the time.'

'She is safe now.' Jatin held Maya's hand. 'All that matters.'

He spoke those words, but another voice inside chanted a prayer. *Let her come out of this, make sure she's all right, and I'll do everything I can to please You, Rabji. Spare her. Give her back to me, and I'll do right by her. I'll do right by everyone, I promise.*

Sill murmuring to his sister, he tried to imagine his life without Anjali. His days would collapse on themselves with no pillar to hold them up. None of it mattered, not his job, his home, son, his sister. This feeling had crept up on him unawares, like a leopard, stealthy and dangerous, and he felt its jaws at his throat.

'How did you come here?' he asked. When you chat about the other person, you don't dwell on what's eating at you.

'With Pawan. He came to our place because I needed help with Nikhil.' She wiped at her face, but still didn't look at him.

She said earlier that she'd fallen asleep. Had Pawan begun staying nights at her place?

Maya moved out of his arms and buried her face in her hands again. He checked his phone: no call from Anjali's mother. She must be on her way.

'You *know* how unsafe the roads are. You shouldn't have come on a bike.'

'I'm tired, Bhai. I pay taxes on my business the same as any man, yet I'm the one who must stay home at night. Why don't men cower at home for a change?'

'You can't not take precautions. It just isn't safe.'

'No place or time is safe, Bhai. It wasn't safe for Anjali in front of a cake shop at eight in the evening.'

Jatin had no answer to that. Anjali was on the brink of death through no fault of her own. No precaution would have saved her.

'I'm sorry.'

He held her hands in his. The words startled him as much as they shocked Maya. He meant the apology. Maya gaped at him.

'All this has everything do with me, not you,' he said. 'I'll fix whatever I can, and you must try to accept what I can't fix.'

Like Varun. Varun hadn't replied to his email or picked up his calls. He needed to allow Varun some space, maybe the time away in Manila would give him that. Jatin tried to ignore the throb in his shoulder. He could use another painkiller.

'No, Bhai. She went to pick up that cake for me.'

'Don't be stupid.'

'I shouldn't have told Drishti Bhabi about you and Anjali.' Maya sobbed. 'I'm so sorry. I was mad.'

'I think Drishti deserves better.'

After almost losing Anjali tonight, it felt like a no-brainer. If he wanted to stand by Anjali's side, he couldn't stay married to Drishti. If that meant letting his job go, so be it.

Maya nodded, her eyes trained on the floor. She might take her time, but she would accept it one day.

'Anjali's mother is on her way here now,' he told Maya, 'I'll need you around.'

'I'm here.'

Maya's face looked puffy, her curls spread like a huge nest around her face. He saw his little Gudiya, the one who made him *rakhi*s, threw tantrums so she could wait up to eat dinner with him, brought her school progress report to him before anyone else. Reaching out, he pretended to tweak her reddened nose.

'Go wash all that snot off your face,' he said. 'I'll get you some coffee.'

Maya returned a watery smile.

'Where were you? You were not at home when I called.'

So he told her about the chase after Lahiri's car and everything that followed.

'What a night.' Maya rubbed her eyes. 'I hope we can nail Lahiri.'

'Come back soon.' Jatin said. 'They'll update us about Anjali in an hour.'

In the men's toilet, Jatin washed his face. He looked at himself, bits of paper stuck to his hair, his eyes red. Jatin Bhatt, the unfit *nikamma* who let a suspect, a possible rapist and killer, escape.

Earlier, on his return to the car, all had seemed under control. The blue Maruti van belonged to Lahiri. The other man was Lahiri's driver. They found a gun in Lahiri's possession, but he hadn't used it. Both men sat handcuffed—Lahiri in his car, and his driver in the Santro. Lahiri asked to speak to Jatin in private, but Jatin glanced at Dilawar, who told the fat man to shut up, or else. Jatin couldn't compromise the case by talking to a suspect off the record.

The woman, though, was barely conscious. They tried to revive her with water, with no success. Kusum called an ambulance, and once it came, she left with the woman to the nearby Lok Narayan government hospital. Dilawar had taken Lahiri and his driver to the Jamia Nagar station so Grewal could interrogate them.

Having called Pawan for help with Kusum's interrogation, Jatin had rushed to the hospital. To Anjali.

***

Anjali's mother stood near the door to Intensive Care when Jatin returned. She marched up to him.

'How is she now?' Dorothy's white face was paler than usual, her eyes baggy. Decades ago, she used to wear her hair long, and a pair of thick glasses. Her short hair, and eyes without glasses made her look surprisingly vulnerable and insecure.

'The doctor should be here any minute,' Jatin said.

'May I see her?' Dorothy's hair stood askew, as if she had combed her fingers through it.

Before Jatin could respond, Dr Singh stepped out from Intensive Care, and asked for Anjali Morgan's attendants.

Anjali wasn't conscious, but she hadn't slipped into a coma either. They would know by morning. Nothing to do but wait, the doctor said. Jatin wanted to collar Dr Singh and shake him. When Dr Singh called him aside, Jatin followed him.

'I'd just like to apologise again in person.' Dr Singh said, his expression alert, but his clothes wrinkled. He had clearly rushed to the hospital after his call with Jatin.

'You really can't say if she'll recover?'

'We are doing everything we can, but septicaemia can be very unpredictable.'

'You let her get injured on your watch.'

'I know it does not make up for the danger to Dr Morgan, or the stress caused to the family, but the hospital has decided to provide heavy discounts for her treatment. We would charge everything here on out at fifty per cent.'

Jatin wanted to tell the good doctor where he could shove his discount, but he held himself back. This doctor would be the one to make sure that Anjali woke up, so Jatin bid him a brisk goodbye instead. He wasn't good at waiting, especially not when the outcome could change his life.

If he stayed away from her, she might wake sooner. He left Maya behind with Anjali's mother, asking them to keep him updated, promising to return soon.

For a moment, Jatin considered taking a walk in the fog, getting lost in the night, away from the disaster. A bike started up behind him, and screamed away. It sounded like Varun's. He checked his watch. 4.30 am. Varun must have already woken up in distant Manila. Jatin dialled his son's number, but it kept on ringing—that low, long tone of phones on international roaming. Jatin could call one of the teachers and demand to talk to his son, but he didn't want to force matters. Not just yet.

He glanced up at the windows, some of which must belong to Intensive Care, where Anjali lay unconscious.

'Make her well, *Rabji*, bless us all,' he whispered to himself as he got into his car and headed out to see Grewal.

41

For about an hour after Bhai left, Maya sat debating whether to dial Pawan's number.

It was past 3 am, but, she reasoned, if he had gone back home and drifted off, he wouldn't pick up. Simple as that. And if he did, she would tell him about Anjali, and ask him about the raid. Again, quite straightforward. She called him, and he picked up at the second ring.

'Maya?'

She spoke the lines she had rehearsed about Anjali and the hospital.

'Jatin sir told me,' Pawan said, 'I'm coming over.' He cut the call.

For the second time on that long night, Pawan had chosen to stand beside her. She wished this were real, that he actually did care. She wanted to pretend Pawan was her boyfriend and imagine him walking in, a huge glass of cafe latte in hand.

She managed to persuade Anjali's mother to go back home and took up her post outside Intensive Care. She had left Anjali alone earlier this night. Not again.

Maya awoke with a start to a soft voice calling her name.

Pawan. And he *had* brought her coffee from the hospital canteen.

'How is Anjaliji now?'

Maya took the coffee and sat up. 'She's stable, but not yet out of danger.'

Pawan took the chair next to her. He looked sharp, as usual, but Maya noticed a change in his posture tonight. Around her, he normally remained alert, as if waiting for her next instruction. But right now, he seemed to have dropped by to meet a friend.

'How did the raid go? Did you find anything useful?'

'I don't know what SHO Grewal told his men, but they were very nice to me.' Pawan sipped at his coffee, 'Hope he didn't tell them I'm Jatin sir's brother-in-law.'

Maya laughed, a laughter of surprise as much as anything else. Pawan never ever cracked a joke in all the time she'd known him. As she thought about what he'd said, she tried to contain her blush. Two ways to be Bhai's brother-in-law: his wife's brother, or, his sister's husband.

'Where is Jatin sir?' Pawan said, 'I thought I would see him here.'

'He has gone to the Jamia Nagar police station.' Maya stretched her stiff legs and twisted her feet one way, then the other. 'They are interrogating Lahiri and his driver.'

'I just spoke to the woman they found in Lahiri's car.'

'And?'

'This woman, Roli, she hasn't seen their faces. The doctors say they injected her with Propofol.'

'Same as Sujni.'

'Yes.' Pawan said. 'She remembers hearing two voices at first, and later, three. Two of them spoke English.'

'Lahiri, his driver, and that third man.' Maya said, 'Lahiri speaks English, and unless his driver speaks English as well, the man who got away must be the other English speaker.'

'The only way to identify that man is to get the other two to talk.'

'I guess so,' Maya said. 'All we know is that he is tall and well-built. Bhai followed him for quite some distance.'

Poor Bhai. To return to the field after so many years and lose the man he was chasing. That must have stung. And right after that, he heard the news about Anjali. No wonder his hair and clothes were ruffled when he came in.

'Lahiri owns that van and employs a driver,' Pawan said. 'He didn't use that van once in the time we've kept watch.'

'I know. And I kept telling Anjali he's a grumpy but good man. That apartment in Lajpat Nagar must be the hideout, the den where they took the women.'

'What car does Lahiri own?'

'A blue Maruti van, according to Bhai.'

Pawan stood up. 'He may have made Radhe disappear— my informer last spotted Radhe entering a similar van.'

'You think Lahiri kidnapped Radhe because the boy found out about his mother?'

'Well. If Lahiri is one of the gang members involved in the Sujni case…'

'Anjali said the hospital has records of the bite-marks on Sujni's body. And with DNA evidence, we can confirm if Lahiri was responsible in Sujni's case, and Roli's.'

'I'm sure Jatin sir is on it already.'

'Radhe fought with Anjali, do you think Lahiri put him up to it?' Maya said. 'Maybe he got Radhe to attack Anjali?'

'Why would Lahiri do that? Anjaliji always helped him. And Chander says Radhe couldn't have done it.'

Anjali. Maya had been so angry with Anjali for the past ten days, but tonight, in those panicked moments when she was rushed to Intensive Care, Maya understood what Anjali meant to her. Would Anjali recover?

As if in answer to her question, a nurse walked out of Intensive Care and asked for Anjali's attendants. She had regained consciousness but she was in a lot of pain, so they had sedated her. They would have to postpone the next operation on her face, but her chances of recovery looked better. The medication had kicked in, and her body was holding its own against the infection.

Maya thanked the nurse and turned to find Pawan grinning. She launched herself at him, laughing, tears streaming down her face. He grabbed her and she loved how strong his shoulders felt under her cheek, how he picked her up and swung her before putting her down. Head buried in his jacket, she realised where she was, and pulled back. But she couldn't contain her smile, and in his eyes she saw…she didn't want to analyse the moment and ruin it.

'I'll be back,' she hurried off.

When she returned after washing her face she found him poring over his phone, his expression grim.

'What is it?' she laid a hand on his shoulder. 'Pawan?'

'I asked my cousin to work on the photographs I took at Sanjay Colony.'

'Yes? So?'

'I can't see the enlargements on my phone.'

'Wait, let me get my tablet.'

She took it out of her purse and flicked it on, and the screen, much larger than the one on Pawan's phone, lit up.

Once the pictures downloaded, Pawan scrolled through them one by one. Maya looked over his shoulder, and for a split second she thought she saw something weird on the screen. She stopped Pawan and asked him to scroll back.

'Oh my God,' her voice caught in her throat. 'That's *him*.'

When she glanced up at Pawan, she knew she was right.

42

Jatin Bhatt had worked for seventy-two straight hours while on special assignments before, and his body had never betrayed him. But this time, no sleep and a few days of stress had killed his shoulder. Despite all the diet and exercise, age sapped at his strength. He parked his car at a tea stall on the way to Okhla, and stepped out into the cold air.

In the past few years, he'd spent most of his time in heated rooms with well-dressed colleagues, watching presentations on rising crime rates and how to combat crimes against women—far removed from the pulse of the city. Standing here by the roadside at dawn, and the last week of working with Pawan and Kusum, felt much more real.

Jatin Satyaprakash Bhatt had felt good about trawling through the slums and visiting Grewal's station. Funny how his middle name dropped away during the years of service, and he'd become *Jatin Bhatt, Commissioner of Police (Crime)*. Satyaprakash—*satya*- truth, *prakash*- light. The light of truth. He started out wanting to stay on the straight and the narrow, and yet rise—to show by example that goodness and honesty could take you places in India. But he ended up following his Papa's example instead, focused on prestige and money, never mind where they came from. Last night, he'd failed to catch that suspect, and landed head first on a heap of rubbish. Served him right.

He sipped his ginger tea, warming his hands with the paper cup, missing the earthen tumblers of yesteryear—everywhere you looked, Delhi was trying to get 'with it': shiny, plastic, disposable. He slurped his tea, and stopped. Papa used to slurp too.

At the Jamia Nagar police station, Jatin found Grewal at his desk supervising the sorting out and recording of the haul seized from Sanjay Colony. Grewal showed Jatin the list so far. Ketamine, ephedrine and pseudo-ephedrine in bigger quantities, but also some brown sugar, and opium. They found cooking equipment for drugs, stored in various parts of Hridayog. It wasn't a record haul, but not that bad either: almost all of it in commercial quantities, enough to send Lahiri in for at least ten years.

'This will look good on TV. The Joint Commissioner will be happy.' Jatin said.

'Helping you has its benefits.' Grewal gave his trademark paan-reddened smile.

'What is Lahiri's story?'

'A strange one.' Grewal pushed his chair back and stretched his beefy arms in front of him.

'Meaning?'

'The *behnchod* says he sent one of his boys to pick up some equipment from his Lajpat Nagar flat, but the boy called back: he heard noises inside, and didn't dare enter. Lahiri asked his friend Manoj to receive the shipment and rushed to the flat.'

'So he says he suspected a thief in the apartment?'

'Yes, *saala tharki*.' Grewal shrugged his massive shoulders. 'He is lying, I know it.'

When he entered, Lahiri said he found two men in the basement assaulting this woman. He threatened them with his gun, only to find that one of them was his own driver, and the other man carried a gun too. The other man had covered his face with a muffler. Lahiri asked them to return the woman, because he ran a business and didn't want trouble. They bundled the woman into the boot of Lahiri's car—so they could drop her back home—which is where she was found when police arrested him. Lahiri claimed he couldn't identify the man who ran away, hadn't once seen his face. He didn't know Radhe or Ram Sharan's whereabouts, either.

'So he's innocent, he says?'

'No, no. He doesn't deny the drug charges.' Grewal said. 'But not the woman in his car-boot. He was only saving her life. He wants to give his DNA, *gaandu saala*. Thinks he can fool us.'

'What about the driver?' Jatin took the chair opposite Grewal.

'He says Lahiri called him there for some work, promising overtime.'

'And Manoj?'

'Manoj says he ran a prostitution racket, but denies anything else. He and Lahiri are supporting each other. Their statements match: Lahiri ran a drug supply chain, and Manoj his business. They sometimes served common clients, but that was it. Neither believes the other kidnapped and raped women.'

'What about Radhe?'

'None of them knows.' Grewal said.

All Jatin's fault; he hadn't managed to catch the third man.

'We've worked all three of them, separately, non-stop, Jatin. And we've kept it low profile so far. My trusted men are questioning them, but we can't keep this hidden for long. You're sure you don't want to go public with the serial murders?'

Grewal made sense, as usual. Jatin might have to talk about the Sujni case at the department. But he wanted one last shot.

'Use your forensic team at the apartment, since you're on the case already,' Jatin said, 'and I'll send a doctor to get their DNA taken. Take swabs from all the men. I'll get it compared with samples from Roli, and Sujni. Let's find out if Lahiri is telling the truth or his driver is. I have someone in Mumbai who can do this quickly, and on the quiet.'

Jatin sent a text to Kusum, asking for the doctor who had processed Sujni's post-mortem to visit the Jamia Nagar station. He would need Maya to work with the contact in Mumbai.

'Let's go see Lahiri one more time.' Grewal stood up, and tugged up his trousers over his stomach.

'If nothing else works,' Jatin said, 'tell each of them they can make one phone call.'

'I extracted all their phone records, and we are processing them. Lahiri and his driver have called the same number many times. The number leads to a fake ID. And it is switched off.'

Interesting. This switched-off number might belong to the

missing man who escaped Jatin. Maybe Ram Sharan, Radhe's disappeared brother. If Lahiri's driver and Ram Sharan were friends, they could have lured Radhe away. But Sujni was Ram Sharan's mother—it didn't add up. Or maybe Ram Sharan had fought with his mother, and then taken her to meet her murderers. He was now terrified and on the run.

'What about Chander?'

'He's talking nonsense now. Too far gone with his addiction. Don't know if we can trust anything he says.'

'Asked him again about Anjali?'

Pawan had spoken to Nikhil, and he felt he needed another chat. But in the meanwhile, Jatin wanted to look at other suspects. Chander and Radhe had motive.

'All of them. Chander, Manoj, Lahiri, the driver Deenu. None of them knows anything.'

'Lean harder on this driver, but let's be careful with Lahiri. He may not be able to take much questioning.'

'You calling fat men weak, Jatin?' Grewal seemed to have regained his smile.

'Would I dare?' Jatin patted his friend's doughy shoulder.

***

Jatin found Lahiri slumped over the table in the interrogation room, his thin kurta pyjama torn, feet swollen. Had Maya or Anjali seen him, Maya would scream 'Police Brutality!' and Anjali would demand a lawyer. But they didn't know what it took to keep people safe, maintain law and order. He stood back in the shadows and watched.

Grewal picked the fat man up like he was a light bag of clothes, and shook him. Lahiri sagged against the table, his head bowed.

'*Dekh*, time *khottee na kar, ugal de jo bhi hai, wo ladki agar gujar gai to phir…*' Threatening Lahiri with murder charges. Telling him the woman from his car boot might die. Grewal's voice remained flat, but the way he shook Lahiri showed he meant business.

'I didn't touch the woman,' Lahiri sobbed. 'I was trying to save her.'

'You will have not even one single mark on your body.' Grewal said, 'My man here is an expert. But it *will* hurt.'

Grewal and his man smiled at each other over Lahiri's head, looking like ferocious tomcats with a fat bird. Grewal did most of the talking, and his man did the heavy hitting, but beyond groaning once in a while, Lahiri gave no response. The pictures on Manoj's phone proved him and Lahiri guilty. Sakhi was there, and other little girls, lipsticked, their stomachs showing in *ghaghra-cholis*. Lahiri operated a drug ring, and had allowed Manoj's business to operate under his nose. Jatin had never batted an eyelid at such interrogations before, but after the attack on Anjali something inside him had shifted, a knot of an unfamiliar feeling. The relentless violence played out before him turned his stomach.

When his phone rang, he stepped out with a sigh of relief. Kusum sounded worried. She had returned to the office and found a picture during her regular scroll through ZIPnet. The face looked like Radhe's. A constable had found the body cut up in two parts at the Delhi Junction railway station.

'Are you sure?'

'I'm looking at the face sir. It is Radhe.'

'Take charge of the body.'

Why would Radhe go all the way to Delhi Junction?

Did his older brother lure him out there? Jatin needed to ask Grewal to step up the pressure on all four men in his custody.

'And sir...' Kusum hesitated.

'What is it?'

'Mehra sir asking for you twice. He's saying he's wanting to meet you before leaving for Chennai tonight.'

Great. Radhe, a possible witness to the Sujni case, dead. And now he must handle his father-in-law. Jatin ran his hands through his hair, tugging at it. He needed to stay on top of things. Maybe Grewal could get hold of a clue to break the Sujni case, so he could talk about that to Commissioner Mehra, instead of the Sabharwal issue, or Drishti. Time to stop acting like a pansy and go watch the interrogation.

The stuffy air in the room, the moans from Lahiri, the dim light, the stench of sweat: Jatin wanted to head out as soon as he entered. Lahiri rolled to the floor after a slap from Grewal's man, who now lifted a wide leather strap, and brought it down on Lahiri's buttocks. After two of those, Lahiri curled up in a ball, his small legs bent near his paunch. He looked like an upturned beetle.

'I did not touch that woman,' Lahiri clutched at his chest, breathing hard, 'You can check, run tests on her.'

'Stop with your lies!'

'Why would I rush off with a shipment on the way?' Lahiri gasped, 'You know I can't call police when I'm robbed.'

'Where is Radhe?' Grewal kicked one of the legs of the table with his steel-toed boots, making Lahiri cower back.

'Radhe used to work for me, it is true,' Lahiri rolled up, slowly, and leaned against the wall, '...but he stole from me. Ran away. Unhappy customers. No supply. I was afraid. They can…go to someone else. That is why…I accepted the shipment.'

'You are lying.'

'I run…small business. Not a greedy man.' Lahiri clutched his chest and drew a long breath. 'No family.'

Rivulets of sweat trickled down Lahiri's face. His eyes were unfocused, his breath came in long gasps. Jatin wanted to stop Grewal from hitting the man again, but Lahiri seemed on the point of giving up. Grewal wouldn't stop now.

'My chest hurts.' Lahiri groaned. 'I…take care of the orphans.'

'And turn them into dealers?'

Another slap from Grewal, and just as Jatin was about to halt the interrogation, Lahiri's head lolled back against the wall. He opened his eyes.

'I own a gun, saab,' Lahiri's voice came out strangled, 'Didn't shoot. Did no harm. Ask them…who arrested me…I…gave no trouble.'

'Do you even know how to shoot one?' Grewal gave Lahiri another shove, 'Or you just kept it like that, for show?'

Swaying, Lahiri fell back against the wall. 'You're…here' he gasped, his gaze lighting on Jatin. He hadn't spotted Jatin in the shadows all this while. Now he seemed desperate to talk. 'I'll talk to…' Lahiri clutched at his own chest, '…*him*.'

Lahiri must have recognised him from his arrest.

'We've been trying to talk to you for the last half an hour,' Grewal roared, 'and now you will choose who you blather to?'

Lahiri slumped down to the floor with a groan, and his

body lay prone. Grewal's man kicked at Lahiri's back and the wide stomach, but Lahiri just lay there in a heap.

'Stop this.' Jatin reached forward and touched Grewal.

For a moment, Grewal didn't react, then nodded at his man to run out and get help. Between Jatin and Grewal, they turned Lahiri over. His head drooped when they tried to make him sit up.

'Let him handle this,' Grewal gestured to one of the three men who rushed in. 'He has medical training.'

They stepped out from the cramped room. Grewal headed to his desk and poured them water, and drained his glass in one go. Jatin held his glass, wishing he'd stepped in earlier. If Lahiri came to real harm, word of it would become ammunition in Mehra's hands.

The man under whose charge Grewal had left Lahiri ran up to them.

'I'm afraid that man is having a heart attack, sir,' he said.

43

Anjali opened her eyes to pink roses, plump with health, standing proud on long stems in a vase.

She turned, and found Maya asleep in the chair beside the bed, her mouth open, emitting those cat-purr sounds Anjali teased her about. She tried to rise, intending to put a cushion under Maya's lolling head, brush her hair away from her face. But the effort of sitting up dizzied her and she toppled back. The bed creaked and Maya sat up with a start.

'Anji!'

Maya rushed to her, stumbling. They hugged, half-sitting-half-standing in a maze of arms. Maya held her softly, but her fingers dug into Anjali's back.

'I'm sorry, Anji. I'm so…so sorry.'

The husky sobs reminded Anjali of the teenaged Maya who had wept, inconsolable, at her mother's death.

'Hey. Shush.' Anjali held Maya close, though it hurt her throat and set her face tingling with burns. 'I'm the one who screwed up.'

'I came to the ICU yesterday, too, but you were asleep. This morning I went to Nikhil's school.'

'Shh…Shh…Maya.'

'I was so scared.'

'I'm so sorry, baby, so so sorry.' About Jatin. About not telling her. About everything.

Anjali called Nikhil *baby* on the good days, when he finished his homework on time, or ate his dinner without a fuss. Maya was her baby too, her baby sister and her daughter. She had no words, only her body clogged with tears, with the sort of tenderness she'd felt in her breasts post birth, the fullness, the heaviness of new motherhood. She held Maya. She could not shed tears herself, because the acid had damaged her eyes, but her Maya could still cry.

This girl needed her. Nikhil needed her. Better not think, she told herself. Feel the mat of your friend's hair, watch her eyes fill with tears, her breath falter. *Deep breaths*. In and out, One, Two, Three. There. Much better.

It strained her to keep holding Maya, but Anjali didn't want to let go. In India, they believed in reincarnation, in *karma*, in debts incurred and repaid. If you hurt someone, or received a favour, you incurred a debt. You then paid it back, big or small, in this life or next: no escape, no negotiations. She owed Maya in this life and the next, for forgiving her. With the way Maya helped raise Nikhil, Anjali owed her for the next few lifetimes.

'I'm sorry, I shouldn't have talked about you to Drishti Bhabi. I hurt Bhai, and I hurt you.'

'Not your fault.' Anjali patted Maya's shoulder. 'Nothing to be sorry about.'

'I stayed away when you needed me.'

'You're here now,' Anjali surprised herself with how deeply she meant her words. 'That's all that matters.'

She murmured on, making sense at first, then uttering soothing nonsense till Maya calmed down. Yes, Maya had told Drishti about the affair, but in her place, Anjali might have done far worse.

Much later, the room filled up with Maya's voice, light and airy. It chased away the shadows. Maya told her how Sakhi and Nikhil sat together at dinner these days, but how Nikhil resented his grandma.

'When will she come to see me?'

Anjali had never imagined she would ask for Mom.

'She was here all of yesterday. She may come in tonight.'

Maya moved out of the bed and into the chair, and belatedly strapped on her hospital mask. 'I can't hug you too much. Sakhi has a cold, I might give you an infection. You gave us quite the scare.'

'Has Nikhil asked for his Christmas present?'

'Don't worry,' Maya smiled, 'I'll take care of that.'

Christmas in four days. How would Nikhil cope with his grandma, with Sakhi and the puppy, without Anjali around? Vibha came into the room, and pushed an injection into the cannula. It didn't hurt, not any more. The cannula was a part of her now.

'What about Mr Lahiri?' she said, to keep Maya talking, and so she herself wouldn't have to talk.

Maya broke into a long, animated account of Lahiri's arrest and his testimony. The man dealt drugs, and police found an unconscious woman in his boot. Anjali lay back as she listened, Maya's voice a hum against the background.

The myriad shades of reality, all impermanent. Lahiri: a former do-gooder now a crook, a drug-dealer, maybe a rapist and a murderer. Her affair with Jatin now common knowledge, Jatin to get divorced soon. Her face, her very identity changed by her own son, a secret she must carry to her grave. Maya, who loved her, then hated her, now loved her again. Delhi was not far enough a city to run away from Mom. No certainty in this world, nothing for granted. Nothing mattered to the universe, it went about its business, uncaring, indifferent.

Disfigured. Outcast. Rehabilitation.

Words floated about Anjali, like dust motes rising and falling, till each one found a place to settle on her. The doctor had said some of the medication would send her into a sort of euphoria. Euphoria this was not. Was it today or yesterday he said that, before or after Maya visited her? Days and nights seemed to melt into each other. She must have slept the entire day, because outside the window, it was dark. She closed her eyes again, unable to keep them open.

She heard words murmured, susurrated around her. She listened to the ones everyone around her carried within them. She understood the silenced, the concealed, the coerced. So many of them: *Corrosive. Matriderm. Noumen. Post-Traumatic Stress Disorder. Marriage. Dress-up. Christmas. Courage. Bandage. Divorce. Humiliating. Whore. Side-effect.*

These words touched Anjali.

Long-term. Abandoned. Tomorrow. Affair. Who knows? Surgery. Yesterday. Maybe still. Painkiller. She deserves it. We cannot say. Two lakhs. Twenty thousand rupees.

She tried to snag all of the words but they escaped her. *You cannot touch words and phrases, Anjali Morgan, but they touch you.*

Anjali wanted to hold on to some words, let go of others. *Deep breaths*, for instance. Or, *Be in the Now.*

What if her *now* didn't bear scrutiny? Could she escape into the pink roses that bloomed next to the window where Maya had arranged them? Sakhi's mouth on her fingers when she'd fed her? Nikhil, when he danced like a drunken horse on receiving a new airplane? Run away back to the *then*? Into the *before*? Anjali closed her eyes, and waited for her Mom.

'You had drifted off,' Maya said when Anjali opened her eyes, 'So I dropped by the office for a while.'

'What time is it?'

'7 pm.'

'Why isn't Mom here yet?'

'She's down with a stomach bug.' Maya looked away and seemed to consider her next words.

'What is it?'

'I don't know. It feels almost as if she's scared to meet you. She wants to, and doesn't. I don't know if I'm making any sense?'

In a way, it made sense, all right. That was what Anjali herself was feeling, too. But in another, it didn't. Mom was always very sure of herself, her beliefs, her prayers, her faith in God. She was always the better one, the one with the right to tell everyone what to do. But no point in discussing it with Maya.

Maya had a real mother, one who opened her heart not just to her children, but to others. To Anjali. Anjali wanted to be such a mother, unselfconscious, all love and no hesitation or self-doubt. Nikhil brought doubt with him; with him she always needed to be careful. To watch herself. Watch him.

'Keep an eye on Nikhil.'

'He's settling in, don't worry.'

Maya didn't know. Nor would she, if Anjali could help it.

44

Jatin Bhatt had hidden from his father-in-law the last few days.

Today, he couldn't avoid the meeting any longer. He decided to tackle it first thing that morning. Several officers had left for their Christmas breaks—if Jatin ended up in a showdown with his father-in-law, fewer ears would listen in. He didn't need the gossip.

Varun would land tonight. Come what may, Jatin must see his son. He called Varun in Manila twice daily: once when he woke up, and after lunch. By now, he understood Varun wouldn't pick up his calls. They needed to meet face-to-face.

He knocked at the door of the conference room and heard Mehra's voice calling him in. Rathi sat across from Mehra, with files and empty cups of tea strewn between them. The Home Minister's stooge stood up as Jatin walked in and wished him a good morning. Jatin made himself smile while returning the greeting. Rathi gathered his papers and left.

'Hello, sir.'

Mehra nodded but didn't speak, nor offer him a seat. Jatin took one opposite his boss.

'You want to tell me what's going on?'

Jatin chose to misunderstand and gave an update of the major cases in his department that week.

'Jatin.' Drishti's father sat up straight, and it struck Jatin—from the older man's chin, the angle of his nose, the way he frowned when angry—how much Drishti took after her father.

'Let's just keep it straight, shall we? What's going on between you and Drishti?'

Jatin noted his father-in-law's pursed lips and steepled fingers. He needed to stay calm, because for once, he felt on the back foot. Mehra had added leverage: the grandson.

'We have had problems.'

'Or you are giving her problems? I never liked that foreigner half-breed girl, and now it seems she's to blame for this mess.'

Jatin itched to lash out at the insult to Anjali, but he spoke instead in the flattest of voices.

'I'm going to offer Drishti the best possible terms.'

'You realise the bad name a divorce will bring the two families? Drishti's sister isn't married yet, nor is yours. Consider the effect on your son, for God's sake. Getting married is easy, staying that way is the hard part.'

My parents stayed married, Jatin longed to say, *look where that got them.*

'Drishti enjoys her job.' Jatin placed his hands on the table between them. 'She can move forward if we can settle this. Varun will take time to adjust, but he's almost a grown-up now.'

'I suggest you think about it again. Men stray from marriage from time to time, that's nothing new.' Commissioner

Mehra stood up. 'You have a bright career ahead of you, and we have to deal with this Sabharwal case together. Try and evaluate if this woman is worth it. Especially *now*.'

So now that Anjali's face had burned, *muh kala*, her face blackened quite literally, she wasn't supposed to be worth Jatin's time. Mehra had made his terms clear: *stay married to my daughter and I'll wrap up the case for you.*

'Her son is dangerous.' Mehra continued. 'He attacked Varun, and you did nothing about it.'

That attack had puzzled Jatin. Varun was twice Nikhil's size. A karate brown belt, he could easily have controlled Nikhil if he wished to.

'I'll talk to Varun after he returns tonight.'

'Do what is best for him.' Mehra rose. 'For all of us.'

Jatin didn't rise, staring instead out of the window at the old wall of the building opposite. Paint cracking in places, the wall stared back at him, cold and grey. Behind him, he heard his father-in-law leave the conference room.

Twenty-two years of service in the Delhi Police, in various departments ranging from Traffic to Vigilance. For the first time, Jatin wanted to quit. He didn't want any more medals and felicitations, the personal use of a vehicle, the burden of the cash he tossed inside his safe.

His Varun had become a bargaining chip. And Anjali.

Ghalib's verses provided the right words for every situation:

Rahee na taaqat-e-guftaar, aur agar ho bhee,
Toh kis ummeed pe kahiye ke aarzoo kya hai?

With no *ummeed*, hope, Jatin seemed to have lost the will to talk about what he wanted, his heart's desire. *Arzoo*, what a beautiful, heart-breaking word for dreams and longing. Jatin stood up, his days of Urdu *shero-shayari* long over. That was a different man. Jatin had buried him for the sake of his Ma, and Maya.

He would go to the airport today, meet Varun, and explain how things stood between him and Drishti. Varun would understand, he must.

Kusum had taken charge of the body they found at Delhi Junction railway station, and got Chander to make an identification. She knocked and entered right after lunchtime.

'Chander saying it is not Radhe, sir, but his brother, Ram Sharan.'

'Ram Sharan?' Jatin stood up, 'How did he get there?'

'Not sure, sir. Chander also not knowing, sir.'

The Delhi Junction railway station wasn't very far from Geeta Colony where that suspect had escaped from Jatin. Was Ram Sharan that man?

'How tall was this Ram Sharan?'

It wasn't an easy question to answer, given that a train had cut the body in two, but Kusum answered without a pause.

'Tall, sir.' Kusum's expression didn't change. 'Taller than Radhe.'

A post-mortem would take too long, but Jatin needed a doctor's opinion on the body. He asked Kusum to shift the body to the Safdarjung morgue, and get a quick examination, a determination of the cause of death, if possible.

Radhe Shyam Misra had disappeared, but that wasn't hard to do in Delhi. Thousands of people entered the city each morning and left each night, making it a challenge for police and administration. Jatin ambled to the window, and turned to stare at a lone Semal tree standing still amid the river of traffic on the Connaught Place circle and the stream of people on the pavements hurrying to work. Parasite ferns grew on its trunk, but its crown towered above the buildings. Jatin longed to be like that tree, aloof, standing his own ground. He turned his gaze back to the passers-by. Any one of them could be Radhe. Radhe was the key to the Sujni case, he knew it in his gut—that boy had disappeared for a reason.

On the map, he looked at the quadrilateral that joined Pul Mithai, Madipur Colony, Dilshaad Gardens and Sanjay Colony. Both Lajpat Nagar, where Lahiri owned an apartment, and Geeta Colony, where the suspect escaped from Lahiri's car, lay within that area.

He sent a text to Grewal, asking for updates on the men in his lockup.

The day before, Jatin had sat in on Manoj's interrogation at the Jamia Nagar station.

'I'm telling you,' Manoj had taken a look at Anjali's snapshot, 'I've seen her at Sanjay Colony. She used to come and work at Hridayog.'

'So you didn't know this little girl was staying with her?' Grewal's man showed Sakhi's photo to Manoj.

'This girl got into some police *ka lafda*, they picked her up.' Manoj stroked his thin nose, one side of it swollen. 'She wasn't delivered to me.'

'But you showed her picture to clients. Where did you get her pictures?'

'It is not difficult. Everyone has phones these days.'

'You were showing her pictures to clients.'

'Clients are ok if we replace the girls.'

'So you're saying you've never met this lady?' The policemen placed Anjali's picture in front of Manoj again.

'I have seen her, she's good-looking, white. Out of our league.' The policeman shoved Manoj, but he winced and smiled. 'I'm telling you, I have nothing against her.'

He had clearly been in the pimping business for a while, and was no stranger to police tactics. In all this time in the lockup, his statements hadn't changed.

Pawan's theory that Manoj might have organised the attack on Anjali didn't seem to pan out. Jatin needed a meeting with Pawan to discuss the Sujni case. Pawan had called earlier asking to meet him in private, but very politely refused to tell him what it was about. Jatin hoped it was about the Sujni case.

45

When Anjali woke up, Mom sat by the corner window, straight-backed, her angular jaw in sharp relief, like an Evil Queen from a story, surveying her kingdom. Part of a dream.

'Hi Mom,' Anjali said, not expecting a reply.

The figure started and stood up. 'They said you wouldn't wake up until late.'

It was Mom. *You asked for me, Anjali*, the Mom inside her head spoke up, making her dizzy. One Mom was enough.

'What day is it?'

When did they finish with the surgery? How long ago?

'The twenty-second.' Mom walked towards her. 'Should I call the nurse?'

'Yes.' Anjali croaked out, 'Water.'

The burns had caused scarring on the inside that made swallowing uncomfortable. Mom didn't ring for the nurse. Instead she filled a glass, and helped Anjali drink. A first, in as long as Anjali could remember.

Once Anjali settled back, Mom went to her chair by the window. Anjali needed the distance, and maybe Mom did too. Anjali had always been in Mom's orbit, unable to let go, but never too close.

'Are you insured for the entire treatment?'

Mom, always the asker of questions. Anjali was glad she asked this one instead of the ones others asked: how are you feeling? Or worse: how are you? The doctors asked, the nurses, Fareeda. A polite greeting. The reply? My face is gone. I find it hard to stand up. I'm a homewrecker. My son has put me here. I almost died. I may not be able to afford my medical expenses, nor my son's.

She kept quiet. *Focus on the positives.* What did Fareeda usually say? '*Find one thing you feel good about.*'

Mom was here, and Anjali could talk to her, just as she had pictured in the past weeks. Ask questions, find answers. Apply them to her life with Nikhil. Those were the positives here. Mom had taken a flight and crossed continents to talk to her. Anjali needed to take that into account.

'I have something for you.' Mom dug into her handbag, and took out a large brown envelope.

That was new, too. Mom never got her anything.

'What is it?' Anjali stretched out her hand.

Mom placed it on the bedside table instead. Typical.

'You can look at it once I've left. For now, I want to hear what you have to say. You did not come to your father's funeral because you didn't want to talk to me.'

Of course. Mom wanted to manipulate all conversations between them, so why should this one be an exception? Anger rose within Anjali, like fire in a roomful of curtains. She took strength from it, because it felt familiar. A few hours of counselling couldn't keep out years of hatred, that came rising and swelling, inhabiting her. But Anjali was no longer a young girl, nor a young mother. She had lived, burned and almost died, she held a secret within her belly that ate at her from the inside, and gave her nightmares. She gathered it all in a breath, let it out in a sigh. She needed calm. When her voice emerged, it did not shake or murmur.

'Nikhil's therapist has been working with him, and me. He felt it would help to talk to you. To understand myself. To understand Nikhil.'

Mom did not reply, just watched her from her chair by the window, her face mask-like, even paler than Anjali remembered.

Why did you never love me, Anjali wanted to say. *Why not a word of praise, always that shunning, angry judgment?* She was a psychiatrist, she told herself, she could use her trade now to get what she needed.

'Tell me about when you were pregnant with me.'

'I was never pregnant with you.' Mom turned away from her, towards the window.

Of all the answers.

Anjali pulled herself up, and did not feel her pain, her mind a slate wiped clean. She tried to form a word, but her mouth did not move.

'I met Ashok in Goa, on a backpacking trip to India,' Mom spoke to the window, 'at one of those crazy parties. It was the sixties. We were all high, all the time. He took me to a rally the next day. We held placards. I don't remember what we protested against, only that my throat was sore by evening, and we did not drink. He was a university student, and he wanted to save the world. When I returned to Florida, we kept in touch. I married him the following year, and he moved in with me. Two years later, he got a job at our local university, and I miscarried for the first time, and then every few months. My mother took pity on me, and sent me Vivian to help around the house the next time I fell pregnant. I was frail, clinically depressed. I was to rest, and Vivian was to take care of the household.'

Mom cleared her throat, then went on.

'She'd turned seventeen that summer, on a long break before she was due to start college, and she came over to help. I had a late miscarriage and recovered, but the doctors told me I could never conceive again. I began to attend church. Vivian stayed on, got enrolled at the university where Ashok taught. By the time I found out about her pregnancy, it was too late to have an abortion.'

Aunty Viv. Short-skirted, her hair cropped close to her skull and dyed red, her laughter loud and unapologetic, her heels high and her belly-button pierced. Aunty Viv for whom Anjali made birthday cards and who she saw once a year. Mom grumbled about having to prepare the guest room whenever Aunty Viv visited, and Dad barely spoke a word.

So Aunty Viv gave birth to a baby. Big deal. In the seventies, bearing a child out of wedlock was news. Not anymore.

'Why are you telling me this?'

'You are that child.' Mom still did not turn and look at her.

Anjali had not made that connection between herself not being Dorothy's daughter, and Aunty Viv's pregnancy. A pall of silence fell over the room, and Anjali used her voice like a hatchet to cut through it.

'The father?'

'Ashok was your father.'

'You're lying.' It was not a shroud that smothered her, but a smog, black, and without form. It entered her, because how do you fight a smog? Even as she spoke the words, Anjali realised their futility. Dad, who put band-aid on her when she fell down and cut her knees, who drove her to school, made her dinner on the nights Mom went out for church meetings. Babysat Nikhil. That *was* her Dad. It *couldn't* be right though. She swallowed, and her throat hurt. At the back of her neck, a low throb built up.

'Why did you keep me?' Anjali said. *Why not give me up for adoption? I would have found a family.*

'Because I thought I was better than I was. It seemed right. Ashok wouldn't lose his job to a scandal, Vivian could go on with her life as usual. I could have the child I wanted.'

'You didn't want me.'

'I did, at first.' Mom turned to face her, 'I thought I could forget, make you my own daughter. But I didn't take into account the fact that I had helped bring up Vivian. You were the spitting image of her as you grew up. You had the *same* gurgle, the same way of widening your eyes when someone spoke to you, the same cry when you were hungry. The same bald baby head. Same face. Like I said, I thought I was better than I was. I wasn't. And all the praying in the church didn't change that. I couldn't forgive him. Them.'

Anjali closed her eyes. Threaded between Mom's shaking voice and the throb inside her head, words hovered about her again, close, but out of reach.

Forgiveness. Truth. Dirty girl. Never mind her. Prayer. Bad blood. Here's some ice cream. Mud. Slaps. She's like that. There, there.

Dad. Her Dad, the good one. The one who bought her chocolate milkshake after Mom raged out of her bedroom and banged the door shut. Who iced her knee when Mom lost her cool and shoved her against a table. Anjali didn't blame him then. What could a mere man do with someone like Mom, except hide?

Forgiveness. Anjali must remember that word, in case she needed it to sort out her *what now*, before she untangled the *you remember when*.

'You need to forgive. For yourself, not them.' Maya had said that, long ago. She had parroted her mother's standard advice, given each time Maya exploded after being teased about her skin. Anjali didn't have a mother. No mother, only an aunt. No father too, now, not even a dead one. This man had seduced his wife's sister, a seventeen-year old. Made her pregnant. Better an orphan than a daughter to that man.

'You kept his last name. Why stay with him at all?'

'You still go by Nate's name.' Dorothy's voice was quiet.

'That's because of my certificates. My job depends on them.'

'I didn't change my name because of the church. It would have been a scandal—I might as well have divorced him.'

Orphan. Outcast. No restraint. Rootless. Freedom. Pancakes. Vodka. Take care of your face.

The window, the air-conditioner, the curtains, and the television; all of them remained in their respective corners, still and indifferent. The bed did not tilt, the door remained closed, the daylight outside did not dim. How was that possible?

Freedom. Joy. Normal.

There was nothing wrong with her, nothing at all. She could love, be loved. She was born to the wrong people.

This woman she had tried to please all her life...Mom, was not her Mom. She didn't need one either. She was Anjali, burnt-in-the-fire Anjali, Nikhil's mother Anjali, Doctor Anjali, Maya and Jatin's Anjali. Dorothy Gupta, with all her advice on 'keeping your man' hadn't kept hers. All those years, she had projected her fears, her anger, her jealousy and grief on the girl she'd adopted by law, but not with her heart.

'I'm sorry.' Mom's voice fell, 'I'm so, so, sorry. For everything.'

She saw the top of Mom's head, the spaces where hair didn't grow, the strands of white, and turned away. No, not Mom. She wasn't Mom.

Forgiveness. Retaliation. Normal. Orphan.

Anjali swept the words away. She didn't care for those. New ones bubbled up.

Tomorrow. My Self. Now. Family. Friends. Nikhil.

A blue blur floated into the room. A nurse.

She didn't want any of it, Mom or Dad, she saw that now. Morgan or Gupta or anything else didn't matter. She saw herself, Anjali, who could smile and fight, a mother, a creator of her own family, though not all her own blood. What did blood matter?

Besides, all this could disappear any moment—her, this bed, the hospital, the people she knew and loved, all of it. Nothing lasted. Not her face. Not her Dad. Not the aunt who was her mother. Not the Mom she thought she was born to. All of life a brief blooming and wilting in a huge indifferent space, and she a small, insignificant speck.

A brief singe of pain in her forearm. When she tried to talk, her words melted into each other, refused to leave her lips. She made one last effort, to speak to the tall, hunched figure now standing in the middle of the room. *Freedom*, she wanted to say, but no words came.

46

Jatin leaned forward to listen closer as Pawan talked about the pictures he had taken at the drug den behind Hridayog. After a long week, he hoped for good news.

Across the table, Pawan went into detailed descriptions of how he got the photographs enlarged, explaining how careful he'd been about the process, how he'd verified each picture.

Jatin needed to meet Rathi in less than an hour for their next meeting on the Sabharwal case. If Pawan had found a clue to the Sujni murder, he needed to get to it faster.

'Come to the point.'

'*Haanji,* sir,' Pawan handed him a thumb-drive, 'It is better if I just show you.'

Jatin plugged it in. Pawan walked around the table, and scrolled down the folders on the drive. The same photos Jatin remembered, only clearer.

Pawan pointed to a boy in profile. He scrolled down to three more pictures, none from the front, of the same boy, holding a syringe.

That slouch, the way his neck was bent, how he leaned forward to point at someone. Jatin would have picked Varun out of a line-up of a thousand boys, based on his posture alone. How could that be? How could a boy look so like his son? This boy wore a t-shirt that fitted his broad shoulders and showed off well-defined biceps, just like Varun's. *Gabru jawan*, Jatin whispered to himself.

'It can't be.' He leaned back, 'Varun's in Manila right now.'

But Varun was very much in New Delhi at the time those pictures were taken.

'This is an enhanced one, sir,' Pawan clicked another picture open.

Unmistakable. Varun's hand, and on his wrist the same bracelet Jatin had gifted his son. As Pawan enlarged the picture further, Jatin saw the engraved script. It said Varun Satyaprakash Bhatt at the back. Varun. His son. At a drug den in Sanjay Colony. He slumped in his chair.

'And sir, look at this one also.'

Opposite Varun in one of the enhanced pictures, Jatin saw another boy, laughing.

'Who is that?' Jatin said.

'Radhe Shyam Misra.'

47

Maya didn't know Dorothy very well and wished for it to remain that way. That woman was too much. She wanted everything done her way, scrambling like a mad ostrich between the living room and the kitchen, driving the household crazy. She ordered poor Ira about, making her drag out the Christmas tree, grumbling that they should have set it up weeks ago. She demanded a Christmas wreath be put on the door right that minute. Maya wished she could book the annoying woman into an asylum, or at the least, a hotel.

Dorothy upset Nikhil this morning by trying to change the seating arrangement at the dining table. He ate only a large slice of fruitcake for breakfast as a result, and kept up a constant chatter with himself. To top it all, Nikhil's counsellor had taken a three-day break.

Untangling the Christmas lights, Maya cursed, but under her breath. Sakhi sat beside her, trying to help. Manku's head rested on the girl's lap. This wasn't like other Christmas Eves, when the entire Bhatt family dropped in for lunch. One splash of acid had changed so many lives.

Bhai would come in later today. She didn't expect the rest of his family. Varun was scheduled to return from Manila tonight, but he and Bhabi were staying at the Mehra's for the holiday week. Drishti Bhabi hadn't taken Maya's calls or returned her messages.

Bhai's family, all scattered now. Maya stifled a sigh, and forced herself to keep at the tangled wires.

Sakhi pulled at her sleeve, 'May I have lunch early?'

The soft question in Hindi yanked Maya out of her thoughts. She brushed the girl's hair, loving that Sakhi felt comfortable enough to ask for food now, almost a month after she arrived.

'Are you hungry?'

Sakhi had developed a big appetite—her body making up for all the years of want.

'No, but Pawan Uncle will come to pick me up soon. He promised he will take me on a bike ride.'

Pawan hadn't told Maya about this. She felt a surge of temper, but quelled it. He was on leave today, he could spend it with whoever he wished.

'Ask Ira to give you your lunch in her room.' Maya pulled Sakhi into a hug. 'But you have to be quiet.'

'Because of Nikhil Bhaiya?' Sakhi knew to keep out of Nikhil's way.

Maya nodded. Nikhil never said he missed Anjali, but when he sat at the dining table, he shot glances at Anjali's empty chair, and threw a fit if everyone didn't join him for meals. According to Dr Bhalla, Nikhil didn't want anyone else disappearing from his life.

Maya watched as Sakhi skipped off to find Ira.

Yesterday, she had taken Sakhi to see her little brother, Chotu. Usha, the woman who had fostered Chotu for the past few weeks, greeted Maya with a big smile and invited her to sit on a small bed in a tiny one-room home. Between racks and the kitchen, with a folded bed and tiny television all stacked on top of each other, and hardly enough standing room for four people on the uneven floor, the couple had cared for a toddler for about five weeks. When Maya pressed them with groceries, Usha's husband looked shamed instead of pleased. Maya never visited Sanjay Colony, though Anjali asked her often. Now she wished she'd met Usha and her husband earlier. Maya watched Sakhi play with the gurgling Chotu, and tried her best not to cry as Usha said they didn't mind Chotu, just that Hridayog had closed down after the raid, making it difficult to care for three children all day. Maya waved her goodbyes and carried a weeping Sakhi back to her car.

Earlier she had argued against taking Sakhi in. Now with Manoj and Lahiri behind bars, Sakhi was safe, so to speak. But Maya couldn't return Sakhi to the slums, not now. If Usha could care for a small child not her own, so could Maya.

***

'It can't go on top of the Christmas Tree.' Nikhil's voice sounded an octave higher than usual. Maya kept her fingers busy with the wires, but her ears pricked up.

'Think how nice it will look.' Dorothy stood on the stool beside the tree. 'It will light up the whole room.'

Maya rose. Any more of this and Nikhil might scream. He didn't like strangers in the house, and he didn't like change.

'Anjali never put it there.' Nikhil's voice took on an edge. 'This star hangs by the main door.'

Maya stood up, careful not to make any sudden movements. She picked up a squeeze ball from the table, and pressed it into Nikhil's left hand. But Nikhil's voice rose with each word he spoke.

'Anjali. Anjali Anjali Anjali. Anjali-AnjaliAnjaliAnjalian jalianjalianjali…'

'Dorothy, why don't you check on Ira in the kitchen?'

Dorothy climbed down, and went into the kitchen without a word.

'Here, Nikhil. You want to help me fix the star?'

Nikhil nodded and rushed up to Maya. She forced herself to stand her ground. This boy had grown taller than her. He would soon be much stronger. She let go of a breath when Nikhil stopped and picked up a roll of scotch tape.

At the main door, Maya tiptoed on a stool. The door was flanked by potted plants. Her gaze followed the row of greenery down the driveway, all the way to the gate. Ma loved plants and took care of them whenever she found a moment. Some of her ferns and palms still thrived.

'Maya,' Nikhil tugged at her sweater. 'Focus on the star.'

The morning cold nipped at her bare ankles. She had better get this done fast and return to the heated living room. The scotch tape stuck to her fingers, and she gave it a jerk, making her stool wobble.

'Do you need help?'

Without her hold on the door frame, the sound of Pawan's voice would have made her topple.

In an English movie, Pawan would have caught her as she fell, before kissing her. Movie characters kissed under the mistletoe on Christmas, but this was no movie. Maya smiled at him and passed the scotch tape, letting Pawan and Nikhil hang the star.

She went back to the mess of wires—she had managed to tangle the Christmas lights even further. The more she tugged at them, the worse they got, but she kept at the hopeless task. Something to keep her distracted from the fact that Pawan was now hanging decorations on the tree behind her.

Dorothy's raised voice floated out from the kitchen. That woman didn't give the household a moment's rest. A crash came from Ira's room. Maya ran, her heart in her mouth. She remembered the last puppy. Had Nikhil caught hold of Manku?

In the dim light of Ira's room, she shoved Dorothy aside to find Ira struggling to keep Nikhil away from Sakhi, but he held Sakhi's hand. 'She can't eat alone, we eat at the table, Sakhi, we eat at the table,' he said in his singsong multiplication table voice. Pawan had followed her, and she wanted to step back and let him take charge, but any movement might set Nikhil off.

'Nikhil. It's ok,' Maya said. 'If you let her go, we'll have lunch together.'

She tried to calm herself. Her panic might affect Nikhil. She kept her distance from both Nikhil and Sakhi, and gestured to Pawan to do the same. If Nikhil felt threatened, he might react, and end up hurting Sakhi.

'No, let me go.' Sakhi gasped in Hindi. 'Pawan Uncle has come. We will go out.'

'You can't go out today. It's Christmas tomorrow. We all stay together.'

Sakhi screamed. It choked into a cough, because Nikhil now had her by the throat. Pawan stepped in and tried to grab Sakhi, but something seemed to have entered Nikhil, a strength greater than any fourteen-year-old's. When he saw Pawan reach for him, he flung Sakhi, hard. Maya made a grab for her, but Sakhi fell with a dull thud. Maya rushed up to the limp girl on the floor. Blood welled up at her right temple. Sakhi's head had banged against a steel trunk.

Behind her, Maya heard bangs and crashes as Nikhil continued to throw bottles and boxes around the room, chanting, 'No one goes out, no one goes out, noonegoesout!'

Ira passed her a white towel, and Maya held it to Sakhi's lolling head. The red stain on it spread. From the corner of her eye, she saw Pawan carrying Nikhil away, smothered in blankets. She heard Ira phone Bhai. Bhai's distant voice said hello, but she couldn't form a reply.

At the door Dorothy muttered, 'That boy is mad, he should be locked up!'

Ira made shushing noises.

Bhai asked her to give Sakhi what first aid she could—his driver would be at the gate in ten minutes. Maya nodded, then realised he couldn't see her. She whispered an ok past her dry throat.

'Take her to L.K.,' Bhai said in a calm monotone. 'Easier to admit her to the same hospital as Anjali.'

Maya found Ira standing next to her, holding the first-aid box. In her housekeeper's eyes, Maya saw her own fear reflected: what was Nikhil capable of?

48

Three years ago, when Jatin first sat in the office of the Special Commissioner of Crime, his nameplate replacing that of his predecessor, he thought he'd made it. So what if all his other dreams had died? He got to indulge his son. People called him successful.

All the medals and certificates lining his office walls made sense back then, and seemed worth the shit he'd gone through during his career. The bullets he took during various encounters, the sucking up to dozens of bureaucrats like Dayal Sisodia, the number of times he missed Varun's school events, the way he slogged during the period of mourning for Ma.

After the photos Pawan showed him, all his medals seemed dull and fit for the scrap heap. His Varun, his golden boy, the *gabru jawan*. Jatin snapped the laptop shut, and paced his office. If the world came to know that his son, the son of a special commissioner of crime, used drugs, he would become a laughing stock in the corridors of Delhi police offices and in the media. Years of distinguished service, flushed down the drain, like so much refuse.

Come what may, Jatin needed to leave early this evening:

meet Maya and Anjali at the hospital, and reach the airport to pick up his son. Lots to talk about, not the least of which was Radhe's whereabouts.

Jatin checked his watch: 1 pm. He called Kusum and told her he would skip lunch, and not to disturb him. Dr Bhalla called, greeting Jatin with his usual bluster. The sudden changes in Nikhil's environment resulted in this incident, he said. Too many upsetting factors: the absence of his mother, a new child at home, and the grandparent staying with him. He suggested they either admit Nikhil for the night for observation, or move in his therapist to stay with him, to intervene and monitor as required. The grandmother needed to leave, as she clearly upset the boy.

'So this could happen again?' Jatin said.

'We can't say, but it is best to be careful, Commissioner saab.'

'Is he a danger to his family?' Jatin said. 'Or himself?'

Jatin would remember Dr Bhalla's reply.

'We're all a potential danger to ourselves and our families, one way or another. We just learn how to hide it.'

***

At the L.K. hospital that evening, Jatin met Maya first. Sakhi was stable, but they wanted to monitor her overnight for concussion. He left his sister with words of reassurance, and headed to Anjali's room. He needed to talk to her about Nikhil, his violent episode, get her to sign some papers to keep the boy under observation.

Jatin sank down on a sofa in one of the lobbies. Large fake sunflowers in a vase stared back at him. His time spent frequenting this building must amount to years, not weeks. The same felt true of the Sujni case, with no credible leads so far.

After those gasped words asking for Jatin, Lahiri had lost his speech due to a stroke following the heart attack. In the last four days in hospital, that man could slur and groan, but not much else. Doctors hoped he would recover more brain function and speech in the coming days. His reports looked positive, they said, but they could not comment further.

At Anjali's door, Jatin drew a breath to collect himself, and knocked. Anjali's nurse said she could talk, but only for a while. The last surgery had left her very weak.

'Jelly?'

Anjali raised her bandaged right hand a little and waved, but didn't speak.

'I couldn't come by earlier—I'm sorry.'

The 'sorry' word never reached his lips earlier, even when he reached for it. But after the first one to Maya the other night, he now said it to Anjali. A first again. Maybe it got easier once you started.

'Are you ok?' Anjali said.

Jatin was surprised at Anjali's old sense of humour, and the sarcastic twang in her voice. She tried to rise, and he helped her by cranking up the bed. He sank down on a chair, drawing it near her, but not too close. Her doctor still feared infections.

'You're on a roll.' Jatin's routine comment for Anjali when in one of her chirpy moods, after a triumph at her clinic, or at Hridayog.

'Never knew orphanhood could liberate you. Don't have parents any more, did you know?'

'Jelly!'

'Yep. Didn't she tell you?'

Anjali told him about her Mom and Dad, her voice normal, as if discussing a work trip. Ashok Gupta, a man who seduced his teenaged sister-in-law. Got her pregnant. Dorothy Gupta was Anjali's aunt, not her mother. Her real mother was dead these ten years. Jatin tried to absorb it all, but a part of him kept listening for a note of hysteria in Anjali's voice, while another shrank back in disbelief. He had thought Professor Gupta to be a great man, generous with his time and his hospitality, patient with his wife, concerned about his daughter, his students.

When Anjali stopped, Jatin hugged her, infections be damned. He let go after a few moments, but not before he'd stroked the velvet clumps of her hair growing back.

'I'm so sorry, Jelly.'

'Hey. Don't make it a habit with the sorry.'

'You seem…'

'I know, right? It's like a load I've been carrying all my life has lifted.'

Over the years, Anjali spoke often of Dorothy. She shed tears, ranted at the injustice of it all. But right now, her tone carried a minor annoyance, like picking up groceries from an out-of-the-way shop, or getting a plumber to fix the toilet.

'I think some of *this*,' she pointed to her face, 'has its benefits.'

'You don't mean that.'

'I do. Look, if not for this, I would never have spoken to her.'

Jatin couldn't read her face, but her gestures remained unchanged, and the look in her eyes. She meant every word.

'All my life I've wondered what was wrong with my family: why everyone else's parents were different from mine. Why I got more from your mother in that one year I spent with her, than from mine all through my childhood. Now I know.'

Knowing someone. How *do* you know you know someone?

He hadn't recognised his own son. Those pictures of Varun in a drug den, a syringe in hand. His smiling boy, with that open face, the boy who always asked permission, never got into scrapes.

'What's wrong?'

He longed to tell her about all the troubles swimming about in his head: Varun. The Sabharwal case and Rathi. Commissioner Mehra and the divorce. He just wanted to lean in and hold her—he was growing used to the way she looked. It didn't bother him now as much as a week ago.

'It'll do me good to listen, Jatin, trust me.' She waved her hand about her face and the bed. 'A break from thinking about all of this.'

The scar on Jatin's shoulder bothered him, the pain moving down into his arm.

'Varun.' It burst out of him before he could stop it.

'He's in Manila, right?'

He had boasted to her about his son all this time. But today he told her about his son's misadventures, about the photographs, his disbelief at Varun hanging out at a slum with users and dealers. That Radhe was possibly his dealer. Anjali listened as he filled her in on the latest from Lahiri, Radhe, and Chander. It was strange to see her go so still after her earlier animation. It was as if she was far away.

He could hear the distant sound of traffic from the

window. When he couldn't take it anymore, he called her, gently, and she surfaced, as if from a dream. Her medications were taking their toll.

'We can only try our best, Jatin.' She seemed to have lost that upbeat tone she had moments before. 'Children come with their own spirit. They make their own destiny.'

'I didn't know any of it. How could I not know? I've dealt with druggies half my life.'

'You don't see it when you don't expect to. But his friend… Bunty, right?' she said. 'Do you think he got Varun into all this? He is the only one I've seen Varun with.'

'Not Bunty.'

As he uttered them, he realised that those were the very words he would have used for Varun this morning, before he'd seen those photos from Pawan. After he spoke to Varun, he must meet Bunty, talk to Dayal Sisodia if needed. Maya had warned him all along, but he never listened.

Varun needed rehab, and that wouldn't work unless Jatin knew what all his friends were up to. Jatin checked his watch. Three hours to Varun's flight. He needed Anjali's signatures on the permission form for Dr Bhalla before he left.

When he mentioned Nikhil and Sakhi, she sat up. 'What about them? What is it?'

'He hit her. She's here, in the paediatric wing.'

'What do you mean? Is she ok?' She seemed to topple back, and he rushed to her.

'I'll call the nurse.'

'No. I'm ok. Where's Nikhil?'

He explained the options Bhalla had suggested. Nikhil would stay calm this evening on strong medication, even drowsy, and sleep well at night. They needed a measure in place by morning.

'I need to talk to you about this.'

'Sign it for now, and we'll talk tomorrow? I must leave for the airport. Varun lands tonight.'

'All right. Later.'

She signed the papers, her bandaged hand dragging on the page. He looked away. Once she was done, he patted her shoulder and left. Walking away sapped all his strength, because it felt like staggering across the deck of a ship in a storm. Body struggling for balance, he tried to calm his breath. Watching Anjali suffer hurt in a strange way, like nothing he had experienced before.

Lagaye na lagey aur bujhaye na baney: Ghalib's famous words, quoted in so many Bollywood movies, now made grim sense. *Try as you might, love is a fire you may not wilfully light, nor snuff out at your will.*

He recognised the intensity of this from another memory made seventeen years earlier: the time he first held Varun and gave him a drop of honey to suck, following family tradition. It terrified Jatin, his feelings for that tiny human shorter than his forearm, as if his beating heart had suddenly gone for a walk outside his body, with nothing to protect it.

He returned the salute of the security guard on the way out, using the gesture to keep a straight expression, and stumbled out to his car. He needed to put Anjali out of his mind for a while. Varun would land in less than two hours, and Jatin needed to ask him a few hard questions.

49

9 pm on a miserable Christmas Eve. Anjali stared at the large clock in her room, the two hands at perfect ninety degrees.

Don't say 'miserable,' Anjali. You said that the year Nate left you. Look where you are now. It can always get worse.

She had decided to protect her son, and Sakhi had paid the price. At five years old, she lost her parents, and was taken away from her siblings. The family where she thought herself safe put her in the hospital. Where do you find a happy ending when your son hurts a little girl under your care?

Anjali thought of Jatin, so broken up about his son. She remembered the lines she had said to him: *We can only try our best, but children come with their own spirit and they make their own destiny.* She had tried with Nikhil.

No one else should have to pay the price. She couldn't just keep quiet, do nothing.

She slid off the bed, and made her way to the door, with no destination in mind. Outside, the deserted corridor stared back at her, a Christmas tree at the far end, with blinking magenta lights. She set off towards it, not knowing why. All the Christmases of her childhood came back to her, those Christmas trees, the presents from Aunty Viv. She couldn't bring herself to call Vivian anything other than Aunty. Had she never wanted to be called *Mom* in all those years? To Anjali's right, a door marked 'Female'. She turned the knob with her crab-like hands. The toilet was empty, but on top of the basin hung a white-framed mirror. She needed to sit down. Her stomach cramped, her legs were wobbly. She needed to see what Nikhil had done to her.

Having locked the door, she lowered the lid on the toilet seat, and sank down. She took deep breaths, smelling the bleach, stale perfume left by former users, the faint stench of urine and menstrual blood. Her mouth dry, her head empty, she counted to five, and pushed her forearms against the counter to heave herself up. She must do this at one go. *Deep breaths.* She closed her eyes and took a few, her toes cold in hospital slippers.

In the mirror, the right eye looked smaller than the left. This wasn't Anjali Morgan, but a demon-god, a *kijinmen* mask from Japanese theatre. She touched a finger to the bandaged nose. The lips on this face had shifted to the right in a permanent grimace. The neck was a brittle trunk of a sapling at the edge of a desert, its skin peeling. The hair receded, and grew back in ragged clumps. When she turned, the face in the mirror turned too. She ran scarred fingers over her head, stroked the clumps of hair. She tried a smile. The lips broke into a sneer. This is what she'd been doing to everyone in the last week—sneering at them. In the mirror, the image wavered, like a screen on low battery. Her head swam, and she sank down on the toilet seat.

Many breaths and false starts later, she rose and tottered out. She trailed her right forearm on the wall for support, and passed beneath a dozen framed prints and numbered doors before reaching hers, the last one down the corridor. She lay back on the bed, but did not close her eyes. She knew what she would see, the sneering *kijinmen*. Nikhil had done this, probably without meaning to, just as he had hurt Sakhi. Anjali had to see Sakhi, now.

When Vibha came in to check the charts, Anjali asked her if they might visit Sakhi before her nightly injection. She expected Vibha to refuse, but Vibha said she could steal away a few minutes before her shift ended. She dressed Anjali in a hospital coat, and brought a fresh scarf to wrap around her head. They came to a halt in front of the nurses' station at the Children's Ward, and a few queries later, Vibha steered her wheelchair inside. Anjali drew the scarf closer, and lowered her face. If children saw her this late in the evening, it would spook them. She had become a Boogeywoman, a creature harried mothers used to scare their kids into good behaviour. Perversely, this made her smile. Dorothy used to call her 'ugly' and 'witch', especially when she put on make-up or a short skirt, making her feel dirty and wrong, inside out.

Her face now put any ugly witch to shame, and all of Vivian's advice or Dorothy's abuses wouldn't make her any better or worse looking. She sighed and took a deep breath: a soothing massage, but from the inside. Maybe this was what *deep breaths* meant, this sense of 'being', of paying attention to the inside, uncaring of others' opinions, or their definitions. She grinned, remembering her face from the bathroom mirror—her grin was a sneer now, but why should she care? No matter what make-up she used or how many surgeries she went through, she wouldn't get her old face back. If people found her ugly, that was their problem. She must stop worrying about her face. Focus on important things; what Nikhil had done to Sakhi, for instance.

In the dimly lit ward, Anjali glimpsed Sakhi from a distance—eyes closed, head bandaged, body covered under a dark blanket. Vibha moved the wheelchair closer.

With her pale translucent skin, Sakhi appeared drained of blood, her forehead held together by strips of white gauze. Anjali patted Sakhi's hair, and gestured to Vibha to take her back to her room. She didn't want to scare Sakhi if she woke up. Vibha turned the wheelchair around.

'Jali Aunty?'

That voice, so soft and small, and her name, so apt now. A *jali*, burned aunty, yes, that's exactly who she was. Vibha turned the wheelchair around before Anjali could stop her. Anjali closed her eyes and braced for Sakhi's scream, but none came. She opened her eyes to find Sakhi gazing at her.

'*Sar dukh raha hai?*' Anjali said. Vibha stood beside her.

She liked the way her mouth felt around those Hindi words. She asked a specific question, about a headache, requiring a 'Yes' or 'No' answer. A non-scary question, hopefully.

'*Nahin. Apka?*'

This kid's head must hurt under those stitches and bandages. But Sakhi asked after Anjali, her pain. Anjali caught Vibha's eye, who understood the unspoken request, and pushed the wheelchair closer to Sakhi. She walked off to the nurse's station, leaving them alone.

Anjali stroked Sakhi's hair fanned out on the pillow. Thank God they hadn't shaved it off. Her bandaged hands snagged on the hair. They resembled monster limbs, but they comforted this girl. As two orphans, they should stick together. Laughter bubbled inside of her at the thought. *Am I going hysterical?*

'Nikhil Bhaiya was very angry.'

Anjali may not have a mother, but she was one herself, and right at this moment, this girl needed one—she looked like she might cry. Anjali weighed each Hindi word before she said it. One mistake now, and she might hurt Sakhi instead of reassuring her.

'He's different. You know sometimes when you catch a cold, you sneeze?'

'Yes.'

'Can you help it?'

'No.'

'Same thing. Nikhil sometimes gets angry and can't help it. They are treating him.'

Anjali stroked Sakhi's forearm in circles, using her own right pinkie finger, the only unhurt part of her hands.

'Are you sleepy?'

'No.'

Sakhi's droopy eyelids said otherwise. Anjali kept stroking the strands of Sakhi's hair, combing them out. The rhythm soothed her, and in turn, it seemed to soothe Sakhi. Sakhi's eyes fluttered closed but she opened them again.

'Go to sleep. I can tell you a story if you like.'

A child sobbed somewhere behind her on one of the beds, but she kept her eyes on Sakhi. Anjali's face hurt and her jaws felt numb. When she lifted her gaze again, she thought she spotted a shadow. Her eyes burned. She began the story of Little Red Riding Hood. In the end, Sakhi's eyes were wide open.

'Why did Red's mother send her alone into the woods?'

Anjali never asked that question as a child. The person she thought of as her mother would send her into the jungle, so it seemed natural Red's mother might, too.

'Didn't she have a brother? Radhe Bhaiya would have killed the wolf.'

Anjali's lips felt dry, her mouth gummy, but she forged on.

'Radhe Bhaiya would go with you. And others too.'

Anjali thought she caught a movement from the corner of her eye, but she wasn't sure where. Her mind seemed to play tricks on her. Medication and exhaustion—she needed sleep.

'Can Nikhil Bhaiya come here?'

That soft, whispered question sucked the breath out of Anjali.

'You have nurses here. Doctors. Outside, you have guards. No one can come in here.'

'Merry Christmas, Jali Aunty.'

'Merry Christmas! Who told you…?'

'Maya Aunty. She said tomorrow is Christmas. We say Merry Christmas to everyone and get gifts.'

'Yes, we do.'

'Will I get a Christmas gift?'

'You will.' Vibha had returned. She stood beside Anjali's wheelchair.

'Thank you, Nurse Chachi.'

The two words made no sense together, the first in English,

the other in Hindi. Sakhi must have thought 'Nurse' was a name, so she called her 'Nurse C*hachi*'. Nurse Aunty. Vibha turned the wheelchair away as Anjali waved goodbye.

The curtain behind Sakhi seemed to flutter and move. Anjali's overworked brain had begun to hallucinate. She kept waving towards Sakhi, till she couldn't see the girl any longer. With no parents or siblings, all alone in her hospital bed on Christmas Eve, Sakhi had cobbled together a new family.

Change your words, Anjali. Learn from Sakhi. Watch how she changes her words, and so her world. Anjali drew in a long, steady breath. *Change your words, reconfigure,* she repeated to herself. Breath and words coming together, that was the secret. She must teach Nikhil this trick once she mastered it herself. She must figure out what was good for him, what he needed, not what she needed of him.

50

The heaviness, Jatin hadn't felt it in years, not since Ma's death. That weight which used to press down on his eyelids and gather in his stomach, had returned. He wanted to touch, be touched. He craved Anjali's body next to his. So many years since he had woken up next to someone.

Anjali bent over him on the bed, with her pillowy, golden breasts, pebbled nipples. His palms cradled each breast, flicking at the wet nipples with his thumb. He heard her soft moans in the semi-dark of the morning. Behind her, a Christmas tree, its lights dipping and blinking.

Jatin sat up with a start. She was burned, and here he was on Christmas morning, dreaming like a pervert. The bedside clock showed 5.10 am. Two hours of trying to sleep. Last night he had missed Varun's flight. Right after Jatin left the hospital, Dayal Sisodia called, quickly followed by a call from Jatin's father-in-law. New intelligence suggested the possibility of a terrorist attack on certain locations in New Delhi. The Home Minister had convened an emergency meeting—the police must consider beefing up security measures. The minister stepped out by midnight, but the meeting continued till 3.00 am. Jatin had called Pawan, requested him to set a watch on Varun, follow the boy if he left the Mehra mansion.

Jatin threw off the blanket and swung out of bed. He needed to get a head start on the day, sort out all the piled-up paper work and then talk to Varun, grill him about Radhe. Mehra had been unpleasant during the meeting last night, second guessing Jatin's decisions, overruling any suggestion he made, making it clear he would make things difficult. Jatin needed to nail Lahiri on the Sujni case, find the other man who ran away. The woman from Lahiri's car, Roli, had died—so a murder charge might stick. But first, he needed that puny rat, Radhe, who continued to elude Grewal's men, and Pawan's informers.

After a quick shower, he took his time brushing his teeth. His eyes felt sandy and his breath reeked of the dozen or so cups of tea he'd tossed down in an effort to stay focused last night. He looked exactly the way he felt—lost and cold. Laddoo, his son's dog, pattered into his room and looked up at him with its large, swimmy eyes. Jatin bent down to pat her.

***

The traffic signal loomed ahead, an armless scarecrow with a single red eye. One hand on the steering wheel, Jatin stared at the tall, straight Ashoka trees by the roadside, and the outlines of men waiting at the bus stop under yellow street lights, muffled against the fog at 6.30 am. His phone buzzed on the dashboard.

'Varun just left the Mehra mansion, sir.' Pawan's voice sounded hoarse, but alert. 'My man is following him now.'

Jatin parked his car by the roadside. Varun was not an early riser; he went to the gym in the evenings.

'Which way?'

'Outer Ring Road, sir.'

The Mehra mansion was a few minutes' drive away, and the Outer Ring Road meant Varun could be headed home. Varun had avoided his father for ten days now. Why rush home this early?

Jatin turned his car and drove back, but he parked two streets behind his own. Careful not to make any noise, Jatin took off his shoes, shut the dog in Varun's room, and waited. The guest room opposite his study gave a clear view of his son's door.

Laddoo whined from inside the room when Varun came in, but despite a week of being away, Varun didn't pay the dog any mind. Strange. He unlocked the study instead. Jatin had given a copy of his study keys to Drishti, but not Varun. He clenched his teeth. He couldn't let a sound escape, not yet.

Varun flicked on a flashlight, unlocked the safe, hauled out a few files and stacked them on the table. He reached in further and took out a black bag.

Jatin wanted to step out, but stayed crouched in the darkness. Switching his phone to silent, he snapped pictures of his son. The boy's hands shook, but not from nerves. Jatin had recently seen this shaking on Chander, Lahiri's man.

Varun dropped his phone, picked it up off the floor. He scrambled around in the bag, and took out a wad of notes.

Sweat soaked Jatin's shirt as he watched his son stuff the money into his schoolbag, and rearrange the files. Jatin ducked out of sight, and heard his son lock the safe, then the room. Varun opened his door, and for a while Jatin heard Varun with his dog. Jatin closed his eyes and relaxed all his muscles one by one, even his jaws, a calming trick he had learned over the years. The main door closed and the gate clanged shut.

Varun had looked like he craved a hit. This early in the morning, he might well be on the way to meet his dealer. Radhe. Lahiri had mentioned that Radhe had stolen a big stash from him.

Jatin called Pawan. While on the phone, he put on his shoes, stepped out and locked the door. On the street, Varun's bike revved off.

'Varun is on his way.' Jatin's breath fogged in the cold, damp air. 'Tell your man not to lose him.'

'Bunty just stepped out of his home in jogging clothes, sir. But he's pacing in the park, not running.'

'How do you know?'

'You asked me to stand by, sir, and I thought maybe Varun might come here, to Bunty's place. I was with Beeji at the hospital. The hospital is not far, so I decided to come and keep watch.'

'Well done.'

In the cold silence, Jatin set off, his long coat flailing in the morning mist. His phone rang as he started the car and reversed it out of the street.

'Sir, Varun is headed this way, he just turned into the Rajouri Garden Road.'

That road did indeed lead to the Sisodia Mansion in West Punjabi Bagh, a posh colony where at least two security men guarded each bungalow.

'Someone is bound to recognise my car in that neighbourhood.'

'Let me follow them out, sir. I'm on my bike.'

Jatin parked at a roadside tea stall, ordered a cup and settled down to wait for Pawan's update. On the opposite side of the road, an old man in a pugree hunkered in blankets inside his tent, smoke billowing out of his shiny brass hookah. The smoggy air carried a chill, but it was colder still in Jatin's heart. He wanted to close his eyes, and open them again to find everything as before. Anjali unhurt, Varun still the polite, obedient son. He sipped the too-hot tea, scalding his lips and tongue. He put the tea on the dashboard and pictured what might go down in the next hour.

Varun and Bunty—both as tall as him, well-built. Varun, a karate brown-belt. If they headed together for a delivery, it could mean they were wary. If it was Radhe, he might not come alone. Jatin checked his gun. But he didn't need a gun battle, nor even a fist-fight—he must keep this quiet. He had Pawan, but they needed backup. Pawan's man? No. someone Jatin could trust, who lived within a ten- to fifteen-minute driving distance. Dilawar. Grewal, but he stayed too far away in South Delhi. The only other person he could count on: Kusum. Jatin tended to keep women away from the main action while planning operations, but given the time on hand, he saw little choice.

The traffic on the road beside him snarled up, and the fog cleared. 7.15 am. He needed to nab his son and Bunty with very little fuss. He could not call Mehra. Dayal? No, better handle everything first. Dayal and Jatin went on golfing weekends together, but Dayal never left him in any doubt that this was a kindness, a favour. Jatin must play this very carefully—make sure Dayal understood that Jatin had not put Bunty at risk.

His phone pinged a message: *Behind the Delhi Junction railway station. The burned jewellery shop.*

Jatin knew the shop before it got gutted in a fire several years ago. The owners had let the burned walls stand, bricks and doors missing, banyan saplings sprouting out of windows.

Switching on his hands-free, he called Kusum, asked her to get Dilawar, and told her the reason he needed it kept unofficial. Without missing a beat, she offered to bring a batch mate who owned a second-hand car. A woman, big-built, Kusum said. Jatin said yes, and to hurry up and pick up Dilawar on the way. Better two women, than no one.

Despite being a woman, Kusum grabbed Lahiri and his driver, his own voice taunted him, *but the famous Jatin Bhatt, a man and a ranking police officer, failed to make an arrest.* Dilawar had helped her, but Kusum had acquitted herself very well on the field in the last few weeks.

He found a left turn into an old alley, more potholes than road, but a shorter route to the Delhi Junction. Driving with one hand, he washed down two aspirins with a swig of water, re-checked his gun. The car bumped along the thin, winding road and Jatin swerved every once in a while to avoid schoolchildren, goats, chickens, stray dogs.

As Jatin made the final turn on the road behind the Delhi Junction railway station, his phone buzzed again. Pawan said the boys were on the other side, much further down from the gutted jewellery shop. Jatin could drive all the way up without alerting them. He reached for his gun, slid it into the holster. Pawan sneaked out from one of the doors, and jumping over piles of glass and trash, reached the car before Jatin could step out of it.

'They are waiting for someone.' Pawan said. 'This way, sir.'

Jatin padded up the littered steps, and walked through the back door of the abandoned shop—floor tiles cracked in places, cigarette butts, rusted spoons, crumpled papers, foil, and empty bottles in the corners. They took the broken stairs up to the first floor, past the walls covered in chalk and paint, swearwords, ugly stick figures in violent sexual positions labelled with lewd Hindi words.

Peering out from one of the windows, Jatin spotted them. His handsome son sat at the window of a building opposite, schoolbag slung across his shoulder, Bunty beside him. Both took drags from a cigarette, passing it to each other. Builders had abandoned the two-storeyed shop house mid-construction. The walls were all brick on the outside with rotting door and window frames, no panes. A huge banyan tree, dark roots hanging from its branches hid their side of the building from the main road. Their faces unsmiling, the two of them sat near a window at the lower floor. They kept glancing at all the entry points.

'They look worried.' Jatin said. 'One of us should stay here. To keep an eye on their movements, and all approaches to that building.'

Pawan shifted on his feet, crossed and uncrossed his forearms, very different from his usual calm.

'You think we can't handle it?' Jatin said.

'No, sir. We'll be five of us, and they won't know we're here.'

'But?'

'I can get hold of the boys, sir, and between your driver, Kusum Netam and her friend, they should be able to take care of any others.' Pawan pointed at Jatin's gun. 'But whoever they're expecting may have guns, sir. You can cover us from the outside.'

Jatin stared at the two boys at the window, their faces bent together, lighting their smokes.

'It will be easier to handle them later if they don't spot you now, sir,' Pawan said. 'Bunty is Dayal Sisodia's son. Dayal sir is your friend, but…And if they meet you, they'll…Then there's Drishti Didi and Mehra sir. I'll make sure no one is hurt. Varun is my nephew, too. *Beeji*'s grandson.'

Pawan made sense. The faster they were able to wrap this up and get the boys out of here, the better.

'All right. Once we have them, everyone can go to the farmhouse. We will have space and quiet to talk to them, and I can call Dayal.'

'I will organise with Kusum Netam, sir.'

'If the boys are not to see me, you take them to the farmhouse.' Jatin handed Pawan his car keys. 'I'll meet you there.'

Dayal Sisodia and Commissioner Mehra would like someplace discreet, and his farmhouse at Sainik Farms was quiet enough to fit the bill.

Kusum messaged to say that Dilawar and her friend waited across the main road for instructions. After Jatin directed them to their positions, Pawan asked to go join them.

'Once I spot whoever is coming to meet the boys, I'll go down, and take position behind that door.' Jatin pointed. 'Keep an eye on your phone.'

Jatin rotated his shoulder in a bid to ease the stiffness. *Keep your head in the freezer*, he reminded himself, *there will be time enough later to think about your son.*

The air reeked of alcohol, ganja and urine. From another window, he could see the Pul Mithai flyover. No matter how many times police raided the area, filthy beggars high on drugs came back to sleep under it. This place seemed a country away from his green, peaceful street in Punjabi Bagh. Yet only a few kilometres separated the two. On the other side of the flyover was the Pul Mithai slum, where police had found one of the women in a trash bag. Ram Sharan's body was found at Delhi Junction. Once he sorted this entire Varun episode, Jatin needed to add more pins to the Delhi map at Vigil. His shoulder hurt, and the pain seeped down into his arm. He focused on the spasm. Better that pain than the anguish of what lay ahead on this bleak Christmas day.

A teen stepped out of the straggly bushes near the railroad and made his way towards Bunty and Varun, followed by a tall man. Jatin checked his gun, and hurried downstairs. Bending low so as to keep out of sight, he ran across to the other building, and took his position alongside an open doorway. His hunch was right. The boy was Radhe.

51

Fareeda ended her counselling session with Anjali, and stood up to leave.

'Dorothy is here,' she said, almost as an afterthought. 'She wanted to know if it would be okay for her to see you.'

That was unlike the Dorothy Anjali knew. She never asked permission, believed she knew what was best for everyone.

'She's at your clinic?'

'Yes.' Fareeda picked up her files. 'She is leaving India tonight.'

Dorothy. The woman who had hated her with all her heart, faked being her mother.

'Ask her to come in.'

Mom came in a few moments later, thin and upright as ever. Wait. Remember the change of words. Not Mom any more.

'I came to say bye.'

Anjali and Dorothy had never really talked, other than to say *pass the butter* or *I'll be back late* or *we've run out of milk*. Her father had mediated between the two.

Questions swirled in Anjali's head, but none of them made it past her lips. Fear took hold, as if she were a child again, and Dorothy a huge, looming figure. Anjali had shrunk, after all, still needing help with eating and dressing. Dorothy had changed too. She still wore no make-up or jewellery, her gaunt white face bare, but something in her seemed softer today.

'You've got good friends here.' Dorothy patted Anjali's bed. 'You'll be ok.'

Without another word, she walked back towards the door.

'Did she want to tell me?' The question burst out of Anjali. 'When she died? Was she in a lot of pain?'

Dorothy stilled. She took slow steps back.

Vivian had died after two months in the hospital. Anjali had wanted to visit, but the thought of Dorothy had stopped her. Aunty Viv was dying anyway. Anjali wanted to remember her the way she was when Anjali left Florida—full of life, dancing around at parties. She had missed saying her final goodbye to the woman who gave birth to her.

'You didn't let her?'

'They kept her sedated, on pain medication.'

'Did she ask for me?'

'I could tell you she did, but the truth is they diagnosed her much too late. Most of the time, she slept.'

'Were you with her?'

'Yes.' Dorothy dragged a chair and sank into it. 'The hardest two months of my life. I watched my sister die at forty-seven as her body turned against her. You begin imagining those things happening to you. Putting yourself in the past tense gives you perspective.'

'You didn't call to tell me.'

'I sank into another depression. Your father informed you.'

Anjali turned away to the blank wall, and tried to picture her mother, her real one on her deathbed.

'Why did you come this time?'

'After your father died, I could not grieve. The man I had loved had become a shadow. I wanted to put things to rest, I suppose. I felt tired. It has been hard, praying, singing at the church, organising bake sales, but hating him. Staying angry. With him. With Vivian who was long gone. You. I just wanted some peace.'

'Have you found it?' Anjali didn't know where the question came from.

'There's no on and off switch to emotions. But I'm aware of what I've done, yes. And I'm sorry, Anjali. Just wanted to get that off my chest.'

Anjali didn't reply, because there was nothing to say. Maybe some day, but all she felt right now was an emptiness.

Dorothy stood up. 'It occurred to me last night. All my life I've given you advice, told you what not to do, been convinced you will make mistakes. But I've never blessed you.' Dorothy placed her hand on Anjali's new-growing hair. 'Be well. Merry Christmas.'

This time, with brisk steps and without looking back, Dorothy Gupta, the woman Anjali had called *Mom* all her life, left the room.

So many of her waking hours and even her dreams spent trying to bond with this woman, unable to set her aside. But as Dorothy walked out, a sense of lightness flooded Anjali. Nothing tied her down anymore, no one to hold her back.

She had seen the world through Dorothy's eyes, all these years. Nothing matched her standards, because they were not her own. It was Dorothy who craved perfection, who advocated piety, who saw a lack in Anjali.

No Anjali Morgan now, other than on paper. And what did papers matter? It was this easy. All along. Anjali sank into the pillows, and toyed with a few words. She tried to apply the lessons learned from Sakhi—reconfigure words, their meanings. *Grown-up. Possibilities. Here I am. Anonymous. Not afraid. Motherhood. Independent. New Year.*

Here I am, she whispered to herself, and sat up in bed. She would no longer look at Nikhil with Dorothy's eyes. He was not perfect, but she didn't need perfection, only her son. Bhalla was right all along—it was how she saw him, wanted to shape him that made him angry. If they wanted to keep Nikhil at an institution, she would find the very best one, a place where they would give him ways to cope with his autism, calm his anger, and give him the tools to interact in society. Where she could be present for him all along if he needed her. She rang the bell to call the nurse. She must speak with Jatin, find a way forward.

52

When Pawan met Radhe Shyam Misra for the first time, the boy had wanted to pick a fight.

Today, sitting in a windowless room under a dull celing lamp at Jatin sir's farmhouse at Sainik Farms, Radhe slumped in his chair. His eyes stared out from dark pits. His shoulders drooped, and he sat with one leg wrapped around the other, as if trying to hold off peeing.

'Where were you all this time, Radhe? Why did you run from Hridayog?'

With a man the size of Dilawar looming over him in a small room, Pawan expected the fifteen-year-old to crumple. But it didn't affect the boy, because he didn't look up. Kusum sat beside him, making notes. Radhe didn't take any notice of her, either.

'The smack we found on you is enough for you to go to jail for years.'

For Radhe, a juvenile, drug charges did not carry a jail sentence, only a stay at a rehabilitation home. Radhe must know this because he had worked as a courier, but he didn't say a word.

Pawan's phone vibrated and Maya's name came up on

the screen, but he ignored it. He could not tell Maya his whereabouts till Jatin sir let him. Pawan needed to check the progress of the downloads. Jatin sir wanted all the boys' phones downloaded. Radhe did not have a phone on him, and his friend's phone took less than ten minutes to copy. Bunty and Varun's smartphones presented the challenge: strong passwords and encrypted folders.

Pawan zipped up his jacket against the chill in the room. What was he even doing here? He needed to go back to his Beeji. Time to try a different tack with Radhe.

'Don't you want to meet Sakhi?'

For the first time, Radhe raised his head.

'I saw her yesterday with madamji.'

Impossible. Both Maya and Sakhi were at the hospital.

'Where?'

'With the tall madamji.' Radhe said in clear, Bihari-accented Hindi.

Kusum and Dilawar stepped forward from the shadows, their faces keen. Radhe shivered despite his jacket, but Pawan recognised this kind of shivering. This boy would sweat in the coolest room before retching, unless he got his hands on his next fix.

Radhe shut up, fear of having spoken too much plain in his hunched shoulders. His feet danced, and he stared at them.

'Either you talk or I can leave you with this man here.' Pawan beckoned to Dilawar, who stomped forward.

'The one who was with me today,' Radhe looked up, but did not meet Pawan's eyes, 'he got me into the hospital. Manoj's man. Manoj is in lockup now.'

'Why did he help you?'

'They want Sakhi: she listens to me; she would have come with me quietly.'

Radhe continued and Kusum recorded him on her phone.

After his mother vanished, Radhe promised to sell Sakhi to Manoj. He received an advance of five thousand rupees, which he spent on food and on buying drugs from Lahiri. He was to hand her over to Manoj the day he and Sakhi got picked up by the police.

Pawan remembered Sakhi's face, her smile when she ran to him, yelling 'Pawan Uncle!'

'So why didn't you take her yesterday, if you managed to get into the hospital?'

'She was very hurt.' Radhe bowed his head. 'I couldn't carry her out without alerting the nurses.'

Radhe shifted in his chair. Lahiri and Manoj, two men who exploited this boy, and turned him into this: a brother who sold his little sister for drugs. Pawan couldn't allow himself to feel sorry for the boy. He asked Radhe about his village, their journey to Delhi. Radhe answered in short sentences, talked about his father's death, and the evening his mother disappeared. Now that he was lulled Pawan asked Radhe the question that mattered. He may not have done it, but he had the motive.

'You were the one who threw the acid on madamji, weren't you?'

'No, saabji! *Kasam se*, I didn't know it would hurt her!'

This was not what Pawan had expected.

'So you did throw the acid on her?' Pawan stood up, making Radhe quail in his chair.

'They told me it wouldn't hurt.' Radhe said, 'Just scare her. Then Sakhi will return to me. I swear, saabji.'

They. More than one person was behind this. But if he asked Radhe a straight question, he would clam up again. So Pawan kept quiet for a while, handed Radhe a glass of water. Radhe did not reach for it.

'Where did you buy the acid?' Pawan said.

'I didn't!'

This time Radhe lay his head on the table and broke down. Pawan let him sob it out.

'Did Chander buy it?' Chander had gone along to threaten Anjaliji.

Radhe shook his head.

'Did someone pay you to do it?' Pawan stood up and paced beside Radhe. 'Lahiri? Manoj? Someone at Sanjay Colony? Your brother, Ram Sharan?'

At the mention of Ram Sharan, Radhe peered all around, as if searching for someone.

'Do you realise Ram Sharan is dead?'

Like his Sensei said, *If you must break something, you must keep hitting it till it is broken.* He didn't want to destroy this teenaged boy, but he had to dig out his secret, no matter the cost.

Radhe stood up, ready to run, but Pawan pushed him back down on the chair. Radhe clamped his hands to his ears.

'We found his body in two parts, Radhe.' Pawan pried Radhe's hands from his ears so the boy heard him, 'The train cut Ram open at the chest. There was a lot of blood.'

'They killed Ram Bhaiya.' Radhe's voice rose, 'I can hear the train engine all the time. Put me away, take me to jail. Just stop this, please. Make it go away.'

53

The arrest had turned into a blur for Jatin. They had rushed in through different doors and windows. Kusum pointed her gun at them, her friend stood behind Radhe, Dilawar caught Bunty by the arm, and Pawan got Varun. Bunty struggled, but Pawan knocked him out.

Jatin hadn't been able to get a clear shot, but Kusum shot Radhe's friend in the leg, and as suddenly as it had begun, it was all over. Jatin had directed the arrest of his own son, but it didn't seemed real.

His shoulder throbbed now. For a moment he stopped under the banyan tree, and stared up at all the aerial roots reaching for the ground. One day they would become trunks, and support the tree, their frail appearance now not to be mistaken for their lack of strength. All his life he thought women weak, exotic beings in need of his protection: his mother, his sister, his wife, lover. Today, two women helped bring down Radhe and his friend, and helped rescue his son. Maya had wanted to join the force; he had stopped her. She had warned him, time and time again, of Varun's excesses, but he chose to ignore her. Witnessing his son steal, stalking and arresting him, and arranging for his phone to be hacked—this was the beginning of Jatin's punishment.

Maybe Maya was right all along. Bunty brought Varun to this hell-hole, ready to poison himself for the sake of a ten-minute high. Jatin coughed, unable to keep in his queasiness, the tea he had drunk a while ago roiling in his empty stomach. He strode through the shrubbery towards the main road to try and find a cab.

Adrenalin leached out of him, replaced by shock and shame at the morning's events. *Dil hi toh hai na sang-o-khist, dard se bhar na aaye kyon?* He murmured. *A heart is a heart not a brick or stone*, Ghalib rightly said, *why should it not brim over with pain?*

Grewal called Jatin just as he got into a taxi from Delhi Junction.

'Lahiri can talk,' he said, 'I think you should meet him. I'm with him now.'

Jatin considered refusing, but decided against it. The hospital where they had kept Lahiri was on the way to Sainik Farms, and Jatin needed a chat with Grewal anyway. Radhe and his friend needed to be put away, and Grewal could also give advice on how best to deal with the problem of Varun and Bunty's addiction.

Grieving over losing his polite, well-behaved *gabru jawan* to drugs could wait.

Lahiri had shrunken since Jatin first saw him at Hridayog. Tubes connected his arms and chest to beeping machines. Jatin veered between wanting to punch the man and feeling sorry for him. 'The woman we found in your car died two days ago,' he informed Lahiri, 'you will be charged with murder. You also carried an unlicensed gun in your car.'

Lahiri said he would tell Jatin about the woman in his car, if Jatin took care of him—a charge sheet for a reduced sentence for the drug case, and witness protection. The 'protection' bit sounded interesting—it meant Lahiri had powerful enemies. Politicos or drug lords, or both. In Delhi, they often went to the same parties, checked in at the same spas.

'I can't promise anything.' Jatin sat back, folding his arms. 'You tell me all and then we can talk.'

Lahiri repeated his earlier story. He didn't know who the other guy in his car was, but that man had warned Lahiri to keep his mouth shut. He'd instructed Lahiri to talk to Jatin Bhatt alone and no one else if he wanted to live. No matter what happened.

'I tried to talk to you,' Lahiri cried, his tone accusing, 'but you won't listen.'

'How did you know I was Jatin Bhatt?'

'He showed me your picture on his phone.'

'My picture? When?'

'When we were driving. He told me if I told anyone about the woman, he would get me arrested for my business.'

'But why my picture?'

'He said I had nothing to fear if I didn't open my mouth. That you will save me if I ever got caught. Protection, he said.'

So the man had offered Lahiri police protection. It wasn't common, but it happened. Some policemen took *hafta*, just like goons. Jatin had never been directly involved, so how did this man know about him? Why would he think Jatin would protect Lahiri?

'What was his voice like? A young man? Old? Did he sound like he was from Sanjay Colony?'

'Why don't you ask my driver? He knows that man, I'm sure.'

'He says he does not. He says you asked him to go there. That man was your friend, he says.'

'He's lying!' Lahiri sobbed now, his voice high. 'Because of him I am in this mess. I always kept my business small, never got into trouble with women, and now...'

'You must have seen that man.'

'When I first went in, they had a dim light on. Later he wrapped a muffler on his face. I did not see him, I swear.'

'Was he young?'

'He sounded young. Younger than me or you. He said you will know. He spoke English. You will get me out of here, he said, if I talk to you alone.'

This man, whoever he was, knew Jatin, carried his picture in his phone. Dread weighed Jatin's stomach. Was he from the police, is that how he knew how to burn the women's faces, and dump them far away from their homes, to avoid police detection? If he was so confident Jatin would help him, why did he run?

Grewal, in a t-shirt and trousers, waited outside. Jatin told Grewal about the morning's events, leaving nothing out. Shame and anger warred within him as he spoke of Varun. Grewal didn't reply, but placed his arm around Jatin's shoulder.

'We have to bring Lahiri to the court now,' he said, 'and also the others. We can't keep them in lockup much longer without a charge sheet. Your father-in-law has made enquiries.'

'I know.' Jatin entered the cab, 'Just let me sort out this mess with Varun today.'

On the way back to Sainik Farms, his phone beeped with a message from Maya: *The DNA of Lahiri's driver is a match to the rape kit on Roli. No match with Lahiri or Manoj.*

Maya had come through, rushing out the results in less than a week. The fat *babumoshai* spoke the truth when he said he didn't molest that woman they found in his car boot.

54

'Do your best.' Pawan patted his cousin on the shoulder. 'Jatin sir is on his way.'

His cousin hadn't expected the phones to contain folders with high-level encryption and passwords. To crack those, they needed additional software, and more time.

Bunty was asleep with a headache, but he would wake up soon, and start kicking up a fuss. Varun had kept his voice low so far, but he demanded his phone.

Pawan hurried back down the corridor, to Radhe's room. The farmhouse was a rambling old bungalow, built by Jatin sir's father. Jatin sir got married here. Pawan's very first memory of Maya was from Drishti and Jatin sir's wedding reception held on the lawns outside. He was five years old, Maya a skinny girl of nine. She laughed, wore normal clothes, fancy frocks that showed her arms and legs. The rooms stayed shut for most of the year now, other than on weekends when Drishti Didi called some of her friends. The air smelled stale.

Pawan had requested Kusum to take over the talk with Radhe. The boy loved his mother, had lost her recently. Maybe a woman could get through to him. Pawan hated to do this, but they needed to find out exactly who got Anjali attacked. Lahiri or Manoj? Or both? Pawan could not afford any mistakes this time; he needed Jatin sir to trust him again.

He drew a breath and entered the room. Kusum sat next to Radhe, with water, a cup of tea, biscuits set on the table.

Pawan sat on a packing box behind Radhe, and let Kusum continue. Radhe sipped tea, holding the cup with shaky hands.

'Radhe.' Kusum's Hindi copied Radhe's Bihari accent. 'You know that whoever made you do this, they are to blame. If we don't catch them, you will be in a lot of trouble. A juvenile home is not as safe as you think.'

Radhe put the cup down and hid his face in his hands.

'Tell us, and we will make sure they are punished.' Kusum reached out and touched Radhe's hand.

'They said they will kill me.' Radhe's voice took on a defeated, hollow tone. 'They will, madamji. They killed many people before, Chander told me.'

'We can protect you.'

Radhe bowed his head, and started off in half-whispered Hindi.

'Chander is related to my father. He introduced Ram Bhaiya to them. Chander met these rich boys at a rock concert in one of the college festivals. He used to deliver drugs there, and made friends with them.'

If Radhe was telling the truth, Chander had not told Grewal the whole story.

'They went out together,' Radhe continued, 'along with Deenu, who worked for Lahiri as his driver sometimes. Ram Bhaiya and I sat with them in the evenings at roadside restaurants. They paid. *Bade aadmi*, madamji, we liked their style.' Radhe smiled for the first time, 'Sometimes we got their old clothes, got to ride their bikes. In return we saved a little extra for them. A little here, a little there.'

Radhe drummed his fingers on the table.

'After I lost Sakhi, Manoj's men came after me. Ram Bhaiya used to protect me, but he had gone, just like Mai. Chander said they knew where Ram Bhaiya was.'

Radhe had gone along, but not before taking with him a stash of drugs from Lahiri, and hiding it. Once he reached Madipur, he found that they held Ram Sharan locked up in a room. When he said he didn't have the drugs on him, they locked him up, too.

'Why did they lock up Ram Sharan?'

'They had a fight.'

'What about?'

'Ram Bhaiya won't tell me. But it was bad, he said. Best for me not to know.'

'What are their names? Who are these boys?'

'Vicky and Vish.'

Pawan held on to the table. The room spun for a second. This had to be a mistake. Vicky was Varun's pet name at school, and Bunty sometimes went by Vish, a shortened version of his formal name, Vishal Singh Sisodia. Pawan stood up. This *could not be* Varun. Yet, Radhe knew Varun well. They were in that drug den together; he had met Varun today to sell him drugs.

'Vicky and Vish. Who are they?' Kusum said, 'Do you know their full names?'

'You brought Vicky and Vish here this morning.' Radhe

looked surprised. 'I needed money to pay Manoj back, so I agreed to sell to them. Manoj's man wanted the money straightaway.' Radhe shuddered. 'I was happy about that, saabji. I would never meet Vish and Vicky alone.'

Pawan looked up at Dilawar and Kusum. They wanted Radhe to stop. Pawan wanted Radhe to stop, but Radhe now seemed determined to get it all off his chest.

'Vicky gave me the bottle, saabji. He said it won't hurt madamji, and he gave me money. I was too scared to do it, but he sent Chander with me to make sure I didn't back out at the last minute. He paid us both. Ten thousand rupees each.'

Pawan sank down on the chair, and put his hands on his lap to hide their trembling. *You cannot let fear win*, his Sensei said, but Pawan was afraid. Afraid all of this was true. That this wasn't the mad ramble of a drug addict. Everything fit, though Pawan didn't want it to. Why would Varun get Anjaliji attacked?

'Chander was with you when you did it?' Kusum said.

'He talked to madamji. We didn't like it when she shouted at us when we went to her clinic. I was angry too. *Kasam se*, I didn't know it would hurt her that much.'

'What happened to Ram Sharan?' Kusum asked, her forehead covered with sweat, her finger on the recorder button of her phone.

Dilawar coughed once, then tamped it down. In the small room, Radhe's sniffles and his jerky, Bihari-accented Hindi were the only sounds.

'They let him live because he told them he had a stash of smack hidden away. He told me he did, too. But they lost patience. Vish hit us all the time. Vicky too. What Vish asked, Vicky did. Ram Bhaiya and I tried to run away that day, and Vish shot at us with his gun. I managed to hide because I am small, but Ram Bhaiya ran into…into that train.'

Radhe's head sank into his arms on the table, and this time, Pawan left him alone.

While everyone waited for Anjaliji at dinner that evening, Varun and Bunty coordinated the attack on her. Later, they ran around the vicinity of the cake shop, trying to buy water and salt. All this time, Varun had walked around, life as usual, worked on his karate practice, went to Manila.

Maya's nephew. Drishti Didi's son. Beeji's grandson. How would all these women cope with this? At seventeen, just a boy. Someone must talk to Jatin sir, but Pawan didn't want to be the one. A strangled sound, and a bump made him turn.

Jatin sir stood at the door.

55

Jatin checked the picture gallery on his phone, his feet up on the kitchen table. He scrolled down the snapshots of Varun, the safe ajar behind him. Varun and Bunty. Maya and Drishti, posing together on the night of the party. Varun's thumbs in the Devil's sign behind Bunty. He turned the phone to silent and shoved it into his pocket.

The people Radhe spoke about. Other people. Not Varun. What Radhe said about Bunty and Varun, not true. Impossible. Stealing, drugs, these Jatin understood—Varun was young, and the young can be stupid—the hatred, the viciousness of the attack, why would Varun hate Anjali so much?

Because of you, Jatin's own voice taunted him, *you laughed at her. You said Varun was too young to remember. He has used your sins to attack her.* The hush money piling up all these years had funded Varun's addiction, and the attack on Anjali. She lay suffering in the hospital because Jatin's son wanted to punish her.

It wasn't her son, as he had suspected for so long, but his.

Jatin lowered his head on the kitchen table, and tried to collect himself. He looked up when he heard a knock.

'Could you please come with me?' Pawan stood at the kitchen door. 'We have managed the download.'

He looked pale, his forehead shiny with sweat.

'Anything interesting?'

'You need to see this yourself, sir.' Pawan's voice shook.

Pawan took him to the computer and showed him the button to click in order to scroll down. On the screen, a selfie—Varun and Bunty. Then another, Varun, Bunty, Chander, and Lahiri's driver. Shirtless pictures of Varun and Bunty, comparing their abs and biceps. The next was another selfie with the four of them, bending over a woman. The woman wore no clothes. Bruises coloured her thighs and stomach. Jatin turned to Pawan, to find himself alone. Pawan had left.

He made himself look. Varun and Bunty bending over her, laughing, their hands on her breasts. The woman's eyes shut, her mouth swollen, drool escaping her lips. The next picture of Lahiri's driver pouring a liquid from a can on the woman. Jatin couldn't tell from the picture if the woman was unconscious or dead. His hands shook, but his gaze did not stir from the screen. With the sort of helpless fascination of someone watching a horrific road accident, he kept scrolling. So many pictures, selfies and other posed photographs, candid shots. Always with a naked, bruised woman in a dark room somewhere, on a small bed, with men's hands on her breasts, her thighs, Jatin turned away for a moment, but forced himself to look back, scroll through each picture. The eyes of the men were red in most of the pictures. Varun smiled and made victory signs, as if posing for photos on a family vacation.

56

The physiotherapist greeted Anjali when she woke up on Christmas afternoon. She relished the movement in her fingers. They had recovered enough for her to type on a big keyboard, where she could respond to a few emails. The physiotherapist chatted with Anjali about Bollywood gossip: which star dated who, who cheated on their spouse. All of it seemed so far away, as if Anjali had slipped into an alternate universe, one that smelled of disinfectants the cleaners used, the coconut oil the nurses massaged her healing scars with, where the loudest sound was the honk of a car in the parking lot outside.

Dr Singh would operate on her once again by the end of the week, and afterwards they would keep her in an induced coma. She needed to speak to Jatin before that, ask for his help with Nikhil, and talk to him about his divorce. She hadn't heard from Jatin the entire day, despite asking the nurse, and even the doctor, to get in touch with him. She'd spoken with Maya, but Jatin wasn't picking his sister's calls either.

When Vibha announced a visitor a while later, Anjali expected Jatin. Typical of him to not pick up calls, and then just show up.

'It is a Commissioner D.M. Mehra,' Vibha said.

What did Mehra want with her? He'd made his dislike for her very clear, and made no effort to hide it. Did Mehra think Anjali could stop the divorce?

When he came in, Anjali didn't recognise the old man straightaway. From the few times she had met him, Anjali remembered Mehra as a ramrod-straight, broad man, who carried his years well. This man stooped a little, and walked slowly.

'Hello Anjali,' he held out a huge bouquet of lilies and chrysanthemums. 'This is for you.'

Vibha took the flowers from him and set them near the window.

'Thank you, Mehraji.' Anjali said.

'Let me come straight to the point,' Mehra said, having waited for Vibha to leave the room. 'I have an offer for you.'

'Offer?' What did that mean? Anjali sat up straighter.

'I know what happened is wrong, and nothing will bring your life back to you, but I can help you move forward. All of your treatment, the expenses, you don't have to worry about any of it.'

'Excuse me?'

'I can help, that's all I'm saying.'

Mehra looked desperate, his eyes bloodshot, his hands trembling.

'I understand your situation.' Anjali tried to reassure him. 'I'm sorry about what Drishti is going through.'

Anjali remembered her face in the white-framed bathroom mirror. A *kijinmen*, a mask of terror. No man would ever want her now.

'So Jatin hasn't told you yet?' Mehra looked taken aback.

'I'm sorry?'

Mehra closed the conversation as abruptly as it had begun. 'Wish you a good day, Anjali,' he said, and walked out just as Vibha came in with Anjali's dinner. 'I'll let him do it then.'

57

Jatin collapsed into a chair in the kitchen, poured himself a tumbler of water and guzzled it down, uncaring of the spill on his sweater. The churning in his stomach made thinking difficult, but he couldn't just sit there. He must talk to Varun and Bunty before Dayal Sisodia and Commissioner Mehra got there. He had called both men about ten minutes ago.

He headed out of the kitchen, Anjali's face mocking him from the family frames hanging in the corridor.

Jatin entered the room upstairs to find Varun with his feet up on the sofa, his head between his knees.

'Daddy!'

Varun uncurled himself and stood up. Pale skin, dry lips, rumpled hair. Jatin had never seen his son this unkempt.

'Sit down.'

Varun sank back on the sofa.

'Daddy, I promise, it wasn't a big deal ya.' Varun made an effort at a smile, then gave up. 'I tried a few things. Nothing much.'

'Why are you sniffling? That jacket not warm enough?' Jatin sat down opposite Varun, his usually straight-sitting teen, who now slouched, his jacket zipped up tight.

'Daddy, Bunty and I were just having a little fun. Mostly it was light stuff. Please don't be like that ya.'

'You call what you have on your phone, "a little fun"?'

Varun straightened up, his eyes wide. He looked younger now, and scared. 'But, Bunty said no one will ever be able to crack it!'

Realising what he just said, Varun shut up. He lowered his head, and sat glaring at his hands, clenching and unclenching them on his lap.

When he watched or read true crime stories, Jatin wondered how the criminals' parents, wives, children didn't know who they were living with. How did a wife not guess that her husband returned home after torturing women? Now he understood it was possible.

'You need to tell me everything.'

'Will you let us go, Daddy? Bunty said you will help, if something went wrong ya, you will never let us go to jail. Bunty's father, too. He will be very angry, but he will bail us out of trouble. Bunty said that.'

Varun crouched back into the sofa. His right knee jerked up and down, in short, quick movements. Jatin wanted to slam that knee down. He curled his fist till his blunt nails dug into his palm. All of this was his doing. He had pushed Varun into friendship with Bunty, hosted Bunty at his home, invited him on family occasions, all for the sake of closeness to Dayal.

'You will tell me all of it, leaving nothing out.'

'But you already know.'

'Varun.' Jatin crossed his arms.

They sat in silence for a while, Varun's hands shaking

so bad now that he slid them under his thighs. His knees continued to jerk once in a while. When Jatin was about to prod him again, Varun spoke almost to himself.

'I told him not to do anything stupid when I was in Manila, I told Bunty, told him to be careful. Chander could squeal. But he said *doston ke liye jeena marna*, and he was right, Chander didn't open his mouth. But Bunty had to go and take Deenu to Geeta Colony...if not for that...'

Varun paused for a while, sniffling.

'I told him, let's not take pictures. Pictures become evidence. But he said that's why we did it, for the pictures. He liked looking at them. He used the best software, he said, FBI standard, no one could get into it, his hacker friends can't crack it, he said. But...now...Daddy, you have to help. You have to help him, help us. Between you and Dayal Uncle, and Nanaji, you can handle this, can't you? Nobody has to know, Daddy.'

Varun's words echoed loud in Jatin's ears, louder than all the dirty words he had heard from his Papa in his childhood: *Nobody has to know.*

Those women, their bodies bruised, their faces burnt off. Anjali. Anjali's face, her life as she knew it, gone. *Nobody has to know.*

The pictures from Varun and Bunty's phones proved Varun went with Bunty, Chander, and Lahiri's driver, Deenu. The question remained: to what lengths? The pictures showed 'before' and 'after'. No photos of Varun assaulting the women. Varun was in Manila during the last kidnap and rape.

'Tell me everything,' he must stay relaxed, in his calm space. Must remember to focus. 'You alone. Not Bunty or the others. You.'

'Will you help us if I do?' Varun's knees danced, and Jatin tried to ignore it.

'I'm the one asking questions here, Varun.'

'Why should I answer, Daddy?' Varun's knees sped up, going up-and-down faster now. 'How about you answer some instead?'

His son had never spoken to him like that. Jatin focused on keeping his jaws relaxed. Varun stared back, but his sniffle defeated him. He wiped his nose on his sleeve. 'Why ask me a question when you know the answer?'

Jatin smiled, but he knew the angle of his lips made it look like a half-snarl. For the first time since the day Jatin first held his baby son in his arms, he wanted to cause him real harm, to twist Varun's arms till he cried out. Jatin's voice grated inside his head when he spoke.

'*You* are the criminal here.'

'Really?' Varun leaned back, his voice polite and soft. 'Where's all that cash from, Daddy? Why do you have wads tucked away in your safe? What happens if all that comes out in the open?'

Jatin sat rock solid, but the words hit him like punches to his stomach. He took them without flinching.

'That does not explain your actions.'

'You pay more mind to that woman's son, that freak, that *saala chutiya* than you do to me. I'm your son ya, but you think you should take him to the hospital, bring him to our house. He kills a puppy, everyone salutes him and says *oho* poor boy, let me take you to eat some icecream-wicecream and take you home where you can stay and pat my son's dog. He's crazy so he gets all the prescription drugs, but if

I bought a few pills or smoked a few joints, that's such a bad thing ya, Daddy. Different standards for different people.'

Varun stood up, and paced, sniffling all the while. So much poison in his son, all bottled up, now spilling out. It burned Jatin. He remembered how throughout Nikhil's childhood, Anjali had suffered for no other fault than having given birth to him. But Jatin had fed and moulded this monster; Varun wasn't born this way. All of it was Jatin's fault, all the women Varun hurt, and Anjali. Jatin was responsible for all of them.

'I'm old enough now ya, I know what's what. Everyone is different. Bunty says he can't stand women, women are such bitches. You know what his Mom did when his father wasn't there? You don't ya. His father doesn't. So what if he picks up those women, they're *randi*s anyway, they'll give it to anyone for money. Don't look so shocked, I know what a *randi* is. If he takes care of me, he's with me when I need him, why shouldn't I do what he says?'

Varun choked, then rushing behind the sofa, threw up in great big heaves. The room stank now, a bitter-black ugly stink, like a dead animal rotting.

Varun came back, wiping his face on his sleeve.

'You think it is so good you give me everything, your card ya, what else can a boy ask for? How about the times I waited for you at cricket practice? The times you never came on parent-teachers' days? What about those, Daddy darling?'

Jatin shut out the smell of vomit and the reek of his son's words. He was trained, years, decades ago. *Never let your feelings show during an interrogation. Not anger. Definitely not heartbreak.*

Varun laughed and sniffled, his eyes red, and wiped his face on his sleeve again, streaking it with vomit. He made as if to throw up one more time, but went on, half choking, half crying.

'For years, you spent more time with *that* woman than you did at home with your wife and child. You think I don't know ya, I don't remember anything, I'm just a child. But I've grown up with it. You bring *her* son to my house. You want me to be buddy-buddy with him. Gave him a few nice ones, didn't I? *Saala gaandu* he thinks he can stay in my house and hurt my Laddoo-dog? Just…a few punches in places you can't see but really hurt, and he was all over me.'

All those words, half-sobbed, with tears streaming down his face, snot down his nose. Jatin's big *gabru jawan* son.

'I fixed him. I wanted to fix his mother, too. But Bunty said it will be too risky ya. Women in the slum, no one will know no one will care, but you take your father's *randi*, he will find you. So easy to make a person die when they're still alive. Just make sure they can't ever come out of their house ya, so they can't show their face. How do you like her now, Daddy? Does the thought of fucking her…'

One minute Jatin was in his chair, the next, he was up, and Varun was on the floor, bleeding from his nose and mouth, choking, laughing, coughing.

Over the ringing in his own head and the sounds his son made, Jatin heard a knock at the door.

'Jatin sir.' Pawan's voice, pitched low.

'Give me a minute.'

'Sir, the home secretary and Commissioner Mehra are downstairs.'

58

Maya sat by Sakhi's bedside at the hospital with the little girl drugged to sleep after the morning's excitement of Christmas gifts and carols. Each year, by this time in the afternoon she was stuffed with Anjali's cooking and slumped on the sofa at the Safdarjung Enclave home—listening to hushed chatter from a few family friends, Bhai, Bhabi, Varun sprawled on the sofa, Anjali and some of her colleagues lingering at the dining table.

In sharp contrast, she had spent all of this morning trying to reach Bhai, because she wanted to take him along to wish Anjali Merry Christmas. He wasn't at home or office—she'd checked. Late morning, she had received a message, *Don't pick any call from the Mehra household, never mind who it is.* She'd tried to call him, but he didn't pick up. Pawan's phone was switched off as well.

When the light outside began to fade, she picked up the bouquet of pink roses she'd bought for Anjali, and headed towards the Burns ward. Anjali sat reading through a file, a huge bouquet of fat chrysanthemums and pink lilies standing beside her on the table. Bhai had sent her flowers?

Maya tamped down on her resentment, and walked towards Anjali.

'Merry Christmas, Anji.'

Anjali looked up and Maya steadied her smile so it wouldn't tremble. She was still not used to Anjali's face, her lips burned off, bandages where her nose had been, her dark blond hair growing in patches.

Anjali thanked her for the flowers and asked her to ring the nurse for another vase. She followed Maya's gaze towards the bouquet at the window.

'Those are from Mr Mehra.'

'Bhabi's father?'

That was strange. Bhabi's father didn't like Anjali—why had he sent her flowers?

'Yes, he came to visit, out of the blue, then left as quickly as he came.'

This was getting worse. No Bhai, flowers from his father-in-law, in person.

'Why was he here?' Maya said. 'Have you heard from Bhai?'

'I don't know, really,' Anjali said. 'Mr Mehra said something about Jatin talking to me, but Jatin hasn't come in.'

Typical Bhai, disappearing just when everyone needed to talk to him. Nikhil was due to be released from the clinic that evening and the hospital would discharge Sakhi tomorrow. How did Bhai expect her to manage alone?

'How is Sakhi?' Anjali placed her file on the side table. She had begun reading case notes, to help with a consultancy job. Bhalla knew someone who could do with online help with his caseload.

Anjali, the fighter.

Maya had loved Anjali all these years, admired her for her grit, but this was on another level. Dr Singh had asked

Anjali to rest as much as possible, but she had taken his permission to work two hours a day.

'I'll take care of her, Anji, don't worry.' Maya said, 'Even if that means we have to close down Vigil for a week. With Dorothy gone, Nikhil will be easier to handle.'

Anjali went absolutely still and Maya realised what she'd said. 'Sorry, Anji. Didn't mean it that way. Dorothy asked me to keep this for you.'

Dorothy had left the large envelope with Maya, asking her to pass it to Anjali and no one else. Maya held it out.

'I had asked the nurse to trash that.'

Maya couldn't imagine what Anjali had gone through—all those years thinking her aunt was her mother—and her mother, her aunt, but Dorothy had looked desperate when she spoke to Maya, asked her to take care of the envelope for Anjali.

'She said it is for Nikhil. From your father.'

'About Nikhil.' Anjali put the envelope on the side table, and continued. 'Keep him at the clinic for now.'

Anjali's calm made Maya want to shake her. It felt unnatural, like someone else—Anjali always spoke of Nikhil with a lot of emotion, with anxiety, earnestness.

Maya approached the bed. 'You've never wanted him there before.'

'I went to see Sakhi.'

'I can have Sakhi stay with one of my friends for some time.'

Maya could do more than that. She was planning to keep Sakhi with her, for always. Adopt her. Adopt Sakhi's little brother, Chotu. She wanted to tell Anjali, but not now. Anjali's hand trembled over the bed sheet.

'This isn't just about Sakhi.' Anjali said.

'What is it Anji? Did Mr Mehra say something to you?'

Anjali turned away. Her body shook.

'Anji? You're scaring me.'

Maya watched as Anjali took a long breath, and straightened, as if steeling herself to speak. Maya wanted Anjali to stop, not say another word.

'Nikhil did this,' Anjali pointed to her own face. 'It was him.'

59

The day after Christmas, Anjali waited for Jatin. Dr Singh had said Jatin would drop by in the evening.

Maya had promised she wouldn't talk to her Bhai about Nikhil. It was Anjali's story to tell. Only now, sitting on her bed in the weak morning sunlight, she felt undecided. It was the right thing to do—tell Jatin, get his advice on how best to deal with this. Had her case been registered at a police station? Would the culprit be tried even if she didn't press charges? Would the fact that Nikhil had autism be taken into consideration? She closed her eyes, and tried *deep breaths* once again.

When she opened them, Jatin stood at the door to her room. He looked lean and handsome from a distance, and he had taken care with his clothes: a crisp white shirt and blue denims. But as he approached, she noticed the bags under his eyes, the pallor of his skin.

'Hi Anjali,' he said, 'I couldn't come in earlier.'

Something was off. He never called her by her given name, always Jelly.

'Are you all right?'

'Yes, I'm on leave today, so I woke up late. I got your messages from the doctor.'

They still didn't allow her a phone. Not good for eyes, a hotbed of infection, and even though they didn't mention it, the camera. They didn't want her looking at herself. She remembered her face from the mirror, but the nurses had no way of knowing that. She watched as Jatin drew the chair near her bed. He'd worn perfume, and it gave her a rush of memories. All ash, now.

'I spoke about it to Maya, but she wouldn't believe me at first. It can't be him, she said.' Anjali didn't look at Jatin as she spoke. She needed to get this out of her before she clammed down. 'But you already suspected him, didn't you?'

Jatin went still, his eyes wary. 'What are you talking about?'

'I didn't put it in my statement to Kusum. I didn't see him clearly, but I heard my attacker's voice. It was Nikhil.'

Jatin leapt out of his seat, but still didn't say a word. Anjali couldn't meet his eyes, so she stared instead at the red scars on her arms where some of the wounds had begun to heal.

'Hear me out. I'm sorry I didn't say anything before. Not even after Varun got hurt. But I saw Sakhi last night. It wouldn't have happened if I'd said something. I'm so sorry.'

Jatin made a choking sound. Anjali called out to him, but without a pause or turn, he rushed out the door.

60

Jatin ran down the corridor, and out into the open at the back of the hospital. He took long, harsh breaths, and tasted the smog upon his tongue. The bitterness in his mouth matched his thoughts. Anjali had offered him on a platter exactly what he needed to get Varun acquitted from her case: a witness statement identifying another suspect. Not his son who had confessed to the crime, nor the boy who had carried out the attack at Varun's bidding.

What of the other case—those molested, disfigured dead women?

The good thing is, Dayal and Mehra had said, *there is no official investigation into this. No one needs to know.* If things did come out, they could prove Varun was in Manila when the last woman, Roli, was kidnapped. They could easily remove traces of Bunty and Varun's DNA from Lahiri's car, and his apartment. Then they would plant evidence against Lahiri and Manoj in Roli's rape kit. No one would believe their words in the face of concrete evidence. Bunty and Varun could finish their studies abroad. *No harm done, no one needs to know.*

Jatin had agreed. He had not given suggestions, but he had agreed to all of theirs. For his son.

Work on your marriage, Mehra had said as he walked down to the farmhouse gate, while Dayal strode ahead, with his arms around Varun and Bunty. *I'll explain everything to Drishti, how you're leaving that half-white woman. No one will know any of this.*

No one will know. All last night with his bottle of scotch, and even at dawn with a hangover from hell, those words hadn't left Jatin alone. And the minute he closed his eyes he saw those pictures, the battered, naked women's bodies. Just as he saw them now. He put his face in his palms and tried to breathe. After a while, having calmed himself down, he headed back indoors.

Fareeda Saigal walked down from the opposite direction and stopped. 'Have you seen Dr Morgan?'

'I'm going in now.'

'She has been very upset.' Fareeda stared up at him through her black-framed glasses, which made her eyes look huge and swimming. 'She has refused all cosmetic surgeries, you know. I recommended she talk to you.'

'I'll talk to her.'

'How are you holding up, Mr Bhatt?'

Never had such a simple question seemed so difficult to answer. Jatin nodded, but couldn't say a word.

Fareeda smiled. The creases on her face reminded Jatin of another woman with fat, comforting, saree-covered shoulders. His Ma.

When Jatin re-entered Anjali's room, her eyelids fluttered. He felt wetness streaking down his cheek, and wiped it off.

'What's wrong?' Her eyes were like darkened pools. He wanted to reach out and stroke that bandaged face.

His mind went blank, a high-pitched sound keened inside his head. He watched her wrecked face, the meshed-together skin and bandages, the bone of her nose, her melted ears, the eyebrows and eyelashes singed away, and the red-brown slash of her mouth.

'Nikhil did not do this.' The words spilled out of him.

The sound in his head didn't let up. He felt his knees give way and he staggered back into the chair at the foot of her bed. She sat up, her eyes wide. He waited for her to ask questions. But she did not move or blink.

'What did you say?'

'It wasn't Nikhil.'

The words burst out, cutting at him as he spoke, like shards of glass.

Anjali shook her head. 'Nikhil...'

'Nikhil had nothing to do with this.' Jatin closed his eyes, trying to get rid of the ringing in his ears. 'I'm so sorry.'

'But I heard his voice.'

'Did you see him?'

'It was foggy, and my eyes were burning, you know the problem with my contact lenses. I saw the shadow of him. It was him.'

'No. You saw Radhe. They are the same height. They wore similar clothes that night. Varun's.'

He had pieced it together last night. Drishti had given Varun's clothes to Nikhil. Varun had given his old clothes to Radhe.

'But his voice!'

'It was Chander.' Jatin raised his hand when Anjali was about to continue, 'Chander spoke to you, Radhe has described it. You mistook his voice for Nikhil's. Nikhil calls you by name, too. He calls you Anjali, not Mom, right? Nikhil was there, he was close enough that some of the acid splashed on him, but no one saw him in the fog. He must have tried to follow you to the cake shop. When we reached, he was there, not in your car.'

Anjali hid her face in her hands, then seemed to remember she wasn't allowed to touch her face. She took them away.

'All this while,' her voice broke, 'all this while, I've thought it was…I've always…' She broke into sobs.

Anjali's eyes could not produce tears. He stood at the foot of her bed and tried not to flinch at each dry sob that wracked her.

'If not him, then who?' she met his eyes. 'Do you know who did this?'

'Varun.'

With that one word, he knew he had changed everything. All of his agreements with Dayal and Mehra, his son, his job, his life as he knew it. He could not have done anything else, he realised, not when confronted with Anjali's ravaged face. He went on, and watched Anjali's eyes widen as he described how his son had orchestrated it, had paid Radhe and Chander, how they had tried to hit her at the Safdarjung hospital parking lot, but it was still daylight, and her assistant had showed up instead of her. How they had followed her car, and seen an opportunity when she stopped at the cake shop.

She sat there, listening. He could no longer read her expression, because she had no expression left, only a criss-cross of bandages and a patchwork of skin and scars.

'When Nikhil hurt Sakhi—' Anjali looked towards Jatin, but her gaze was far away '—every time he hurt anyone, when he killed that puppy—I thought—'

Jatin tried to open his mouth, but gave up. Words meant nothing. He surrendered to the pain that had sliced into him ever since he saw Varun stealing from the safe. Varun waiting at an abandoned building for his drop. Varun with those bruised, battered, raped, murdered, burned women.

'Every time Nikhil did it—but he's my son—so I tried to—'

'Nikhil has a problem he was born with. I made Varun what he is today.'

In the end, tears said it all. Tears he had held back for years, and tears that had built up each moment since yesterday, bled out of him. He didn't know how or when, but his head ended up in Anjali's lap. She patted his hair. He tried to stop himself but his body refused to listen. He sat back a while later, still shaking.

'Jatin.' She held his hand.

'How can you be like this?' Jatin said. 'How can you not be angry?'

'I am. Oh I am. But we always knew we would have to pay, didn't we?'

'Not this. Not this way.'

'I spoke to Dorothy yesterday. She was angry with her husband and her sister for so long. Still is, after they're both gone.'

Anjali picked up a pillow and hugged it to herself.

'Is it that easy to let go?'

'No, it isn't. I'm sure I'll be angry a few hours from now when they change my dressings and I scream in pain.'

He had no answer to that. She would face agony every day, every living moment for the coming months and years all because of his son. Because of him.

'For now, I want to see Nikhil. I thought—and it's not him.' Anjali looked up, 'It wasn't him, it was someone else. Oh I'm sorry, I didn't mean it that way.'

'I'm responsible.'

'Don't say that. He did this on his own.'

'Because he saw me, each day. He saw me go after what I wanted. He saw me not care who I hurt.'

'We'll find a way.'

Anjali spoke like his Ma, who went on forgiving, all her life. But whereas Ma decided to stay and take the abuse, Anjali left. And now, she was rising above it all, her childhood, the attack that ruined her.

'There's more.'

'What more?' Anjali nudged his forearm. 'Jatin? What more?'

Before he could change his mind, he flicked on his phone, and showed her the photos downloaded from Bunty and Varun's phones. He switched it off at her first harsh moan. He had changed his clothes, bathed and disinfected his hands before entering her room. He'd wanted to coax her. The cold, calculating Jatin had done all of that.

'How did you not know?' Anjali burst out, 'He's your son!'

Jatin had no answer. He had seen in Varun what he wanted to. He had gone after what he thought was important.

The woman from Lahiri's car; Sujni—Sakhi's mother, and the others who were lost. Varun, Bunty, Chander and Deenu had tortured and burned them. Taken selfies. Varun was the youngest, but he wasn't just a boy. He had followed where Bunty led.

Jatin stood up, trying to contain the storm building inside him. He had laughed when Varun called Maya a *feminazi*, when he had disrespected his mother. He did not set Varun right, not once.

'Those women...Jatin, what are you going to do?'

This question had eaten into him since yesterday, ever since he showed Commissioner Mehra and Dayal Sisodia the pictures from the phones.

Anjali had hidden her suspicion of Nikhil, but when she saw Sakhi hurt, she had been ready to give her son up to the law, not wanting anyone else to get hurt.

Where did that leave Jatin Satyaprakash Bhatt? If he sheltered Varun, lied—if he sent him away with no repercussions—would Varun stop being a monster? Won't there be other women? Jatin had come here after making a pact with Mehra and Dayal, to make sure his son escaped punishment.

'So that's why Drishti's father came here.' Anjali's voice startled him. 'For Varun.'

'He came here?'

'Yes, yesterday evening.' Anjali's voice broke. 'He offered to pay for my treatment.'

The very same offer had been on his mind earlier, when he entered this room. He reached out for her then, and held her in his arms, her back to his front, taking care not to touch her face or throat.

'*Shaq ho gaya hai seena,*' he whispered over her head, her hair tickling his chin. '*Khushi lazzat-e-firaaq. Takleef-e pardadaari-e-zakhm-jigar gayi.*'

'What's that?' she asked him. 'It sounds so sad and happy at the same time.'

His love for poetry came from Papa. Jatin couldn't stand his father, but the Urdu words in his father's baritone voice had charmed him as a little boy. In college, he'd thought it was original, his love for Ghalib, Rumi, and Sahir. But Papa had made a home inside of him. Papa lived in his body, in pain, in humiliation, but also in poetry. Jatin would never outgrow his Papa, or get rid of him. Some day he would translate for Anjali these lines from Ghalib, about how a heart torn apart leaves you carefree, because then you don't need to bother hiding your wounds.

He hadn't told her all of it yet. He must strip, lay each wound bare, spare nothing.

'I hit Varun yesterday,' he said, 'and dislocated his jaw. He's in the hospital now.'

But that wasn't all. Nor was it enough. It would never be enough.

'Varun hit Nikhil.'

She sat up straight, and turned to him. He watched her eyes blaze in anger as she listened.

He wanted this. He was done with life as he knew it—*paani mein rehkar magarmach se bair* was exactly what he had to do now, make enemies of the big crocodiles in the pond. He needed her anger, not forgiveness. He needed it in order to tear his world apart with his own hands, and let everyone watch him as he did it.

61

Nikhil. Anjali repeated her son's name to herself. Nikhil. Her Nikhil was to visit her today, her second visitor on the day after Christmas.

She wanted to hug him, knew she couldn't. Setting her eyes on him would soothe some of the ache in her heart. Each time Nikhil had acted out—when he ran away, after the incident with the puppy, when she couldn't find him the evening of Drishti's party—she had wanted someone different, longed for a different son, a perfect son. She thought he had attacked Varun. She was terrified the day he ran away from Fareeda's clinic, injuring her in the process, feared he would deliberately attack Sakhi, again. He needed understanding, she had passed judgment.

No more.

Today she would look at her son, begin the process of unlearning all she had taught herself about him, see him as he really was. She would go in for her next operation this afternoon, and not wake up for a week. Before that, she would fill her eyes with the sight of him.

A nurse walked in. 'You have a new visitor, madam.'

'My son?'

'It is a lady. Mrs Bhatt.'

What would Drishti have to say to her now? Whatever it was, Anjali wanted it over and done with before Nikhil came in.

'Ask her to come in.'

Drishti walked in wearing a white mask, and the sort of little black office dress only the skinniest women could wear. Anjali caught herself. She had no business judging Drishti.

'Hi, Anjali.'

Didn't sound like a greeting, more of a challenge, the cracking of the whip. Drishti lightly swung the bag she was carrying, as if slowly gathering momentum to lob it.

'Hello.' Anjali met Drishti's eyes, and Drishti took a step back, as if Anjali had pushed her. She stalked to the bed.

'What are you planning now?' Drishti's voice shook with fury. This had to be about Jatin, the divorce.

'Would you like to sit down?'

To her own ears, Anjali sounded like she was treating one of her patients at her clinic, as if Drishti needed the care of a doctor, not her. Drishti didn't back down this time.

'Answer me.' Drishti said. 'You took away my husband, isn't that enough? Now you have to drag in my son, too?'

Anjali's heart raced, and under the bandages, her face flamed. 'You know what your son has done?'

'My father has told me everything. You won't rest till you ruin our family, would you? You're saying my Varun did this?' she pointed at Anjali's face. 'My son is not a psycho like yours. Dad says he has witnesses. They saw your son attack you.'

'I don't know what your father told you. He came here

to bribe me the other day, pay for all my treatment. Why did he do that then?'

The pictures on Jatin's phone with Varun, Bunty, other men, and those burned women came back to Anjali.

'You think I'm going to believe the woman who slept with my husband, and still ate dinner at my table? For years, Anjali.' Drishti scoffed, 'Ten years. You should be ashamed. Varun knew. He has shown me pictures of you going into hotels.'

'I'm sure he has. And I was wrong to do that. But why don't you ask him to show the other pictures from his phone? What he has done to so many women?'

'I know what my husband has done to protect you and your freak.'

Anjali stepped out of bed, and faced Drishti down. 'Don't you dare call my son names.'

Drishti stepped back, but she didn't lower her gaze. 'Get this, Anjali-half-breed-Morgan. If my son comes to harm, I won't spare yours either.'

Drishti left, softly closing the door behind her.

Anjali's hands shook as she laboured her way back to her bed. She rang the bell for the nurse so she could call Jatin. *You better sort this out, Special Commissioner Bhatt.* She whispered to herself. *I'll not be parted from my son again.*

62

Maya paced the conference room at Vigil, craving a smoke. Quitting cold turkey on New Year's night had not been her smartest move, and in the last week it had all but driven her crazy. She needed to finish this meeting with Pawan and Bhai before dropping Sakhi to her friend's place, and picking Nikhil up from the clinic.

Nikhil, Anjali had whispered, before being wheeled yet another time into the operation theatre. Maya had taken videos of Nikhil for Anjali to watch, promised she would help her Bhai protect him. Anjali had recovered from her coma, and the doctor said she was ready for the grafts. She had still not agreed to the cosmetic procedures later, but she would. Maya would make her. For Nikhil, Maya would say. So Nikhil could lead a normal life with her—she needn't worry about money for him, Professor Gupta had left him more than enough. Nikhil asked for Anjali, but he understood now that she was unwell and in the hospital.

Nikhil asked for Pawan, too. But Pawan hadn't come to Vigil since before New Year. His mother died two days before New Year's Eve. Maya hadn't seen him since. She missed him like she craved cigarettes. Pawan would only come in today because Bhai needed help with the chargesheets against Bunty and the others. She hurt for Pawan, having known the pain of losing parents. The chimes at the door jingled, and the object of her thoughts walked in moments later. He tried to grin, but the smile didn't reach his tired eyes. He hadn't shaved or combed his hair, because of the thirteen-day period of mourning. He had lost weight.

'Hi.' Maya walked up to him. 'Once again, so sorry about your mother.'

She wanted to reach out and hug him, but didn't know how, nor what else to say.

'Thank you.' He was hunched over, his arms hanging by his sides. 'Is Jatin sir on his way?'

'Yes, we'll sit here today. Bhai needs that map.'

She pointed at the map of Delhi on the conference room wall. Pawan's hair looked a mess, his eyelids puffy. He didn't seem to understand her words, but nodded and sank into a chair.

'How is Bhabi?'

'She isn't talking to us.' Pawan opened his bag. 'No one in their family came for Beeji's...'

His voice choked up. Maya wanted to step closer, but held back. Bhabi didn't attend her own aunt's funeral? Maya thought Bhabi had visited that day, after she and Bhai left Pawan's place.

'She thinks I cooked it all up about Varun and Bunty. Planted evidence against my nephew. That's what Mehra sir told her.'

So much anger and hurt in those words. Maya needed to remain professional but she took another step towards his chair. Pawan took out his pen and notebook, and laid them on the table. Had she not been watching him, she wouldn't have noticed the slight tremor in his fingers. She laid a hand on his shoulder. He caught it, and drew her in for a kiss.

Maya kissed him back, his lips soft, then firm on hers. Part of her revelled in his touch, his hands in her hair, on her back, delighted in the heat of their mouths, in the sounds they made, the stifled groans. The other part kept saying, *He's kissing you, Maya, this is your first kiss. You're twenty-seven and this is your first proper kiss, are you listening? Feel this, you stupid girl, remember it.*

The chimes at the door tinkled for the second time. She pushed Pawan away, and ran. Once in the washroom, she stared into the mirror, her flushed face, the bright eyes.

***

When she returned, Bhai stood by the kettle pouring hot water into cups. Pawan looked composed, with sheaves of paper spread in front of him. Kusum had come in, and sat beside Pawan, taking notes. With Kusum and Maya present, Bhai had decided to make tea—Maya wouldn't believe it if she hadn't seen it.

'So you're saying we don't have enough to charge Radhe for the acid attack?' Bhai stirred his tea.

'They're using him, sir.' Pawan said, 'If he testifies that he knows Lahiri and Manoj were behind the murders, then Varun and Chander will say Radhe didn't throw the acid. Chander might also testify that Nikhil did it. They have taken charge of Nikhil's clothes from the night.'

It had become about *Us* vs *Them*. Everyone in this room, against Commissioner Mehra and Dayal Sisodia.

'They would anyway be charged as juveniles, right?' Maya said.

'Varun, yes.' Bhai arranged the papers in front of him, 'But Bunty is twenty-one, Deenu and Chander are older.'

'The pictures are solid evidence,' Maya said.

She couldn't forget the images burned into her mind, couldn't imagine her nephew was part of this. She'd considered Varun a spoilt brat for years, but poor Bhai, who used to call Varun his pride, had helped file charges against his son last week. One on behalf of Anjali, and another, from Roli's husband.

Bhai served them all tea, waved at Kusum to sit down when she rose.

'Yes,' Pawan said. 'But even though we took backups of the downloads from Bunty and Varun's phones, they might be able to get those marked inadmissible in court. We didn't use a warrant for their phones, or their arrest.'

Pawan looked so pulled together. This was not the same man who grabbed her a few minutes ago. Maya's face heated up at the memory.

The discussion went on. They must fight against huge odds. All the evidence from Sujni's post-mortem, and the woman found in Lahiri's car had been tampered with. Rathi, the new in-charge for the Sujni case, claimed Manoj and Lahiri had done it all. Their DNA was found in the car, on Roli, and at Lahiri's apartment. Sujni and Roli's bodies had been cremated. Commissioner Mehra and the home secretary had not missed a trick.

'Radhe might change his tune.' Bhai looked at Kusum, who nodded. 'Netam managed to get access to Radhe. We've

YOU BENEATH YOUR SKIN

shown him the photographs of his mother, what Bunty and the gang did to her. We told him they really took Ram Sharan because he found out about his mother's murder.'

Maya recognised that firm tone in Bhai's voice. He hid behind it when he felt emotional. He looked exhausted and new lines marked his face.

'I can go chat with Lahiri if you like.' She put her teacup down and stood up. 'We can work on his and Manoj's testimonies. Also, I want Hridayog to open its doors again.'

'We'll discuss that later, Maya.' Bhai stopped her. In some ways, Bhai would never change.

For the next fifteen minutes, they discussed the details of the case. At the end, Bhai asked them for questions and comments.

'We saved the backups in a secure place, with various copies on the internet,' Pawan said. 'If things come to a head, we can release those pictures.'

'We're talking about the home secretary's involvement here.' Maya said.

'Social media can be very effective.' Pawan looked around the room at everyone. 'At the very least, those pictures will keep us safe.'

Bhai and Kusum left, leaving Maya to wrap up before she set out to collect Nikhil.

The conference room felt cramped, even though it was just her and Pawan now. With her back to him, she put away the cups and files, but remained aware of the shuffling of papers, the zipping of his bag, the thump of files, and finally, the tap of his shoes approaching her.

'Maya.'

Her name felt like a caress at her neck. She didn't turn around, but her hands stilled on the table.

'I wanted to talk to you.'

She didn't turn, didn't move or breathe. He turned her to face him.

'About earlier...' he stopped.

Rabji, no, he would say sorry now.

'Maya, I can't talk to you unless you look at me.'

Anger. She would take that. She turned and raised her eyes to his, saw them widen and smile down at her.

'I need to tell you something.'

She liked how he flushed, how that made him look so alive, not like the defeated man he'd seemed when he came in.

'I want—' Pawan fumbled with his words, 'I would like—' and gently led her to a chair. He made her sit down, sat in front of her, and held both of her hands in one of his.

This had to be a joke; he was mocking her. She tried to pull her hands away from his grip.

'I'll let you go, if you say so. But only if you say so.'

She had to tell him. She couldn't lead him on, not now. She bowed her head, reaching for the right words. He let go of her hands and stood up.

'Pawan, it's not that—well, it's just that—' Maya peeled back the sleeves of her sweater and showed him her skin. He sat down again.

'I've known for a while,' he said, breaking into Hindi, running a finger over a discoloured patch on her forearm. 'I've got them too. Can't show you, because they are on the inside.'

She couldn't meet his eyes, not after having hidden herself from him for so long.

'*Sabke andar daag hotey hain.*' Pawan's voice shook. 'All of us have scars, secrets. We can take our time finding out about each other, if you like. I'll wait for your answer.'

Maya met his eyes.

'But there's another thing,' he said. 'I have to go away.'

'Go?'

'Not too far from you,' he kissed her hands, 'but from this office. I have spoken to Jatin sir…Bhai. He will help me with my Civil Service exam.'

'Police?'

So they had discussed this behind her back.

'I've always wanted to join,' he said, loosening his grip on her hands, 'but never went for it because of Beeji.' Before she died, she said I could do whatever I wanted, be whatever I wanted. I want to be good enough for you, Maya.'

Pawan's eyes were moist. He had released her hands, but Maya reached for him.

63

Varun lay curled up with Laddoo-dog in his bedroom at the Mehra mansion, feverish and groggy. He checked the swelling on his jaw in the mirror. It had gone down. You had to give it to Daddy ya, man could throw a punch. They'd kept him at the hospital for three weeks for his 'withdrawal symptoms'. New Year's puking into a bucket, that was a first.

Today he felt better, and had talked to Mummy who was away on a work trip, told her he still had the flu. That's what Commissioner Mehra, his dear Nanaji, told everyone, including his wife and daughter: that he admitted his grandson Varun to the hospital because of an infection. No one was allowed to see him. Liar. *Keep your head down, betey,* Nanaji said, *and do not try to find your phone, or drugs, if you don't want to go to jail. I will fix everything.*

He sat up when he heard his Nanaji come in. Bunty's father, Dayal Sisodia, was downstairs, and wanted to meet him. *Just shut up and sit there, don't open your mouth, all right?* As if Varun wanted to talk. What a bore ya, this Nanaji.

Varun took the stairs down to the study. Bunty's father sat on the sofa in his usual Nehru jacket, but there was also someone Varun hadn't expected—Daddy, in an old sweater and jeans, he seemed to have grown older in the last three weeks. His shoulders stooped, and he looked tired. He didn't say a word.

Varun heard Laddoo-dog bark to be let out of the bedroom—he wanted to finish with this and go lie down again. He felt dizzy, and craved a hit.

'Sit down, Varun.' Dayal Uncle said. 'You kids need to realise precisely what we're doing to keep you out of jail.'

'We're doing nothing of the sort.' Daddy said.

'Commissioner Mehra here tells me he has tried everything to persuade you. He has already suspended you on the basis of the findings of the Sabharwal case. Yet you insist on this mad idea of putting those pictures online.'

'I only want my son to go through the due process of law. I've tendered my resignation.'

'What process?' Dayal Uncle turned to Nanaji. 'Based on what evidence?'

Daddy leaned forward. He was something else ya. He had resigned from his job, broken his son's jaw, and now wanted him sent to jail.

'You've tampered with the evidence and transferred Grewal out of the Jamia Nagar station, but once your son's photos go online, news channels will pick it up.'

Bunty's father was not as tall or big as Daddy, but boy when he smiled now, he looked scary, you wanted to call him Dayal Singh Sisodia, not Dayal Uncle. This man was no one's uncle.

'Jatin, I don't understand. Commissioner Mehra has only taken the measures all three of us planned together that day at your farmhouse. You were part of it.'

Dayal rose and walked to where Varun sat. He put an arm around Varun's shoulders. 'I want your son to listen in when I say it, so you know I am serious. My family has too much at stake. I'm not defending what my son has done, and I'm not saying you're wrong to demand that he face the law, but the Sisodia family can't afford it.'

The room was silent other than the whir of the heater. Daddy and Nanaji exchanged a glance. Varun unzipped his jacket, Dayal's heavy hand still on his shoulder. He wanted to plead with Daddy to listen to Dayal, but a hard-faced man had replaced his Daddy darling.

'It does not please me to say this in Commissioner Mehra's house, to his son-in-law. But if those photos go online, we'll make sure we begin with this boy here.' Dayal patted Varun's head. 'Anjali, who used to think so much of herself she refused me. She'll never come out of her induced coma.' Dayal leaned back, 'Ah, don't be surprised. You know I have my ways. Her crazy son will be shut in an asylum, or worse. Your curly-haired sister with the vitiligo will be next.'

Daddy stood up, his fist clenched. Varun remembered what that fist had done to his jaw. But Bunty's father did not care—a scary but *dhansoo* man, this Bunty's father. Varun shifted out of his grip, and backed into the sofa.

'Sit down, Jatin. You know that I may only be the union home secretary, but my family goes back a long way. Keeping the photos safe is the only way you can protect your *gabru jawan* here.' Dayal reached out to squeeze Varun's shoulder, the way he had done so many times over the years at family parties. 'You were proud of him. I was proud of Bunty too.'

Daddy listened, his eyes angry and red.

'We'll find you if you go public.' Dayal Sisodia said. 'How far can you run with that burned woman, anyway?'

If Daddy was still before, he seemed to freeze now. Like a statue only he was, made of stone. Always after that woman only ya. Threaten his own flesh-and-blood, he didn't give a shit, but talk about that tall bitch, all burned and ugly now, and suddenly he couldn't speak.

'Think about it, Jatin. As my friend, you know me well enough to understand that this gives me no pleasure.'

Walking up to Nanaji, Dayal Sisodia shook his hand. He patted Daddy on the shoulder and walked out. Daddy's shoulder hurt each winter, and he couldn't bear for anyone to touch it. Maybe Dayal Singh Sisodia knew that.

64

'There must be something we can do.' Pawan jogged along with the former Commissioner Bhatt. 'We can't just give up.'

Jatin sir did not reply. They cut across a stone path, and jogged down the pavement along the Hauz Khas lake. The air was filled with bird calls, the screeches of the water fowl. This early in the morning, they had the stretch to themselves, other than a few other joggers. The outlines of the surrounding historical tombs and pavilions reflected in the lake's calm waters. Jatin sir, or Bhai as Pawan now called him, put on the pace, and for a while they ran side by side, focused on their breathing and the path they took.

They completed the circle, and stood next to a bench, panting and stretching their legs when Jatin sir spoke.

'I have not given up.'

'Then?'

'It has taken Anjali so long to sit at the dining table to eat with us. It's been five months, and she still doesn't like anyone but Maya driving her to the hospital. She's working online, insists on paying all her bills not covered by the insurance. I can't put her at risk. They can have Nikhil put away, Pawan. I promised her I would keep him safe.'

Jatin sir loved Anjaliji, that much was clear, and the guilt of his son attacking her had tied his hands. Pawan knew Mehra and Sisodia: they would stop at nothing to hurt Anjaliji. But what of those women who Bunty and his gang had killed?

'Bunty will leave the country soon.'

'I know. So will Varun.' Jatin sir looked away. 'But you and I both know Nikhil is doing better now than he has for months. The new school suits him.'

Bunty and Varun going free haunted Jatin sir. Pawan's man had followed Jatin sir one night after Maya called Pawan. Her Bhai had driven out way past midnight again. Jatin sir had parked his car under the Modi Mill flyover, and walked into Sakhi's former neighbourhood. He trawled around like a shadow, a ghost looking for something.

After that night he had agreed to go to the doctor, who in turn referred him to a psychiatrist. Maya had got the diagnosis out of him—clinical depression. He had lost weight. With his hair turned grey, he seemed to have aged ten years in five months. This man, who had towered over Pawan his entire life, now looked defeated, like a runaway in hiding. He had moved into the Safdarjung home in order to help care for Anjaliji, but in truth, he had run from his life, his career. *Beda garak.*

Pawan sank on his haunches. 'I want to join the police so I can fight for justice, protect those who need it. If people like Mehra and Dayal run the show, I might as well do something else.'

Rathi was tipped to succeed Mehra, as a reward for all the cover-ups. Each time Pawan thought of that, he felt his bile rise.

Jatin sir laid a hand on his shoulder. 'It's only been a few months. Give us time.'

'What about Vigil?' Pawan said. 'I could be useful there.'

'Kusum is joining us next week, so we will have help. I'll try not to mess things up at the office, and bring in a few cases. We need more people like you in the force.'

'What will I manage, Bhai?' Pawan looked up, 'What difference will it make?'

'You won't turn out like me, you will stick to your principles. You will have love—you won't need to rise in the ranks to fill up a hole in your life.'

'All that is idealistic.' Pawan stood up.

'The world needs idealism.'

'If Sisodia gets away with this…'

'For now. We need you on the inside for a reason, Pawan.' Jatin sir smiled, 'And quit having me followed.'

Pawan had told Maya he would stop having Jatin sir tailed, but kept his man on the lookout. He couldn't bear to think of Maya losing her Bhai.

'You know?'

'Of course. I can take care of myself. Maya gets scared and calls you, but you must trust me.'

Jatin sir still had it in him—a strong man trying hard to keep it together. But something inside him had broken. Pawan turned away, so Jatin sir couldn't see his eyes.

'Race you to the gate?' he said instead.

He set off, and Jatin Sir joined him. Pawan recalled his Sensei's words from a lesson the week before: *Follow the example of water: pause and gather strength, until an obstacle no longer presents a challenge.*

65

Two years to the day after her last major procedure, Anjali stood gazing at the mirror. The face staring back at her smiled as if it knew secrets of its own, and of those who watched it. Glowing, peachy skin, arched eyebrows, a pert nose, thin but lustrous lips, high cheekbones, and glowing, kissable cheeks.

The *noumen*.

She removed from her face the only Japanese mask she'd kept for memory's sake. She'd given away all the others in the past two years, to Sakhi's school and to the Hridayog theatre group. But this *noumen* had moved with her: from Bhikaji Cama to the clinic they had built at the Safdarjung Enclave house. Today she'd taken it down to clean while she waited for her next client.

Anjali hung the mask back in its place, and straightened the frame of the photo taken the previous Christmas: two kids, a teen, four adults, and one dog. Her family. Maya sat in the centre with Sakhi on her lap, Jatin and Anjali on either side. Pawan stood behind them, carrying Chotu on one arm, his other hand on Maya's shoulder. Nikhil, now taller than Pawan, stood beside him, a model airplane clutched in his hand. Manku the dog lounged as usual, his head on Sakhi's knee. The second that picture was taken, the two kids had squirmed away, along with the bounding Manku, eager for cake. They had reached the table in an explosion of squeals, laughter, and excited yips from the dog. Anjali had stood next to Nikhil and watched them.

'That was fun, Anjali.' Nikhil had looked away, as usual, but hadn't winced at her touch.

He hadn't had a meltdown in a very long time, although he still struggled with his mood swings and medication. He got nervous every time she needed to stay at the hospital, so she tried to space out her surgeries.

Dr Singh had operated on her more than a dozen times in the first year, and given her deep discounts. *We put your life in danger, Dr Morgan. Let us help in any way we can.* Anjali had flown to Singapore for a few more operations. Thirty-four of them in all now. The antibiotics gave her allergies and side effects. This meant she could no longer run, and was only allowed the least strenuous of exercises. Playing with Chotu and Sakhi was out of the question for a while yet. *They grow up so fast*, she protested, but the doctor and Maya insisted she wait. Maya had adopted Sakhi and Chotu, and was their Mom now, so Anjali had little say.

Walking into the living room, she found Jatin at his usual chair poring over a file.

'The kids have settled down for their nap.' He put the file away, 'They demanded a story as their price.'

Pawan and Maya had gone on a two-week honeymoon, leaving Sakhi and Chotu with their nanny, in Anjali's charge. Jatin Uncle had become a firm favourite, because he gave them rides on his back, tossed Chotu up in the air, and of course, the many stories he acted out for their benefit.

'Thank you.' Anjali said. 'They turn so cranky without their naps.'

He poured her a glass of coconut water, and himself a large measure of whiskey.

'You're back early.' Anjali accepted her glass, 'everything okay at Vigil?'

'Yes, I just took some time off.' Jatin clinked ice into his drink, 'Also, I wanted to talk to you.'

Jatin cleared his throat and took a deep breath. Must be another crisis at Hridayog, an issue with the women. With Maya away, Jatin found those tricky to navigate, and often came to Anjali for help.

'Sure.' She leaned forward.

'I'm planning to go away for a while.'

'A vacation? That will do you good.'

Jatin had changed, his eyes hollowed out, his greyed hair cropped close to his skull. He still worked out, but it was a punishing routine, against all medical advice. It caused frequent fights with Maya. He ate little, slept even less—Anjali heard him pacing the corridor upstairs when she woke up in the middle of the night.

'No.' Jatin said, 'Away from Delhi. From everything.'

'Is this to do with what I said earlier?'

A month ago on Valentine's day, Jatin had gotten down on his knees and asked for her hand, but she'd kneeled right next to him—told him they were just friends now, and she wanted them to stay that way.

'No. You were right.' Jatin turned away from her.

Anjali rose and walked to the mirror opposite the dining table. She stared at the uneven skin, the shiny spots where the latest scars had healed. She'd worn makeup last night, during the dinner out with the kids. Fareeda said that keeping stares to a minimum did her good, and helped Nikhil. Her face must have looked smoother in the softer light of the night lamp, but Jatin knew what she looked like—the changing landscape of her face for the past two years. He had been at her side through it all. She remembered the verse Jatin whispered often:

Dil mera soz-e-nihan se bemuhaba jal gaya
Atish-e-khamosh ke manind goya jal gaya.

She had caught a few words, and looked them up on the internet. This poet from another time and place, knew what she felt. Ghalib's words, she'd made them her own now. *Atish-e-khamosh*, the *silent, inward blaze*. It had burned away her grudges, old fears, and the craving for touch, for acceptance. She had changed the words in her life, like Sakhi, and built from them her new world. Sakhi said it best years ago: *You are pretty in the morning, with your real face.*

She was her Self now. She was her own validation, had no need of another. She did not regret her decision.

'If it isn't to do with me,' she walked back to Jatin, 'then why now, all of a sudden?'

'I've been thinking. Maya is married now, and Pawan can be here for the family. I can focus on sorting everything out in my head. I need the distance. From this city. From everything that has happened.'

She had become so used to having him around. For her

hospital appointments. Each time she had a panic attack. When Nikhil needed support at school. But she couldn't say that, so she asked the next obvious question.

'What about Vigil? And Hridayog?'

Jatin ran Vigil with Maya, Kusum, and two assistants. He helped Maya at Hridayog, teaching classes, filing documents, raising funds.

'I'm not leaving tomorrow. I'll make sure everything can run smoothly before I leave. Once Maya and Pawan settle in, after you come back from your next procedure. In two months or so.'

'Where will you go?'

Jatin's son was in London now, in the same college as Bunty. He had been rushed again to a hospital yesterday for another episode of drug overdose. Pawan knew this from the family grapevine, but they didn't tell Jatin—he didn't want news of his son, never mentioned his name.

'I couldn't get you justice, Anjali.'

Not Jelly, Anjali. Jatin was already distancing himself. He hadn't answered her question.

No, she hadn't seen justice, and sometimes late in the night, it bothered her—all those women, Sujni, Roli and others, picked up, mutilated, binned like trash.

In a documentary on acid attack survivors, Anjali had faced the camera and spoken about the attack on her. She worked with other survivors and had set up Swarupa to help them, a foundation to raise awareness on acid attacks. Whenever she could, she organised fundraising events, and ran a page with followers from India and all over the world, where she hosted campaigns to ban the easy availability of acid, and to support the rehabilitation of those who survived an attack. Maya helped by taking the women to Hridayog to learn skills, and Pawan, set to be posted as an Assistant Commissioner of Police soon, helped with police formalities when needed. She was doing her bit, and Jatin helped. With Swarupa, with Hridayog.

She watched as Jatin poured himself another drink, his face all planes and hollows in the weak afternoon sunlight from the window. He didn't look at her, but she knew the rage in those eyes, the helpless impotence. She didn't address it, because Jatin was not a man you could reassure.

'I'll make sure you're okay even when I'm away. And you'll have Maya and Pawan. Nikhil.'

She wanted to ask him how long he would be gone, but her phone rang, and Nikhil's picture flashed on the screen, his vivid blue eyes looking somewhere else.

'Anjali, can you pick me up?'

At sixteen, other boys would have taken a bus or cab home by themselves from their karate class, not called their mothers. But other boys his age had other problems, and didn't spend quite as much time with family. In another two years, she would hand him over the large brown envelope from his grandfather. Professor Gupta had made Nikhil, not Dorothy or Anjali, the beneficiary of his will.

'Is it ok if Jatin comes over? I have an appointment in a few minutes.'

'Ok. I'll wait.'

Jatin put his drink down. 'I'll be back soon.' He had heard Anjali speak, and knew he had to pick Nikhil up from his karate lessons. He grabbed the car keys and strode out.

Soon, Anjali would be without this man who had stood by her side these past two years. Even with him gone, she told herself, she could hold her own. When she felt a burst of frustration at a job not done or at Nikhil refusing his dinner, she knew to remind herself that the world would go on; it was okay to let go of control, stop short of perfection.

Jatin needed to focus on himself for a while. He was still her friend, would always be one.

In front of the mirror, she twirled in her dress, setting her hair loose, and let a smile work its way down her body. She had a job to do, a life to live, and a hell of a story to tell her grandchildren.

The bell at the reception rang. Ira would get it.

Anjali walked to the window, and stared out at the Flame of the Forest. Branches swaying under the weight of its vermillion blooms, the tree stood in a riot of colour and light. Nikhil collected the blossoms fallen on the grass, pasted them in a scrapbook along with snapshots of the family, and his new karate friends.

She settled herself down on her chair. Sunlight played on her scarred hands as she flipped open her last client file for the day.

Acknowledgements

The writing process is lonely, often touched by utter despair. But a novel is not a lone effort, and many hands held mine on the writing and publication journey for *You Beneath Your Skin*.

It began with Sharon Bakar, who gave me the permission to write. It continued with those who read messy early drafts: Lim Shee Pinn, Durba Dhyani, Mou Sarkar, Aditi Mitra, Sarah Carlson, Vikram and Kiran Tandon, Michael Dellert, Marc deFaoite—thank you. Over the years, I learned a lot about writing from the Forge Writing group: huge thanks to Sommer Schafer who read the manuscript twice, to John and Yosh Haggerty for their constant support, and to everyone in the group who read *You Beneath Your Skin* and showed me ways to improve.

Julia Bell from Birkbeck University mentored me during the early stages, Rose Gaete and Sanjida Kay from The Literary Consultancy gave excellent feedback—all of which was made possible through the support of National Arts Council, Singapore. A word of thanks to author Jake Arnott, a brief chat with whom during a Curtis Brown bootcamp changed the entire novel.

You Beneath Your Skin came about thanks to Anouradha Bakshi and my experiences at Project WHY, her organisation that helps women and children in New Delhi's underprivileged communities. Discussions with acid attack survivors at Chhanv Foundation, and Alok Dixit, shaped a large part of the narrative. Thanks to Smita Barooah and Damien Lai for the help on the chapters that involve autism. Special thanks to Vikramjiet Roy, who helped with crucial local research. Mr V.N. Singh, Former Commissioner of Delhi Police, vet the storyline for me, and Mr Rituraj, Inspector, Delhi Police, explained police hierarchy and investigation procedures. Dr Shahin Nooreyezdan gave excellent guidance on plastic surgery procedures for acid attack survivors. Thanks and appreciation for Manisha and Adarsh Bhargava, and Mahua Ghosh for their love and hospitality in London.

No thanks are enough for my sterling agent Ed Wilson who has kept me going with much-needed doses of good advice and humour. Much gratitude to the kind, patient Himanjali Sankar for believing in *You Beneath Your Skin*, and choosing to champion it.

My parents as well as so many mentors and friends have cheered me on this journey, but I would not have been an author but for my better half, Swarup Biswas. I hope I grow to deserve him some day.